REBEL DHAMPIR

REBEL DHAMPIR

THE ROYALE VAMPIRE HEIRS, BOOK TWO

by

GINNA MORAN

SUNNY PALMS PRESS

To Jazmin,

Without you, this book would've been written fast-
er. But thank you for fueling my imagination. Keep
being YOU. ;)

1

GIFT TO HUMANITY

THE SCENT OF BLOOD PULLS me from the blood hunger paralyzing my body. I lost track of time in this dark room, but I'm nearly certain I've been in here forever. Without windows to the outside world, there is no way of telling. All I know is that I keep falling in and out of sleep...or consciousness. I can no longer tell the difference. I expect to close my eyes and never wake up, but my body just keeps surviving.

I shouldn't expect death to be so easy.

I am half vampire after all.

Hunger doesn't kill those starved of blood, but it does turn them wild, feral. Untamable. And I'm on the verge of losing the human part of myself.

"Gwen," a soft voice whispers. "Wake up. I don't have a lot of time."

Snapping my eyes open, I stare at the silhouette of a female vampire. Her dark hair spills around her shoulders as she leans over, looking down on me. Silver flashes in her eyes, and she takes an automatic step away. It's now that I realize her eyes weren't flashing at me. My eyes were flashing at her, and I could see the reflection.

"Stay back," I say. "I don't want to hurt you. I'm so hungry. It's taking everything in me not to rip your throat out, and I don't want Corona to punish me."

The woman shifts on her feet. If I didn't know any better, I'd think she was nervous. "That's why I'm here."

I jerk upright. "Please, you don't have to. I haven't done anything wrong. One of the staff members let me out of the cage."

"You misunderstand, Ms. Royale," the woman whispers so quietly that only I'd be able to hear her. "I'm not here to hurt you. I was sent to feed you. Now, please. Try not to attack me. Bronx warned me how aggressive you get when you're hungry."

The sound of Bronx's name on her lips sends my heart crashing around my ribcage. The woman doesn't let me ask any questions as she bites her arm, the scent of her blood overpowering everything. It wasn't the scent of blood that stirred my consciousness. It was just her. I'm *that* hungry.

Sitting down beside me, the woman extends her bleeding arm to me. I lock my fingers around her wrist without hesitation, bringing the syrupy smelling bite mark to my lips and suck. Her free hand slides across my shoulders, and she combs my messy hair without making a single sound. Not like all the vampires I've ever drunk from before.

"I need you to listen very carefully, Ms. Royale," the woman says. "The sun will rise shortly, so you don't have a lot of time. Upon my brother's request, I have mind manipulated one of the staff members to retrieve you to escort you outside. It will be up to you to get past the daylight security. Head north to the far side of the estate. You'll know you're in the right place if you see the orchards."

I don't know how I get my mouth to cooperate, but I manage to ease my lips away from the woman's arm. "Is this some kind of test? What does Corona expect for me to do?"

She frowns. "Corona is away until dusk."

I flare my nostrils, my stomach still all sorts of angry that I resist snatching her arm back to drink more of her blood. "But you said your brother."

"Bronx," she says, sighing. "I suppose you wouldn't understand, considering the infrastructures of covens. Bronx is my biological brother from before we transitioned and were separated."

"Oh." He never mentioned having a sister. But why

would he have? Laredo, my old blood source, claimed that most vampires forget about their human lives.

"You can ask him all about it when you get out of here," she says. "I have to go. If I'm caught with you, I'll be sentenced to death for treason."

The woman vanishes without so much as a goodbye, shutting and locking the door behind her. I stare at the crack of light seeping in from the space under the door until my eyes water. My mind whirls with a dozen thoughts. I knew my guys said they'd come for me, but I did not expect it to be like this. I thought they'd come blasting in this place, killing everyone in sight. Why they haven't? I hope to find out.

Getting up from the cot, I stand and stretch, my body aching from hunger and not being used for so long. I've never been this inactive in my life, and my muscles scream at me that I better pull my shit together.

I do a couple of floor stretches to loosen up, but my muscles remain tight with nerves. I have no idea what to expect from the daylight security. I can't imagine they'll just let me go. It's never that easy. Humans working for vampires take their jobs seriously. They wouldn't risk breaking their contracts and facing their final donations. I wouldn't want them too, either. Despite what the elder Blood Rebels think, I'm not a traitor to humanity. Fuckers.

I return to the cot and sit down, crossing my legs. Closing my eyes, I focus on the sounds of the house. I'm not the only human locked in a room. I've heard at least three other people—all men—and they sound a million times more miserable than me. I bet they're in cages or chained to a wall. Probably on the cusp of dying. I've seen such conditions a dozen times before, and without having to know much about Corona, I can tell he's a true monster and the type of vampire that deserves a stake through the heart.

The thuds of footsteps draw my attention from my thoughts of Corona and to the hallway outside. By the sounds of the heavy clomping, the woman vampire wasn't lying. Someone is coming.

I stand up and move near the door, pressing my back to the wall. I don't have a weapon, so I need to be close to the door in case whoever comes in my direction turns out to be a threat. At least it's not another vampire. That's the only thing I'm certain of by the noise the person creates.

Fisting my hands, I prepare to fight. A key jingles, and the shadow of a figure blocks out the light pouring in from under the door. It creaks open, but no one enters my room. The person remains in the hallway without speaking.

I turn my body and lean toward the doorway to peek out. A man stands there, his eyes glassy, his face expressionless. It's eerie to see him under mind manipulation. I had expected him to be normal, but he's a total puppet under the female vampire's influence.

"Follow me."

I startle at the sound of the man's voice cutting through

the air. He sounds as creepy as he looks. I don't get much of a chance to think about it, because he swivels on his feet and starts striding down the hallway without even looking to see if I follow.

I do.

Chasing after him, I stay close on his heels, glancing around me every few feet as I try to concentrate on my surroundings. A soft groan sounds from a closed door, and I can't stop myself from trying to open it.

"Hey, wait," I say to the guy. "I need you to open this door."

The man continues down the hallway without responding.

Ah, hell.

Racing ahead, I stand in front of him with my palms raised. "Stop."

He doesn't. He plows into me, pushing me back. I fall, the force of his body knocking me flat on my ass. I screech as his boot steps right between my legs, nearly kicking my vagina, and I can't stop my hand from swinging out and punching him right in the junk.

He yelps and trips, colliding into me to knock me onto my back. I knew that a person could break from mind manipulation, but I never really knew how to do it. I guess a dick punch is an effective method. Unfortunately, it's a little too effective, because the man thrashes and grabs me by the hair. He rolls off of me and drags me to my feet, locking me to him.

"Stop fighting, and I won't hurt you," he says, shaking me.

I do as he says, going slack in his arms. "You're already hurting me."

"What are you doing out of your room? Do you want the both of us to be killed?" he asks, shoving me in the direction we came from.

I swallow my desire to punch him in the junk again. "Hey, asshole. You're the one who let me out."

His eyes widen. "What?"

I take advantage of his sudden confusion and jerk my knee up, hitting it into his stomach. He heaves a breath and bends forward. I break away from him and thrust my fist down into his back. He drops to his knees. The set of keys flies from his hand, and I rush to snatch them off the ground.

The man's quick to get back to his feet, and he charges me. "You bitch! You better get back in your room before I alert security."

I spin out of his way. "Yeah-fucking-right. I'm leaving."

"The hell you are."

The man reaches for a weapon on his belt, and I jump at him, risking closing the space. Knocking him off his feet again, I ram my hand into his chest to pin him in place while I swing my arm and punch him so hard in the throat that his face reddens.

And then he blacks out.

I swipe the dagger from his belt and scoop up the keys. Voices murmur from the nearest door, and I scramble to shove a key in the lock. It takes four different attempts to get the door open, but I can't just leave whoever is inside the room here.

Three men turn their wide eyes to me. None of them react as I bolt into the room and to them. Silence fills the air, and I concentrate on listening to my surroundings as I mess with the cuffs on their ankles, finally finding the key to free them. A part of me knows I should just leave them. I'm better off alone in my escape especially since I broke the person who was supposed to guide me out's mind manipulation, but the part of me that was raised to help people wins. I can't just leave these prisoners here. They don't deserve such a fate.

"You're Gwen," one of the guys says. "The dhampir."

"You know me?" I ask and then shake my head. "Actually, never mind. We don't have time for this. Come on."

I offer my hand out to the man, and he gets to his feet and helps the other two guys up. One man can barely walk, his sallow skin sagging on his too-thin body. He looks like he's been here a long time, just taken care enough to be kept alive.

"Can you guys carry him?" I ask, peering over my shoulder. "I'll protect us."

"Yeah," the two men say in unison.

"All right. Let's go. The sun should be up any minute if it's not already," I say.

I stroll to the door and peer out, nearly losing my shit as the staff member tries to grab me from his place against the wall. I was too distracted by the guys that I didn't hear him get up. Locking his fingers to my wrist, he drags me forward, looking hell-bent on causing me as much pain as I inflicted on him.

Without thinking, I jab my hand out and stab him with the knife I stole from him. He grunts and throws himself away from me, hitting his back on the wall. Blood seeps through his white shirt. My heart slides to my feet. I've never hurt another human so badly before.

"Gwen, hurry," the man from the locked room says. "He's a traitor and doesn't deserve your sympathy."

I blink a few times, the man's words digging into me. "You're a rebel?"

He brings his index finger to his lips and smiles. "Call me Augie."

"Is that why you were imprisoned?" I ask. I can't help it. A small part of me fears that this guy is a Blood Rebel, who also knew who I was, because of the fact that I've been deemed a traitor to humanity. If he knows that I am, he'll kill me.

Waving his arm, he motions down the hallway. "No, but I'll explain. Later."

I lead us in the direction he points, trying to ignore the

groans of the guy I just stabbed as he drops to the floor with a thud behind us. The hallway curves left to meet with a set of concrete stairs. Nerves bunch my stomach, and I stop and take a breath. It's at least two flights up, and I have no idea what to expect.

"At the top of the stairs will be a guard," Augie says from behind me. "He might be waiting for us."

"I think that dude was the guard," I say, pointing my thumb behind me.

Augie tightens his mouth. "Just be prepared."

Fumbling with the keys, I take a moment to unlock the door. It clicks open, and silence greets us. Cool air wafts in from another hallway, and I inhale a long breath. I had no idea how musty and stale the basement air was until now.

I stick my head out and glance around. "It's emp—"

A vampire materializes in front of me, twisting my arm to knock the dagger away. He flashes his fangs with a growl. My fear instincts ignite in my chest, going off like crazy, and I kick my leg up, aiming for the guy's balls, but I'm too slow.

He hooks his fingers around my leg and hoists me up, dangling me upside down. My shirt rolls up, exposing my bra. He spins me around with a smile that digs into my skin. Fucking creep. The action is enough to set me off, and I swing my body, managing to surprise the vampire by hooking my leg over his shoulder. I risk getting bitten right in the thigh, but he freezes and inhales a breath at my closeness.

He hums in his throat. "You smell deli—"

Jerking my arm out, I hook it around his leg and pull myself closer. I'm not sure whether or not I'm about to make a huge mistake, but I link my fingers to the waist of his pants and tug them as hard as I can.

He shivers, making a strange noise in his throat. "What are you doing?"

"What does it look like?" I ask, my face flushing.

"Corona will be displeased if—"

Tilting my head, I sink my teeth into his thigh, biting him so hard that blood pours from the wound. And damn my mouth. I'm still so hungry that instead of ripping his flesh away, my lips mold onto his leg and I suck.

And shit, I wish I didn't. The vampire grips me tighter, getting turned on by my closeness and I can feel his boner graze my boobs. It's enough to get me to release him and throw myself back. I thud on the ground, the wind escaping my lungs. The vampire steps closer, his eyes flashing crazy silver with both hunger and desire.

"That was quite the experience, Gwen," he whispers, saying my name. "Allow me to help you up. Corona won't return until tonight. Perhaps you'd like to join me until then?"

"Uh..."

The vampire concentrates so hard on me that he doesn't see Augie come up behind him. The man stabs the vampire through the back with my discarded dagger. The vampire releases a roar, swinging around. He's too fast for the man, and the vampire thrusts Augie against the wall, bending his neck.

I hop to my feet. "Wait."

The sound of my voice makes the vampire hesitate.

"Don't hurt him. He's only trying to protect me. He doesn't know...how much I like vampires," I say, keeping my voice low. "You can deal with him later. I don't feel like waiting for you."

The vampire drops Augie and turns to me. "Is that so?"

I comb my hair from my neck and expose my throat. "Don't you know what I am?"

His jaw twitches. "Just what I've been told. That you're supposedly a dhampir."

"Which means watching you try to bite someone else...makes me incredibly jealous," I say in my sweetest voice. This guy is way easier to manipulate than I expect. He gobbles up every bit of my attention and charm.

The vampire hums under his breath. "We can't have that now, can we?"

I curl and uncurl my finger at him, getting him to come closer. Trailing my hand up his stomach, I stop at the blood spot staining his chest through his shirt. He licks his lips, watching me as I bring my hand to my mouth to glide my tongue over his blood now staining the tip of my finger.

"No, we can't," I say, biting my lip.

The vampire reaches up and pushes my blond hair from my shoulder, exposing my neck to him. My heart picks up speed. The vampire looks at me exactly how Laredo always had after I bit him, like it's taking everything in him not just to bite back.

He leans in and inhales a breath by my ear. "May I take you to my suite, Gwen?"

I exhale, my nerves disappearing. I can't believe he just asked me instead of biting. I mean, I knew not all vampires were crazy-ass lunatics on a mission to drain people, but I struggle with the concept. Even Corona hadn't tried to bite me. The fact that he asks makes me feel a teensy bit because of what I plan to do next.

"Actually..." Swinging my fist, I clock the vampire right in his bleeding chest.

He hollers and thrashes at the strength of my punch, hitting his back to the wall. Thrusting his arms out, he shoves me forward, knocking the wind from me. He links his fingers through my hair and bends my neck, no longer playing nice.

Augie and the other man come up behind the vampire, but he spins to face them, throwing the man, whose name I don't know, into the frail, half-dead guy now sprawled across the floor. The vampire rushes Augie again next, but I push off from the wall and ram my shoulder into the vampire. The three of us fall forward, Augie wrapping his hands around the vampire to try to hold him in place.

Pressing my palm flat on the back of the vampire's neck, I pin him down with one hand and aim my fist at the stab wound Augie inflicted. I punch down as hard as I can, my strength crazy-powerful—so much so that I gasp at my hand sinking into the vampire's back.

The vampire screams and bucks, managing to throw me off. I wince and close my eyes. I brace to have my throat ripped out at any second. But silence sounds through the hallway until Augie groans and a body thumps on the ground.

"Gwen, you okay?" Augie asks, drawing my attention to him.

I gasp a few breaths and open my eyes. "Yeah," I manage to say. "You killed him."

Augie pushes to his feet. "That was you."

"Me?"

"You're holding his heart."

Lifting my hand, I stare at the organ oozing in my fingers, my body wanting nothing more than to pulverize it. And then it does. I drop the soft, bloody tissue to the ground and pop my fingers into my mouth to lick off the blood.

All three guys stare at me—a mix of surprise and something else, possibly horror—crossing their faces. I wipe my bloody mouth on my shirt and get to my feet, hugging myself instead of offering to help Augie up.

"Such a gift to humanity," Augie murmurs, still staring

at me with wide eyes. "I've heard the rumors but have never seen anything like it."

"She's not," the other guy says, drawing my attention to him. He stands a few feet away, clutching my discarded knife. "She's a traitor."

Augie frowns. "What are you talking about, Cody?"

"She's responsible for Kyler's death," the man, Cody, responds. "She's here because she abandoned our people."

Glancing from Cody to me, Augie searches my face for answers, a dozen thoughts morphing his expression. "But she helped us escape."

"Doesn't matter," Cody says, inching closer. This bastard. He must be deep in the rebel life if he's willing to try to kill me here before we've even escaped. Someone could find us at any second. "She can't come with us. She chose vampires."

Augie frowns, the wrinkles on his forehead deepening at the accusation. "Is that true, Gwen?"

"No," I automatically say, fisting my hands. Annoyance rushes over me. "It was all a misunderstanding." It wasn't, but none of them have to know.

Cody points the dagger at me. "Because they betrayed you. They gave you away."

I tighten my jaw. This guy.

"She deserves to be here," Cody says to Augie. Cody's hand shakes as he clutches the dagger tighter. "Frankie died because of her too. She refused to leave. She chose the Royale Coven."

I take a step back, my muscles tensing even more under the man's accusations. How he knows? I don't have a clue. I've never seen him before. "Please, let me explain."

Augie raises his hand at Cody. "Let's give her a minute."

"No."

I don't get a chance to react as Cody flies at me.

2

ESCAPE

THREE GUNSHOTS RING THROUGH THE air, piercing my ears. I startle at the heavy weight of Cody's body slamming into me. The knife falls from his fingers before warmth blooms over me, his blood seeping onto my stomach.

"I found her," a man says from somewhere above me. "The rebels were trying to kidnap her."

I pat my hand across the floor, feeling for the dagger. The cool hilt grazes my fingers, and I snatch it up without pushing Cody's body off me.

"Ms. Gallagher, are you hurt?" the man asks.

"Y-yes," I say even though I'm not. "Please help me. If Corona finds me out here, he'll kill me."

"You're going to be okay, Ms. Gallagher. Your survival is Mr. Anderson's top priority. You should not fear him."

The hell I shouldn't.

The man kicks Cody's body off of me, and I groan and roll to my side, clutching my stomach while hiding the knife under me. With all of the blood, there's no way for the guard to tell for certain if I'm truly injured.

"We need a health keeper," the man says, calling into his com device. "Human. There's a lot of blood."

The man kneels next to me and touches my side, gently easing me onto my back. Without hesitating, I jam the knife into his side, but the blade scrapes off his body gear and misses its mark. I swing my arm out and punch him in the face instead, sending him back. Hopping on top of him, I pin him down and sock him again. And then again.

He slumps under me, surprised by my move.

A few voices trickle through the air along with more thudding footsteps. I scramble off the guard and reach for his belt, not managing to grab anything before another pop sounds through the air. Bolting to my feet, I dash down the hallway with no idea where I'm heading. I don't stop to try to break the tinted glass windows, knowing I'd be unable to.

"Running is pointless, Ms. Gallagher," another security guard calls from behind me.

A man releases a whistle. "Just let her wear herself out. She's not going anywhere."

As the words come out of the man's mouth, I reach a foyer far less impressive than the grand entrance of the Night Palms Castle. A blank wall, a black metal chandelier, and a single wooden door greet me. I yank on the handle, despite what the guards said, and attempt to force it open.

The world spins around me, and I screech as bright light stings my eyes. Warm sunshine engulfs me, and I land on top of the first female human I've seen here. She gasps under my weight and covers her eyes with her hands.

"Don't hurt me," she says, her soft voice pushing me into action.

I roll off her and get to my feet. "Tell me where the orchards are. I need to head north."

Loud alarms blare through the air, and my soul nearly jumps from my skin. The young woman quickly points in what I hope is the right direction, and I push my legs to run as fast as I can without looking back. Voices yell out, prodding at me to move faster even though all I want to do is bend forward and catch my breath. The days locked inside the room wreaked some horrible havoc on me. Or maybe it's my still burning hunger. No matter what, I feel like shit and am afraid I'm not going to make it.

More gunshots ring through the air, and I try my best to weave back and forth as not to give the guards a clear shot. If they manage to shoot me, it'll be the end. Because

I'm not going back. I'll not be imprisoned a moment longer. Only torture will await me. The guard already said that Corona wouldn't kill me, which means that he'll try to break me. He nearly did by starving me.

"Come on, Gwen. A hundred more feet. Don't make me face the sun."

I jerk my head up at the sound of Everett's encouragement. I don't know what I expected from my sudden release, but it sure as hell wasn't finding Everett waving his hands at me from the shade of a tree.

My heart races, my breath quickening. I've never been so relieved in my life. Except for the relief I feel flees away with the stretch of a long shadow closing the space behind me.

"Don't stop," Everett says.

But it's too late. The surprise of someone getting this close distracts me, slowing me down. A deep, threatening growl rips through the air. Two hands lock on my shoulders, yanking me back. I lose my footing and hit the grass, tumbling a dozen times. My head spins when I finally stop, and I dig my fingers into the grass in an attempt to get to my feet.

Someone grabs my leg, and I jerk my head up to stare at a man training a gun at me. "Stop fighting. It's over."

Everett releases another growl, causing the man to draw his attention away from me. He pulls the trigger on his gun, and I screech, pulling my knees to my chest. I expect pain to blast through me like the other time I was shot, but nothing happens. The man's gone.

Heaving a breath, I push my hands into the ground to get to my feet. I spot Everett and the man in the shade of the trees. Everett flashes his fangs, looking ready to chomp down on the guard's throat. Fear trickles through me, my human instincts going off like crazy. I can't help it. Seeing Everett so intense and snarly freaks me out a bit.

Whipping his head in my direction, Everett catches my gaze. His chest heaves with a few deep breaths, and he locks his fingers around the guy's throat and leans into him, capturing his stare. The man slackens in Everett's arms. I shuffle my way closer, pushing past the panic engulfing me, causing my hands to tremble.

"Ms. Gallagher was taken by Blood Rebels," Everett tells the man, breaking into his mind. He flashes his fangs, growling again like he can't help himself. If I didn't know any better, I'd think he was about to bite him.

The man stares at him without a word.

I inhale a small breath at the memory of how awful it was to experience such a thing by the hands of Mr. Bevaldi. It takes everything in me to keep walking to close the space to Everett, though my mind wants me to hurry the hell up. His tense muscles bulge against the fabric of his long-sleeved shirt, his blond hair hidden under his hood. His cheeks glow light pink, a few blisters peppering his jaw from his few seconds in the sun to get the guard away from me. I want so much to tackle him and attack him with my lips. If he wasn't focused on the guard, I would.

"You will return to your post and forget I was here. Do you understand?" Everett asks the man without looking at me, though I know he senses my closeness. His shoulders relax just a bit, hearing me come up beside him.

I touch my fingers to his sides, resting my head on his back between his shoulder blades. It's so amazing to breathe in his scent, to touch him, to hear the sound of his heart picking up speed for me.

"Yes," the guard says, his voice even, robotic almost.

"Now go." Everett releases the man, pushing him back into the sun.

I don't have a second to react as Everett spins and engulfs me in a hug. He lifts me off of my feet and kisses me. I cling onto him, devouring his affection. He breathes softly into my hair and takes off, blurring the world around us. I can't stop my eyes from burning with tears—summoned from both my fear and relief—and I tighten my arms around Everett, pressing my face into his hoodie to muffle my sniffles. I've been suppressing my emotions, so focused on my hunger that Everett breaks my walls down, sending me spinning through everything that happened.

"Gwen," he whispers, his soft voice humming in my ear. "I'm so sorry."

I don't respond to his apology. I can't. If I try, I know my voice will break. The last thing I want is for him to see how out of control I am right now. I want to be tough, strong. Not some whimpering mess.

"I wanted to come sooner, but—"

Instead of letting him finish, I pull away from his shoulder and meet my lips to his again, silencing the words I'm not so sure I want to hear. I know the way the world works. I understand that Everett and his brothers probably had a mess of things to deal with...and that their region takes precedence. I just—I push the thought away.

"I get it," I finally say without pulling away more than an inch from his lips. Resting my forehead to his, I breathe in the sweetness of his breath, mingling with mine.

He kisses me again like he can't resist the closeness of our mouths. I had no idea how much I missed him, his touch. Just everything about him. Being away from him and now returning to his arms cements the fact that my decision to choose the Royale Coven and let them claim me—claim them as my own—was the right one. I don't want to imagine any other future.

"There is no need to explain. You have to take care of your coven first." I don't look at him as I say the words.

Everett huffs against my lips. "Gwen, no. It wasn't like that. Let's get out of here and I'll explain."

The world suddenly stops, and Everett slides me into the backseat of a car. He climbs behind the wheel and taps a few buttons, sending it jolting forward as he engages the autopilot. Pushing down the seat, Everett maneuvers his way into the back with me and lifts me into his arms to hug me on his lap, not even caring that I'm covered in all sorts of blood.

"You have been our priority," Everett says softly, combing his fingers through my dirty, messy hair. "Not the coven or the region. You."

I lick my lips and nod. I don't know what to say. My brothers used to claim that I was the priority, but it never felt that way, not like it does now. I can feel the truth to Everett's words deep in my soul.

His eyes flash silver as he turns his attention from me and out the windshield, keeping his attention split. "I know it felt otherwise, and I'm sure Corona said some things—"

"Like how you willingly gave me to him," I say, resting my ear to his chest to listen to his heartbeat.

He releases a soft growl. "We'd never. Mikkalo thought your chances of survival would be higher if we didn't fight. If we didn't...reveal how much you mean to us. Corona already has Zaire to use against us."

I shudder, inhaling a ragged breath. "I never want to be your weakness, Everett."

He shifts me on his lap so that I face him, straddling his waist. "It's already too late for that. You're our girl."

His claim brings a smile to my mouth. It's the first time I've managed to do so. "Everett."

Leaning forward, he caresses his lips to mine. "You are. And so you know, I don't think you're our weakness. You make us stronger if anything. You have no idea how relieved I am to hold you right now. My brothers are probably going crazy."

"Where are they, anyway?" I ask, easing away.

My heart beats wildly just thinking about them—about how Jameson will smother me in his arms and let me bite the hell out of him. How Mikkalo will be so proud of me for getting my ass out of there when not only Corona's security was after me, but the damn rebels too. And Bronx? I can already feel the weight of his arms around me. How his ever broody face will light up just for me.

"With Corona," Everett says, tightening his jaw. The throatiness of his voice cuts through me in a good way. The way he says Corona sounds like he can't wait for the moment to rip that asshole's heart out on my behalf. He'll probably hold me down to let me do it now. "Our plan took a bit longer to kick into action, but it had to be this way. We can't give Corona a reason to suspect we had something to do with your disappearance, so they're all there. Even an ounce of doubt could complicate things."

A loud ring cuts through the air, and Everett stiffens in my arms. Bronx's picture flashes on the navigation screen. I bounce in my seat, excitement rushing through me, knowing I'll get to talk to Bronx at any second.

"I need you to get on the floor, Gwen. Don't make a sound, okay?" Everett says, quashing my anticipation to mush it into fear.

He slides me off his lap and onto the floor without giving me a chance to answer. My chest tightens with more panic, and I swear my heart will never even out again. I thought life going from city to city to save humans was intense and sometimes freaky as hell, but I'm more on edge. Maybe because my secret about being a dhampir is out.

Everett climbs back into the front seat and gets behind the wheel. He turns off the autopilot and picks up speed before answering the line. I clench my jaw and cover my mouth with my hand just in case.

"What's up, Bronx?" Everett asks, his voice even, strong.

"Checking in. Is everything all good?" Bronx's smooth voice echoes through a speaker, and I silently beg my heart to chill out. "What's your ETA?"

It takes everything in me not to sit up to try to glance at Bronx's face on the screen. I can already imagine his dark eyes now. His chiseled jaw. Full, soft lips. So kissable.

Damn. The rest of my body needs to chill out too.

"Would be better if it weren't the fucking afternoon," Everett says, raising his voice in agitation. "Other than that, it's all good. I'm seven minutes out. Be ready."

"And what of the transfers?" The eerily familiar voice of Corona stops Bronx from responding.

I tense, squeezing my eyes shut.

Everett clears his throat. "I've signed off on the health statuses of the new Anderson donors. All Bronx needs to do is to confirm the transfer."

"Very good. Always a pleasure working with the Royale Coven. I do hope our alliance remains strong for the unforeseeable future," Corona says.

The words dig into me. I wish I could yell that it'll only be strong until I bite his throat out.

"Yup," Everett responds flatly. The car shifts as he turns. "Five minutes, brothers. I'm not waiting all day."

"Got it, Ev," Bronx says.

Corona clears his throat. "Actually, I would like you to go over the paperwork with me. I'll come to the garage. It'll be quick."

"Sounds good. Three minutes."

Everett smacks his hands on the steering wheel, startling me. One second I'm on the floor, and in the next, he's pulling me into his arms again. He hits a lever on the backseat and pulls the seat forward to the cargo space of the trunk. I'll have to curl on my side to fit in it, the space not as big as the trunks of the cars from the back-world that I'm used to.

"I'm going to make this up to you," he says, tightening his jaw.

I purse my lips. "This isn't the first time I've had to hide in a trunk. Just be quick. I'm really over small, dark spaces."

His lips curl in a frown, but he doesn't have a chance to say anything as the vehicle navigates into an underground garage beneath a tower. I've never been into this city before, which means it probably belongs to the Anderson Coven.

"Hurry, get in," Everett whispers, helping me slide through the small opening. "I swear, I will make this up to you. Anything you want. I'll do it."

I twist my lips. "Feed me on the way home?"

He smiles. "You bet."

The car comes to a halt, and I curl my knees to my chest, pulling what looks like a sun blanket over me just in case. Vampires can handle short bursts of direct sunlight, so keeping a blanket like this helps somewhat if they have to abandon the car during the day. Everett must've been antsy if he just used a hoodie. The tree coverage helped.

"Everett, love. It's so good to see you." The sugary voice of Francisca muffles through the trunk, even over the hum of the music Everett flicked on.

"Francisca," he says. "What a pleasant surprise."

I press my lips together as not to react. I can't believe how jealous I am. I mean, what the actual hell? I guess I'm more vampire than my family would ever like to admit. The strange need to burst from the trunk to tell Francisca off consumes me worse than the fear and hunger colliding in me.

"Yes, yes. There is no time for pleasantries," Corona says. "I'd like to have the transfers signed off on. Please go over the donors with me one more time."

I hold my breath, trying to concentrate on listening for

Bronx, Jameson, and Mikkalo. If they're around, they're too quiet for me to hear. A door slams, and I startle.

"Gigi," Jameson whispers. "It's taking everything in me not to yank this seat down to grab you. I've missed you."

I want so badly to respond to his quiet voice, but I know if I try, I'll give myself away. There is no chance I can control the volume of my words right now. Not with my wild emotions running rampant. I'm freaked out enough as it is that my stomach chooses now to roar and send pain through me.

"Damn," Jameson murmurs under his breath. "Just hold tight. One more minute."

I grip onto my knees, holding my breath to listen to the outside noise. A com device chimes, and then another and another. Corona growls, and something thuds on the trunk of the car. Hands—the hit so hard that I hear the crunch of the metal under the force.

"Was this you?" Corona asks, his voice deep with a threat that scares me worse than him smacking the trunk.

"Back off, Mr. Anderson," Mikkalo says, his voice cutting through the pounding of my heart. "Don't be ridiculous. We've been with you all day and most of last night."

"Your brother—"

"Was in Crimson Vista," Everett says, speaking up. "Do you want proof?"

"What I want is your cooperation in helping get back what belongs to me. My head of the night security is dead.

My daylight too," Corona snaps.

Bronx sucks in a breath through his teeth. "Shit."

"That bite," Mikkalo adds.

I nearly lose my shit, listening to them watch what I can only assume is security footage from my nearly failed escape. And not just any footage, the video of me chomping on that vampire guy's thigh.

"Looks like Blood Rebels got her," Bronx says, a master of acting in control. I can only imagine how much seeing any of my time at the Anderson Coven's estate makes him want to rip some heads off.

Something crashes and Corona snarls, the sound of his voice ripping a wave of panic from me. I heave a few breaths, trying to calm myself down to stay quiet. A thud hits the top of the trunk again, startling me. I hear the latch click, and I curl up as small as possible, praying the blanket covers me completely.

"Calm down, Corona," Francisca says. The taps of her heels grow closer. "It's one donor."

"You don't understand—" Corona snaps his mouth shut and something thuds on the trunk again. It bangs closed. "I—I liked her."

"And we'll find her, right, Mr. Royale?" Francisca asks.

Bronx hums gruffly. "I'll put out all available guards to sweep the area."

"And when you find her, you'll call me immediately," Corona says.

"Yes."

A car door slams and tires screech across the concrete of the underground garage. I release a breath at the sound of three more car doors closing. My body shifts as someone puts the car in gear and drives out of the parking structure. I can't see anything, but I can sense it. Relief washes over me the longer I remain in the trunk.

"Gwen, you're safe," Jameson says, shifting the blanket from my face.

I cover my mouth with my hand, trying to keep my shit together. But damn. It's so good to see Jameson.

His green eyes widen, drinking me in for a second before he hooks his fingers under my arms and tugs me into the backseat. Silence greets me as four gazes smolder over me, making me squirm under the intensity. If I didn't know any better, I'd think I look like I just dolled up with the way they peer at me like I'm the best thing they have ever seen—even with my messy hair, dirty clothes, and soaked in blood.

"Damn, Gigi," Jameson says, pushing my hair over my shoulder to get a better look at me. "Are you hurt?"

Everett slides his fingers through mine, unable to resist touching me. "None of the blood belongs to her."

I glimpse myself in the mirror and grimace. I knew I had blood on my face, but shit. This is worse than I thought. I look nasty as all get-out. Heat burns up my cheeks, and I cover my face with my hands, hoping the four of them will get the hint that I want them to stop looking at me. This wasn't exactly the reunion I imagined.

Cool fingers lace around my wrists, gently easing my hands away. Everett smiles at me. "Don't mind my brothers. You're fine. Still stunning."

"The best thing I've ever seen," Bronx says softly, meeting my gaze in the rearview mirror.

My heart flutters at his words. I can't wait to hug him.

"He's right, but Gigi, you're confusing the hell out of me. I can't decide if I'm jealous or hungry just looking at you. I mean, I thought I was the only one you'd ever use those teeth on ever again." Jameson wipes the dried blood on my bottom lip with his thumb.

Mikkalo swivels in his seat and grabs onto Jameson's shoulders. "Knock that shit off. I'm proud as hell of Gwen. She strategized perfectly. Used what she knew. Our girl is bad-fucking-ass."

Jameson groans. "I *am* proud of her. I'm just, get over here, Gigi. I need you to bite me. I need your mouth all over me."

I release a breathless laugh, my stomach roaring at his suggestion, proving how much I want to. "Jamie."

He holds his hands out to me, but Everett hooks his hand to my waist. I catch the scent of his blood before I even see it, and I moan so incredibly loud that Jameson doesn't even release a growl at his brother. His eyebrows shoot up on his forehead, and he looks away as I swivel and grab onto Everett's arm, pulling it to my mouth without hesitation.

"So good," I murmur, sucking hard enough to pull a sexy as hell moan out of Everett. I find myself on his lap with my back resting on his chest, keeping him pinned under me in a way that turns the both of us on.

"Damn," Mikkalo says, keeping his gaze trained out the windshield. "Me next."

"I'll fight you for it," Jameson says, scooting closer already.

Their need to take care of my needs prods at my dhampir nature, and I hum under my breath, reaching out to dig my fingers into Jameson's leg.

"Give her space. We don't even know what she's been through. This is probably so much for her to handle," Bronx says, keeping his voice low like if he dares raising it, it might set me off.

I meet his gaze in the rearview mirror. He's the only one who looks at me as I drink from Everett. His mouth tilts in a frown, and I blink my eyes, stopping any tears from falling. Pulling away from Everett's arm, I manage to control my still furious hunger.

"I'm okay," I say, my voice barely coming out a whisper. "I'm just so happy you came for me."

"I promised you we would," Bronx says, still not gracing me with the smile I love. He looks more sad than anything, even though I'm here now. "You're our girl."

I bob my head, any form of response staying locked in

my throat.

"Now let the rest of us take care of you," Jameson says, wiggling his fingers at me. "I could use your arms around me."

A smile breaks across my face. "Okay, Jamie. Just be prepared. I'm starving."

He tilts his head, showing off his neck. "Take as much as you need. I'll gladly die under those kissable lips of yours."

I kiss his throat. "It's a good thing I want more of you later."

He hums. "Hurry up, Bronxy. Let's get our girl the hell home."

3

MIND MANIPULATION

"THIS IS THE WEIRDEST BONDING experience of my life," Bronx says, reaching over to touch my cheek. "But thanks for inviting me. I know it's Everett's time with you."

I cup his hand, pressing it into my skin just to feel the weight of his fingers. "I think it might be the best one for me."

"Which is why I agreed." Everett slides his hands around my hips to shift my body slightly so that my back faces him. It takes everything in me not to react to his stiff boner poking my back, and I'm nearly certain my constant wiggling gives it away.

"This would be better if Mikkalo didn't go crazy with the bubbles. I can't even see your tits," Jameson says across from me. He scoops up a handful of bubbles and blows it, sending the foam into the air.

I flick water at him. "Behave."

"Yeah, the bubbles were more for our benefit," Mikkalo says, pulling my legs to sprawl over his lap, risking me turning him on.

I grin at the three of them while sneaking my hand underwater to trail it over Everett's leg as he massages shampoo into my hair. He leans into me, his soft moan tickling my shoulder.

"And you think we need to behave," he whispers, tugging my hair gently so I sink more into him.

I laugh. "I can't help it. I've missed you all. You have no idea."

I hadn't planned on taking a bath, intending on just going straight to bed after my shower, but I couldn't sleep over the soft murmurs of Bronx, Mikkalo, and Jameson as they hung out in Bronx's room while I snuggled with Everett. I could tell they all wanted some attention, so I mused that I was still achy and wanted a bath in Mikkalo's tub since it was the biggest.

I couldn't just intrude on Mikkalo with Everett, so here we are, the five of us sitting together and proving how big the tub really is. And hot. I love getting to peek at all the muscles and delicious bodies every time the water shifts. I'm the luckiest ever.

"And I really love the bubbles," I add, sliding my leg across Mikkalo's now raging erection. I'm nearly certain no one's going to leave the tub at this point. "After the...week?" I frown, thinking about the time locked away on Corona's estate.

"It's been two and a half days," Bronx says, keeping his voice even.

"But it felt like fucking eternity." Mikkalo runs his hands up and down my legs. "I was going crazy."

"We all were," Everett murmurs, moving my wet hair from my shoulder to brush his lips to my skin.

No one reacts to his affection, though Jameson looks like it's taking a whole bunch of self-restraint not to try to move to sit between Bronx and Everett to get closer himself. And not because he wants attention. He looks ready to smother me.

"Well, I'm back and everything's g-great." My voice hitches with my words. "Like that nightmare didn't happen." Except it did. The harder I try to suppress the memory, the more it fights to return to me.

The four of them fall silent, turning their gazes from me to each other. Talk about pouty as hell vampires. Even my brothers could never master such brooding expressions. It gets to me more than it should. Because I have nothing to be upset about. I wasn't mistreated that much nor was I with psycho Corona for long. So many more people are worse off. Grayson would smack me upside the head if I even dare feel sorry for myself.

Jameson risks reaching out to touch my leg under the water. "Gigi, you don't have to pretend you're okay if you're not. What happened with your brother—"

"Please, don't." I grab his hand and scoot away from Everett to face Jameson. "I'm fine. He betrayed me. Told Corona what I was in an attempt to free my other brothers and punish me for being a traitor to humanity. He was a stupid, stupid jerk. He should've trusted me."

I heave a breath, suddenly feeling too hot in the water. I stand up, dripping bubbles everywhere in an attempt to get out, but I don't make it far. There are too many legs to climb over that I end up slipping. Jameson catches me, my body sliding against his. He tries to hand me to Everett, but I clutch him tighter.

"You know, I don't know why I'm so messed up over this. Look at what he did to us. You almost lost your heart," I say to Jameson. And then I swat him. "And I can't believe you were going to give it up for me."

Jameson doesn't respond. He doesn't look at me either.

"You barely know me, Jamie. I'm not worth dying for. I'm an anomaly, and you guys probably can't help the attraction you feel for me. Laredo always said he thought part of my predatory nature was to hypnotize—"

Jameson spins me away from him and toward Everett,

who interrupts me with a kiss that leaves my whole body buzzing. Everett doesn't pull away until he's sure I won't continue with my rant. "Why don't we get out of here, Gwen? You've been through a lot."

"I've been through worse," I say, lowering my voice. Everyone's tense as hell now. I've ruined what was supposed to be a time to relax and forget, but my head just wants me to remember. I've never had such a difficult time shoving something to the back of my mind. "Spending a couple of days alone in the dark doesn't compare to Laredo killing..." I squeeze my eyes shut. I can't even remember my one and only sort of...boyfriend? Lover? Distraction? Whoever he was. "Or...damn it." I can't remember my former blood source's name before Laredo either. "What is wrong with me?"

Bronx gets out of the tub and grabs a towel, wrapping it around his waist. "All right, dandelion. Time to get out. This was too much."

I place my hands on my hips. "Was not. I'm just...fuck. I can't believe this shit. Why can't I suppress it like every-thing else?"

No one responds to me right away as Bronx hands his brothers their towels and holds one out to me. Everett helps me from the tub so that I can step toward Bronx. Bronx wraps me up, taking a moment to hug me. It's the first one he's given me since I've returned because Everett has barely stepped away from me, except for Mikkalo and Jameson to give me more of their blood in the car.

"Gwen, I think I know why you feel so overwhelmed," Everett says softly. He wraps his arms around both me and Bronx, resting his chin on the crook of my neck.

"Isn't it obvious?" Mikkalo asks. "Our girl—"

Everett turns and shakes his head at his brother. "Yes, she's been through a lot, but I think it's more than that."

I frown. "What do you mean?"

Bronx eases away from me so I can turn and look at Everett. I glance at the four of them, taking a minute to study their faces. Bronx and Mikkalo remain expressionless, but Jameson can't control his grimace, his eyes flashing silver as he realizes whatever thought Everett has about me—a thought I can't guess.

Everett sighs. "You keep saying you don't understand why you feel what you feel."

"Well, yeah. It's not like I'm a stranger to losing people. It's my life," I say. "I mean, I watched my former blood source rip my dad's throat out, and I didn't feel this bad. Kyler doesn't deserve my grief."

Jameson groans. "Fuck. You're right, Ev."

I hug my arms around myself. "Just spit it out. I can't read your minds."

"Gwen, I think Laredo manipulated your mind so that you never had to deal with these kinds of emotions," Everett finally says.

"It wouldn't be the first time a Blood Rebel had dealt

with something like this," Bronx adds. "From what I know, some rebels ask to have things manipulated from their minds. They think it makes them stronger. Allows them to do things they wouldn't normally do otherwise."

I shake my head. "No. That's not true. A Blood Rebel would never allow or ask a vampire to get into their heads."

"Maybe you did. I can't imagine dealing with the death—"

"I'd never," I say, jerking my attention to Mikkalo.

Jameson clears his throat. "I think it was Grayson. He was her keeper."

"He'd never..." Ah hell. Yes, he would. Grayson cared the most about our purpose in life. If I feel this way about Kyler now, even though he betrayed me, I can only imagine how I was after Dad's death. It was enough to push me into killing my blood source, and Grayson found Laredo quickly after that. I don't even remember how. Grayson just showed up with Laredo a couple of days later, and that's when we started putting all of Dad's training to use.

I blink a few times, trying desperately to remember. But the harder I try, the more my head hurts.

"Gwen?" Everett says, drawing my attention to him. "You okay?"

"I don't know," I respond. "I—I can't think."

He hugs his arms around me. "Can I take you to our room?"

I slowly nod and glance into his blue eyes. "Will you fix

me?" My mouth asks before my brain can catch up.

"Fix you?" Everett asks, confusion lining his brows.

I press my fingers into my temples, wishing with everything in me that I knew what the hell Laredo did. Losing Kyler messed me up. It was easy to not dwell on him when I was dwelling on my hunger, on being imprisoned by Corona, but now I can't stop it. It's hard to process. I don't want to feel like I do, but I don't like the strange feeling of my past being locked from me even worse. "Something's wrong with my head."

Everett frowns and looks to his brothers. He rubs his scruffy face, a dozen thoughts consuming his handsome features.

"You can do that, right?" I ask, hooking my fingers around his neck to get him to look at me again.

"I can try, but Gwen, you should—"

I press my lips to his to cut him off. He's not the only one who can silence an argument. "Please, Everett. Just try to help me."

Everett releases a small breath and turns to Bronx. "What do you want me to do? We never discussed the possibility of her giving us permission to open her mind." That's what his look to his brothers was for. I know that Bronx made it clear that under no circumstance were they ever to manipulate my mind. Not that they would. Except now. It's the first time I've asked.

Bronx's jaw tightens, his dark eyes roving over my face

without looking at me directly. Without him having to say anything, I can tell he might have a problem with it. "I don't think it's a good idea."

I huff and jerk from Everett to glare at Bronx straight on. "This isn't your decision. It shouldn't be anyone's decision except mine and Everett's, because I'm asking him to do this." Shifting, I turn back to Everett and puff air through my lips. "I trust you, Everett. Please, please do this for me."

Bronx releases a soft growl at me. "But Gwen."

I hold my hand up. "No. I want this. I want Everett to open my mind. I think it might be the only way I can deal with this."

"It could change things..." Bronx is worried how it'll affect us. But that is the last thing I'm worried about.

"Not what we have," I say, my voice sounding more confident.

Bronx's eyes soften. "Are you absolutely sure?"

Everett squeezes my hand. "There's no going back once it's done. I will not take a part of you away."

Tightening my mouth, I hesitate to respond. Am I sure? No, not really. But I need this. If what they say is true, then I want to know to what extent. What exactly did Grayson have Laredo do to me? What if it's far worse than I can imagine?

"Yes, I'm sure," I finally say.

Bronx looks at Everett. "All right, Ev. Give our girl

what she wants."

"So, your brothers aren't going to join us?" I ask, resting my back on the pillows Everett propped against the headboard so that I could eat the dinner Jameson made for me in bed.

"They can if you want them to." Everett removes my empty plate and sets it on the nightstand. He scoots in front of me, crisscrossing his legs to face me. "I understand if you're nervous to do this alone. This can't be easy for you."

I lean forward and take his hands, twining our fingers together. "I'm good. I trust you. I just thought they'd want to be here."

"I don't know if you realize this, but you're giving everyone a bad case of feelings." He moves a bit closer, choosing to open his legs for me to sit between and then adjusts my legs to rest over his. "They're afraid of not only how you'll take this but also how they'll take it. This isn't exactly something they can strategize to get through until we know for sure what we're dealing with."

I smirk. I can't help it. "Oh, no. Feelings. How awful."

He chuckles. "Jameson is especially a mess."

"And Bronx hates surprises," I say.

He leans into me. "Not as much as Mikkalo."

"What about you, Everett? Am I putting you in a terrible position? If you're uncomfortable with doing this...I don't want you to feel like I'm forcing you." I fiddle with the sheets, messed up from the little bit of sleep I got while we waited for the blood I drank to wear off.

Everett decides to close the space completely, pulling me so close that I can wrap my legs around him. He runs his fingers over my cheek and tucks my hair behind my ear. "Nothing with you is uncomfortable to me. I'm confident in my ability to care for you on every level, even if you think I'm somehow only attracted to you because of what you are."

I crinkle my nose. "I'm sorry I said that. I just...I sometimes wonder. I don't know any other dhampirs. There was a vampire at Corona's, and he made it so easy for me to attack him."

"The guy you bit?" he asks, smirking.

I scrunch my face more, closing my eyes at the thought. "Desperate times. I did not enjoy it."

He chuckles. "We were proud as hell watching that, though Jameson might be a little jealous."

"He would be," I say, meeting his gaze.

"And not because of what you are."

I suck in my top lip to stop from frowning. "If you say so."

"I know so. Even if your being a dhampir might've ignited our attraction to you—which I'm certain would have happened regardless—it doesn't change the fact that you're amazing. You're quite lovable, Gwen."

"Are you sure it's not because I smell delicious to you?"

I tease.

Everett releases a soft hum. "You forgot taste. Do you know how hard it is for me to resist not kissing you?"

"What about touching?"

"Gwen," he murmurs. "I've missed you. So much. I've never been so...I wanted so badly to destroy the Anderson Coven. It kills me that Bronx won't allow us."

"He has his reasons," I say. Bronx hasn't said as much, but I know he didn't wage a war because the Royale Region already faces problems with the death of Zaire. I can't imagine the board will take kindly knowing that my guys acted without authority. I think Corona knew that too and that's why he risked it.

"I know, it's just... Can I kiss you?" Everett cups my face, capturing my gaze, his intensity hot enough to awaken my body as I sit so closely to him.

I answer him by closing the space and brushing my lips to his, jumping head first into the desire that crashes over me at the memory of being with him. Everett devours my affection, slipping his tongue into my mouth, allowing me to taste the sweetness of his deep kiss. His hands travel to my waist, and he plays with the hem of my shirt, twisting it to tighten against me.

I graze my fingers down his chest, touching his tight muscles through his shirt. I tug it over his head and break my mouth from his to draw my tongue down his neck until I reach his shoulder.

"We should stop," he whispers. "I don't want you to risk biting me and consuming my blood just yet."

I suck his skin just hard enough to leave a mark. "Okay, but I won't bite you."

"Gwen." He groans softly, still playing with my shirt. "I want you so badly. You're all I can think about."

"You're all I want to think about." I push him back to straddle him, my body wanting nothing more than to experience everything that is Everett all over again. "The mind thing can wait a bit longer."

"Are you sure?" he asks.

I nod, bending down to kiss him. "Mmmhmm."

He drags my shirt over my head, leaning up to kiss along the cup of my bra while unclasping it. His tongue flicks across my nipples, tracing around them, and I grind against him. Even through his pants, I can feel the length of his erection. It teases me, setting me off in a desperate way that has me rushing to unfasten his jeans.

Everett sucks my nipple into his mouth just hard enough to send tingles through me, and I clutch onto his head, panting and shifting, my body begging me to hurry up already. I reach between us and slide his boner from his jeans, tightening my fingers around it to feel him flex in my hand. He releases a deep moan, his fingers digging into my back as he finds my mouth again.

Trailing his fingers down the length of my body, he unbuttons my pants and slides his hand between my legs, moaning again as he feels exactly what he does to me. I gasp at the amazing pressure of his fingers tracing slowly over my clit as he explores my body.

Everett kisses my jaw, his fangs grazing across my skin, just teasing me and sending goosebumps over my body. I arch up and allow him to tug my pants down more until he lifts my legs to undress me completely. I do the same for him and kneel between his legs to take a moment to drink in his naked body. His eyes flash silver with desire, and he reaches for my hand to pull me back against him.

He kisses me deeper, and I purposely graze my tongue to his fang to draw a little bit of my blood to tease him with. His fingers tighten on my hips as he guides my body to his, slipping inside me while I sit on top.

I moan so loud at the sensation of him inside me. I've never been on top before, and just feeling every inch of him leaves my body buzzing. Everett hooks his fingers to my ass, helping me rock against him until I get the hang of what he likes and move on my own, picking up speed, my breath gasping through our motions.

Leaning down, I meet my mouth to his and kiss him again. He trails his hand over my pelvis and puts a bit of pressure on my clit, working me over as I roll my body against his, enjoying the pleasure cascading over me.

Everett whispers my name and reminds me how beautiful he thinks I am, how good I feel, how happy I make him. I can't stop from smiling, the look in his eyes speaking volumes without him having to say anything more.

I savor his closeness, the sweet scent of his skin, his fervent yet gentle touch. My emotions run wild as the intensity between us builds and builds until I feel like I'm going to explode at any second.

I inhale a deep breath, my whole body igniting with the best sensation ever. I throw myself closer to Everett, and he moans again in my ear, kissing my shoulder and moving my body for me when I slow. My body tingles everywhere with bliss, my heart crashing against his. He kisses me passionately, rolling me over until I hit my back to the pillows. He thrusts deeper inside me, propping himself up on one hand while the other keeps me close to him, our chests touching, our hearts beating wildly as they thump against each other.

Everett releases a deep, throaty hum that tickles my skin as he cums and slows down and puts more weight on me. Tilting his head, he meets me for another kiss, just light and sweet. He pants for a moment, smiling while hugging me close like he can't find the will to pull away.

"I can't ever get enough of you," he murmurs, brushing the strands of messy hair from my face. "You're just so perfect to me. I hope you know that, Gwen."

I smile. "You're perfect to me too. I love spending time with you."

"I hope you always feel that way."

Everett slides off me and pulls me close, hugging his arms around me. We lay together, our legs entwined, our hearts finally slowing down. A dozen thoughts cross my mind as I look at him, his gaze never leaving mine.

If it wasn't for the sudden growl of my stomach, I'm sure Everett would never let me go until it was my time with Bronx. Heat warms my face at another rumble, making him chuckle. He touches his cool finger to my cheek, smiling wider.

"I don't know if you realize this, but it's such a turn on to know that you have the same deep-seated hunger for me that I do for you," he says. "I know you think being a dhampir makes you a predator to me as a vampire, but I'm nearly certain it's neither for us. I wouldn't even think of hunting or preying on you. I want nothing more than to just take care of you. It feels like we were made for each other."

His words dig into me as I think about them, about the possibility that we can survive off each other. "Fate." This isn't the first time I've thought such a thing, that it was my destiny to find a coven that holds me as their equal. That doesn't freak out for what I am and instead appreciates me. It's what cements my thoughts in knowing that my family was wrong about vampires.

"Fate only led you to us, Gwen. You chose to stay," he says.

"How could I resist your claim?" I tease. "It never felt right before I met you guys."

"Maybe because your blood sources weren't right for

you," he says. "We don't claim you as a possession, Gwen. We claim you as our girl, someone we want as our mate, and someone we can see a future with. I don't know exactly what Laredo's motives were, but with how you speak of him, you don't sound like you were on the same page with him."

"I know he desired me," I say.

"I think it was more than that. The more I think about your situation and your brothers, how things went down...it doesn't really add up. You said that you were trying to save some humans from an outcast, but we don't have outcasts in Crimson Vista. The vampire wouldn't have run from you either."

"Most outcasts ran from us," I say, turning more to face him.

He twists his lips to the side. "Which doesn't make sense. Outcasts didn't even run from Zaire."

I swallow, reaching out to run my finger over his jaw. "Well, why don't we try to make sense of it now? I don't know how much longer I can resist biting you."

He smirks, though his eyes don't light up. "Are you sure you really want me to do this? It can be overwhelming, and it can take your mind a bit of time to adjust."

I think about his words, wondering if it's worth it. I mean, I'm okay now. But what if something changes? I can't help thinking about the elder Blood Rebel who claimed to be looking for me before he deemed me a traitor. What if

Bronx had been right all along and that Laredo had been using my family? What if I'm not who Everett thinks I am? What if he opens my mind, and I turn out to be just like my brothers?

"Gwen?" Everett asks softly. "We don't have to do this now. If you have even an ounce of doubt, it might be better to wait."

I shake my head. "I need to do this. If I don't, I won't. It's probably better for everyone. I mean, what if Laredo messed with my head so much that I'm not so perfect to you?"

He puffs out his bottom lip with a breath. "Gwen."

"It's still early enough that you guys can salvage your region and not have to worry about what my life means for your coven," I add.

"I've never worried about what your life means for our coven." He holds my hands. "It's the one thing I don't worry about."

Our coven. He says it like I'm included, and I can't stop my heart from racing. "You sure?"

"Yes." He doesn't hesitate or think about his response at all, just says the words like it's the truth. I hope it is.

I kiss him. "Okay. Let's get this over with then. I'm hoping you're right."

"I am."

"If you're not, all that I ask is that you let me go. Please don't cage me." The words come out softly, the thought hard even to admit.

His eyes narrow with his frown. "I'm not agreeing to either of those. If you change, we'll work through it. Together. I'm not giving up so easily."

"Why not?"

He releases a soft sigh. "I'm just not. Now, please. Look at me and don't look away."

I slowly draw my gaze to his, letting him capture me in his silver stare. My body relaxes next to him, and my heart remains even.

The sensation of him locking me with his gaze is nothing like the moment I experienced before. I'm neither scared nor threatened or feel like I'm imprisoned in my body. If anything, I feel closer to him. His thoughts clear on his face. He feels the connection too.

"Gwen, I want you to remember anything Laredo made you forget," he says, his voice even. "Remember anything that had been taken away from you."

I startle at the pain bursting behind my eyes. It's enough to make Everett break his gaze.

Covering my eyes, I hold my head in my hands, the throbbing pain growing worse. My eyes leak with unbidden tears, the edges of my vision darkening.

"Fuck," I whisper.

"What's wrong? Tell me what you feel," Everett says, adjusting me.

"I—" My words turn into a screech, my head pounding

so hard it feels like it'll explode at any second.

"Gwen!" Everett calls. "Gwen, look at me."

But I can't.

I black out.

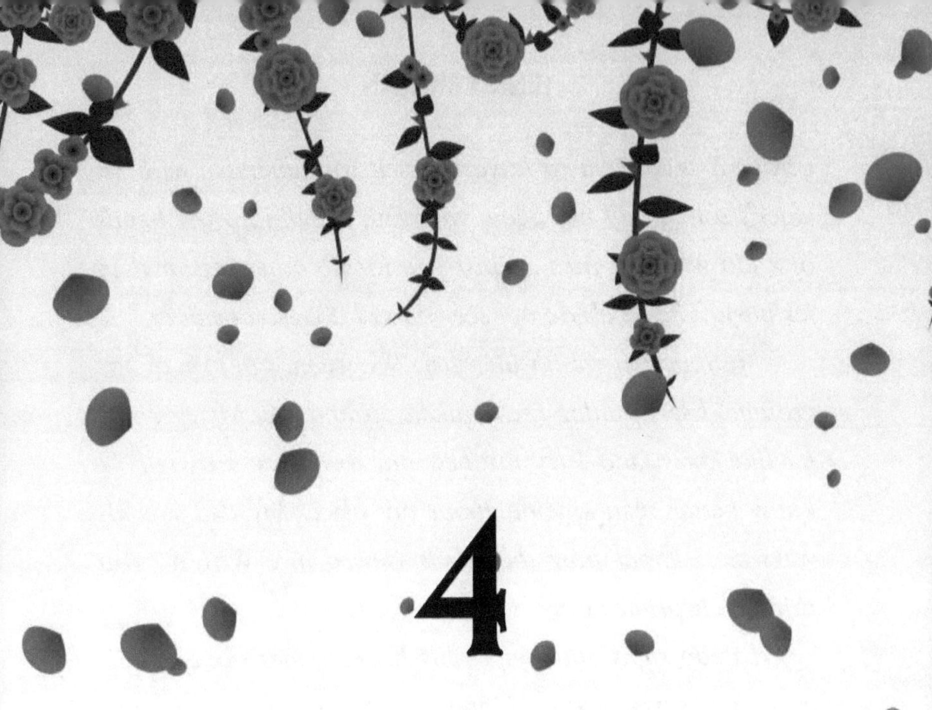

4

PREVIOUS BLOOD SOURCE

"HOW COULD YOU DO THIS to me, Gwen?" Laredo says, dragging Nathaniel's body off me before I can even scream. Leaning in, he captures me in his silver gaze, stirring terror inside me. "Shhh. We don't want your brothers to hear now, do we? Keep your voice low."

I blink my eyes, shaking away the strange feeling washing over me to suppress my oncoming yells. "You killed him." It's all I can manage to whisper.

"Of course I killed him. He should've been nowhere near you," he says with a growl. "Don't you know how dan-

gerous it is for you to leave yourself so vulnerable with an elder's son? I will not allow your fate to fall into the hands of a kid who can turn against you for no other reason than jealousy. The rebels do not see you as I do. No one does."

"Jealousy? It wasn't like that. We weren't in love or anything," I say, pulling the blankets around me. My eyes water like crazy, and I try my best not to let my tears fall. "I know better than anyone about my place. My dad was always clear about how the rebels viewed me. Why do you think he kept me away?"

Laredo sighs and swipes his finger under my eye. His eyes flash silver again. "Don't cry. He wasn't worth your tears."

And like that, my eyes dry.

"You will not feel sad, either. You were just having fun with him."

Laredo breaks my stare, and I scrunch my nose and backhand him in the shoulder. "You asshole. We were just having fun. Porter is going to stake you for this, you know."

Narrowing his eyes, he says, "Highly doubt it. I thought he was hurting you. Grayson said you were a virgin, and I assumed...you had better taste. You know I'd be happy to satiate your every need."

Laredo runs his tongue over his bottom lip before sinking his fangs into it. Blood dribbles onto his chin, and I inhale a small breath, unable to draw my eyes away. Before I can think about what's happening, I crash my mouth to his, *gliding my tongue over his lip. I suck it into my mouth, making him moan, the noise vibrating through me.*

His hands travel under my ass, and he lifts me up with him, carrying me across the room and to the couch. He trails his fingers over my legs, drawing them toward my thighs, still exposed under my long T-shirt. Snatching his hands, I lock my fingers through his and draw them up to restrain him.

"You smell so good," he whispers, trying to close the space to me to kiss me for real.

I don't let him. I know better than to give him what he wants. If I give him even an ounce of control, he'll take advantage of it and try for a cup of it next.

"And you taste good," I murmur, trailing my mouth over his throat. I nip his skin between my teeth just hard enough so that he shifts under me to show me what my words to do to him.

"Perhaps you'll let me experience how incredible you truly are." He draws his fangs over the sleeve of my shirt, tearing it to expose more of my shoulder. Gently grazing his lips against my skin, he tests me for a reaction.

"You'd like that, wouldn't you?" I sink heavier onto him, grinding against his erection through his pants. He knows I'm not wearing underwear, and I bet he's trying so hard to seduce me. There is something I enjoy about the games we play.

"More than anything."

I hum. "I'll think about it. It would be so easy."

He breaks my hold on him and hooks his fingers to my waist, rocking me harder, making my body buzz. "Maybe after you get another taste of me..."

"Should we find out?" I tease, licking up his throat.

He moans again and bends his neck to make it easier.

I bite him hard, sinking my teeth into his skin until he bleeds for me. We both moan at the same time, and I don't resist as he trails his hands lower to squeeze my ass, drawing his fingers incredibly close to my vagina. Warmth floods my mouth and sends tingles to my stomach with every swallow.

A door slams. "Hey, Nathaniel. Have you seen Gwen?"

Porter's familiar voice cuts through the small house, and I throw myself off Laredo and pull a pillow from the couch to cover my face. I heave a few breaths, my wild emotions getting the best of me. And oh shit. What the fuck? I was close to giving into Laredo's desire to be with me.

"Nathaniel?" Porter calls again.

I pull myself together and get to my feet. Laredo staunches the bleeding on his neck, pressing Nathaniel's discarded shirt to it. He twists his lips to the side, giving me a look like I better deal with this.

Striding across the room, I stand in the doorway and block the way. "Porter, I'm here. But something happened."

Porter appears from the hallway, coming in from the back door. His eyes widen as they lock on me. "Fuck, Gweny. Is that blood?"

I touch my fingers to my mouth, feeling the stickiness of Laredo's blood on my chin. "I—I'm so sorry, Porter."

His eyebrows furrow. "What happened?"

A strong hand touches my shoulder as Laredo stands behind me. "It seems I couldn't tell the difference between your sister's yells for pleasure from the ones of her in pain."

Swinging my elbow back, I hit Laredo in the stomach, making him gasp. He releases a small growl but stops at the silver stake Porter snatches from the front pocket of his jacket. I take an automatic step back into Laredo's arms. Porter scowls, his face distorting in anger I've never seen directed at me before.

"How stupid are you, Gwen?" Porter asks, tightening his lips so they hide under his unkempt beard.

"Me?" It takes everything in me to suppress my anger.

"Yeah, you. Fucking my best friend—an elder's son— knowing about the delicate relationship you've formed with your blood source." He bares his teeth at me. "This is your fault. You ruin everything."

"Are you kidding me? My fault? Relationship? I'm not in a relationship with Laredo. He feeds me. Nothing more." I clench my jaw as my own fury gets the best of me. "And so you know, who I choose to be with is none of your damn business. You sleep with whoever the hell you want. I'm an adult. You are not my keeper."

"You are a dumbass. Dad was too overprotective of you. Laredo feeds you, yeah, but you have to fulfill your end *of the agreement as his companion and protector at some point. Grayson used your virginity as part of the deal. You're not supposed to go around fucking people."*

I jerk my head toward Laredo. "What?" This is the first time I'm hearing of this. The contract I'm aware of only assures that my brothers feed Laredo while Laredo feeds me.

Laredo shrugs. "It was for everyone's safety. I...I get jealous. You know how enthralled I am with you."

I scowl. What the hell? "No one told me this bullshit. Had I known—"

"Because we thought you were better than this, Gwen," Porter snaps. "We only thought that we had to worry about Laredo, and only because of his possessiveness. Now, my best friend is dead. His life is on you. You're lucky if I don't report you as a traitor."

Rage cascades over me, darkening my vision. "Shut up. I'm not."

He jabs me in the chest. "You are. You're a monster. I don't even know why Grayson bothers. We should just let the elders take you before you're responsible for more deaths."

"Porter!"

Before I can react, Porter slaps me across the face. Laredo roars and hooks his fingers to my waist, ripping me away from him as I attempt to retaliate. Everything happens so fast that I don't have a chance to react. Laredo shoves Porter into the wall, lifting him off his feet. He snarls in his face.

Porter tries to stake him, but Laredo's quick to unarm him. He stabs the stake into the wall next to Porter's ear.

Leaning in, he captures Porter in a gaze. "You will not speak of this again, nor will you ever touch Gwen. The elders are never to be brought up. She does not belong to your family or them. All of this was an accident. You will not so much as look at me or Gwen in the wrong way again. Do you understand?"

Porter bares his teeth. "I understand."

"You will also take care of Nathaniel's body. Tell the elders he succumbed to his destiny. Tell Grayson we have an assignment. He can see me about it." Laredo drops Porter to the ground and looks at me. "Now, come along, Gwen. Let's get you cleaned up before your other brothers realize how much you enjoy devouring me. It is in our best interest to keep such things a secret."

I take a step back. "I—no. I need to get out of here. I need space."

Laredo blocks my way and takes me into his arms. I can't fight against his strength or do anything to get him to let me go. "You can have your space in a few hours."

"Please, don't do this."

"I'm sorry, Gwen. For my sake, it must be done."

"No!" The sound of my voice screeching through the air startles me awake.

I flail my arms, looking for something to grab onto but only touch empty air. The world drops out from under me until big hands catch me by my waist. I thrash for a second, forcing my eyes to get with the program to open up. Gasping, I gulp in air, my mind whirling as I try to figure out what the hell is going on.

"Hey, I got you, Gwen. It's okay. You had a nightmare," Bronx says, shimmying further onto the bed until I'm on the mattress and between his legs.

I cover my face with my hands, trying to orient myself. The vivid nightmare felt utterly real, even though I know it wasn't. Laredo is dead. Porter is...I don't even know. "Shit."

Bronx scoots closer and pulls me into his arms to stroke his hand up and down the length of my back. His familiar scent loosens my muscles. He hugs me tighter, his own soft breathing tickling my neck. "Take it easy. Just breathe. In and out."

I swallow the burning in my throat. "What happened? Why am I here?"

Glancing down, I take in my satin and lace shorts and tank top. I don't know why I look at my PJs. I know Everett wouldn't have brought me here butt-ass naked. It's not like Bronx hasn't seen me either. It's just disorienting.

And then I remember Everett's mind manipulation. The pain of how intense it felt. But I also remember how intimate the moment was, especially after our passionate lovemaking. I wasn't scared at all. I just...

"I'm sure you're a bit confused." Bronx must notice my reaction. "I hope it's okay that Everett brought you here.

He...needed to clear his head."

"Is he all right?" I ask, frowning. The last thing I expected was to wake up next to Bronx, but it's not bad. I just didn't expect it.

He hugs me closer, brushing his lips to my temple. "Yeah, don't worry about him. He'll stop by for breakfast. Promise."

My damn stomach. I don't even clutch it for more than a second before Bronx offers me a thermos of blood. He doesn't let me take it, just holds it to my mouth and watches me sip the warm liquid. The sweet flavor bursts over my tongue, and I release a soft moan.

"Is it good?" he asks, studying my expression. "Just mine and Everett's this time."

I can't get myself to pull away to respond to him. The blood mixture tastes so amazing, fulfilling me with exactly what I need now that I realize how starving I am. I must've been out for a while. Everett did warn me that things could be a little intense.

Lacing my fingers around the thermos, I help Bronx tilt it more. I start to gulp, making Bronx's eyes flash silver. His Adam's apple bobs in his throat as he swallows, and I can't stop myself from staring at his mouth and how his fangs peek out from under his lips. My desire for him rises inside me, but it's not all-consuming like it was before when I drank only his blood. It's just enough to make me feel a ton better.

When the thermos is empty, I rub my lips together. "Can I have more? I'm just—I don't know. I feel out of control. My head. Fuck." I throw myself back onto the mattress and gaze at the overhead lights. My nightmare comes crashing back to me all over again, except now that I've had a moment to process, I realize it wasn't a dream at all. It was a memory. One that had been manipulated by Laredo.

Bronx doesn't get a chance to answer me. An alarm blares through the air, piercing my ears. Scooping me up, Bronx presses my face to his chest, using his hand to help silence the noise of the shock alarms going off.

His bedroom door swings open, and Mikkalo flies in, clutching two scary-ass swords. His wild eyes blink silver as his gaze sweeps across the room until he stops to stare at me in Bronx's arms. His mouth moves, but I can't hear anything over the screeching alarms. Neither Mikkalo nor Bronx reacts to the noise, and I can't help wondering if they even hear it.

And then the alarms shut off, leaving my ears ringing.

A familiar woman materializes in the hallway just outside the door, and Mikkalo swings his swords. He cuts through the flowy fabric of her long dress, and she snarls but only steps back. The world blurs, and my back hits the mattress. Bronx abandons me to step between the woman and Mikkalo.

"Brooklyn, what are you doing here?" Bronx asks.

I sit up and stare at the woman. I know her. She was

the one who helped me escape from my room at Corona's. She's Bronx's biological sister.

"She betrayed you," Mikkalo says. "Corona's here. He's threatening to contact the board if we don't let him sweep the premises."

Bronx growls, flashing his fangs. "What?"

"Calm down," Brooklyn says, holding her hands up. "He doesn't know I'm here. I only came to warn you. Corona thinks he can test you. Without Gwen, he plans to use Zaire's death to his advantage."

"Why should we trust you?" Mikkalo says, aiming his sword at her.

"Because I'm risking treason to be here." Brooklyn flashes her fangs. "I don't know exactly what the hell is going on and why my brother wants to risk everything for—" She flicks her gaze to me. "Whatever she is. But if he thinks she's worth it, then I think she's worth it. Not to mention that Corona denied my request of a Blood Vow to Neihart."

"You want me to push it through to Donor Life Corp?" Bronx asks.

She nods. "A favor for a favor. You want me to be happy, little brother. Don't you?"

Bronx's com device chimes from the nightstand, and he sighs as he looks at the screen. "If you take Gwen to our old hideout and protect her with your life, then I'll see to it."

"You can't just let her take Gwen," Mikkalo argues, looking fully prepared to battle him over the decision.

Bronx flashes his fangs at him. "What other choice do we have?"

Mikkalo raises his sword.

I scramble off the bed, drawing everyone's attention to me. Rushing forward, I get between Mikkalo and Bronx, holding up my palms to each of them. My fear instincts go off like crazy, and it takes everything in me not to start gasping for air. They look ready to jump at me to steal me away from each other.

"I'll go," I say, darting my gaze to Brooklyn.

"Gwen." Mikkalo growls at me this time.

I turn to Mikkalo, suppressing a shudder. "I'll be fine, Mikkalo. Give Corona what he wants so that he'll back off. Tell him you located a rebel hideout."

He frowns. "But—"

"I'll explain later. Just get him out of here." I can tell it takes everything in him not to lock his arms around me to steal me away. I don't think we have time for me to tell him that whatever Everett did to me has weird thoughts—bits of knowledge long forgotten—seeping to the forefront of my mind, one of them being the community we stayed in where I was hooking up with Nathaniel. Fuck. Thinking his name sends my mind whirling.

Bronx nods to Brooklyn, pulling me from my thoughts. "Take her. Now."

Brooklyn doesn't even give me the chance to say good-bye. If only I could suppress the fear leaving me out of control. Or the desire to bite.

"We'll be there soon," Brooklyn whispers into my hair, holding me to her.

Sunlight engulfs us.

5

REBEL DHAMPIR

I LAND ON MY ASS with a thud, my hands scraping along the rough ground of a cave. Brooklyn presses her body to the wall and out of the sunlight trickling in from the mouth. I don't move and just blink under the warm glow of the afternoon. I had no idea it was already daytime, which means I must've been knocked out for hours.

"Uh, are you okay?" I ask, keeping my voice low. I consider moving deeper into the shadows, but the darkness behind me freaks me out just a bit. This is definitely the type of place shadow dwellers might use to take shelter.

Brooklyn releases a long breath. "I will be. It's been a while since I've exposed myself to the sun. Hurts like a bitch."

"Oh." I push to my feet and dust the dirt from my bare legs. "What is this place?"

"Just a secret lair." Brooklyn eases from the wall and struts a few feet deeper into the cave. Turning on her feet, she squints her eyes to look at me. "A place where Bronx and I could devour any donor we wanted in peace before The Divide."

My mouth falls agape.

Tipping her head back, she laughs. "I'm just kidding. Mostly. You know Bronx was my brother before we transitioned. This is only a place we used to meet after we were separated."

A dozen questions flit through my mind. Bronx never mentioned Brooklyn before I met her. Only Jameson has gotten into great detail about his life, and even then, it was only from his life as a Royale. Discovering this new information about Bronx ignites some crazy curiosity inside me. I'm desperate to know more.

"What do you mean by separated?" I try to keep my voice from rising. "Did the uprising force you apart or something?"

Brooklyn's brown eyes flash silver. "No."

"No?" Jeez. "What happened?"

"You ask too many questions. I do not want to face the

wrath of the Royale Coven if I say something I shouldn't. You'll have to ask Bronx yourself." Damn. Who knew I could be so disappointed by an answer? I'm curious now. I don't want to wait to ask. I get easily sidetracked under Bronx's attention—his brothers' too.

"Not even a hint?"

I regret my words immediately. Brooklyn materializes in front of me, startling me from her quick movements. Narrowing her eyes, she captures me with the same intensity Bronx sometimes does. The more I look at her face, the more I can see the resemblance she carries to Bronx—from her deep tan skin and oval brown eyes to how expressive her brows are.

"I don't know where your place lies with Bronx, and until he decides to share that information, which I doubt he ever will considering the fragility of our covens' alliances, no. I will not give you even a little hint."

I shift on my feet, the scrutiny of her stare setting off my fear instincts like crazy. Brooklyn straightens her shoulders, her fangs showing, and if I wasn't certain that Mikkalo wouldn't rip her apart, I'd think she'd risk locking her fingers to me to give me a good shake. She looks like she wants to.

"Now, if you can please just be quiet. I don't want anyone to discover we're here. I'll lose my head if we're caught," Brooklyn says, gazing past me.

"Corona—"

"Not my coven leader. Mikkalo," she says. "Because as much as it would pain me, I'm not risking my life for you."

"You said—"

"That was for his brother's benefit. I'm sure Bronx knows that if we're caught, he will have to take full blame. I'd be the one who found out he was hiding you here." She already has her story all figured out. Now I regret thinking that a former human bond actually meant something to her.

Ah hell.

Her sultry voice lowers into a whisper. "You don't think Bronx was serious about me protecting you with my life, do you?"

I guess I should've expected as much. I mean nothing to this vampire. While she might have once been Bronx's sister, things have changed. I can see why he never mentioned her. They're not even in the same coven. Shows a lot about where their loyalties are.

She blows a few strands out of her face. "Don't take it personally. While I think Bronx might've lost his damn mind risking his power and control of the region for you, I do like seeing him fighting for someone other than Zaire. He was a prick."

Yeah, he was. Her admission makes me like her just a little bit. "You mean a dickhead asshole," I mutter. "So glad he's dead."

Brooklyn tilts her head at me. "As much as I agree with you, I'd be careful with what you say. The Royales carry a fierce loyalty toward their leader."

I twist my lips. "Must not have been that fierce."

"What's that supposed to—"

A moving shadow catches my attention behind her. I don't get a chance to point before a strange vampire rushes from the darkness. Without thinking, I charge forward and ram into the gross-smelling man, knocking him back into the cave wall. He snaps his teeth at me, snarling, but doesn't get a chance to bite me.

Brooklyn drags me away and tosses me outside the cave where I catch sight of the sun fading into the horizon. From my spot, I glimpse the enormity of the Night Palms Castle. I also realize that the sun sinks into the ocean. I had no idea it was so close. I doubt many people do. I can only see it because of how high up the mountain this cave hides.

"Gwen, watch out," Brooklyn calls.

I don't get a chance to react as two strong hands dig into my shoulders and drag me farther from the cave. I hit the ground with a thud and peer up into the pure silver eyes of a different vampire. His skin blisters and smokes in the sun. It slows him down but his hunger pushes him to risk it.

Bucking my body, I kick my legs up over my head, striking him in the stomach. He catches my ankles and tugs me so hard that if I didn't cover my face with my arms, I'd have scraped my chin on the rough terrain.

Panic squeezes my chest, but all it does is make me fight harder. I flail and twist, trying to grab anything I can hold onto. I know the second he manages to get me into the shade, he'll bite me. There's no way I'm letting that happen.

Another growl sounds through the air. I realize the vampire isn't moving this slow only because of the sun. Hanging out between two nearby boulders, a guy waits for his chance to rush us. The other vampire is just as creepy and dirty as he hovers in the shade created by the boulders. All it would take is the guy dragging me to slip up for a second. This is more than a game of who claims the woman in PJs. These assholes look vicious as shit. Feral. They'll rip me apart if it means my blood spills.

The thought gives me an idea, and I slump against the dirt and stop fighting. I do my best not to react under the annoying pain of being hauled along the dirt burning across my skin. Just as I predicted, the vampire stops and drops my legs. He'll pick me up instead because running is faster.

"Gwen!" Brooklyn yells, her voice ripping through the air. "Damn it. Wake up and fight. Don't make me go out there."

I ignore her, remaining placid on the ground. It takes everything in me not to flip over and lash out even as a hand runs along my bare leg to lift and drop it. Pain bursts in my knee from hitting a rock, and I accidentally suck in a breath through my teeth.

The vampire grabs me by the waist too fast for me to react and flips me onto his shoulder. Something inside me snaps—annoyance and frustration, fear, everything bad that has happened to me in my life crashing over me in an intense wave that makes my head spin.

My shoulder slams into the ground, and I somersault onto my back. The edges of my vision shadow as I gasp, trying to breathe while getting to my feet. A screech cuts through the air, startling me. I scramble to search for anything I can use to fight. I can't let my life end like this. I didn't escape Corona only to die at the hands of disgusting, starved outcasts.

The vampire roars. I squeeze my eyes shut, my mind whirling with fear and the need to survive. I punch him as hard as I can. He falls on top of me, and I shove him with my free hand, throwing him off with strength elicited from my nature as a dhampir.

My head pounds, the world spinning. Rage still clings to me, my vision burning. I can't see anything clearly. I can't get to my feet either.

The quick thud of footsteps draws closer, and I tense, expecting to get yanked off the ground and devoured. Another shriek rips through the air, and I cover my neck with my hands to try to protect my throat the best I can.

"Fuck," a familiar voice says, pulling me from my haze of fear.

"Stay back, Jameson," Everett says, his voice low in warning. "She might attack. Look what's in her hand."

Jameson sucks in a breath. "Is that—"

"Yeah, it's a heart." Bronx's voice hums to me, pushing

through the pounding in my head. "And I'll get her. Just stay back in case." More soft footsteps sound out. "Dandelion, you're okay. You're safe. Open your eyes and look at me. I need you to see me so that I can pick you up."

I hadn't realized I couldn't see because I had squeezed my eyes shut or that I curled in on myself. I slowly blink and stare in shock at the heart squished in my fingers. How in the hell? Where did it even come from?

A cool finger touches my cheek, drawing my attention away from the pulverized organ. "You can let that go. That was one helluva punch." Bronx remains expressionless, though something indecipherable flickers through his eyes.

I drop the heart onto the dirt and wipe my hands on the front of my nightshirt. Bronx reaches out for me and lifts me up, cradling me in his arms while wrapping the both of us in the blanket he uses to shield himself from the last few rays of sunlight.

I can't find my voice to say anything, so I just rest my head on his chest and let him carry me back toward the cave where Everett, Jameson, and Mikkalo wait with Brooklyn. She stands against the cave wall, her hair barely mussed from her fight with another dead vampire in pieces on the ground.

The second Mikkalo gets a good look at the dead guy, he releases the scariest noise ever and kicks the vampire's head so hard that it flies down the steep terrain to smolder in the dirt. I think I must whimper or something, because he freezes and turns to me with wide eyes. A dozen emotions sweep across his face, but he doesn't rush to me even though I want him to. I just can't get my voice to work to tell him it's not him who scares me. It's just my adrenaline leaving me, knowing I'm safe.

"Mikkalo, take Jameson with you and do one more sweep of the area. Make sure we're really clear," Bronx says, keeping his voice even. He adjusts me in his arms, turning me so I can hug him with my whole body the way he likes. I think he needs my embrace as much as I need his.

Mikkalo opens and closes his mouth like he's about to argue, but another look at me stops him. Jameson motions for Mikkalo to follow him, and they both disappear. Everett closes the space to me and eases the blanket away from my body, tugging it from the death grip of my fingers.

"Gwen, may I examine you?" Everett says, keeping his hands to himself, though I can tell he wants nothing more than to steal me from Bronx. He touches my shoulder to ease me away from Bronx's chest a bit more. "I can't tell if all the blood on you belongs to the outcast. I want to make sure you're not injured."

"I—" I stop myself from telling him I'm fine. Now that my adrenaline dissipates completely, pain radiates through me. I'm certain I'm cut and bruised along my back, my legs. Most definitely my ass. "Okay."

"Why don't you escort Brooklyn from the premises?" Everett asks Bronx, keeping his voice low. "I need to give

Gwen more blood."

Bronx bows his head to me to whisper in my ear. "You okay with that, Gwen?" He doesn't have to admit it, but I can tell that he doesn't want to give me to Everett. His deep-seated nature flares as much as mine.

So despite my aches, I glance to Everett and say, "I can wait. I'm just a little scratched up. I'd feel more comfortable if we were back home. I feel too vulnerable out here."

Everett and Bronx share a look, and then Everett nods at me. "It's probably better if you get cleaned up anyway. Bronx can help you with that." He turns to Brooklyn, tightening his jaw. "Let me show you out. I don't want my brother to act irrationally and try to attack you for allowing an outcast within a foot of Gwen."

She straightens her shoulders. "Perhaps you four need to take better precautions. I was not expecting an attack right outside your property. Might I suggest you tell your brother that he was at fault for failing to secure your estate?"

I frown. "Hey, don't you—"

"I'm sure he's aware, Brooklyn," Bronx says, cutting me off. His com device beeps, and he tugs it from his pants to glance at the screen. "Looks like the place is clear. You should probably hurry back to your coven. Send me the Blood Vow application. As long as Corona doesn't threaten us again before we figure out what we're going to do about our situation, I'll send it through with region approval to the board."

"I hope you know what you're doing, Bronx," she whispers. I don't think Brooklyn realizes I can hear her. Reaching out, she risks getting close to me to pat his shoulder. "I already lost you once. I don't want to lose you again. Not for some infatuation you have with a donor. Please make sure she's truly worth it, okay?"

Bronx doesn't respond to her, and Everett nudges Brooklyn toward the mouth of the cave. I squeeze my eyes shut and concentrate on the sound of Bronx's heart beating, trying my best not to let Brooklyn's words get to me. She poked right at my insecurities.

"Gwen," Bronx whispers, hugging me close. His lips brush my ear. "You are worth it to me, you know. I don't want you to ever doubt that. You're not some donor to me. You're our beautiful, smart, sometimes insanely infuriating rebel dhampir."

I peek at him through my eyelashes. "She might be right, though. I don't even know if I am. I've only caused you trouble."

He shakes his head. "Don't blame yourself for the decisions I make, okay? I'm aware of the consequences."

I rest my chin on his shoulder. "That was before you knew what I was."

He eases his head away, his eyes begging for me to look at him. "Doesn't matter."

I straighten my aching back to meet him straight on. "You sure?"

Leaning closer, he brushes his lips to mine, not even caring if I'm filthy from being dragged around. "Absolutely certain. Now can I take you home? All that other guy's blood on you is making me crazy. I want it off you."

I release a breathless laugh. "If it helps, it tastes disgusting."

He grins. "That does a little. But you know what else would help?"

"Hmm?"

"If you'll let me try to give you blood again."

I can't stop my heart from racing at the thought. "Only if you let me do the same."

6

JUST A TASTE

APPARENTLY RIPPING HEARTS OUT IS a real bitch on the hand if you smash right through a bunch of bones. Light bruises and scratches decorate my knuckles and wrist, my whole hand now tender. I don't even know what really happened or how such a thing was possible. It was like my dhampir side decided to take over to protect me. Almost like an out of body experience.

Bronx clears his throat, drawing my attention to him. He looks hot as hell, just looking at me with longing and anticipation. "Are you ready?"

I play with the strands of my damp hair while I sit on the bed. I give him an extra-long once-over, trailing my gaze from his flexing muscles to his gorgeous brown eyes. "You're nervous." I keep my voice light, teasing.

He licks his lips, and now I can't stop staring at his mouth. "No, just anxious."

"Mmmhmm," I say, smiling at him.

He chuckles, relaxing his shoulders. My teasing helps lighten his intensity. "Okay, just a little bit. But don't tell anyone."

I stretch my hands out to him, motioning for him to come closer. "Don't be. If you managed to handle my crazy ass during that freak out, you can handle this."

"This is far more difficult, dandelion. I can handle your ass being feisty."

"But not turned on." I bite my lip. "Or a little wild. In desperate need of your attention and affection...and that's before getting a taste of you."

Rubbing his hand on the back of his neck, he says, "Careful or I'm going to have to prove that I can handle that too."

I bow a bit forward, letting my hair veil his view of me. I can't help squirming under his desire. "Maybe that's what I want."

Bronx releases a sexy, throaty noise, his eyes flashing silver with my words. I know better than to tease a vampire, but I can't help it. I love it. I love how he makes me feel under the weight of his gaze, how his heart beats out of control like mine, how he can't stop himself from moving closer.

He sits on the bed next to me and brushes the hair I let fall in my face out of the way to expose more of my skin to him. "I love when you're playful. Always teasing me."

I reach out and run my fingers over his shoulder, exploring his muscles. "You think I'm teasing you? I've been staring at that empty thermos for at least three minutes."

Bronx surprises me by biting his arm.

I suck in a breath through my teeth and shift closer, dropping my hand to his leg. His chest rises and falls with his deep breathing as he drips his blood into the thermos to fill it up. I know just touching him like I am drives him wild. A mixture of emotions swells through me. It takes everything in me not to jump on him and intercept the blood to drink directly from him.

Anticipation makes me dig my fingers into his thigh, making him release another sexy as hell noise. My body tingles, remembering how incredible his blood alone makes me feel. How amazing it tastes. But another part of me is nervous as all get-out. What if the side effects are just as strong and I lose control? What if my dhampir side runs wild and not the kind he might like?

"If you're too nervous, I can call one of my brothers to...stand by," he says, balancing the thermos between his legs as he staunches the blood on his arm.

"You know, you're risking a lot even keeping that

thermos where you have it."

Damn him with that sexy noise. It's driving my body wild. His attraction to me is so palpable that I can feel it in every part of my body.

"And I'm not nervous. I'm anxious," I say, licking my lips. I use the same words he used on me.

Except he doesn't tease me like I do him. He rests his hand on mine, pressing it even more into his leg. "Everett thinks it'll be okay since you already have blood in your system to dilute the effects."

I suck my bottom lip into my mouth and pry myself away from him to lean on my elbows. I know if I don't put at least a little bit of space between us, I might climb right on him. "Are you sure you want me to? This is your last chance to change your mind. I can't promise I won't attack you with my lips because I already want to."

His face lights up with his chuckle. "You not only like teasing me, but you also love testing my restraint, huh?"

I nudge him with my hand. "You like it."

Joking with him helps get my racing heart back in control. All I want to do is forget the mess that happened earlier. I want to forget Corona and Brooklyn. Laredo. The other memories trying to break free if I don't distract myself. Being this close to Bronx, inhaling the scent of his blood, feeling the weight of his hand as it touches my leg—it's all I could ever ask for. He makes it feel like there isn't a world outside his room.

"I do," Bronx says, turning his attention away from the thermos and fully on me. "I also really want you to try. You have no idea how torturous it is that I can't give you blood like my brothers can. I want to be able to take care of you in every way you need, Gwen." His voice turns soft with the words, his eyes flashing silver.

There goes my heart again. It beats wildly in my chest, and I reach out and touch Bronx's cheek.

I knew that exchanging blood was personal, intimate even, but it didn't dawn on me that it would bother him that the side effects made us both want to be cautious. I didn't realize this was the reason he wanted to try again. Now his hesitation in the cave makes sense. He wanted to be the one to give me his blood to help me heal. It's more than what he teased me over about the gross blood of the outcast driving him crazy. The fact that he wants me to try again speaks volumes about where he stands with me.

"You've been nothing but caring of me," I say, leaning forward. "So much so that I feel like I haven't done enough for you."

"You don't owe me or my brothers anything."

I play with strands of my hair. "I know, but I wasn't kidding earlier. I want to reciprocate and take care of you if you'll let me. It's just—you risk a lot and your sister's words got to me. I need to understand why. I've never met a vampire who freely gives with nothing in return."

"I know you think you give me nothing, but you do.

You've changed my life, given me unexpected power, and brought my brothers and me closer than any of us knew possible. It has strengthened our bond. Most covens fall apart without their leader, even with a first in line in place. Now, I feel like we're stronger. Powerful. Better than ever."

"Even with everything at risk? What if what you feel is...?" I let my words trail off. I don't know if I want the answer.

"What I feel is more than just what you make me feel, Gwen. I'll be honest. I can't explain what drew me to you, and even if it does pertain to what you are like what you said before, well, that shit doesn't matter to me. I didn't realize how much you being here and choosing to stay meant to me until Corona took you."

I nearly forgot my conversation I had with him and his brothers in the bathtub, a moment that feels so long ago. And him saying this? It means more to me than I thought possible. Because being here, spending time with the four of them, agreeing to see where all this goes without choosing someone to take my Blood Match contract is still ludicrous to me—but in the best way possible. I've never felt so wanted for who I am and not what I am in my life.

"Thanks for saying this. I worry about what will happen. Corona knows about me," I say. "He thinks I'm the key to getting power."

He closes his eyes in thought. "We're going to take care of him. I promise. We just have to go along with him for a bit longer until his suspicions diminish. Today was a little too close for comfort, but your idea about telling him we have information on a rebel nest worked perfectly. I'm proud as hell, to be honest despite Mikkalo freaking out a bit over falling through."

"You're not going to fall through. I have one for you."

He frowns. "But—"

"They're not my people, and I don't want to think about it anymore right now." I hug myself.

"Me either," he says, grazing his fingers over my leg. "Not with your eyes flashing at me like that."

I blink a few times. "I'm sorry."

"Don't be. I let my nerves distract me." He offers me the thermos. "Here. Drink."

The second I take the thermos from him, he disappears off the bed and stands near the couch. He offers me a small, almost shy smile. He's more nervous than he lets on. The distance between us nearly steals my breath away. I want him close more than I want to drink his blood.

I wave the thermos. "And you say I torture you. This space? Come back here."

He raises his eyebrows. "Drink first. In case."

Bringing the thermos to my mouth, I take a long sip, savoring how delicious his blood alone tastes. My body tingles, my heart picking up speed the longer Bronx gazes at me in anticipation. I finish the whole thermos and set it on the nightstand. Glancing into its mirrored glass top, I check to make sure it's not all over my face.

Bronx's soft footsteps draw closer, and I remain still, letting him close the space. "Well?"

I grin to myself, but I don't turn to look at him. "I'm not sure. I think you need to come closer. Don't be scared. I only bite if you ask."

He releases a soft laugh, his shadow moving in on me. I wait until I can feel the subtle shift of the bed, and then I make my move. Twisting, I grab onto Bronx's shirt, using it to pull myself toward him. His dark eyes widen, the golden flecks catching the light just right. He freezes as I land on top of him and press my hands into his chest.

I just couldn't resist messing with him. He's super sexy, just bracing himself for what might happen next. He looks fully prepared to let me bite the hell out of him. "Not even going to put up a fight?" I tease, smiling wider. The warmth of his blood settling in my stomach does all sorts of crazy things to me, but it's not as intense as before...or maybe I already was tense with desire. Either way, I'm not throwing myself at him. I still have control.

"Not unless you try to devour me." He relaxes beneath me, hooking his hands to my hips. From his growing erection, he realizes the same thing I do about my control and how I'm not acting this way due to the side effect of his blood. This is all me.

Bending down, I brush my lips to his, kissing him harder. His hands slide to my ass until he digs his fingers into my ass cheeks to tug me an inch higher so that I can really feel his desire for me. I hum under my breath and pull back only enough to speak. "What about if I kiss you until you beg for mercy?"

Flipping me off of him, he rolls over, holding his weight above me while lying between my legs. And hell if I didn't wish we weren't both still dressed. I can't stop my rebellious hands from trailing down the length of his back until I reach the hem of his shirt to touch his skin.

"Pin me again, and I'll let you," he says, leaning down to suck my bottom lip into his mouth.

My hips arch up in response, and I rub my body to his. "And if I can't?"

He caresses his lips to mine again like he can't resist, not that I'd want him too. "Then I get to do it to you."

Tingles burst between my legs, and I moan at just the thought, the idea sounding like the best thing ever. I don't know if it's because Corona took me or what, but Bronx lets his guard down for me, letting himself risk losing control. And I love it. So does my body.

I flop deeper into the pillows and pull his hips to mine so that he presses harder between my legs. "Okay, you win."

My words surprise him, and he studies my face, searching my eyes. "Maybe we should put on a movie or something. My blood—"

"Was delicious, and Everett was right," I say, trying to keep my voice even. I guess I was wrong. He still clings to caution at my attempt to drive him wild. "I don't feel any more out of control than I did. Your playfulness helps distract me."

"From what? Are you still hurting?"

Shit. His desire morphs into concern. I shouldn't have mentioned anything.

"Oh, no. I'm fine. I feel great actually." I smile with the words because it's true. "All I meant is that I really needed to get my mind off things. Helps me suppress all the bullshit of my life before you." I groan and tip my head forward to rest it on his shoulder so that he can't see my face.

He shifts onto his side, stopping me from hiding my face for long. "You remember more?"

"I do. The nightmare earlier—it was a memory. The worst. You were right about Laredo, but I don't know to what extent. I guess it doesn't matter much. What he did to me...I just, I don't want to think about it."

"That's why Everett needed to clear his head," he whispers to himself.

I frown. "I don't understand. Why would my memory mess with him?"

He groans. "I should really let you two talk about this."

"I will when I see him, but I want you to tell me now."

Bronx's jaw tightens as he looks away, not allowing me to lock him in my own stare. I link my fingers through his and let him work through his thoughts without pushing.

"I'm not sure you know this, but a vampire can put a

sort of block on a human's mind to ensure long-term manipulation. It takes a lot of power to do something like that, and it seems Laredo had. I don't know exactly what Everett saw opening your mind, but it was enough to have him ask me to take you."

"What do you mean that Everett saw something?"

He brings my hand to his mouth and kisses it. "There are different kinds of mind manipulation. Everett used what I can only describe as a mental link."

My mouth forms an O. "Shit. This is awkward." If he somehow saw my memory as I had, then he got to experience me sleeping with Nathaniel. Biting Laredo. Ah, hell.

Bronx runs his fingers over my shoulder, his closeness helping to ease my nerves. "And it's fine if you don't feel comfortable telling me. Just know that you can. I won't think differently of you."

I press my lips into a line and close my eyes. "But Everett might." I mean, if he saw what I remember. It wasn't good.

"No, I can promise you that. I know my brother. He might not show his empathy like Jameson, but he's probably the most empathetic out of the four of us. It's what makes him good at his job as the head of the Donor Division and also mind manipulation." Bronx shifts again, looking at the side of my face.

"Laredo manipulated my emotions so that I wouldn't hold things against him," I blurt. "He murdered an elder's son out of jealousy because I—we—ugh. If Everett saw..."

"He's fine, really. I promise."

"Apparently I was supposed to be a virgin or some bull-shit." I groan, unable to keep the thought to myself. "He made an agreement with Grayson."

"But you're not a virgin." I can't tell if it's a question or statement, his voice remaining even.

My cheeks burn like the gates of hell, and I sit up and gawk at him. "No, I'm not. I never slept with Laredo, though."

"So with a Blood Rebel's son?"

I don't answer him. Instead, I say, "And now I know why Porter hasn't even looked at me. He wanted to call me out as a traitor then. Told me some things that Laredo didn't like, so he manipulated him too."

"I hate to say this, Gwen, but he probably manipulated all of you."

"Yeah. It's not like I drank his blood all the time ei-ther." I sigh. "And there's something else."

He hums under his breath, letting me know that I can continue if I want to.

"I don't think my dad was a Blood Rebel. Not the kind you think about. He knew how to fight vampires and kept records of our history and the back-world, but he kept us—*me*—in the bunker to hide me."

He doesn't respond.

"I still can't remember much else, but I think it was Laredo who pursued my brother to get Grayson to bring him to me. I think he was trying to free me before the elders found out. He said something about my place and what they think of me." I close my eyes, trying to summon a memory that refuses to come. "Ugh, I don't know. I wish I could ask Grayson."

"When we find him, we will," he says.

"What do you mean? Corona—"

"Didn't kill them. Our sources say they were separated among the different regions."

"Really?"

He nods. "Don't worry, dandelion. Now that we have you back, they're our next priority."

I throw my arms around him and kiss him. "You have no idea what this means to me. I know my family isn't easy, and I'm sure they're going to put up a fight."

"But they're your family," he says.

I kiss him again. "Thank you."

He smiles. "Anything for you."

"Even though I'm a dhampir and might accidentally devour you?"

He chuckles. "I don't think you realize how hot that makes me. Just thinking about your mouth on me."

I snap my teeth at him. "Careful what you say. You might just think that because of what I am."

Reaching out, he touches my cheek, tracing his finger to my chin. He gently holds my face and leans in but keeps an inch of space between our lips. "I'd be lying if I denied that I find that part of you appealing. But not because of why you think. You're feisty yet soft. I don't know how to explain it."

I grin at him. "Just admit it. You just like how delicious I am. Your edible dandelion."

"That's still up in the air," he says, closing the space completely to suck my lip into his mouth, just teasing me for a second.

"Is it now?"

He shrugs, pressing his lips together to keep a straight face. "Maybe after I get the chance to taste all of you."

My. Damn. Vagina.

My smile disappears with the look of desire that crosses his face, his gaze leaving mine only to drink in my body, my boobs totally showing off their excitement without my bra. I can't stop myself from sinking deeper into the bed, curling my fingers around the sheets, trying to get myself in control.

"Gwen," Bronx whispers. "Will you look at me?"

I tip my head slightly to meet his eyes.

"I'm sorry if I got carried away."

"You didn't." I inch closer to him.

His eyes flash silver, but he doesn't say anything.

"And I've missed you. More than I knew possible."

My words ignite something wild inside Bronx, and he rolls me on top of him, sliding his fingers under my shirt. I lean in and kiss him, dragging my fingers down the hard planes of his stomach until I link my fingers to the hem of his shirt and get him to sit up enough for me to take it off. My shirt lands with his on the floor, his desperate movements prickling tingles over my skin.

"You're so enchanting," he says, his voice deepening, his hands gliding up my sides until they brush over my breasts. "I want nothing more than to kiss every inch of you."

I release a breathless moan and scoot back until I can kneel between his legs. "Me first."

The sexiest noise ever escapes his throat, and he sits up and grabs for me. I laugh and move out of his reach, tugging his workout pants with me. One second I'm kneeling in front of him and in the next, my back hits the fluffy pillows.

"Those aren't the rules of the game," he murmurs, sucking my throat just hard enough to quicken my breathing.

"I'm a rule breaker, remember?"

I shimmy lower, tracing my tongue over his chest and to his abs. The hardness of his boner grazes against my pelvis and then my stomach as I work my way lower while he holds his weight over me, remaining utterly still until I can't go any farther because of his knees. He rolls off of me, taking me with him, and I press against the length of his shaft until I lace my fingers around it and stroke him, watching him as intently as he watches me.

His lips part slightly with his deepening breath, his

heartbeat thumping as hard as mine.

"Is this okay?" I ask, licking my lips.

He reaches down and combs his fingers through my hair to push the stray strands from my face. "Only if you want to."

"I have to warn you—"

"I'm not afraid of your teeth."

Blush warms my skin, and I can't control my nervous laughter. "I'm a little afraid of yours. But also...I've never done this. And I don't know why I just admitted that."

He doesn't react to my words, just keeps playing with my hair. "Like I said, whatever you want. I love being with you."

I smile and lick my lips, suppressing my nerves. Bronx intakes a soft breath when I bend forward and graze my mouth to his tip, just tasting him with my tongue, drawing a slow circle around the ridge until I finally mold my lips over his erection and suck him into my mouth.

"Gwen," he whispers, my name coming out with his moan.

I rest an arm on his thigh and tighten my hold just enough to draw him in and out of my mouth, tasting the building sweetness of his excitement trickling across my tongue. I don't know what I was expecting, but it wasn't for him to taste similar to his blood, sweet and sugary, almost like the vanilla frosting of the first cupcake I ever got to eat on our first official day together.

"That feels amazing," he says, playing with my hair, the intensity of his gaze sizzling over me though I don't look at him. I can just feel the weight of his stare, his desire, and I feel so incredibly sexy in this moment, any nerves I had now gone.

I suck a bit harder, working my mouth up and down, listening to his breathing and soft moans. His fingers turn desperate, combing through my hair until he props himself up to run his hands over the length of my back. He reaches down my sides and grazes his fingers over my breasts, the sensation drawing a moan from me.

"I'm going to cum soon," he murmurs, tightening his hands around me.

The click of his fangs sounds in my ears, and I shiver as tingles wash over my skin. I dig my fingers deeper into his thighs, holding him still when he tells me I can stop if I want. But I don't stop. Excitement builds inside me, his breathing quickening even more. He moans my name again, easing to lie back. I peek up to watch his expression, his eyes flashing crazy silver at me. He pants, arching a bit, moaning as I suck and lick, feeling his hard-on flex in my mouth.

Closing his eyes, he scrunches his face in pleasure, tightening his hold on my shoulders as he finishes in my mouth. Sweet flavor bursts over my tongue, and I ease my mouth away and automatically swallow. He tugs me up to straddle him, kissing my throat and hugging me, wanting more of my affection that I gladly give him.

"I want to taste you," he whispers against my shoulder. His fangs so close to my skin send my heart racing in a good way.

I ease away from him to meet his eyes. "Will you be careful?"

"Always with you."

I swallow my nerves and shift my hair from my shoulder to send it cascading down my back. Bronx inhales a small breath as I expose my skin to him. His eyes flash silver again, his hunger and desire hardening his features as he trails his gaze from my eyes.

He licks his lips and leans forward, sliding his hand down the front of my body to touch me between my legs. I moan and close the space at the pressure of his finger slipping inside me to feel exactly what he does to me. He hums from his throat, enjoying my reaction to the pleasure he elicits with just his touch. Grazing his mouth to my shoulder, I tense a little, but then he only kisses me, drawing his tongue over my heated skin, pulling me to lie back with him in the process.

And then he's on top of me.

"I'm not going to bite you unless you ask me to. Even then, I'm going to savor you inch-by-inch first if that's okay," he says, kissing me softly.

I nod, squirming a bit at his words.

Leaning down, he kisses me again, sliding his tongue into my mouth with a fervent passion that leaves me gasping. He breaks away and glides his tongue along my jaw, sending my skin buzzing. He was serious about kissing every inch of me. His slow, almost torturous pace makes me pant and moan and squeeze my legs together until he draws his hands to my thighs and guides my legs open for him.

Hooking his fingers to my panties, he slides them down and kisses each of my hips until he undresses me completely. He licks his lips, devouring the sight of my body as I lie before him. He retracts his fangs and smiles at me, massaging his fingers into my thighs as he makes his way to my hips to guide me onto my side.

He positions his body diagonally and bends my knee toward the ceiling to rest my leg on his shoulder. I clutch the blankets between my hands, feeling him use two fingers to spread me open so that he can trace his tongue over my clit in such a way that I accidentally squeeze his head between my thighs and gasp.

He hums deep in his throat, moving his hand to massage the back of my leg, getting me to relax. I moan so embarrassingly loud as he sucks and licks, creating sensations unlike anything I've felt before. My whole body trembles as he works me up with his mouth, murmuring his enjoyment every time I moan.

Bronx shifts me from my side and onto my back, pulling both my legs over his shoulders while he lifts my hips higher, curling my body slightly as I lie against him. Heat flushes my skin, and I can't stop wiggling under the incredible sensations he creates with his tongue and lips.

A wave of ecstasy explodes through me, and I reach for something to hold onto. Bronx eases me down and takes my hand, linking our fingers together as I orgasm. He slows down, watching my face, just taking an extra moment to kiss between my legs again as I get my breathing under control.

"That was the best thing I've ever experienced," he says, sliding up next to me to take me into his arms. "You're so incredible. Everything about you."

I smile and kiss him. "I love our time together. I hope you know that."

He tucks my hair behind my ear. "Even when bullshit stuff happens?"

"That just makes moments more meaningful to me," I say, running my fingers along his chest. "But you know what would make this even better?"

"Hmm?"

"I wasn't joking about wanting to take care of you. I want you to bite me. I'm ready to try, and I want it to be you. I know you'll be gentle. I mean, if you want to."

He doesn't respond right away, his dark eyes searching my face. "Are you sure?"

"More than anything."

He swallows and nods. "I want you to bite me too."

"You sure about that?"

"It's what I want."

"Okay," I say with a smile, excitement washing through me.

Bronx grins back at me and helps me sit up so that we face each other. He adjusts my legs over his, pulling me so close that my thighs meet his hips, though he doesn't push his body between my legs.

Gently brushing my hair away from my shoulder, he traces his finger down my neck, making me inhale a soft breath. He extends his fangs, the action setting my body off like crazy, and his eyes flash silver at my reaction.

"You can tell me to stop at any time," he says, holding my gaze. "And I won't drink too much."

I bob my head and tilt my neck to the side, giving him silent permission. My heart thrashes around my chest the closer his mouth gets, and he starts by kissing the skin of my throat softly and then works his lips to my shoulder.

"Take a breath, Gwen," he whispers.

The second I inhale, Bronx's fangs pierce my skin. It happens so fast that I barely feel a pinch before he glides his tongue over my skin and molds his mouth over his bite. I moan so fucking loud at the strange yet good sensation, the noise making Bronx dig his fingers into my sides. I had expected more pain than pleasure, but there is nothing about this that hurts. It turns me on. I feel so good, so desired, in this moment as I finally allow myself to fulfill his needs as a vampire the way he fulfills mine as a dhampir.

"Bite me, Gwen," he murmurs against my skin.

"Please."

My body buzzes under his words, and I don't hesitate to give him what he wants. I shift closer, feeling his arousal awaken again between my legs, enjoying just the friction of our movements. He moans as I kiss and graze my teeth along the skin of his shoulder.

His lips tighten on my shoulder as I sink my teeth into him, but he releases his mouth with a moan. Sweet, sugary blood dances across my taste buds, tasting so good that I hum and suck harder.

And I keep sucking.

And sucking.

"Gwen," Bronx murmurs. "That feels..." His words trail off.

I slowly ease away to look at him. A strange expression crosses his face, and he blinks his eyes a few times.

"Shit," I whisper. "I drank too much, didn't I?"

Bronx slumps back onto the pillows, sending a blip of panic through me. I quickly hold my arm up to his lips, and he links his fingers to my wrist and bites me. Something snaps inside me, sending hunger pain through me, and I press my hand into his chest. He releases his lips from me, his eyes widening.

"Jameson!" Bronx yells, grabbing for my other arm.

Two hands grab me from my waist, yanking me back. I scream out and thrash, fear kicking my body into action.

"It's okay, Gigi. It's me," Jameson says, twisting me in

his arms.

The second our eyes meet, he startles. He rips the collar of his shirt and bends his neck for me. I don't even have a chance to think before I bite him too.

I can't stop sucking.

My body wants nothing more than to drain Jameson dry.

7

SAVAGE

"FUCK, DID YOU REMEMBER TO feed her?" Jameson asks, keeping his voice even despite the fact that I curl my naked body around him and drink.

Bronx materializes next to us and drapes a blanket around me. "I did."

Jameson strokes his hand up and down my back. I feel so out of control and annoyed at myself. What the hell happened? I wasn't even that hungry. And now I can't even summon the strength to pull away from Jameson. I feel as I did after being starved with Corona, but even then I still managed.

"More than just your blood?" Jameson shifts me, hugging me tighter. He still manages to remain calm, despite how rigid he stands.

Bronx groans and shifts behind Jameson to look at me. Our gazes meet, and I can't handle the strange look he gives me, so I close my eyes. "Gwen, you have to stop. You're drinking too much."

Bronx reaches to touch my cheek, but Jameson spins me away. "Let her. I'm good."

"She'll get—"

Jameson releases a soft growl. "You have to let her. She needs to learn the consequences herself."

Bronx growls back at Jameson. "But—"

"Trust me, Bronxy," Jameson says, cutting him off. "Now go get some fucking clothes on. Your naked ass won't help Gwen chill the hell out, and I've seen enough of your damn cock."

Jameson strolls with me in his arms to the leather couch and sits down with me on his lap. He continues to stroke my back, letting me satiate my need for his blood. I don't know what the hell happened—if Bronx drank too much or if his blood really set me off—but I still can't seem to get myself in control. My stomach screams if I even consider pulling away.

"I hope you know it's taking everything in me not to touch you how I like," Jameson whispers, the softness of his voice tickling my skin. "You're driving me crazy. That bite on your shoulder isn't helping."

I finally pull away from him to meet his gaze. "I'm sorry."

Jameson smiles at me and leans forward to rub his nose to mine. "Don't apologize. This is your time with Bronx. What the two of you do is none of my business, though I'd prefer not to have to get in the middle. You're way too hot all wild like this. I love how you cling to me."

I pat his chest. "You're ridiculous. I can't believe you were willing to risk me draining you."

He smirks. "It's because I knew you wouldn't."

"How are you so sure?"

Jameson stands up and sets me on my feet, adjusting the blanket around me. His green eyes sparkle in the light, and he flicks his gaze past me. I turn to catch sight of Bronx standing a few feet away, his shoulders straight and his posture stiff. From Bronx's expression, I'm sure Jameson isn't the only one preferring he didn't have to get between me and Bronx.

Jameson nudges me in the back, getting me to take a step, and I immediately regret it. My stomach sloshes, the pain erupting in it not from hunger but something else. Bending down, I clutch my belly, which only makes it worse.

"What the hell?" I ask, the question more for myself. I've never felt this bad in my life after drinking blood.

Jameson comes up next to Bronx, and the two of them give me a once-over. Jameson squeezes my shoulder. "I'm sorry we didn't talk about this. You were kind of busy trying to devour me."

I blush at his comment. I'm nearly certain I'll never hear the end of his teasing. "I'd have stopped."

Jameson's smirk turns into a full-blown smile, lighting his face. "I know, but I figured I'd help get your sexy wild ass in control."

Bronx steps closer to me and shifts my hair, stopping it from veiling my face. "And I'm going to kick his ass for it."

I hold my arms up, the liquid crashing back and forth inside me. And holy shit is it uncomfortable.

"Everett will probably kick my ass too," Jameson says, dodging away from Bronx.

I attempt to get between them.

Big fucking mistake.

Bronx accidentally knocks into me trying to grab onto Jameson, and I stumble back. Jameson catches me by the waist, sending pain through me. I gag, my stomach heaving. The edges of my vision shadow, and I cover my mouth.

"Shit. She's going to throw up, you asshole," Bronx says, closing the space.

Just as Bronx says the words, I heave again. The world spins as he turns me away from him, and I vomit all over the front of Jameson, covering him in blood. He stands in shock, peering down the front of himself and then to me.

Bronx brings me a damp towel and runs it over my mouth while searching my face.

"Can I kick his ass now?" Bronx asks me, pushing my hair away from my shoulder to keep it out of the way. His gaze flicks to the bite mark he left on me, and he gently runs his cool fingers over it like he can't resist touching it.

I puff out my bottom lip, my stomach still screaming. My cheeks burn like crazy in embarrassment. This is so not hot. "Only if you take me to the bathroom first."

Bronx hesitates, and I'm nearly certain he's afraid of getting covered in the blood my body wants to expel in anger.

Jameson sighs and strolls to me, carefully lifting me up in his arms. The sudden jostling of my body causes me to heave and throw up again. I groan, mortified.

"Fuck. I went too far," he says, swiping his hand across his face, flicking blood out of his eyes. He shuffles slowly toward the bathroom, carrying me like a bomb that will explode at any second. "Go get Everett. I'll get her to the shower."

Bronx disappears, leaving me with Jameson. He decides against the gentle approach and rushes us into the bathroom. He braces himself as I get sick again, my stomach so pissed off. I whimper and rest my head back on the cool tiles as warm steam fills the air.

Jameson steps into the shower with me, leaving his clothes in a pile on the floor. Gently shifting my hair, he rubs circles on my back without saying a word. I don't know what he meant by claiming he went too far, because I'm pretty sure it was me.

"As soon as you get over your blood bloat, you can kick my ass. My brothers will help you," Jameson says with a sigh.

I turn to look at him, keeping my elbows on my knees. "What the hell is blood bloat?"

"The only time a vampire gets sick is from over-consumption. It's more discomfort than sickness, and we never throw up. I thought if I let you drink until that point, that your body would realize its limit."

"And now all your blood has gone to waste," I murmur, sticking out my lip more.

He groans. "I'm really sorry, Gigi. You just freaked me the fuck out."

My brows furrow.

I don't get a chance to ask him why when the glass shower door swings open, and Everett materializes in front of me. With one look into my eyes, he flashes his fangs and grabs Jameson by the neck, throwing him away from me. If the shower door wasn't open, Jameson would've crashed through. Instead, he slips across the tiles and lands against the wall, not even fighting back as Everett looks ready to attack him.

"What were you thinking?" Everett yells, swinging his fist into the wall next to Jameson's head. "I am her health keeper. You can't take it upon yourself to try to fix a problem you have no idea about. You jeopardized her wellbeing!"

Jameson protects his face with his arms. "I'm sorry, brother. I just—when I saw her with Bronx, her fingers piercing his chest, I just acted."

"Wh-what?"

My soft voice draws Everett's attention to me. I try to get up, but my body wants nothing to do with it. I can barely lift my head without wanting to puke my brains out. Everett vanishes from in front of Jameson, leaving him naked on the floor. Stepping into the shower in his clothes, Everett kneels on the floor to get a better look at me. Bronx throws Jameson a towel, and Mikkalo motions for Jameson to leave with him. Neither of them looks in my direction like they're trying to give me privacy. And I'm thankful for it.

Because, fucking gross. I didn't want any of them seeing me as a hot mess. At least if they pretend they didn't, it's not so embarrassing.

"Bronx?" I try to get up from my spot in the shower, but my body won't allow it.

Everett shifts my hair and holds me while I get sick once again. He slides his hand around me and presses it into my abdomen to feel my stomach. "Just take a few slow breaths. I think the worst of it is over." His gaze trails from my face and down my neck, stopping at the bite mark Bronx left on my shoulder. Silver flashes in his eyes, but he doesn't react, continuing his exam of the rest of my body. "Come on. Let me help you out."

Bronx stands outside the shower with a towel in one hand for me, and I freeze in my tracks. Everett carefully starts drying me off as I gape at Bronx, hovering before me with only a towel around his waist. He holds another towel, stained with blood, over his chest. My mouth falls agape as Jameson's words from before he left finally sink in. I step forward while Bronx steps back, keeping three feet of space between us.

"Shit," I whisper, trying not to freak out. "What did I do?"

"I'm fine, dandelion. I like a little rough play, remember?" he says, stepping back out of my reach again.

My chest aches more than my stomach. "You're afraid of me." I can't stop the words from coming out, my voice barely a whisper.

Bronx sighs. "No, definitely not."

"Then stop dodging my closeness," I say, trying to capture him with my gaze.

Everett disappears from beside me and stands behind Bronx, not letting him move away from me again. The two of them growl at each other, but Bronx doesn't try very hard to break out of Everett's grip.

"Let our girl take a look at you, Bronx," Everett says. Lowering his voice, he adds, "She's not going to stop pouting until she sees for herself that you're okay. I don't know about you, but I want to see her smile. Your stubbornness about showing signs of weakness will hurt her feelings. She's going to think she did something wrong when this wasn't her fault. You drank too much."

The two of them realize I can hear them, and Bronx groans, shifting from Everett's hold. He lets Bronx turn away from us to link his hands on the back of his head. I step forward and slide my arms around his waist, hugging him from behind.

The bathroom door clicks closed as Everett leaves without needing for me to ask him for a minute alone. Bronx drops his arms from his head and wraps his fingers around mine, squeezing them between his hands.

"Will you please look at me?" I ask, pressing my cheek between his taut shoulder blades. His heart picks up in a melody of thrums that matches mine.

Slowly turning around, Bronx meets my gaze. I automatically flick my stare down his chest to take in five very distinct puncture wounds that still bleed. He holds utterly still as I reach up and brush my finger around the injury I caused. And hell.

"It doesn't hurt," he whispers, relaxing the longer I stare. "You'd have missed my heart anyway."

I scrunch my nose. "But still."

Grasping my chin, he turns my head up so that I meet his eyes. "Apparently we're both a little out of control. Everett was right. I drank too much from you, and I'm sorry.

I'm not used to drinking from anyone."

"You think you drank too much?" I touch my hand to my stomach. "I'm not just out of control. I'm a fucking savage. You can't even properly heal. What if—"

Bronx silences me with a kiss, not letting me spill my anxiety all over the place like I had his and Jameson's blood. "No thinking about stuff that was unlikely to happen."

"Bronx," I say against his lips.

"I hope tonight didn't ruin this for you." By this, he means us. He doesn't have to say it for me to know that he's worried it might have. "This is new, and I know I'll be better."

Without having to ask, I know he hopes that this wasn't it. I know how much he desires my closeness in every aspect. "I hope all my damn grossness didn't ruin me for you," I respond with a grimace. "You looked nervous as hell."

He chuckles and shakes his head. "I was. I'll be honest. I didn't know how to handle...*that*."

"Let's just hope *that* doesn't happen next time. Or ever again." My words lighten his brooding face even more as I confirm that I want there to be a next time with him. I draw my finger across one of the puncture marks, coating the tip in blood. "And maybe Jameson was onto something. I don't feel out of control."

He hums in his throat, watching me intently. "Hopefully not repulsed either."

I pop the tip of my finger in my mouth. "Definitely not. I already feel tons better. Only want to bite you a little bit. A nibble."

Pulling me closer, he hugs me. The weight of his arms around me feels like the only thing I'll ever need. He's not the only one relieved. His hesitation freaked me out. I can't even imagine not being able to devour his attention and affection. "Don't tease me, dandelion. It's going to be hard enough to leave my room with you already, and I promised my brothers we'd join them for dinner. They should see you're okay."

I suck in my bottom lip between my teeth. "You're right. I think I hear Everett pacing."

"That's Jameson probably waiting for you to kick his ass."

I release a small laugh. "I've changed my mind, but I expect to be served dinner shirtless," I call, standing on my tiptoes, raising my voice loud enough for Jameson to hear.

Bronx smiles and picks me up, not even reacting to my request. "Have it ready in thirty. I need some time to cuddle the hell out of our girl."

"Make it an hour," I say.

Bronx smiles. "Nothing has ever sounded better."

"You guys!" I clap my hands, cracking up, as Jameson lies on the narrowest table I've ever seen in only his boxers. He turns his head and flashes me a smile that makes me want to rush and cuddle the hell out of him. I know this had to have been his crazy-ass idea.

Mikkalo cuts up pieces of fruit faster than I've ever seen anyone do so while Everett arranges them on Jameson's chest. It's the most ridiculous and hilarious thing ever. I can't stop the burst of laughter that escapes my throat. Talk about team work. It might be ridiculous, but I love everything about it.

"What the hell is this?" I ask, tugging Bronx along with me. I can't get to my guys fast enough.

"My way of apologizing," Jameson says, straightening his shoulders. "And you did say I had to serve you shirtless. So, yeah. You get what you want."

I laugh again and take an extra moment to appreciate their effort to see to it that they fulfill my every desire, even if Jameson purposely misinterpreted it. His idea is far better than anything I could imagine. "This is so weird...and sweet. I love it. Thank you."

Mikkalo waves a fork at me, drawing my attention away from the mouthwatering array of fruit. "Can I feed you?"

I raise my eyebrows as Jameson groans and tips his head back. Mikkalo looks fully set on jabbing Jameson with the fork in the process as punishment for the whole blood bloat thing. I'm sure both he and Everett might have given him some hell about his attempt to help me, but I know he had good intentions. And this most definitely makes up for it.

Strolling closer, I let go of Bronx's hand to brace on the table. I bend down and suck a grape from the hard line of muscles on Jameson's stomach into my mouth. All four of them inhale sharp breaths at my action, and I can't stop from giggling like a maniac. Seriously. The. Best.

"No thanks. I think I'm going to feed myself." I draw my mouth across Jameson's chest next, grazing his skin with my teeth to pick up a slice of apple. "I hope you have something chocolatey with whipped cream I can lick off for dessert."

Jameson releases a sexy purr from his throat as I glide my tongue over the hard line of his stomach to suck up some of the fruit juice. His body reacts with a hard-on, and he shivers.

"Damn," Mikkalo says, stabbing the fork into the table. "Had I known..."

I tip my head up and smile at him. "I'll gladly eat dinner off you tomorrow," I tease, tossing a grape at him. "Maybe breakfast if you ensure I get my favorite kind of yogurt."

Bronx hugs me from behind and kisses my shoulder. "I love how much you love this."

His brothers watch the two of us with unreadable expressions as I turn to meet him for the kiss I know he yearns for. Our intimacy brought us closer together no matter how crazy it ended. I'm sure his brothers all saw that I let Bronx bite me, which none of them can ask about it. And now it's starting to feel a bit awkward. They don't show signs of jealousy, but I know they all crave the experience.

I shift on my feet. "Okay, you guys. Quit it with all the intensity. I know this is an adjustment, and we're figuring things out, but I don't like feeling like there is some big thing between us. I understand that you're worried about your possessive streaks and jealousy. I get it. I respect it."

"Gwen, it's all good," Mikkalo says, smiling at me, trying to show the truth to his words. "You don't have to say anymore."

I place my hands on my hips. "I do. Especially after earlier. I know you guys are probably thinking about how I asked Bronx to bite me, and you're wondering why I didn't ask you first. You should know that I look forward to getting to that point with each of you, okay? You all make me incredibly happy, and I want to do my best to do the same for you. I just—"

Jameson sits up on the table, spilling fruit everywhere. "As much as I wish that mark peeking from your shirt was mine, I don't expect you to let me bite you. I love our time together already."

Everett reaches across the table and takes my hand. "You know I do."

"Same," Mikkalo says. "But thank you for saying that. I've been struggling a bit with the amount of time between our days."

Jameson whacks Mikkalo on the back. "You're not the only one. Today has been the longest of my existence."

I purse my lips and look at Everett and Bronx. "Do you guys feel the same?"

"I don't know how else we'll do this, dandelion," Bronx says, sitting down at the table.

Sliding onto his lap, I study his eyes for a moment. I know that they all need time with me, and I need alone time with each of them, but they're right about the amount of time that passes. It's forever. Feels even longer since coming back from Corona's.

"What if we do this more often?" I finally ask, turning to each of them to see their reactions.

"Let you eat off Jameson?" Mikkalo says, raising an eyebrow. "Because I don't think he can handle the task. I can though."

I throw a fork at him, rolling my eyes at his joke. Pretty sure Jameson's going to get teased for the rest of time. I know how brothers are.

Bronx hums. "I'd love gathering for breakfast and dinner as a coven."

"If it gives me the chance to see you every day, hell yeah, Gigi," Jameson says, giving me the best smile that uplifts my heart.

I suck in my bottom lip between my teeth. "Maybe I can give you my blood too? I don't want it to turn into you all just watching me eat and feeding me. I want this time to take care of all of you. I know I can handle it. What I can't handle is thinking about not doing it."

"That would stop Bronx from getting carried away," Everett says, keeping his voice even.

Bronx releases a growl, but I cut him off with a kiss. I know he feels badly already, but Everett can't help from mentioning it as my health keeper.

"You mean it'll help me," I say, getting Bronx to relax. "Because as much as I love the thought of devouring the lot of you...please stop me."

"I don't even think I've ever drunk a gallon of blood at once before," Mikkalo says, his fangs peeking out from beneath his lips.

Everett materializes next to me and pokes me in the side with his finger. "It was probably closer to two."

I grimace.

Jameson laughs, risking his hand to poke my belly. "Yeah, our girl can out-drink all of us. That mouth of hers. So hot."

"Amazing," Bronx says, smirking at me.

I blush so hard, knowing he's not talking about my bite. "Okay, okay. Knock it off." I turn to Everett. "Think I'm good to provide blood to you all now?"

"If you want to."

I smile. "I do."

Everett picks up a piece of fruit off the table. "Okay, but let us feed you first."

8

DATE NIGHT

"KEEP YOUR EYES CLOSED," JAMESON says, strolling behind me with his hands covering my face. I couldn't even peek to see if I tried. He remains ultra-close, guiding me along.

"Are you taking me to the car?" I ask, focusing on listening to my surroundings.

I'm getting better at deciphering certain noises. I can tell that he already led me outside because of the elevator ride and the familiar feeling of fresh air. I can't hear much else. Just the slight hum of what I think is the car's engine.

"Stop listening." Jameson shifts his hands from my eyes to my ears, cupping them just enough to muffle the sounds.

"All's clear, brother." Mikkalo's soft voice trickles to me. I turn in the direction I think he stands. "Have fun, Gwen."

Jameson pulls me to a halt, and cool lips meet mine. I catch the alluring scent of Mikkalo's skin and draw my arms around his neck to kiss him deeper. He eases away with a chuckle, and I peek at him through my lashes and smile.

"See you at dinner, Mikkalo," I say, patting his cheek.

"Can I kiss our girl, too?" Bronx asks from somewhere behind me.

Jameson spins me around without complaint, already knowing that I wouldn't deny any of them a kiss—especially outside in what we established as neutral territory. We just finished breakfast anyway. I had no idea how much I'd enjoy such a simple thing, just spending time with the five of us together.

Bronx touches my cheek, caressing his fingers along my jaw. I lean toward him under the weight of his fingers but keep my eyes closed. Something about the anticipation and not being able to see him sends my heart racing. I hum the second our lips meet and sink deeper into his arms for a hug that will linger.

"Try to stay out of trouble, dandelion," he murmurs against my lips.

I suck his bottom lip. "Never."

"At least try not to get hurt," Everett says from somewhere to my right. "Bronx and I will be unavailable for the next couple hours."

I open my eyes and turn to look at him. "Where are you going?"

"Following a lead." Everett doesn't have to say anything else for me to know that he's attempting to find my brothers.

It makes me both excited and nervous. Nervous because I'm afraid of how to handle them, especially after they find out about Kyler's death. Excited because I'll have the chance to fix things. I plan to let my guys try to remove the blocks that Laredo put on their minds. I just hope it helps. It'll make things easier when I beg them to trust in my decision to stay with my guys...except I'm not going to tell them about our agreement. Not yet. They have to see they're not out to get us first.

"Be safe. The both of you," I say, reaching out my arms to get Everett to close the space to me.

He engulfs me in a hug and lifts me off my feet. "Don't worry about us. Our coven got the position of region leader for a reason."

I kiss him, opening my mouth to let him glide his tongue over mine in a way that ignites desire through me. I ease away, heat blossoming up my chest. "Still be safe. I want more of this later."

He squeezes my ass with a smile and sets me down.

"Use the restraints, Jameson," Everett says to his brother. "I mean it. Our girl isn't invincible."

Jameson releases a soft growl and hugs his arms around my shoulders. "I got her. Don't doubt my ability."

"I don't doubt your ability to keep her safe. I doubt your ability to tell her no if she asks you otherwise," Everett says. He turns and smiles at me. "Like Bronx said, behave, Gwen. Please try not to test Jameson too much."

I laugh. "Oh, I will."

Jameson buries his face into the crook of my neck, making me screech. The world blurs for a few seconds, and my back hits the cool leather seat behind the wheel of the car. I don't even have a chance to orient myself to the sudden shift in my surroundings before Jameson quickly snaps my seat restraints into place.

He leans into the car and plants his mouth to mine, kissing me for a long moment until I try to pull him in with me. Chuckling, he eases away and shuts the door only to get into the passenger's seat.

"I plan to let you drive, but we have to wait until my brothers disappear to turn off the autopilot," he says, tapping a few buttons on the dashboard to send the car lurching forward.

I spot three figures standing together in the reflection of the rearview mirror. Bronx lifts his hand to wave a second before all three of them vanish.

"So where are we going?" I ask, shifting in my seat. I

mess with the straps of the seat restraints because I can barely turn my body to meet Jameson's gaze straight on.

He playfully slaps my hand and then takes it between his. "On a date. As much as I wanted to spend all night in bed making blanket mansions with you, I don't want you to get restless from being kept inside all the time."

I smirk. "Mikkalo was wrong about you."

He chuckles. "Okay, he *might* have suggested I take you out for a bit."

"You know, we can make blanket mansions anywhere."

He reaches into the back and tugs a blanket between the seats. "My thoughts exactly. And fuck, I find you so sexy right now. Like you can read my mind."

"Your brothers might have teased that if you had been able to apply to Blood Match with me that we would've rated high for a personality match."

Jameson raises an eyebrow. "And attraction. Nutrients. We're completely compatible, Gigi."

"You think?"

"Oh, I know."

I grin at him. "If only you could truly convince me."

Jameson narrows his eyes at me as I mess with the latch of the seat restraint. He looks torn between listening to his brothers and my desire to take the damn thing off so that I can at least lean a bit closer to him.

"How much farther are we going? I don't care about driving," I add.

He releases a soft hum from his throat and relents to unfastening my seat restraint. I smile wider and hold my hands out to him so that he can pull me into his lap. His seat suddenly reclines, and I laugh and pat his chest. Grasping my cheeks, he leans up to kiss me, his body reacting to my closeness. I can't stop myself from rocking against his boner through his pants, just feeling him through the sheer material of my thong.

Tonight's the first time I decided to give in and wear one of the dresses Jameson had pushed to one side of his closet and out of the way because he was probably certain I'd never wear one. But I gave a few of the dresses a try and loved how perfect a flouncy emerald green one fit, hugging the curves of my breast perfectly while being short and flowy enough around the skirt as to not restrict my movements.

The only thing I skipped was the heels and instead paired it with some flats that I'm nearly certain have real gemstones sparkling on the tops.

"Have I told you how stunning I think you are tonight?" Jameson murmurs, running his fingers down to touch the skin of my legs peeking out from the hiked up hem of my dress.

"Mmmhmm. Three times."

"That's not nearly enough." He breaks away from my mouth to kiss my jaw and then glides his tongue to my earlobe to suck it into his mouth. "You're ravishing. Spectacular. So fucking hot it's hard for me to accept this is not just a fantasy."

"It's not a fantasy," I say, reaching down to touch the button on his jeans. "Unless you want to make it one."

"Gwen."

My name sounds so hot on his lips that I unfasten his pants and pull his cock out to play with him. I had expected him to make a move during the day, but he just cuddled me until I fell asleep in his arms, just being with me, something I had no idea I needed. But now that we're both refreshed and alone, I can't stop myself from wanting to give into his desire, especially because it mirrors my own.

"That feels so good." He draws his tongue over my jaw and glides it down my throat. "I hope you know that I wasn't expecting this."

I bend my neck so he can trail his lips over my collarbone. "I was. Ever since dinner."

Moaning, Jameson tightens his fingers on my hips until he trails his hands up to drag my dress over my head, tossing it on the seat next to us. Jameson leans back in the seat to gaze at me, his eyes flashing silver with more than their usual hunger.

"I feel so lucky to be with you," he says, his voice low, sultry. "I know you might not believe this, but I feel like you're my soul mate. I've never felt such a connection to anyone in my existence."

"Is that why you were willing to die for me?" I ask. I

can't help it. The memory of Francisca giving Mikkalo an ultimatum of losing his brother or losing me, and Jameson not letting Mikkalo make a choice and instead choosing to risk his life—it haunts me. "That's one of the things I thought about over and over while I was imprisoned apart from why Kyler would choose everyone else over me."

Jameson sits up to hug me, pulling me closer. "I hate so much that you went through that. It should've never happened."

"You didn't answer my question," I say, running my fingers through his light brown hair.

He fake-glares at me. "Maybe I don't want to."

I puff out my bottom lip. "Please."

He sighs, releasing a breathless laugh. "My brothers were right. I can't deny you. We're going to get in so much trouble all the time. I can already feel it."

"Well, I am a lawbreaker," I tease.

Leaning in, he kisses me. "So am I. Zaire would kick my ass all the damn time that it turned into almost a competition between me and Mikkalo."

I grip onto the hem of his shirt and lift it to graze my fingers across the dozen tattoo lines decorating his side. "You sleep with the enemy too?"

He raises his eyebrows. "Me? No. These are from various...discrepancies. Zaire didn't always approve of my method of creating and holding alliances. He was an asshole while everyone loved me. These are supposed to be reminders of who was the board member on Donor Life Corp and who—never mind."

I clutch his face. "Who was charming as hell? Way hotter. Sexy. Delicious. Oh, and a great kisser."

His sudden frown disappears at my words. Closing the space, he kisses me softly. "Where have you been all my life?"

"Hiding in a bunker," I say, grinning at him.

"Well, I'm glad we found you. I rarely speak for my brothers, but on this, I know they agree. Just you being here makes us happy. I can only hope that you'll be as happy as us one day. I know this situation isn't ideal, but I promise we'll try everything we can to annihilate the threat of the Anderson Coven, get things settled with Donor Life Corp, and bring your brothers back."

I nod. "So you know, even if you can't make all of that happen...I like being here with you. I've never felt so equal. Free. Close to anyone."

The car slows to a halt, and Jameson groans and looks out the windshield. "I don't know about you, but I'm kind of having fun in here."

I lace my fingers around his erection, gliding my hand up and down again. "Even though we totally got distracted?"

He chuckles. "Nothing like baring my soul along with my body."

I reach behind me and unclasp my bra, letting it drop

between us. "It is fun, isn't it?"

His eyes flash silver with my words, and he leans up and taps his finger to the navigation screen, sending the car lurching forward again. I don't even have a chance to react as Jameson flips me off him and into the backseat on the pile of blankets. He sets the autopilot controls in what looks like an endless loop around the property and then maneuvers between the seats to join me.

"Is this okay?" he whispers, sinking his weight onto me, kneeling on the seat between my bent legs. "Our night is free to do what we want. We'll still have time for me to take you where I wanted to."

I want to ask him where, but the desire crossing his face locks my words in my throat. Because I don't really care. All I want is to enjoy my time with Jameson and to show him how much his soul baring meant to me. No one has ever told me anything like that before. No one has cared about what I wanted or my happiness. Everyone in my life before meeting the Royale brothers consisted of people wanting to use me for what I was. Even my own family. Everyone except my dad.

"It could be better," I say, tugging at his jeans.

His eyes flash silver. "You're right."

He kicks off his pants, setting them with my dress. I lift my hips, licking my lips, giving him silent permission to undress me completely. Shifting out a blanket from beneath us, he wraps it around us, though I doubt anyone could see us at the speed the car races. I can't help smirking to myself that Everett would flip his shit if he knew that Jameson dared take off my seat restraints, let alone take his eyes off of our surroundings.

Jameson kisses me softly, trailing his hands over my breasts and down my stomach, mapping my skin with his fingers, memorizing my body by his touch alone. I do the same, tugging his boxers down until he manages to get them off in the small space. Wrapping my fingers around his erection, I play with him until he slips a finger inside me, making me gasp.

"This okay?" he whispers, moving his finger until a burst of tingles shoots from between my legs and through the rest of me, and I release a moan under the sensation. With his other hand, he traces circles on my clit, increasing my pleasure to such an intensity that all I can do is clutch the blanket.

I've never felt anything like what Jameson does to me, and I can't stop moaning and saying his name. A dozen emotions explode through me—from lust to ecstasy to something new and strange, completely unfamiliar.

I squirm and curl my toes, arching my back, unable to lie still through the sensations he creates with his hands. Opening my eyes, I meet his green gaze, his lips curved in a smile like he's enjoying this as much as I am.

"I want you so badly," I whisper, trying to grab for him.

"Not until you cum for me," he says, his fangs protruding from beneath his lips as he speaks.

I can only respond with another moan, the pressure of his finger inside me growing more intense. I don't even know what's happening to my body, but I can't stop gasping and moaning, my eyes watering as my emotions overwhelm me.

I scream out with the most intense orgasm I've ever felt, my whole body clenching, something insane happening inside me like I can feel the pleasure throughout my whole body. Even my fingers tingle with something indescribable.

Jameson slows down and kisses me.

"That was intense," I whisper through another gasp, my body still buzzing.

"I could tell," he says, smiling. "You got me a bit wet. I fucking love it."

I laugh and shake my head, not even sure what he means by his words. He doesn't let the space stay between us long and meets my lips for a passionate kiss, exploring my tongue with his, teasing me with his tip without fully entering until I reach down and grab his hips, guiding him into me completely.

He releases the sexiest moan, bending into me while holding himself up with his hands. His reaction to our bodies coming together makes me kiss his throat and graze my teeth down to his shoulder. I nip him without breaking his skin, and he rocks harder into me, adjusting my legs up onto his shoulders.

The shift of my body lets him thrust deeper inside me, his movements building toe-curling sensations through me. Jameson whispers into my ear, telling me everything he loves about me and how perfect I am, how hot and fierce and smart I am. I've never felt so good about myself in my life. So beautiful and sexy and like he sees me how I always saw myself—someone deserving of everything the world has to offer. It's why I've been fighting against the ridiculous laws set by Donor Life Corp. Why I was willing to put those in need of help before me.

Jameson props himself on one arm, his muscles flexing with his movements, and reaches under my back to pull me close to him. Our hearts race each other, bumping and crashing in out-of-control beats in an attempt to be as close as the rest of us.

Releasing a moan into my shoulder, Jameson grazes his fangs across my skin, the sudden sensation sending a wave of crashing desire through me. I nearly ask him to bite me, but he slows down, pressing his weight into me, and brushes his lips over my hot skin.

"I'm so crazy for you, Gwen," he murmurs, leaning up to comb the hair from my forehead. "This was better than I imagined."

"It was perfect," I say, sliding my hands around his neck. "I loved sharing this moment with you. I've imagined it myself, too. I didn't think it could be better, but it was.

I'm so glad you're mine, Jameson."

He furrows his brows at my words and releases a deep growl, startling me. I lie in shock as he pulls himself off of me and reaches under the seat, yanking out a hidden dagger. My fear instincts ignite, stealing the warmth burning over my skin.

Something hits the car, crashing into the window.

Jameson stifles my scream with his hand, and we both jerk our attention to the front windshield. An unfamiliar vampire crouches on the hood, peering at us in the backseat. He flashes his fangs in a creepy-ass smile, and then he punches his fist to the glass, trying to shatter it.

Jameson scrambles to give me my clothes, ignoring the vampire trying to get into the car. "Hurry, Gwen. It's resistant to weapons, but with enough continuous force, the douche can break it."

A crack cuts through my heavy breathing.

The windshield shatters.

9

CAN'T BE CLAIMED

JAMESON RAMS HIS BLADE INTO the vampire's neck. Blood cascades over the dash, but the vampire manages to shimmy into the car enough to turn off the autopilot. The car jerks, sending us fishtailing. Jameson punches the vampire so hard that he loses his grip and flies off and under the car.

I screech and slide across the seat, the out-of-control car spinning too fast for me to grab anything to brace myself with. Jameson holds onto the seat and leans forward, jabbing his finger on the navigation screen until the car activates the brakes. Smoke wafts through the air, the tires burning off their rubber from the sudden move. The force of skidding to a stop sends me slamming into the driver's seat. The car comes to a halt, and Jameson cuts the engine and hops out to thrust the back door open to get to me.

"Fuck. Fuck. Fuck!" Jameson's voice echoes through the air as he leans in to look at me on the floor. He waves his hands in my face, his eyes flashing crazy silver. I don't think I've ever seen him panic like this before. "Gwen, don't move, okay? You're hurt, and I don't know to what extent."

I blink a few times and touch my forehead, my skin stinging. Blood coats my fingers. I scrunch my nose and grab one of the blankets to press against the gash. I've seen head wounds gush blood on my brothers but the injury turns out not to be that bad. With the way Jameson looks at me, I'd think my head is about to fall off. I touch my neck next to be sure. "I-I'm okay. It's just a cut. It doesn't hurt too badly. I am a little dizzy from all the spinning though."

He touches the blanket I use to try to staunch the blood. "I think it's worse. You're bleeding everywhere. Fuck. Please don't die on me, Gwen. Just hold on. Mikkalo will be here any second."

I laugh. I can't help it. "Jamie, relax. I've been injured worse. It's not as bad as it looks."

"But this shouldn't have happened. Had I listened to Evere—"

Grabbing the front of his shirt, I yank him to me and

stop him from spilling his guilt like the blood that drips down my face. Jameson sucks in a haggard breath and pulls back, cupping my cheeks to search my eyes to see if I'm lying to him about being okay.

"Please don't kiss me again right now," he murmurs. "This is never how I want to taste your blood, though it's so fucking good."

I raise my eyebrow with a smirk. "I'll throat punch you if you even try to lick my face. Only I can be that savage, but you don't have a single scratch to take care of with my mouth. Kind of rude, to be honest."

Releasing a breathless laugh, he hugs me, lifting me from the floor and back onto the seat. "I'm so relieved to hear you joke around, even if you're such a tease, Gigi. Letting all of that deliciousness go to waste."

"You think I'm the tease? You're the one standing there half-naked, sexy-as-hell, and haven't even offered me a taste to help me heal quicker. Do you know how hungry you make me just standing there?" I snap my teeth at him, hoping the lightness of my voice chills him out.

Without hesitating, Jameson bites his arm and holds it out to me. "I'm fucking failing you all over the place. This should've been the first thing I did."

"Hell yeah, it should've been. What the hell, Jameson? Is our girl okay? Are you?" Mikkalo's voice sounds from outside the car. I hear the soft thuds of his footsteps as he approaches the car to peer at me underneath Jameson.

Jameson presses his arm to my mouth when I'm too slow to react to his offering, now distracted by Mikkalo's arrival. Had he been Bronx or Everett, I'm nearly certain I would have had to get in the middle before they started a fight.

"Gigi says she's fine, but I'm not sure if she's just trying to stop me from flipping out," he says, studying my gaze. "Look at all the blood."

Mikkalo's nostrils flare. "Our girl's tough. If she says she's okay, I believe her. She's not as fragile as Everett thinks."

They talk to each other like I'm not lying here, sucking Jameson's arm. Before, I'd think they were rude, but now that I know how they feel about blood exchanges and how intimate it can be, I know Mikkalo's purposely ignoring me to give us some fake privacy. Kind of like how Jameson tried his best to act like he didn't find me and Bronx naked.

"I just—I fucked up. She should've never gotten hurt. Some asshole came out of nowhere and attacked the car. He managed to shatter the windshield and knock off the auto-pilot while..." Jameson's voice trails off as he looks at me. "We were distracted. I was more concerned about other things."

Mikkalo rubs his hand on the back of his neck. "I'm going to pretend you didn't just admit that you took your eyes off your surroundings."

"It was my fault," I say, managing to pull my mouth

from Jameson's arm.

Mikkalo closes the space to me and reaches out to touch my cheek from over Jameson's shoulder. "And that's why I didn't hear anything. I wouldn't resist you, either."

I grin at him. "Thanks, Mikkalo. You're the best. And I'll remember that."

He meets my gaze. "Is that so?"

I don't get a chance to respond to his playfulness. A beep comes from Mikkalo's pocket, and he tugs out his com device. Frowning, he peers at the screen a moment before reaching into his jacket to pull out a dagger. I don't even see the strange vampire approach until Mikkalo already shoves the blade into his chest and kicks him back.

He yanks the guy off the ground and spins him around, restraining him. "Is this the fucker who attacked you?"

Jameson pushes from the backseat to stand up to get a better look. "No. That guy is probably still bleeding out on the road back there. We hit him." Grabbing the front of the guy's shaggy hair, Jameson yanks it from the guy's forehead, making him wince. The guy growls and snaps his fangs but doesn't say anything. "No marks. Not an outcast."

Mikkalo shoves the guy toward Jameson. Jameson easily snatches him and takes over restraining him. I can tell by how effortlessly they work together that they've done this before. Of course they have. Probably a whole bunch of times. They do deal with all of the problems in the region.

"Listen carefully. I'm going to give you one chance to

give me answers," Mikkalo says, his deep voice sending a chill through me. "What coven do you belong to?"

The vampire tightens his jaw without answering.

Mikkalo jams his dagger into the guy's chest, making him holler.

"Okay, okay!" the guy wails. "I'll talk. Don't kill me."

"What coven?" Mikkalo repeats.

"No coven you know of. I'm not an outcast either. Just unregistered," the guy says.

I sit up on the backseat, and the guy's gaze darts past Mikkalo to glance at me. A weird familiarity tugs at my mind, but I can't place him anywhere. If the vampire is unregistered, he might be a blood source to Blood Rebels, maybe even the same ones who tried to take me.

Mikkalo punches him. "Look at her again, and I'll cut your head off."

"I'm sorry. I just—" The guy snaps his mouth shut and trains his gaze to the ground, though I know he still pays attention to me.

"You what?" I can't stop my question from ringing through the air. Getting to my feet, I clutch the roof of the car to get my shit together. The gash on my forehead has already stopped bleeding, so I toss the bloody blanket onto the backseat.

Mikkalo turns his head to me. "I got this."

I stroll closer. "No, I want to hear what he has to say."

Jameson hooks his arm around the guy's throat, gripping him tighter. He and Mikkalo both stiffen like they wish I'd stay back. But I don't want to. This guy and whoever the hell the other dickhead was just interrupted one of the best moments of my life. And I'm pissed the fuck off. These damn blood sources have been nothing but a pain in my neck the last few years, trying to mess up my life. First Laredo and now this?

"Gigi," Jameson says. "Whatever he has to say isn't important. We need to know why he's here."

I step close to Mikkalo, and he automatically reaches to link his fingers through mine, stopping me from trying to move past him to meet the strangely familiar vampire straight on. I doubt I could get a foot within his reach even if I try, so I relent to Mikkalo's need to protect me and stand on my tiptoes to glare at the guy from behind the sexy solid wall of protectiveness Mikkalo creates with his hard, muscular body.

"He's here because of me," I say to Mikkalo. "So, yeah. It's important to know what he was thinking."

Jameson shakes him. "Go on. Tell us. But I swear to the fucking universe if you say something to upset our girl, I'll rip your head off."

The guy continues to stare at the ground. "All I was going to say is that I can't believe it's her."

"What's that supposed to mean?" Mikkalo asks, aiming his dagger again. "Did Blood Rebels send you?"

Glancing up, the guy meets Mikkalo's expression. "I'm

here to collect the Gallagher descendants." He didn't answer the question.

"My brothers aren't here." My. Dumb. Mouth. I wish I could take back the words.

"I'm well aware of that," he says.

Mikkalo punches him in the stomach, making him heave. "Don't talk to her. And whatever you think you're doing—it's not happening. She's ours."

"You can't claim someone who doesn't belong to you."

Oh shit.

Mikkalo roars and crashes into the guy, knocking him and Jameson into the dirt. Jameson grips the guy, holding him in place while Mikkalo punches him in the face until blood bursts from a split on his lip. I rush forward, and Mikkalo hops up and spins around to lift me off my feet like holding me is the only thing stopping him from pulverizing this guy.

I clutch Mikkalo's face. "Take a breath." I motion for him to breathe with me, and a hint of the vampire's blood trickles to me. And what the hell? It smells familiar, but I still can't place him in my memory.

Jameson manages to launch back to his feet, still restraining the guy. "Let's get one thing straight, asshole. Gwen does belong to us. She has willingly taken the Royale name. She is ours."

The guy growls. "You can't claim someone who doesn't belong to you," he repeats.

Jameson's eyes flash silver, and he throws the guy to the ground and stomps his stomach so that he can't fly to his feet. "Well, we've claimed her. She's claimed us. Now, I'll give you one more chance. Tell us where the Blood Rebels are, and we'll consider letting you live."

"They're just outside the Bellamy Region," he says.

"The old Bellamy Region doesn't exist anymore," Mikkalo says. "And I've heard enough, Jameson. End him. That's an order."

"Gwen!" the vampire yells, using my name for the first time. "You'll never see Grayson again if they kill me. We've already collected him."

I throw my hands out. "Jameson, wait."

"He's lying, Gwen," Jameson says. "We have a lead, remember?"

"I can show you," the guy says. "In my pocket."

"Jamie, please. Just check. That's all I'm asking." My soft voice is enough to get him to relax his shoulders.

"You know if Grayson is with Blood Rebels what it means, right?" he asks me, glancing in my direction.

The guy tightens his jaw, flicking his attention to me for the second time. "He's waiting for you, Gwen. He begged us to bring you to him. The elders want nothing more than to have you home."

I blink a few times at his words. He's lying. I know he is. I've been deemed a traitor to humanity. The elders don't want me home. They want me dead. As for Grayson, he would go along with what the elders say just like Kyler.

Something snaps inside me, and I jump from Mikkalo's arms and rush toward Jameson and the guy. Mikkalo remains right on my back, but he doesn't stop me from approaching. All he does is back me up in case I need him.

"You're full of shit," I say, kicking him in the ribs. "You're not a blood source. The Blood Rebels who want me would never trust a vampire to do a job alone, let alone two. And even if they wanted me, I'm not fucking going. This is my home now. The Royales are the only ones who care about me."

The guy has the nerve to smirk. "That's where you're wrong, Gwyneth Gallagher."

"Gwyneth isn't my name. That was—" My eyes widen as a thought swirls through my head. "Ah, hell."

Jameson and Mikkalo both focus on me as I try to process who this guy is and why he seems so familiar. None of us notice the shadow sneaking up on us until it's too late. Instead of fighting, Mikkalo lifts me off my feet to spin me out of the reach of another vampire. He doesn't even attempt to get me. Instead, the guy rushes toward Jameson and the other vampire. I realize the new guy is the same asshole who tried to crash our car.

I don't get a chance to react as the guy pulls a long-ass sword from a sheath on his back. He stabs it through the other guy and Jameson. Jameson swears, releasing the vampire he restrains in the process. The two asshole vampires flee instead of fight.

"Fuck," Mikkalo says.

I screech as he tosses me toward Jameson.

Mikkalo disappears after them.

"Don't you even think about it, Gigi. You didn't let me lick your face, so you don't get to lick my stomach." Jameson turns and smirks at me from over his shoulder as he stares at the healing wound right at the top of his delectable abs.

"You're no fun," I say, sticking my tongue out at him.

Jameson materializes in front of me. "Sorry, brother. It's what our girl wants."

"I can wait outside," Mikkalo says, sliding me off his lap. "This is your time anyway. I don't want to add to the reason your night didn't go as you hoped."

"Apart from the jerks, my night has been amazing," I say, grinning at Jameson. "And I'm so impressed right now. Your studio is incredible, Jamie. Thank you for sharing it with me."

"Sorry it's a mess. I haven't been here since Zaire got the board position. I had no time for frivolous hobbies, as my asshole brother called it," Jameson says, strolling to plop down on the chaise lounge beside me. "Apparently you have to be bored as fuck all the time to hold power. At least, if you're beneath the guy who holds power and pushes all the shitty work onto you."

"Don't let Jameson fool you into pitying him. It wasn't that bad," Mikkalo says.

"Well, you were given the task of watching the creeper feeds," I say, bumping my shoulder to his. "Those things are nuts."

Mikkalo chuckles. "You haven't seen the worst of it."

Getting to his feet, he stretches his arms over his head, lifting his shirt with him in the process. I can't stop myself from reaching out and grazing my fingers across the dozens of tattoo lines that wrap from his stomach to his back.

"I bet it's given you all sorts of interesting ideas," I say. "No wonder you're a troublemaker."

"I'm the troublemaker, Gwen," Jameson says, sliding his arms around me. "Mik just helps me stay out of trouble."

"He'd have been an outcast by now," Mikkalo says, shaking his head with another laugh. "Some of those videos, man."

Jameson punches him. "Like you can talk."

I bring my hand to my mouth, my eyes widening. "Ah, hell."

The two of them turn to me, trying to figure out what's up.

I grimace and take Jameson's hand. "The car cam." Turning to Mikkalo, I add, "I want you to delete it. No looking. I mean it."

Jameson scoops me onto his lap and tilts me back to

kiss me. "You think I'd let us be recorded? We took out the inside cam."

I shrug. "I don't know. I knew they were there. I just didn't think—" I blush like crazy at the memory.

"That's one thing you never have to worry about, Gwen," Mikkalo says. "I'd never intrude on your privacy without being invited. Which means, I should go."

"You don't have to, brother. I'm good if Gwen's good," Jameson says.

"I'd prefer you stay here so I can keep an eye on you until Bronx and Everett get back," I say, patting the spot next to me. "I can't protect you otherwise."

Mikkalo's brown eyes light up with my words, and he returns to his spot next to us. He grabs my legs and sprawls them across his lap, massaging his fingers into my calves. Silence falls between us, but it's not uncomfortable. It's just the sound of our hearts beating as we spend time together.

It's me who breaks the silence. "So, what should I prepare for when your brothers get back?"

"A whole lot of yelling," Mikkalo says. "I don't think your head's going to heal by then."

"Not yelling, angry whispering. Both of them know better than to yell at us." Jameson plays with my hair. "The look you gave us the last time we yelled...it was terrifying."

Mikkalo pats my knee. "The worst."

I laugh and roll my eyes. "I doubt it could compare to the looks you gave the dickhead who said you couldn't claim me."

"I should've killed him," Mikkalo says.

Jameson sighs. "We both should've."

"I should've let you." I frown at my hands. I can't help it. "And I'm sorry. I shouldn't have let him get to me like he did. I know better than to believe anything anyone says outside the five of us. You're the only ones who have ever truly been honest with me."

Jameson kisses my cheek. "We have no reason not to be."

"He's right, Gwen. You're a Royale now. We don't keep secrets," Mikkalo says.

"Except the whole distraction thing you promised not to tell Bronx about," I say, smiling.

"I'm not keeping a secret. I'm following the rules." Mikkalo takes my hand and brings it to his mouth to kiss the back of it.

"For once," Jameson says.

The three of us laugh.

"I never thought I'd be thankful for the rules...at least some of them." I rest my head on Jameson's chest as Mikkalo scoots a bit closer, massaging his fingers into my arm now.

"Only some?" Jameson asks.

"I know this is your space and our time, Jamie." My voice lowers with my oncoming thought. "But I'd love...to take a moment to kiss each of you."

"What about a drink too?" Mikkalo says, looking at his brother.

I inhale a small breath at the suggestion. "That's a dangerous invitation."

Jameson slides me off his lap to sit between him and Mikkalo. "Which is why you love the idea." He turns his attention to Mikkalo. "What do you think?"

Mikkalo leans closer, touching my chin to get me to look at him. He closes the space and brushes his lips to mine, kissing me softly and just long enough to make me crave more. "I can't deny your needs," he murmurs into my mouth.

Jameson kisses my shoulder, sending tingles through me. "Neither can I."

I shift and kiss Jameson next, sliding my tongue into his mouth to get him to kiss me deeper. Mikkalo's hands trail up my legs, gliding up to stop just before the hem of my dress. I blindly reach for him, grazing my fingers over his pants until I feel the hardness of Mikkalo's erection for me under my palm.

He releases a breath, cupping his hand over mine to guide me to stroke the length of his shaft through his pants. Jameson breaks from my mouth and kisses down my throat and to my shoulder where he nudges the strap away to kiss my bare skin.

I reach and touch his leg with my other hand. "Is this okay?"

"It's fucking amazing," Jameson says, meeting my gaze. He extends his fangs and bites his arm. "Let me give you what you want now."

Fuck. Me. My body tingles, my desire and excitement rushing through me feeling Jameson and Mikkalo turned on for me. Neither of them treats this experience as anything weird, not even showing off the nerves I feel fluttering inside me. I had no idea I'd love to show them both attention, but doing so feels so right. We've been so focused on me getting time with each of them, I never really thought about how incredible it'd be to get time together.

Mikkalo's hand slides up my leg and to my stomach, gently caressing over my boobs as he waits for me to release Jameson's arm. I ease away and lick my lips, smiling at Jameson as he trains his gaze to my mouth.

I kiss him again. "So good."

He sucks my bottom lip into his mouth. "I could kiss your soft lips forever."

I grin. "Maybe I want you to explore the rest of me."

Mikkalo bites his arm, drawing my attention to him as Jameson adjusts himself on the lounge to work his mouth lower and to my cleavage. Touching my chin, Mikkalo guides me in for another kiss before offering his arm to me. I gasp and tilt my head back as Jameson exposes my breasts to kiss me lower, flicking his tongue across my nipple. Mikkalo drips his blood into my parted lips, and I moan and pull him closer to glide my tongue over his blood, sucking harder with the explosive tingles traveling over my body.

Bending down, Mikkalo follows Jameson's initiative and takes my other breast into his mouth. The different sensations the both of them create make me moan so embarrassingly loud that I pull away from Mikkalo's arm.

I link my fingers into their hair, my chest heaving, my heart beating wildly. Mikkalo eases back up, his eyes flashing with his desire. He kisses me again, slipping his tongue into my mouth, stealing my breath. Jameson moves lower, dropping to his knees. He eases my legs open and kisses my knee.

"Gwen," he whispers. "Can I?"

My body reacts to his words, but instead of relaxing, I tense.

He pulls back, stopping immediately. "I'm sorry."

I open and close my mouth. "It's okay. It's just..." I don't even know how to explain my hesitation.

"You don't have to explain anything," Jameson says.

I flick my gaze to Mikkalo, now sitting up. "I need to. I don't want you to think you did anything wrong. But Mikkalo and I haven't gotten past this point yet, and I don't know."

Mikkalo squeezes my hand. "Have I told you how perfect I think you are? Thank you for allowing me to enjoy some of your time with Jameson. And I understand."

I lick my lips and nod my head.

Mikkalo's com device chimes, cutting off the rest that I

want to say, and maybe it's a good thing. I probably should let him know my feelings while we're alone. I like Jameson, and I love the time I've spent with him, and I want to have the same with Mikkalo. Our nights together haven't been exactly easy with my dhampir secret coming out and our last date interrupted. I just—I want to get to know him alone first.

"Hey, I need you to pull up the feeds to all cameras surrounding the Nguyen Coven," Bronx says, his face taking up the whole screen that I peer at next to Mikkalo. "Everett's source said one of Gwen's brothers was there, but they denied it despite finding the transaction we found between Simeon and Corona."

"So he's being hidden?" I ask.

Bronx frowns. "You're supposed to be with Jameson, Gwen. What happened? What did he do?"

Mikkalo and Jameson swap com devices so that Mikkalo can do what Bronx asks.

"Let's see," Jameson says. "I fed her. Made her laugh. Showed her my studio. Now I'm about to sketch her topless if she lets me."

I scrunch my nose and laugh. "Jameson."

Mikkalo clears his throat. "I got something."

"What?" I ask at the same time as Bronx.

"You and Everett should come home, so we can explain," Mikkalo says.

He holds Jameson's com device out so that Jameson

and I can get a look. The video locks on two figures cast with shadows. And I recognize them both.

"Fuck," Jameson says.

"The asshole wasn't kidding. He took Grayson."

"What are you talking about?" Bronx asks.

I clutch the com device. "Bronx, please. Just come home. Now."

10

THE GALLAGHER DHAMPIR LINE

"IF YOU PLAN TO KICK someone's ass, it should be mine." I stand up and turn around, bending to lift my dress just high enough to give both Bronx and Everett a little peek of my ass cheeks.

Mikkalo tips his head back and laughs so loudly that I can't stop from laughing. Jameson releases a cross between a groan and a chuckle, pulling me back to him. He flips me off my feet before I can sit and hangs me across his lap.

"There will be no kicking of our girl's ass. But if you have the need to give her a little spank..."

I full-on giggle as he twists to turn my ass toward his brothers. I squirm on purpose, turning him on for the billionth time tonight while also getting my dress to sweep back and forth with my movement. "I'd deserve it."

I can feel everyone's stares burn across my skin as I test the dangerous line between being playful and seductive.

"But you're going to have to wait for your time," Jameson says, picking me up with him to set me on my feet. "Her ass is mine until she finishes dinner."

Everett closes the space to me, whatever scowl he had for Jameson gone as he trails his finger lightly over the nearly healed wound on my forehead. A dozen questions flash through his eyes, but he doesn't ask any of them. I think he's waiting for Bronx to lead the conversation, but he's also quiet as his own questions and confusion darken his eyes.

"First, I need some hugs," I say. "While most of my night was perfect, parts of it sucked. Like Jameson getting stabbed."

"And you getting hurt," Everett says, taking a minute to trail his eyes over the rest of me. "Are you injured anywhere else?"

I wrap my arms around Everett so he stops looking at me. "I'm fine. It was a little cut. Barely bled."

That makes Jameson chuckle.

"How did it happen?" Bronx asks, finally speaking up.

"We were attacked—"

"You let someone touch our girl!" Bronx's yell erupts through the air, startling me.

I spin and press my hands into his chest. "No, and calm down. You're setting off my fear instincts." Throwing my arms around him, I hold Bronx in place. He remains stiff, locking his fingers to the back of his head, looking toward the ceiling.

"Then how did it happen?" Bronx asks again, taking in a few deep breaths.

Jameson and I look at each other without answering. Bronx gently unhooks my arms from around him and proceeds to tug his com device from his pocket. Without having even to see what he's doing, I realize he's checking the security feeds. I risk snatching his com device from his hands, but he swivels to turn his back on me.

"It's not a big deal," I say, trying to get him to stop. I know that Jameson said there wasn't a camera inside the car anymore, but Bronx will probably blow up at the sight of the vampire smashing through the windshield.

So I do the only thing I can think of. I jump on Bronx's back and cover his eyes with my hands. He has the nerve to growl at me and flips me off him to drop me on Jameson's bed. He surprises me by sitting on the edge. Everett joins him, and I scrunch my nose to glance to Jameson.

"Fuck," Bronx whispers under his breath. "What were you doing that gave this douche even the chance to..."

The three of us watch Jameson launch from the driver's side to thrust open the back door in his boxers. I groan and throw myself back on the bed, pulling the blankets up and around me.

"It's against the rules to talk about it," Jameson says, keeping his voice even.

"Unless it concerns the health or safety of Gwen," Everett says, touching my foot through the blanket.

"Oh, no you don't," I say, kicking him hard enough to know that I'm serious.

"You could've died." Everett's eyes flash silver at me. "If something happened to you—" He sighs. "Jameson knows better. He should've kept his cock in his fucking pants."

Jameson releases a low growl. "Watch it, brother."

"Don't act like you've never been caught up in the heat of the moment," Mikkalo says from his spot at the table.

Everett flashes his fangs. "Stay out of it. This is between me and Jameson. Jameson put Gwen's life in danger. And for what?"

"Stop it, Everett," I say, my voice shaking.

"As our girl's health keeper—"

"Stop!" My voice rings through the air, cutting Everett off. "If you want to get angry at anyone, get angry at me. I knew the danger of taking off my seatbelt in a speeding car. You will not sit here and make Jameson feel guilty after we made love, okay? I'm not a donor, Everett. I'm a dhampir, and you need to start treating me like I'm as tough as you guys are. Because I am."

Silence falls through the room.

Everett palms his forehead, resting his elbows on his knees. "I'm sorry. I wasn't thinking clearly. It wasn't my intent to make either of you feel badly. I just—I don't want to lose you, Gwen. You either, Jameson."

I crawl closer and wrap my arms around Everett's shoulders. "And I'm sorry for scaring you. You too, Bronx."

Bronx purses his lips at me. "You make it so I never want to leave, you know."

Throwing myself at him, I knock him sideways on the bed and straddle his waist. Leaning down, I kiss Bronx sweetly, not letting myself get carried away. "Good. That's how it should be."

Jameson slides onto the bed next to us and holds his arms open for me. I flop onto him, smothering him with my chest as I cage his head with my arms. He chuckles and kisses my cleavage, rolling me onto my back to kiss me again.

"All right, you guys out," Jameson says, peering down at me. "If you eat fast, we can stretch our time together."

I laugh and pat his cheek. "You've distracted me enough. We need to figure out who those asshole vampires were."

"They knew of Gwen but not her personally," Mikkalo says, coming closer to perch on the bed with the four of us.

"And they weren't Blood Rebels," Jameson adds.

"The one guy looked strangely familiar. He smelled it too," I say.

"It's possible that you still have repressed memories," Everett says softly. "I told you it could take a bit of time to bring them all back to the surface."

I squeeze his hand. "Is there anything you can do to help?"

His eyes flash silver. "I—I can't."

"What are you talking about?" Mikkalo says. "You can—"

Everett tightens his jaw. "I mean, just no. I'm not going to. One of you guys can. Last time was brutal. I can't do it to Gwen again. You didn't see what I saw."

Mikkalo, Jameson, and Bronx all look to me. I press my lips together and hug Everett. He sinks against me, and I snuggle close until he pulls me onto his lap to just hold me. I let him even though the others sit and watch us, probably wondering what the hell went down. I didn't get into it with Bronx, but he knows it was enough to have Everett needing time to process.

"I'm sorry my life was a mess," I murmur, bringing my mouth to his. "But I hope you know that I'm okay, really."

He nods. "I know. I just—I'm pissed the hell off that Laredo got an ounce of our mercy. What he did to you, the way he manipulated your entire life like it was some game to him, it was so horrible. How you can still want to be here with us..." His voice trails off.

"I'm here because you guys are nothing like Laredo. I know you would never do anything awful like that. He only gave blood to me when he had to, which gave him the ability to do what he wanted. I'm nearly certain at least Jameson would let me suck on his neck all day, every day, which assures my clear mind." I laugh as I say it, smiling at Jameson.

Everett releases a cross between a laugh and a groan. Mikkalo whacks Jameson on the back, sending him falling off the bed to land in a crouch. Bronx remains ever so silent, just listening.

"I was naïve even to think Laredo wouldn't dare manipulate me. Grayson was just plain stupid to think he had control over him," I say.

"If Laredo had any ties at all to a region, the contract you told me about would be enough for Laredo to play him. You were not raised within the Donor Life Corp territory nor were you raised as true Blood Rebels," Bronx says, finally speaking up.

I inhale a sharp breath at his words. "Fuck. The contract. Those guys tonight. I know why they seemed familiar. I think I've seen them before."

Bronx releases a deep growl. "Laredo wasn't acting alone."

I squeeze my eyes shut. "I just—I can't remember."

"Everett, I know the last time was difficult but I need you to—"

I raise my hand to Bronx. "No, don't ask him. He already made his feelings clear. You do it."

Bronx blinks a few times in surprise. "No."

I frown. "What?"

"No," he repeats.

"I'd do it, Gigi, but I'm terrible at it," Jameson says, pursing his lips.

I sigh. "This is important, Bronx."

"You gave Everett a pass, so I'm taking one too," he argues.

I turn my gaze to his brothers and throw my hands up. Why he won't do it? I have no fucking clue. He tried to do it to me before...shit. He's taking my demand to never ever do it again literally. It's exactly what I told him when he found me with Zaire's body and tried to ease my panic.

"Okay, you know what? I'll do it. It's going to be my time with Gwen anyway," Mikkalo says. He moves closer to slide his fingers through mine. "If you're okay with it. I know you might not want to go there with me yet since—"

"I'd like nothing more than to figure this out with you, Mikkalo. I trust you with my life and my mind." I slide off Everett and kneel in front of Mikkalo to rest my hands on his shoulders. "I know you'll be careful with me."

"Hell yeah, I will," he says with a smile.

"I guess I better go make our girl something more to eat. She's going to be starved," Jameson says. "And maybe one of you two should stand by later in case. As much as I enjoy our girl's blood lust, I've done enough brotherly intervention if she goes wild."

I stick my tongue out at Jameson. "You're no fun."

He raises an eyebrow. "Lies."

I laugh.

"Not it," Everett and Bronx say at the same time.

"Looks like you might need to request a new health keeper since yours doesn't seem to be up for the job," Jameson says, clocking Everett. "I think it was more than about your safety, Gigi."

I play kick him. "Knock it off, Jamie, or I'll be the one to kick your ass." Turning to Everett and Bronx, I add, "And we don't need you guys to hover around."

"Our girl is right. I got this," Mikkalo says, scooping me up. "Now, group time is over. We'll see you at breakfast."

"Give him hell, Gigi," Jameson says. "He likes that shit."

I roll my eyes. "I know what I'm doing."

"Damn," Everett whispers to himself.

Bronx gives him a look that makes him tighten his jaw. "Have a good day, you two. I'm going to spend some time looking over the feeds. See if we can get any other confirmed sightings of these assholes."

"I'll let you know anything I find out," Mikkalo says. "In a few hours. Our girl needs rest. It's been a helluva night."

I hug him tight. "Can we take a bath first?"

"Nothing sounds more perfect."

I moan into the pillow as Mikkalo straddles my waist, massaging his fingers into my back. I had no idea how tight my muscles were until he started kneading through them. And it's the best. I've never had a massage like this. I don't ever want to move again.

"Good?" Mikkalo asks, keeping his voice low.

"So good," I murmur, turning my head sideways. "I think the rest of me needs some attention too."

"Show me where." He slides onto the bed next to me, allowing me to roll over.

I point to my legs first. "Here." Gliding my hands slowly up my body, I stop at my breasts next. "Maybe here." His gaze continues to follow my fingers as I draw them up my collarbone and point to my neck. "A little here."

"Gwen," he whispers, his heartbeat picking up speed.

I point to my mouth. "And most definitely here."

Smiling, Mikkalo leans in to kiss me, playing along with my teasing game. I run my fingers over his muscular shoulders and to his back, lightly grazing my nails along his taut skin flexing as he holds himself above me.

Mikkalo brushes his lips to my throat next. "Like this?"

I hum. "I think you could do better."

He moans and combs his fingers into my hair, bending my neck slightly to graze his tongue over my heated skin.

Molding his lips to the base of my throat, he sucks hard enough to leave a mark without breaking my skin.

And damn does it turn me on.

I slide my hands down the length of his torso until I can touch him through his briefs, showing off every delicious muscle on his body for me.

"Gwen," he says again. "I want to give you everything you desire, but I need a bit of focus to open your mind. If I give into you, you're all I'm going to think about. You want answers, not fantasies."

I pull back slightly to meet his gaze. "You can do that?"

He chuckles. "I can, but reality is much more fun."

I wrap my hands around his back and pull him closer for another kiss. "You're right, so we should get on with this. I might be feeling a little bitey too."

Flashing his fangs, he snaps his teeth at me, making me laugh. "You're not the only one."

I draw him closer and purposefully graze my tongue over one of his fangs. "You can have a little taste if you want."

He nips me and kisses me deeper, tasting the small drop of my blood coating his tongue. "Waking up to you is the best part of my day, you know. Your teasing is a close second."

I smile and pull back. "I won't complain if you wake me up with a full-body massage on our nights."

He groans and presses his weight into me. "Okay,

Gwen. We gotta sit up. If you keep talking to me like this I'm not going to open your mind, and I know it's important."

I scrunch my nose.

He leans in and kisses it to smooth out my features. "I'll be quick. I promise."

I bob my head. "Okay. I'm ready when you are."

Mikkalo rolls off me and sits upright, pulling me in close so that my legs hang over his hips. We sit so close that if we weren't wearing underwear, our bodies would align and nothing would get done. I almost tell him that I changed my mind, that I don't care who those assholes were, and all I want is to explore the next level of our relationship like I've done with his brothers.

I think he considers backing out for the same reason.

Bowing forward, he kisses me again like he can't stand our lips being apart, and I run my hands over his cropped hair, feeling the texture of it under my fingers. The soft lamplight sparkles in the depths of his brown eyes, the copper ring around his irises looking metallic against the darkness of his complexion.

"It's best you remain as relaxed as possible," he says, lowering his voice like any louder pitch will mess up the tranquility he creates.

"I don't think I've ever been this relaxed." I trail my fingers from his hair to rest on his neck.

He smiles, curling the corner of his lips. Hooking his

hands to my sides, he manages to pull me even closer. I try not to react to feeling his bulge so close to me, but he only adjusts me so that he can get his hands on my back to continue to knead my muscles.

Mikkalo meets my gaze. "With Everett, you had your mind completely unlocked. I'm going to try not to do that. If I can get you to answer my questions, I won't create a mental link."

"Will I pass out?" I ask.

He shakes his head. "You shouldn't. Everett already removed the block Laredo put on you. This will be just a little prodding to see if we can summon specific memories."

"I have to warn you. Some of them might be bad." Nerves attempt to bunch my muscles, but Mikkalo kneads them as they tense.

"And I'm here for you if they are. I promise."

"Thanks, Mikkalo. This means a lot to me."

"You mean a lot to me," he says, moving his fingers from my back to cup my face. "Now look at me and don't look away. I will ask you a series of questions to make sure the connection is open. If you feel uncomfortable answering, you don't have to, okay?"

I slacken in his arms, realizing the words were a command. "Okay," my mouth responds before I can even think of it.

A tiny blip of fear tightens my chest, but Mikkalo's dark eyes lessen my nerves. "For the first question. What's your name?"

"Gwen Royale."

His eyes widen and soften at my automatic response. My heart beats faster, the words ringing true inside me. I've already accepted my life and future with the Royale Coven. To hear that even my subconscious agrees brings me more relief and a strange emotion that leaves warmth blossoming in my heart.

"What is your favorite thing to eat?" he asks, keeping the questions light.

"Bronx's blood." Seriously, mouth? That is not what I wanted it to say. If my human half could slap my dhampir half, it would. Because how embarrassing. My answer should've been like pasta or something. The yogurt and fruit mix Jameson loves to make me. Something normal.

Mikkalo's features tighten like he's trying his hardest not to laugh. I can see the amusement clear in his eyes. I'm almost certain I hear a chuckle come from somewhere in the hall. My guys claim that none of them wanted to listen, but I bet Jameson, Everett, and Bronx all hang out in anticipation of my answers.

"There's something comforting about knowing you'll devour my brother first so that I can enjoy you longer," Mikkalo says, breaking into a smile.

I'd whack him if I could.

He must notice my urge, because he adds, "Respond to my comment any way you like."

Swinging my arm, I backhand his shoulder.

Chuckling, he leans in closer to me, our noses touching. His eyes flash silver. "I think we're good to start. Are you ready?"

"Yes." The word comes out so softly that I'm not even sure if my mouth really said it.

"Gwen, I want you to think back to the vampires who attacked us. Imagine their faces, their voices, their scents."

A dozen images flicker through my mind as I recall the first guy who punched the windshield. An image of him settles clearly in my thoughts—brown eyes, thick brows, high cheekbones, slightly tilted, almond-shaped eyes, wide mouth close to a round nose and chin. He smelled of something strange, almost nutty, and his voice rang higher with his scream.

"Tell me, Gwen. Do you know who they are?" Mikkalo asks.

A burst of pain pulses in my head, the thought hanging so close it hurts how I keep missing it. The other vampire's face flashes through my mind—long sandy-colored hair, wide, hazel eyes, a sharp jawline to match his sharp nose. I can still smell the subtle hint of vanilla of his blood, taste it even. The deep sultry tone of his voice hums in my ears. I can imagine him saying my name. I can hear him saying Laredo.

Mikkalo gently digs his fingers into my cheeks, his eyes flashing silver again. "Gwen, do you know who those vampires were."

"Yes." The word rips from my mouth with another burst of pain in my head.

"How?"

How? I repeat his question over and over in my mind, my mouth begging for me to find the answer. Pressure builds behind my eyes, and I can't stop the tears from pooling. My mind and body war with each other, but both want nothing more than for me to shout what I can't remember.

"How, Gwen?" Mikkalo repeats, his eyes flashing more silver.

I groan. "Laredo."

"Did he introduce you to them?" he asks.

"No."

Mikkalo inhales a soft breath, the air tickling across my lips as he presses his forehead to mine, blurring the world outside the lightning in his gaze. "Tell me more."

"I can't."

His eyes flash silver. "I need to prod deeper, Gwen. Is that okay?"

"Yes."

"Tell me how you know those vampires." Mikkalo's stare burns through me, setting off a fire inside me so intense that I inhale a sharp breath at the pulse of agony shadowing my vision. Uncontrollable tears splash my cheeks, and sweat prickles across my skin.

"Mikkalo, stop." Everett's voice sounds through the air.

"You're hurting her."

"Gwen, tell me," Mikkalo repeats.

I release a screech and say, "They're Laredo's coven brothers. I saw them a few times after Laredo arrived. They never saw me, but he made me forget. He wasn't supposed to take over as my blood source after I killed his coven leader."

Mikkalo's brows furrow. "His coven leader?"

"Rochester. My previous blood source. He tried to claim me because of my family. He bit my ancestor. He started the Gallagher dhampir line."

"Fuck," Bronx says from somewhere behind me.

"Do you know why?" Mikkalo asks me.

"Laredo said because dhampirs mature to carry power unlike anything. My dad didn't purposely keep us in a bunker. It was Rochester. He wanted us caged."

11

FRIENDLY COMPETITION

I DON'T KNOW WHAT SHOCKS me more—that my whole life was created for some ominous purpose or that an asshole coven thinks that they can control me. And now I have all sorts of questions I'm sure I'll never get answers to. Like Laredo. What was he actually doing? He claimed we were working for the elders, but he's the one who took us on the road. He kept me away from his coven brothers. He bit me because he claimed it would keep me free.

I wish his actions made more sense.

Something sweeps my legs out from under me, and I

land hard on the blue mat with a gasp. Mikkalo stands over me, aiming his dagger a few inches away from my heart. His fangs peek from beneath his lips, his mouth tilting down with a frown. I don't move. I don't even attempt to fight back.

"Focus, Gwen," Mikkalo says, keeping his tone stern though I know it bugs him having to command me. "I know you have a lot on your mind, but it's important to learn to fight through it. Especially now."

Holding his hand out, he waits for me to give in to let him pull me up. After his mind manipulation, all I wanted to do was curl up in bed. If I were with any of his brothers, they'd have let me. But Mikkalo? Something he saw or felt or whatever during the moments my mind was open to him has him on edge as much as me.

I guess I can't blame him.

"I'm not really in the mood, Mikkalo," I say, hugging myself. "Can't we just go back to your room?"

He shakes his head.

I groan. "I just—you'll protect me, won't you? This isn't necessary. What happened to the guy who wanted to give in to my desires?"

Locking his fingers to my shoulders, he flips me onto my back again. "What happened to my feisty, demanding, sexy-as-hell woman who would never just give in to defeat?"

"She knows you'll protect her," I say, narrowing my eyes.

He growls at me. "Even if you're right, shit happens. I need you to be able to defend yourself and back me up."

"I already can."

"Prove it."

"If you let me bite you," I say, snapping my teeth at him.

"If you can pin me, I'll let you bite the hell out of me however and wherever you like," he says, leaning in closer, pressing his weight into me.

"Wherever, huh?" I ask, raising my eyebrows.

"But the same rules apply to me. If I pin you, I get to bite you." He combs his fingers through my hair, gently tilting my head sideways to kiss my throat.

Tingles burst through me at the sensation of his fangs grazing my neck. "You can't use your vampire strength or speed."

"Fine by me," he murmurs, meeting me for a kiss. "You can fight however dirty you want."

I shove my hands into his chest, pushing him off me to straddle him. "Oh, I plan on it. I hope you're as tough as you act, Mikkalo. I'm pretty hungry."

"I hope you're ready for the best experience of your life," he says, flashing his fangs. He slides his hands to my ass and squeezes. "I'm going to start by biting your hot little ass first."

I raise my eyebrows. "You want to bite my ass?"

"You scared?"

I glare at him. "No."

"Mmmhmm."

"I'm not. But you should be. I'm not gentle."

"It's a good thing I won't find out."

Mikkalo attempts to flip me over, but I throw myself back between his legs, somersaulting to my feet. He stays good on his word and doesn't move at vampire speed. Jerking his legs up, he catapults to his feet and rubs his hands together, assessing me.

He takes a few steps closer while I step back, trying to figure out the best way to knock him on his ass. I don't get the element of surprise, so I can't catch him off guard. Mikkalo rushes me, not giving me another moment to figure out my strategy. Even without vampire speed, he's incredibly fast. Instead of bracing for a collision that'll knock me off my feet, I turn and run.

What a fucking mistake.

Mikkalo chases after me, unintentionally setting off my fear instincts. It happens every damn time someone follows me. I can't shake the feeling of being hunted, even if he isn't doing it to me. My brain knows better, but my body freaks the hell out.

"I think this was a bad idea," I call. "You're scaring me."

"Use it to your advantage, Gwen," Mikkalo says. "I know how a little fear can set you off."

I frown and spin to face him. "You're not supposed to

help me."

Mikkalo launches at me, hooking his arms around me. He flips the both of us midair, taking the brunt of the force onto him when he could've easily pinned me down.

"That's what we're here for. Plus, I want to earn my bite," he says, kissing my neck. "It'll make it ten times sweeter."

"Not happening," I say, shoving my hands into his chest. "My mouth is already set on biting every inch of you."

"Sounds like I'm winning either way," he teases.

I attempt to lock my fingers around his wrists, but he snatches my arms and flips me onto my back over his head. Jerking up my knees, I kick him in the stomach and knock him off course before he can land on top of me.

Locking his hand around my ankle, he tugs my leg, stopping me from getting to my feet. I screech as he pulls me to him by my foot. Twisting my body, I swing my leg with enough force to get him to let me go. I jump back to my feet and dash out of his reach. There's no way I'm going to pin him down like this.

"You know you can't outrun a vampire," Mikkalo says, keeping his distance behind me.

I race across the gym and to the different equipment. Picking up a large rubber ball, I chuck it at Mikkalo. He catches it and throws it right back at me. The ball bounces off my chest, sending me stumbling. I don't even realize

Mikkalo moved until his arms catch me, and he rights me on my feet.

"Throwing things won't work either," he says, grinning at me with his fangs.

He charges me again, locking his hands around my waist. I jab my fist at his stomach in surprise, hitting him right in his solar plexus. It's enough to get him to let me go, the force of my punch making him heave.

I dart away instead of attempting to overpower him. That's when I notice the small folding table with two thermoses and my empty plate from lunch. It reminds me of a trick I had almost forgotten since being away with my brothers. Mikkalo was wrong. Throwing things does work if you pick the right thing to throw.

"Time out," I say, holding my hands in an X-shape.

He raises an eyebrow. "You can't be tired already."

"Thirsty."

I reach the table and try to grab for the thermos, but Mikkalo materializes next to me. He hands me a glass of water instead, and I slowly take a sip, watching him watch me.

Taking the thermos, he lifts it to his lips. "These are both mine."

I can't help scrunching my nose. "Oh."

His eyes flash silver, and he sets down the thermos. "You're jealous."

Opening and closing my mouth, I try to come up with

another reason why I sound so disappointed that he's drinking someone else's blood. I mean, what the hell? He has to eat, and Everett isn't around to draw my blood all the time. He never takes enough from me to provide completely for the four of them anyway because he's afraid of taking too much.

"No," I say, softly. "That would be unfair."

"It's okay if you are. I should wait anyway since you're going to satiate me any minute now." He grins with his words, setting the thermos down without drinking.

I glare at him. "Don't count on it."

"You're going to love every moment."

"Because you taste amazing," I say.

He moans under his breath, his eyes flashing silver at my banter. Closing the space to him, I slide my arms around his waist and risk hugging him though he could easily throw me off my feet. I graze my teeth to his throat, distracting him enough to grab the thermos of blood off the table.

"My mouth's watering already," I whisper, sucking his skin between my teeth without biting.

Dropping his hands to my ass, he tugs me close so that I can feel the arousal my closeness, my teasing, my deep-seated need does to him. "This might work on one of my brothers, but it won't work on me."

Mikkalo releases me and grabs my arm, thinking I'm going to try to knock him off his feet. The sudden movement sloshes blood from the thermos and onto his back. He flares his nostrils and stiffens. I take advantage of his sudden distraction and pull myself free. Jerking my hand forward, I attempt to throw blood in his face. This method worked at least a dozen times in dealing with shadow dwellers. A face full of blood is hard to ignore.

Unfortunately for me, Mikkalo blocks my swing, sending the thermos back at me. The blood sloshes from it and spills across the front of me, covering my chest and soaking my tank top. Mikkalo inhales sharply, his eyes leaving mine to gawk at the blood streaming into my cleavage.

This wasn't exactly the distraction I had planned on, but it's a distraction none-the-less. Charging forward, I ram my shoulder into Mikkalo's chest and knock him off his feet. I land on top of him, dripping blood onto his face.

Laughing, I lock my fingers to his wrists and try to pull his hands over his head to pin him. He realizes too quickly what I'm about to do and hooks his arm around my waist, throwing me off of him. I roll a few times, trying to get back to my feet. Mikkalo pins me down, grabbing my hands to pull them up. Flipping me from my stomach and onto my back, he gets on top of me, straddling my waist.

His eyes rove over me, drinking me in. "Shove me off."

But I can't. My chest heaves, my body squirming under the weight of his stare. I capture his gaze with mine, submitting to defeat.

"You win," I whisper, sucking my bottom lip into my

mouth. "You beat me."

Mikkalo rolls off me onto his back, staring up at the ceiling. His chest heaves as hard as mine, and we lie together on the mat in silence.

"Gwen," he murmurs, lacing his fingers through mine. "I'm not actually going to bite you. I just thought you could use some motivation."

I prop up on my elbow. "But you won. It was the deal."

"I don't want to bite you because I won. It's not how I imagined it to be." He sits up, turning his gaze from the high ceiling and back to me. Reaching out, he combs my blood-soaked hair from my shoulder to look at my cleavage. "Though I wouldn't mind licking my lunch off you."

Heat flushes my skin at his words. "That would only be fair," I say, straightening my shoulders. "Since I did waste it on a failed plan."

Mikkalo scoots closer until he can pull me onto his lap. My whole body buzzes, feeling the stiffness of his erection under my ass. He searches my eyes for a second, and I reach up and pull the strap of my tank top from my shoulder, giving him silent permission to do what he wants.

He grazes his tongue over my shoulder, licking the sticky blood from my skin for a moment. "Do you know why it failed?" he murmurs, continuing to kiss and suck and lick the sensitive skin of my breasts peeking out from my bloody top.

"Hmm?" I ask, tilting my head back, enjoying this way more than I thought I would. I don't even care that someone's—or a bunch of someones'—blood still drips down my skin as long as Mikkalo doesn't stop.

"You lost focus the same time I did," he says, his breath tickling my skin.

"Can you blame me? The way you looked at me..." I guide his chin with my fingers until I meet my mouth to his for a kiss. "I lost on purpose."

He pulls back slightly, searching deep in my eyes to see the truth to my words. "Gwen, careful what you say."

"I want to give you what you want." I trace my finger across his lips until I feel the sharpness of his fangs. I prick my finger and let him suck it into his mouth. "You were right about me being jealous of a cup of blood. I want to be the one to satiate you."

Mikkalo slides his arms around me and lifts me into his arms. He blindly kisses me as he strolls toward the changing room tucked off to the side of the gym. I deepen our kiss, sliding my tongue into his mouth to caress the softness of his tongue. He carries me by my ass with one hand, using the other to tug the bloody shirt over my head. My bra falls off next, and he lifts me higher to trace his tongue over my breasts, sucking my excited nipple into his mouth. I moan and clutch his head, desire pulsing between my legs as I enjoy Mikkalo's mouth exploring my skin.

"Let's get this gen. pop. blood off us," he says through

kisses, turning on the massive tiled shower as nice as the one in his room.

I yank his shirt over his head, helping him undress as he drops his athletic shorts. He slides me a few inches lower until he can rub his erection between my legs, just teasing me through the barrier of my pants.

Setting me on the long sink, Mikkalo kisses me while standing between my legs. I grind against him, so turned on by his closeness, his fervent touch, the constant tease of his fangs grazing my shoulder.

He slows down and pulls back to meet my eyes. "Are you sure, Gwen?"

I nod with a smile and ease up my hips so that he can tug my pants down. He drinks in the sight of me in only my panties before he continues and massages his hands into my legs until he reaches my waist to finish undressing me completely.

I expect him to do the same, but he surprises me by kneeling on the floor between my legs. Goosebumps prickle my skin as he eases my legs open enough to position them on his broad shoulders. I gasp as he pulls me onto his face, drawing his tongue in circles over my clit while holding me in place to stop me from wiggling.

Pleasure cascades through me, and I clutch his head and moan, his mouth as amazing as I imagined. His sexual experience shows as he continues to taste my body, flicking his tongue just right that I orgasm after only a few minutes, my whole body humming with my release that makes Mikkalo moan and tug me to him to carry me to the shower.

He undresses completely without letting me down. Warm steam engulfs us, and Mikkalo steps us under the rain shower faucet. I kiss him deeper, feeling his body slip against mine. It would be so easy to enter me, but he doesn't. He takes his time kissing my throat and exploring my breasts with his fingers as the blood rinses away.

Reaching down, I wrap my fingers around Mikkalo's thick girth and stroke him with my hand. He spins me and presses my back into the cool tile wall, his mouth kissing more desperately across my skin.

He lets me slip from him to touch my feet to the floor and rests his forehead to my shoulder as I tighten my fingers and stroke the length of his raging boner over and over again. Propping his hand against the wall, he leans into me, kissing me and nipping my bottom lip, moaning deeper until his breath pants with the pleasure I give him.

"I'm almost ready to cum. Will you bite me when I do?" His breathless moan tickles my skin.

"You don't want to bite me?"

He hums again, his fingers digging into my hips. "Not yet. You first. When I cum."

His request comes out breathlessly, his muscles flexing as he tips his head back on the verge of orgasming. His cock pulses in my fingers, and the second he releases a husky moan, I sink my teeth into the tautness of his chest hard enough to make him bleed.

He cums all over my stomach, rocking his body with the motion and moaning again as I suck harder while slowing my hand.

His blood tingles down my throat, and Mikkalo presses me into the wall, breathing heavily into my wet hair. He drags his mouth over my shoulder, grazing his teeth to my skin without puncturing me.

I can barely stand the anticipation as he holds me by my waist until I manage to pull myself away.

He meets his mouth to mine. "I've never cum so fucking hard. You're so sexy. So perfect, Gwen. Can I bend you over now?"

I inhale a small breath. "You really want to bite my ass cheek?"

He chuckles. "I want to make you orgasm again too."

My heart races at his words, and I slowly turn around. He presses his body to mine, nudging me toward the inlaid bench out of the steady stream of water. Sliding his hands around me, he trails them up to my breasts, massaging his fingers over my nipples while kissing my shoulder.

"Relax," he whispers. "You can tell me to stop at any time, but trust me. You're going to enjoy it as much as I do."

He maps his hands down my stomach all the way to my pelvis until he touches me between my legs, rubbing circles over my clit to create enough pressure to make me moan. He kisses my shoulder, working his way down my spine, until he kisses my lower back. Parting my legs, he slips a finger inside me from behind, using his other hand to nudge me a bit until I bend over to rest my palms on the bench.

He kneels behind me and spreads my legs a bit more, sliding his finger in and out of me, touching me in a way that leaves my knees weak. I pant at the building pressure he creates as he uses his other hand to massage my clit.

He kisses the line where my leg and ass cheek meet, drawing his tongue over my skin until his mouth takes over for his hands and he tastes me between my legs again. He sucks just hard enough to draw another moan while rolling his tongue to add to the sensation that leaves my body shaking so hard that I find my boobs pressed into the bench as I lie forward.

Mikkalo hums, adjusting my body to spread my legs more. A dozen different sensations wash over me. He works me over with his lips and tongue until I can't stop moaning over and over again. My voice echoes through the shower as Mikkalo takes me to the point of release a second time, but he slows down right before I feel like I'm about to explode, bringing his hand back to replace his mouth.

"Take a breath," he murmurs, using one hand to squeeze my legs together to slip his finger inside me. It takes only seconds for my muscles to tighten and tingle, my whole body igniting in a wave of ecstasy that makes me scream out from the most intense pleasure that explodes through me.

I gasp and moan through more excitement zinging through my body, Mikkalo's lips sucking exactly where he said he wanted to bite me.

He draws his hands from me to slide around my legs, holding me up as my body relaxes completely. He only sucks for a moment longer before lifting me up to cradle me in his arms.

He kisses my throat. "How was it?"

I rest my cheek to his shoulder. "I want to experience it again."

His eyes flash silver. "Yeah?"

"And again."

He hums breathlessly. "Gwen."

"Possibly one more after...if you can handle it. Maybe you can bite me somewhere else new. I'm sure you didn't get that much to drink. You must be hungry." I trace my finger across his damp chest, sparkling with steam.

Shifting me in his arms, he sits on the bench, letting me straddle his lap, his body aroused and ready to continue this wherever I suggest we go. Mikkalo brushes my wet hair from my shoulders to expose my breasts to him.

"I'm only hungry to experience the rest of you," he says, his eyes trailing down my body.

I squeeze my thighs around him. "Is that so?"

He tightens his fingers to my hips, rolling my body

against his. "Everything about you satiates me deep in my soul. Just being close to you fills me up with something unexplainable. I want so desperately to prove that I will do the same for you."

I kiss him softly, letting his words sink in. I had no idea how much I wanted to connect with Mikkalo on every level. His cool yet wild intensity reminds me of the part of myself I try to suppress.

The powerful part of me that's nervous about what I can do as a dhampir. But Mikkalo makes me fearless. He encourages me to embrace the fierceness inside me he enjoys.

A soft tap draws our attention away from each other, and Mikkalo releases a small growl. "We're busy, Bronx."

"One of the leads was solid. I just got visual on one of Gwen's brothers. If we move now, we can try to intercept the trade," Bronx says, ignoring Mikkalo's comment.

Mikkalo doesn't hesitate or look to me for what I want to do. Instead, he stands up with me in his arms and shuts off the water. He grabs a giant towel and wraps it around the both of us.

The changing room is empty when we leave the shower, and Mikkalo sets me down on a bench to open the closet with some clothes in it for me.

"Put her in pants," Bronx calls from the workout area. "She's coming with us."

My eyes widen. "I am?"

"We're a team, Gigi," Jameson calls. "We do things together."

"And we'd never leave our girl behind," Everett adds.

12

WARNING SIGN

NO ONE SAYS ANYTHING, BUT I know I'm walking funny. When Bronx bit me, I was so focused on not dying from my excessive drinking of his blood that I barely noticed the tender skin of his bite. But with Mikkalo? It's reminding me with every step toward the car of the fun we had. My damn vagina loves the memory, but my poor ass cheek says I better be careful sitting in case.

"Is she okay?" Jameson whispers, trying to keep his voice low so that I don't hear him.

Mikkalo chuckles. "She lost a competition with me."

I suppress my embarrassment and straighten my shoulders, trying to walk as normally as possible.

Everett touches my shoulder. "Gwen, I can't help but notice how stiffly you're moving. Did Mikkalo work you too hard?"

I ignore the heat of Mikkalo's gaze boring into my back. He anticipates my response as much as Everett but obviously for two different reasons.

"I'm great. A little tender," I say, keeping my voice even. "Kind of wish Bronx didn't insist on the pants."

Mikkalo's loud laugh echoes through the air, and he materializes in front of me, lifting me off my feet. Strolling the both of us ahead of his brothers, he bows his head, bringing his lips to my jaw. "I'm sorry, Gwen. I didn't mean to laugh. Had I known we were heading out, I'd have picked somewhere else to give you a pleasure bite."

I scrunch my nose and smirk. "Just wait. I plan to repay the favor."

He kisses me. "Maybe not in front of my brothers."

"I'm sure Jameson wouldn't mind," I tease, saying the words loud enough for him to hear.

Mikkalo laughs again and presses his index finger to my mouth to get me to stop talking. Bronx remains expressionless as he opens the driver's side door. Everett doesn't stop giving me what I can only describe as The Look. He's probably going crazy thinking I'm injured, and the last thing I want to ask is for some of that damn numbing cream to put on my ass cheek.

Jameson raises an eyebrow at me from over the car. "Do I even want to know?"

Mikkalo says, "Yes," while I say, "No," and we both start laughing.

Bronx groans. "I know you're welcome to have your inside jokes and privacy, but if you can calm the hell down and focus, maybe we'll manage to succeed."

"Damn, Bronxy. Lighten up," Jameson says. "I think we could all use our girl's laughter right about now."

Bronx rubs the back of his neck. "I'm sorry. You're right. I'm just—I worry about taking her, but I worry about leaving her here. She looks like she might not even be able to keep up if she had to."

"She's not going to have to. I got her," Mikkalo says.

"Are you sure? You look more ready to play around than protect her."

I cover Mikkalo's mouth before he can respond, but my hand does nothing to stop him from growling in his throat. "First, you know I can protect myself or must I remind you? Second, I will be able to keep up. Don't doubt me. And third, I know you trust Mikkalo with your life, so please, you must trust him with mine. I know none of you will let anything happen to me."

Bronx turns to face us and reaches out and whacks Mikkalo on the back. "Our girl makes it hard to be annoyed with you, brother."

"Right?" Jameson says, sliding in the front seat.

"My comment didn't apply to you, Jameson," Bronx says, flashing his fangs in a smile.

Jameson groans. "You just wait, Bronxy. You're going to owe me a big fucking apology when you realize how difficult it is to resist her while she's looking at you with her big, beautiful green eyes."

"Oh, he knows," Everett says.

Mikkalo laughs and sets me on my feet. "Pretty sure you do too, brother."

Everett sits on the backseat and pats the place next to him, motioning for me to get in. My guys might not be obviously staring at me, but I know they're focused on my every movement and sound. I clench my jaw and ease down on the seat, slow as hell, and release a breath at how sensitive the bite is. How every time I feel the dull ache, I remember my body exploding, and I get aroused. Fuck. Me.

"You good?" Mikkalo whispers, leaning into me.

"I would be if my body would chill the hell out." I suck his earlobe into my mouth, nipping it softly. "The slightest pressure to your mark turns me the hell on."

He digs his finger into my leg. "That's what I was hoping for."

I slide my hand over his leg, squeezing him back. "It's only fair if you have to suffer with me."

"It's going to be a long fucking night," Mikkalo whispers, touching my chin to guide me to him for a kiss.

Everett clears his throat, drawing my attention to him, and I blush so hard realizing that everyone remains silent, trying hard as hell to give Mikkalo and me a bit of privacy even in this closed space.

"I need you to sit straight, so I can properly fasten your restraints," Everett says, messing with the straps.

"Um, I am sitting as straight as I'm going to get," I say, twisting my lips. "Why don't you guys just hold me in place?"

"We're heading to the outskirts of our region, dandelion," Bronx says.

I heave the most dramatic sigh. Shit like this is awkward as all get-out. I'm sure I'll get used to it eventually, but I don't want anyone to know that I purposely lost a fight with Mikkalo because the idea of him biting me excited me. I let him bite me somewhere I never thought anyone would consider biting. And I liked it.

"Gwen," Everett says softly. "I know you want to be tough, but what did I tell you before? If you're hurt or need something, it's okay to ask. You don't have to be shy or embarrassed. I want you to feel good always."

"Maybe if we weren't flying away from the estate," I respond. "Or if it didn't involve something personal."

"Damn, Mikkalo," Jameson says. "Our girl slip in the shower with you or something?"

"Jamie," I say.

He swivels in the seat to look at me. "I think my brothers can suck it up if that was the case. I mean, we all heard how loud you moaned. You don't have to get into the details or anything, but if you need something from your health keeper, just say it."

I look at Mikkalo, who remains expressionless but still looks at me.

"I don't mind," he says.

I lick my lips. "If any of you think you might get even slightly jealous, cover your ears."

Jameson chuckles while Bronx raises an eyebrow at me in the rearview mirror. Everett remains calm, waiting for me to tell him.

"You can just show me if it makes it better."

I giggle, and I mean full-on giggle. "Definitely not but whatever. I just need your magical numbing cream for my ass cheek."

Jameson tips his head back and releases a loud-ass laugh. Everett slides his arm between the seats and smacks his hand over Jameson's mouth to shut him up.

He doesn't, though. Talking into Everett's hand, Jameson mumbles, "It was supposed to be Bronx or Everett to spank you, Gigi."

I flick his shoulder. "It wasn't a spanking."

"Fuck," Bronx, Everett, and Jameson all say in unison under their breaths.

I expect Mikkalo to growl at them or something, punch someone, but he breaks out in a cocky as hell smile.

"You bit her on the ass?" Jameson asks.

He continues to smile without comment.

"Damn," Bronx whispers.

I wave my hands, my face so hot. I squirm a bit as silver flashes in all of their eyes, and I'm nearly certain they're imagining all sorts of possibilities for later. "Don't you guys get any ideas. I lost a fight."

"On purpose," Mikkalo says, bumping his shoulder to mine.

"How deep did you bite her?" Everett asks, keeping his voice even. He's definitely in health keeper mode while Jameson looks like he's on the verge of planning some extreme fantasy, and Bronx looks like he's lost in his own memory of his time with me.

"Not deep at all," Mikkalo says.

"I'm not in excruciating pain. It's just...I enjoyed it a lot. And it reminds me just how much every time I get the slightest amount of pressure," I whisper to Everett, keeping my voice as low as possible.

He hums under his breath. "Damn."

I whack him in the leg. "Hello? No mind wandering when you're supposed to act as my health keeper. We're not playing doctor. Will you just give me the cream?"

"You guys play doctor?" Mikkalo asks.

"Of course they play doctor," Jameson says.

Bronx smirks at me. "It is kind of his thing."

I backhand both Bronx and Jameson in their shoulders.

"Okay, I'm enforcing our no details rule right now. The next one of you to comment will be in trouble. And nobody look. I have to pull these damn pants down."

Silence fills the car, and I glare at each one of them, daring them to test me. Jameson looks like it takes everything in him not to turn in the seat, especially when they hear the snap of my pants unfasten. Everett remains expressionless as I shift on the seat to kneel.

"Why don't you lie across my lap?" Everett says, scooting to the middle to give me room.

I do as he says, my damn body tingling like crazy as I position myself. Mikkalo plays with my hair, letting me rest my upper body on his legs. Everett tugs my pants down a bit more, showing off my thong, and a deep, throaty noise escapes Mikkalo's lips. He totally gets turned on just at the sight of his mark on me, which doesn't help my own insistent horniness.

"I'm going to have to touch it," Everett says.

Mikkalo says, "Okay," while I say, "Just be careful."

I tilt my head to look up at him and realize that Everett's comment wasn't even intended for me. And hell. I didn't realize how personal the letting them bite me stuff was.

"There's a difference in the kind of bites we give," Everett says calmly, like he can read my mind.

"Yeah, Gigi. We agreed never to bite you just to eat. If we're drinking your blood for sustenance, it'll be from a glass." Jameson doesn't look back as he says it.

"But you let me bite you," I say.

He chuckles. "I think you underestimate the allure of your mouth anywhere near me regardless of what you're doing."

"We like fulfilling your needs," Bronx says.

"Damn right," Mikkalo says, massaging his fingers into my back.

An intense burst of pleasure rips through me, and I moan so fucking loud that everyone falls silent. "Holy shit," I whisper to Everett. "What did you do?"

"That's what I want to know," Jameson says, swiveling in his seat. His eyes flash silver when our gazes meet.

Another burst of ecstasy washes through me, and I squeeze my legs together, feeling like I might explode in the best way possible.

"Fuck," I say, digging my fingers into Mikkalo's leg.

Everett's hand touches the small of my back. "Almost done."

"Really?" Shit. Did I just sound disappointed? How awkward.

He breaks his serious demeanor and chuckles. "I don't have to be."

"Damn it. Make room back there." Jameson reaches out and touches my cheek. "Me next."

I swat his hand. "Don't you remember what happened the last time we got carried away in the car?"

He fake growls at me.

I smile and wag my finger at him.

He sighs. "Fine. But you're missing out."

"No, just saving all the fun for la—"

The car jerks and Bronx swears, tapping a few buttons on the dashboard. Everett quickly tugs my pants up and wraps his arms around me, holding me in place. I don't have the chance to react as Bronx slams the brakes. Mikkalo, Bronx, and Jameson disappear, the slamming of three doors ringing in my ears.

"What the fuck?" I ask, shifting to try to get a view of what's going on outside.

"Stay down, Gwen," Everett says, locking me in place with his hands.

I dig my fingers into his legs. "Tell me what's going on."

"It's those assholes again."

A shiver trembles through me. "What?"

Everett rubs his thumb over mine, squeezing my fingers. "They must be tracking us somehow."

My brows furrow. "Why do you say that?"

He tightens his jaw and looks at me. "It seems they've left us a message."

I jerk upright, pushing against Everett's attempt to keep me down. Slapping my hand over my mouth, I suppress a scream at the sight of the half-naked man stumbling around the road. And then I do yell out. Grayson's familiar blond hair hangs limply against his head. Blood coats his body from crudely cut words sliced into his back that declares, "She's not yours."

"Grayson!" I screech, trying to open the door. "Grayson!"

Grayson stumbles as Mikkalo, Bronx, and Jameson surround him. He swings out a blade in an attempt to fight, my name sounding funny coming from his mouth.

"Gwen! It's time to go home. If you don't, more will die. Your brothers will be drained dry."

"Grayson!" I shout again.

Grayson waves his blade into the air.

"Shield her, Everett," Bronx calls.

Not even a second later, Grayson slides the blade across his throat.

I scream again and fight Everett as he tries to hug me against him. I swing out, hitting him in the shoulder hard enough to get him to let me go. Thrusting the door open, I dive out. Two strong arms catch me, and Bronx pulls me up and smothers me against his chest.

"Put me down!" I yell, punching out.

"No." Bronx's denial pisses me the hell off, and I manage to uppercut him in the jaw. He growls but still doesn't let me go.

"Everett, I need you to verify," Mikkalo says. "Not all the blood belongs to Grayson."

I release a strangled cry and give up on trying to break

free of Bronx's embrace. Instead, I sink into him, hugging him close. His tense muscles relax, and he moves me to the back of the car to set me on the trunk to stand between my legs.

"We will make them pay for this, Gwen," he says, swiping his fingers over my cheeks. "They have no idea who they've decided to fuck with."

I suck my top lip between my teeth to get it to stop quivering. What had started as an amazing night quickly turns to shit all because of what I am.

"Bronx." My voice barely sounds a whisper. "I don't want you to act on my behalf. I don't want you to put your coven in jeopardy. These guys, they know about me. Who's to say they won't try to ruin everything you've built?"

"You better not suggest that we give you to them," Bronx says.

I crinkle my nose. "Fuck no. You think my brothers would trade themselves for the traitor against humanity? I just—this—I don't want anything to happen to you because of me. Don't feel obligated to handle this."

"I don't feel obligated, dandelion," he says, leaning in close. "I *am* obligated."

"Bronx."

His eyes flash silver. "Let's get one thing straight, Gwen. You're our girl. You picked us. We didn't get our power just by sitting around. And there's no fucking way I'm going to let anyone get away with making you cry. I don't care who they are." Leaning in, he kisses me, pulling me so close that I can feel every inch of his body. "No one else can claim you."

I release a small breath against his lips. "What have you done to me? I'd have kicked you in the junk for saying something like that before."

He kisses me harder. "What do you feel like doing now?" he murmurs, pulling back to smile.

I pat his chest. "I better not say."

"You and your love of torturing me. First that sexy show in the car and now this? Our time can't come soon enough."

I pat his cheek with a smile. "Maybe I'll let you bite my other cheek...if you're good."

"And if I'm not?"

"I get to bite yours."

Jameson heaves a breath, materializing behind Bronx. He squeezes his brother's shoulders and gives him a good shake. "Seriously, Gigi. It's time for you to say something sexy like that to me."

I snap my teeth at him. "Like what?"

He glares.

I stick out my tongue.

"Fuck yeah!" Mikkalo yells, drawing our attention from each other. He jogs in our direction, holding out his com device. "Gwen, it's not him."

I frown and blink. Bronx and Jameson somehow managed to distract me so much so that I nearly forgot why we were stopped out here in the first place. "What?"

"It's not Grayson," Mikkalo repeats.

I slide off the trunk of the car and push between Jameson and Bronx. No one stops me as I close the space to the body lying in a puddle of blood in the middle of the road. Everett carefully kicks the guy over so that I can get a better look at his features.

"Shit. You're right," I say, keeping my hands at my sides. My panic really messed with my head. Because of this guy's build and hair color, I just assumed it was Grayson. I thought he said my name weirdly, but I thought it was because this guy has been manipulated.

"Those assholes went through a lot of trouble to find someone who looked like your brother," Everett says. "I'm sorry you thought it was."

I groan and stretch upright. "It still doesn't change the fact that they have him or that they will kill others."

"But this gives us an advantage. We know what to expect. They plan to go after your other brothers. We can set a trap," Mikkalo says.

"You think so?" I ask.

He nods. "Maybe we can even start tonight."

13

REIMBURSEMENT

"KEEP YOUR VOICE DOWN. GWYNETH will hear you, Jerry. You know she never stays away long."

"Never call her that again. It's Gwen. Don't confuse her with someone she's clearly not."

"Clearly," Rochester says. "You haven't allowed me the closeness it takes to treat her as my beloved."

Goosebumps prickle over my skin. I hide behind the curtain of the storage area near the stairs leading out, peeking through a crack to stare at my dad and Rochester glaring at each other. Neither of them realizes I've already returned after only pretending to follow my brothers to the creek like Dad told me to do.

My brothers didn't want me tagging along, and I didn't exactly want to follow either. The last time, I accidentally stumbled upon Declan jerking off to an old back-world magazine when he was supposed to be helping scavenge the fruit trees. I mean, it's better than if he did it in the bunker, but still. Fucking not a dick I ever wanted to see.

"Because she's not, nor will she ever be." Dad's voice rises with his words. "You need to get that straight or leave."

Rochester releases a low growl. "I think you mistake where your place is, Jerry. Have you forgotten who you belong to? This life is fleeting. I'd hate to have to be the one to tell Gwen that her father couldn't handle what she was and abandoned her."

I blink a few times at Rochester's threat.

"Just because she turned eighteen today doesn't give you immediate claim. I know the deal. I've seen the contract."

"But has Gwen?"

Dad doesn't respond.

Rochester's eyes flash silver. "I can't wait to give her such a surprise."

"You—"

I step from the curtain, stopping Rochester from lifting my dad off his feet. The two of them gape at me. If there was one thing I've learned from Rochester, it was how to be quiet enough not to be heard by vampiric ears. I bet he regrets teaching me now.

Abandoning Dad, Rochester materializes in front of me and offers me a wide smile. "You're back early."

I glance at Dad but keep my attention on Rochester. "I wasn't exactly in the mood to see my brothers' naked asses. It's warm enough to go in the creek, you know. I'm sure they wouldn't mind if you join...never mind."

"You just love to tease me, don't you?" Rochester says.

I shrug. "Wouldn't you like to know?"

"I would."

"Maybe tomorrow."

I push past Rochester and head toward the couch and pull my feet up to tuck them under me. I don't know exactly what I interrupted between Dad and Rochester, but whatever it was leaves not only me on edge. Dad's lips hide under his beard with how hard he clenches his jaw.

Rochester sits down next to me, giving me more attention than usual. It's been only a week, but last time, he didn't even say more than hello. Now, he looks like he has a bunch to say. His sudden closeness tightens my muscles with nerves, and I shift in my spot, considering getting up to leave.

Cool fingers caress my cheek. "Gwen, today is a special day, isn't it?"

I draw my eyes to Rochester. "No, not really."

"You've turned eighteen."

"Have I?" I try to keep my voice even. "We don't celebrate birthdays." It's a flat-out lie, but I wasn't exactly looking forward to this day for the sole reason that once a person turns eighteen, they usually must register to become a donor, something I never plan on doing.

"But I insist we celebrate this one." Reaching into his jacket, Rochester pulls out an envelope and hands it to me. "Please, accept my gift."

I frown and look up to see my dad staring at me, the wrinkles on his forehead so deep they look like black lines under the shadow of the light fixture. He brings his hand to his lips and motions for me to be quiet.

My heart picks up pace, but I turn my attention back to Rochester. "A gift? You didn't have to do this." I force myself to smile. Dad obviously wants me to keep Rochester distracted. I know what his expression means. Something is utterly fucking wrong.

"Of course I did...but technically, you're the gift."

I grimace. "Huh?"

"For me."

Pulling out the papers, he hands me what looks like some sort of contract. I've seen something like this once before at one of the Blood Rebel outposts my dad took me to a few years ago to get my brothers and me a health check. It was in the strange archive building with everything I could ever want to know about vampires. I didn't get to stay long, but the copies of contracts taken and stored were interesting *to look at.*

Except this one freaks me out.

"What is this?" I ask, silently reading over the words.

"Reimbursement for providing for you. Now that you're eighteen, I'd like to collect your dues."

A wave of ice drips down my back, the dread so intense that I shiver. "I don't understand. My dad gives you blood."

"He's been only paying partially until you hit maturity. If you want to continue the life you live, I must insist you pay yourself."

"No."

He growls at my word, flashing his fangs. "This isn't your choice to decide. I've had a deal with your family for decades. We will provide for each other how it should be in every way imaginable. You are going to be responsible for my rise in power, something we can only accomplish to-gether."

Swinging my arm out, I attempt to punch Rochester in the face, but he catches my fist and pulls me to him. The click of his fangs sounds in my ears as he extends them even longer, holding my gaze while turning my neck to the side.

I squeeze my eyes shut, bracing for his bite.

A roar startles me, and Rochester shoves his hands into my chest. He disappears from the couch and smashes my dad into the wall. A silver stake protrudes from Rochester's back. Snarling, he punches my dad in the face, spilling blood from his nose. Dad doesn't yell or scream or any-

thing. All he does is mouth that he loves me and to run.

Rochester bites my dad's neck, sending blood pouring from his throat unlike anything I've ever seen. He's bitten my dad before, but never like this. Something inside me snaps, and I rush toward Rochester instead of away.

He drops my dad to the ground and flies at me. The world spins and blurs, and my vision shadows with the movements. With one hand, I link my fingers into Rochester's hair, bending his neck. The world slows as my back hits the wall at the other end of the bunker. Rochester heaves a few deep breaths, his eyes flashing crazy silver, igniting my fear instincts inside me.

"You are mine, Gwyneth. I did not spend all this time assuring your survival for nothing in return. Submit to me, or I will make you," he says, his deep voice growling the words. "We have a new future to create together."

"Okay," I whisper, leaning forward to hug him.

He relaxes under my action.

And then I bite him.

Blood fills my mouth, the action shocking Rochester enough that he doesn't react in the rage I expect. He doesn't do anything but let me continue to drink his blood. His hands travel to my waist, pulling me closer.

Reaching between us, I tug the silver stake dad gave me for my birthday, one he said that was specially made for me. I pull away from Rochester's neck and lean back to meet his eyes. He puffs a breath of air, caught off guard by my closeness. It's the first time I've ever been in his arms.

"Gwyneth," he whispers. "You're everything I imagined."

Swinging my arm, I stake him so hard that I shatter his sternum. His eyes widen, and he snarls, but he's too slow to stop me. We both fall to the ground with me on top of him. I punch him in the face over and over again even though he doesn't move.

"Dad!" Silas yells.

"Where's Gwen?" Grayson asks. "Gwen!"

Kyler rushes to my side. "She's over here."

I fall off Rochester and land on my back, heaving a breath.

"Fuck, Gweny. Are you hurt?" It's Ashton.

"Declan, get a jar. Hurry. Gwen's going to need this bastard's blood until we find a new source," Grayson says, standing over me. Bending down, he picks me up. "Hey, lil sis. Look at me."

I blink through my tears.

"You're such a badass," he says. "Rochester was powerful as hell."

"You saved us." Kyler shoves his hand into Rochester's chest. He pulls out what I'm guessing is his heart.

"D-Dad," I cry.

My brothers surround me with various expressions on their faces.

"I'm sorry, Gweny. Dad's gone."

"What? No!"

"She's having another memory," Bronx says, his deep voice yanking me from sleep.

"How can you tell?" Jameson's voice trickles to me next.

"Turn her towards me," Everett says. "Hold her tight, Mik. She looks like she's going to wake up fighting."

Jameson groans. "Damn, you're right. Her heart's going wild."

"I don't like this," Bronx says. "Wake her up."

Cool fingers touch my cheeks and comb into my hair. "Gwen, hey. You're okay. We got you. Open your eyes and look at me."

It takes everything in me to drag myself away from the memory of my dad's death as it spins over and over in my head. It's strange, the experience nearly as I remember it but something was different. More clear.

"That's it," Mikkalo whispers. "You're safe. You can relax."

I sink against his taut body and flutter my eyes open, meeting Everett's sparkling blue gaze. His sharp features soften as he suppresses his concern to offer me the smile I love. Reaching out, I run my fingers over his jaw, grazing the scruff on his cheeks. He covers my hand with his and presses it more firmly into his skin, feeling the weight of my hand.

"Do you want to talk about it?" Everett asks, tilting his

head slightly.

I lick my lips and clear my throat. "Can I have a drink first?"

Everett reaches under the seat and pulls out a bag with what looks to be dinner. I wouldn't usually eat until past dawn, but from how neatly everything sits arranged in the bag, I'm sure that Jameson wasn't going to risk not having food for me.

Everett pours me a glass of water from a thermos.

I just stare at the clear liquid without taking it.

Extending his fangs, he pierces his arm and holds it out to me. Mikkalo loosens his grip on me, letting me scoot closer. I bring Everett's arm to my mouth and moan softly as his sweet blood coats my tongue, washing away the bitter taste of Rochester's final donation from my mind.

Everett hooks his arm around me and pulls me sideways into his lap so I can lean against him. I rest my head on his chest and listen to his almost musical heartbeat sounding like it's beating just for me. Usually none of the others would watch me, but tonight, they all capture me in their stares.

It's enough for me to pull myself away. "Thanks, Everett. That helped a lot with the bad taste in my mouth. Rochester's blood to be exact."

"Fuck, Gigi. Let me help too," Jameson says.

I smile and shake my head. "Later when I can drink from all of you."

Bronx glances at me in the rearview mirror, his face remaining expressionless though I know he's glad that I deny Jameson. Not because he doesn't want me to but because he wants to be able to join in.

I lean forward and squeeze his shoulder. Bronx brings his hand up and rests it on mine. "Thanks, Gwen," he says softly.

Jameson punches him in the arm. "You guys need to get your shit together. I never thought I'd say this, but maybe we can help you get past your need to devour each other."

"What's the fun in that?" I tease, gliding my tongue over my teeth.

Bronx hits a few buttons on the dash to put the car on autopilot. "Careful, dandelion. I might ask Jameson to take over if you keep teasing me like that."

"Who says I'm teasing?" Sliding off of Everett, I wiggle my way between the seats and onto Bronx's lap.

"Teasing or not, you should come back here, Gwen," Mikkalo says, reaching over the seat to grasp my hand. "You look ready to start something I'm not so sure we'll be able to stop."

"Plus, there is no fucking way Bronx would seriously let me drive," Jameson says, fake glaring at his brother. "Especially not with how close to our contact point we are."

"Wait, we're almost there?" I ask.

Bronx hooks his fingers to my hips to stop me from

bouncing. From the hardness of his boner, I'm probably driving him crazy.

"Almost, but try not to get too excited," Mikkalo says. "This was only a lead. We can't be certain that we'll get your brother."

I nod my head. "I know."

"You also need to be prepared if things go to shit," Jameson adds.

"Story of my life." I scrunch my nose. "At least until you guys."

The car slows, and I swivel to peer at a tall stone wall with a wrought iron gate. Bronx doesn't move me from his lap, and no one reacts at the small tap of a finger to the window. Something freaks me out, and I can't stop from hugging Bronx and hiding my face. It's the first time I've never wanted to see what I could possibly be dealing with—but this is the first time I know things will be okay. This isn't me and my brothers facing demented outcasts. This is my guys showing me exactly the reach of their power as the force behind the Royale Coven.

"Mr. Royales, what an unexpected surprise," a smooth, velvety voice says, humming through the window. "Mr. Brentwood will be pleased by your arrival. Please, come with me."

Bronx opens the door and slides out of the car with me still in his arms. Mikkalo steps in front of us while Everett takes our side and Jameson positions himself behind. I realize they're protecting me by circling me.

"Don't talk or look at anyone," Bronx whispers in my ear.

"Then maybe don't let me go," I say.

"Wasn't planning on it."

The world blurs, the sudden movement making my head spin for a few seconds after we stop. I can't resist easing my face away from Bronx's shoulder, and I meet Jameson's green eyes. He stands close enough to Bronx's back that if I stretched my neck a little, I could kiss him. I consider it for all of a second, but a loud, warm laugh reverberates through the grand room to soak into my bones.

"What an honor it is to have the Royale Coven grace me with their presence," a man says from somewhere behind me. "But where is Zaire?"

"He's away on business," Bronx says. "And I must ask you to keep our visit discreet, Brentwood. You know how Zaire gets."

Brentwood roars a laugh. "I won't say I'm not pleased by his absence. Now, come on. I have dinner on the table. Join me. I even have something for...that lovely little thing."

Bronx stiffens.

"May I see her?" Brentwood asks.

"No." Bronx's deep tone snaps through the air. "And she will not be joining us. May I request a room?"

"Of course. But what a pity. You know I'll keep my hands to myself, dear friend."

"Your brothers might not," Mikkalo says. "Or must I remind you of the Vaduva ball?"

What the hell is a Vaduva ball?

Brentwood heaves a sigh. "I suppose you're right." He claps his hands. "Ms. Stephanie, please show Mr. Royales to a guest room and retrieve whatever they'd like."

"Thank you," Bronx says. "Now, if you don't mind, I'd like to rejoin you in an hour to discuss a few...regional issues."

"Splendid. My home is your home."

Soft footsteps sound through the air, and Bronx shifts me in his arms. It takes me a moment to realize that the man vanished without as much as a goodbye. Gathering my nerve, I pull away from Bronx and catch sight of a petite woman in a uniform not unlike the one Bronx had me wear that was intended for the staff I still have never even seen at Night Palms Castle.

The woman, Ms. Stephanie, keeps her head bowed, staring at the floor. She guides us up a huge spiral staircase that takes us to an entertainment room with comfy couches, wall projection screens displaying a movie I've never seen, a pool table, a swing hanging from the ceiling, and a group of humans—mostly female—swaying to music on a small dance floor. While I don't see any vampires, I know these people are part of the entertainment. At least they look to be having a great time.

"Some households control their staff by treating them

as if they're above the general population," Bronx says. "It encourages loyalty and population growth. Staff members who procreate usually have a clause in their work contracts that require blood donations to the coven's personal staff. The Hunter Coven rules Sky Canyon in our region and has one of the largest self-made staff—so large that they no longer receive gen. pop. blood."

I raise my eyebrows and turn to look at the women. It's then that I notice the bulging belly of a blonde who doesn't look much older than me. She perches on a chair in only a bikini while a man paints her toenails.

"Don't stare too long, Gwen," Everett whispers. "It's considered rude to focus on the staff."

I avert my eyes. "I've never seen a pregnant woman before. She looks so...happy. Not what I'd expect from someone who...they don't force them to be baby-makers, right?"

"If they were, they'd be stripped of power and most likely sentenced to death. Donor Life Corp favors females and has laws to assure no coven manipulates the population unnaturally. Blood adds to power, and alliances wear thin." Mikkalo leans in closer to me. "Too much population growth requires transfers and adjustments to the regions."

"Sounds complicated," I say.

"With good reason," Bronx says. "But let's talk about this later. You can't control the volume of your voice when you're on edge. This kind of discussion isn't meant for human ears. You'd have to accept a Blood Vow before we could really get into things...at least in other households."

"A Blood Vow?"

"Gigi, later," Jameson says.

I glare at him. He knows how curious I get about everything, and once one of them opens up, I know they'll spill all their secrets. Bronx must realize it or else he wouldn't have said anything.

Ms. Stephanie comes to a stop outside a set of double doors. "Your room, Mr. Royales," she says, keeping her voice low.

Bronx sets me on my feet. "Please show us the accommodations."

Nodding, she opens the door.

Bronx pushes her inside.

14

GETTING ANSWERS

PRESSING MS. STEPHANIE'S BACK AGAINST the nearest wall, Bronx leans close and locks his gaze on her. Her eyes widen, her body going slack. Without having to ask, I know he's opening her mind to be manipulated.

"What are you doing?" I hiss, trying to rush closer.

Mikkalo blocks my way. "Shhh. Keep your voice low."

Bronx cups the woman's face, pulling my attention away from trying to burn Mikkalo's back with my glower. "Don't move. Don't make a sound. I'm not going to hurt you."

Anger explodes through me. I mean, what the actual fuck? Bronx knows how I feel about mind manipulation, and yet he's using it on an unsuspecting woman.

"You will not tell your misters of this," Bronx says, keeping his voice even.

Shoving my hands into Mikkalo's back, I manage to push him out of the way like the time I did when he found out I was a dhampir. He releases a growl, catching himself on his hands. I rush past him toward Bronx, fully determined to interrupt his mind manipulation.

Jameson clasps me by the waist, and I automatically swing my arm out and punch him in the jaw. He growls at me too, the force of my fist enough to get him to release me.

"Bronx," Everett calls. "Brace yourself."

Bronx breaks his eye contact with the woman, and she heaves a breath. I crash into Bronx, knocking him off his feet only to land on top of him. I don't know if he lets me do it or not, but I manage to grab his wrists and yank his hands over his head to pin him in place. Silence falls over the room, the only noise I hear coming from my rapping heart pounding in my head.

Silver flashes in Bronx's eyes and he scowls, baring his fangs at me. "Gwen, what are you doing?"

I swallow the burning in my throat. "What am *I* doing?" My voice rises with my anger. "What the fuck are *you* doing?"

The look he gives me shouts that I should know the answer. "Getting the information we need," he responds, his brows furrowing.

Everett touches my shoulder. "Come on, Gwen. Let Bronx up. You look like you might lose control."

I hiss. And I mean full-on hiss, the noise something strange and unfamiliar, feral, coming from my mouth.

Everett raises his hands in surrender. "You're on your own, brother."

Bronx takes advantage of my distraction and breaks my hold. Flipping me off of him, he thumps me on the floor beside him and pins me down just the same as I did to him. I thrash, trying to kick my legs to throw him off me.

"Mr. Royale, please. Don't hurt her." Ms. Stephanie's soft voice trickles through the room. "I will answer any question you ask."

Bronx stiffens, the woman's words clearly getting to him, because we both know he'd never hurt me. By his expression, he looks ready to attack me with his soft lips, if anything. And damn my body. It should know better than to react, especially when I'm pissed off.

"Please," Ms. Stephanie repeats.

Her pleas dig into me. I've never had anyone, let alone a stranger, beg for mercy on my behalf. She even risks taking a step closer.

Bronx heaves a breath, the intensity of his gaze warming my skin. His hold on my wrists loosens, and I jerk upright and slam my palms into his rock-hard chest, pushing him off me. Because if I don't, I might give into his nearly palpable lust for me and start making out with him, even in front of this frightened woman.

Bronx somersaults to his feet, leaving me a panting mess on the floor. Mikkalo, Everett, and Jameson stand nearby, but none of them come to my side. They watch Bronx straighten his shirt and close the space to the woman. She bows her head again, staring at the floor.

"I'll know if you're lying," Bronx says, keeping his hands at his sides.

Ms. Stephanie straightens her shoulders. "I will not lie nor will I tell my misters. Please, just don't hurt the girl."

Bronx doesn't respond to her request, taking full advantage of her fear. "We're looking for a donor. Would have come in within the last week."

"What's her name?" she asks, lifting her gaze to meet Bronx's gaze. I can't help but appreciate this woman's bravado.

"His name is Silas Gallagher."

"Oh, Silas. Yes. He's been quite the talk among the girls."

I scrunch my nose. Of course he is. He always has been popular with the tiny amount of women we helped escape cities.

"They've been anticipating for Mr. Brentwood to release him so that they can properly mingle." Mingle? Yeah, no. The way she says it sounds more like they're interested in boning Silas. Silas would most definitely give in.

"Do you know how Brentwood acquired Mr. Gallagher? Mr. Royale put a block on transfers of more males to this household. The staff population growth has maxed out for the year." Bronx shifts on his feet to glance at his brothers.

Ms. Stephanie bobs her head. "There was an accident. It opened up a few spots for groundskeepers."

An accident?

She glances at me. "We lost our three eldest staff members. It was unfortunate considering they were only a year away from exemption."

"How convenient," Jameson says.

I sit up on the floor and pull my knees to my chest.

"What can I say? The girls were unhappy with..." She lets her voice trail off.

From the way she says it, it sounds like it wasn't actually an accident and these supposed girls she keeps mentioning wanted a different selection.

"What the fuck?" I whisper to myself.

Bronx straightens his back. "Will you tell me where he's being kept?"

Her eyes widen. "You can't take him. The girls will be so disappointed."

And funny enough, this concept isn't exactly new to me. I just didn't know it until now. Blood Rebels do something similar, at least, according to my dad. He once told my brothers he chose not to join a rebel community because I'd be separated from them and kept with the other women. Women who are treated far better than soldiers.

Vampires aren't the only ones concerned with population growth. Dad said only the best of the best men get the privilege of being among the women. It's where he met my mom and how he found out the truth about our lineage. Dad wasn't chosen because he was an amazing soldier. He was chosen for carrying the dhampir gene.

"The hell we can't," I snap, getting to my feet.

Jameson cuts me off from closing the space to her to give her a piece of my damn mind. There is no way in hell that I'm letting her stand between reuniting me with my family all because some girls will be unhappy. My brother isn't a plaything to be discarded once they no longer find him interesting.

Ms. Stephanie glances at me. "You want him for yourself."

I inwardly cringe at her assumption. "He's my brother."

"Then you should be thankful he's found himself in such a position."

Jameson cuts off my oncoming remarks with a kiss. "Chill out, Gigi. She's only being honest."

I glare at him. "You agree with her?"

He smirks. "Could be worse."

I whack him on the shoulder. The woman gasps from

behind Jameson, and I meet her narrowed eyes. Without her having to say anything, I know she realizes that I wasn't ever in any danger. Her pleas of mercy were unfounded, and she risked her life for no reason.

Opening her mouth, she releases a shout that Bronx quickly cuts off with his hand. He leans into her, trapping her in his gaze. A burst of fear ignites inside me at the deep growl that escapes his throat. I can't stop myself from pushing past Jameson to stand behind him.

"Gwen, do not interfere with me," Bronx snaps.

I take an automatic step back like he physically pushes me even though he doesn't even look my way.

"Do not speak or scream," Bronx says to Ms. Stephanie.

She slackens in his arms with only Bronx holding her up by her waist.

"Tell me where to find Silas Gallagher," Bronx commands.

"He's in Lady Tori's quarters. Down the hall, sixteenth door on the left," she automatically says, unable to resist Bronx's mind manipulation.

Bronx pinches her chin. "Good. You will not speak of this conversation to anyone. If you do, you will suffer great agony. Now, leave us."

Breaking his eye contact, Bronx releases Ms. Stephanie from his mind manipulation. She falls to her knees and gasps a breath, hanging her head for a moment. I don't get a chance to move before Bronx spins and snatches me off my feet. The world blurs at his speed until I find myself standing in the middle of a small bathroom with only a toilet, sink, and shower. I can't even step away from him if I wanted to.

"What the hell, Gwen?" Bronx asks, scowling at me hard enough that I press my back into the sink.

"Are you kidding me? You're asking *me* what the hell?" I snap.

"You could've endangered us all." His muscular body creeps into my space as he bends his head closer. "What you did, interrupting my mind manipulation like that, was stupid as hell."

"And what you did was invasive and wrong." I jab him in the chest. "You could've given her a chance to see if she was willing to answer your questions."

"She wouldn't have."

"How would you even know?"

Bronx growls at me, his eyes flashing crazy silver. "You know what? We don't have time for this. I did what I did for you, Gwen. Do you fucking want your brother back or not? Because right now, I don't give a shit."

The second the words escape his mouth, he closes his eyes.

And then he disappears, leaving me alone in the bathroom.

I spin around and face the mirror, clutching the marble

countertop as my knees threaten to buckle and send me to the floor. Soft murmurs come from the open door, but I can't gather my nerves quick enough to return to my guys. A door slams, and I groan and bend over, planting my forehead to the cool sink.

What the hell just happened? I can't even process things. I feel like shit, and I can't tell if it's because I'm pissed off at Bronx or myself.

Everett clears his throat in the doorway, drawing my attention to him. I glance at him and then back to the mirror without saying anything. Unlike Bronx, Everett remains expressionless. His calm, rhythmic heartbeat helps settle the wild and out-of-control beats of mine.

"You okay, Gwen?" Everett asks, stepping into the small bathroom. "I'm sorry about Bronx."

I flare my nostrils. "Don't apologize for him. What he did—what he said? I have every right to be angry."

Shuffling up behind me, Everett slides his arms around my waist. He rests his chin on my shoulder and stares at my reflection in the mirror. "Of course you do. But so does he."

"Seriously?" I step back to push away from the sink so I don't have to look at his unreadable expression.

Everett follows me from the bathroom and to the empty guestroom. Bronx, Jameson, and Mikkalo have all disappeared. So has Ms. Stephanie.

Materializing in front of me, Everett rests his hands on my shoulders to get me to look at him. "I'm not taking either of your sides, so please stop looking at me like that."

I frown at his words. "Like what?"

"Like you did the first day we met. Like I'm the bad guy."

I puff out my bottom lip, my anger melting into regret. I thought I felt bad before, but now I feel damn right awful.

"I'm sorry," I whisper. "You're not. None of you are. I'm just—I hate mind manipulation."

"I know."

Everett pulls me into a hug and kisses my temple. I breathe into the front of his shirt, smelling his sweet skin until I get my emotions under control. Now is not the time to flip my shit and have a meltdown.

We stand in silence for a few minutes until Everett thinks I'm calm enough to put space between us. But he doesn't allow much. Only enough to lean down and brush his lips to mine. Something comes over me, and I hook my hands around his neck and draw him in closer, kissing him deeper.

One second I'm in his arms, and in the next, my back hits the bed. Everett presses his body to mine, combing his fingers through my hair to kiss me more fervently. I devour his affection, gliding my tongue over his while trailing my hands down his back. I snatch the back of his shirt and yank it off him, setting him off with desire that lights his blue eyes as they rove over me.

Bending up, I nip his shoulder and draw my tongue

over his sugary skin and up his neck. His fingers unfasten the button on my pants, and he pulls them down only enough to slide his hand between my legs to touch me through the soft fabric of my thong. And then he rips it off and steals the gasp from my lips with another hot kiss that leaves my whole body buzzing.

"Gwen, I want you," Everett says, licking his lips as he pulls away and searches my eyes. "Let me distract you until my brothers return. You're all I ever think about, and it's driving me crazy."

I smile and lean back in to kiss him. "Is that so?"

"Mmmhmm. I don't want to pass up any spare moment that I can be with you how I want." Damn. Everett's desperate touch continues, turning me on so much. I'm nearly certain I'd never deny him.

"I want you too," I whisper.

Trailing my hands down his tight stomach muscles, I fiddle with the button of his pants until it releases and I can slide the zipper down. He moans into my mouth, kissing me with a passion that sends electricity zinging through me. I blindly tug his pants and boxers down, wrapping my fingers around his raging boner. He only lets me play with him for a moment before he pulls away and flips me onto my stomach to bend me over the edge of the bed.

I moan so fucking loud into the blankets at the sudden pressure between my legs. Everett thrusts deep inside me, holding my hips to create resistance so that I feel every amazing inch of him.

The spontaneity of this moment, the heat of his desire, and the tangle of emotions coursing through me leave me gasping with every rock of his body to meet mine. He moans softly with each thrust, and I dig my fingers into the bed, enjoying the sensation of one of his hands roaming down my pelvis so that he can rub my clit.

A burst of incredible sensations builds my desire more intensely that it takes everything in me not to scream out my pleasure. I bite the blanket between my teeth as I reach the point of orgasming. His need to assure I get off as much as him is nothing like what I experienced before being claimed. All of them are like this, really cementing exactly where I belong. And I enjoy it.

I shudder with a long moan, my legs shaking so hard at the amazing rush that collides into me to steal my breath. Everett whispers how good I feel, how sexy I am, how happy I make him through his own gasping.

Not long after my body stops shuddering, Everett moans and sinks onto me, pushing as deep as he can as he cums. His breath tickles my shoulder and he kisses my skin through his panting until he gently slides out of me and rolls me over to meet my mouth for another kiss.

"I wish we were home," he murmurs. "I want to ravish you all night. You're addicting, Gwen. Every time you allow me to be close, I want more and more of you."

"And I'm happy to give you more," I say, mapping my

fingers down his back until I reach his ass to squeeze.

He graces me with a smile that I can't resist reciprocating. "My brothers will never give me anymore of their time with you if they knew that."

I tilt my head. "What does that mean?"

"Bronx needed Mikkalo, so Mikkalo picked me to stay with you," he says, grinning.

"Instead of Jameson." I fill in the blanks, realizing that Mikkalo only picked Everett over Jameson because he doesn't know Everett and I have already reached this level of intimacy. While we've all agreed to this, I'm sure their deep-seated nature will always influence their decisions in regards to me. "You guys," I say. "I swear. This isn't a competition."

He bends down and wiggles his nose to mine. "I know, but I would be lying if I apologized. Because I'm not even sorry. After...I just feel so much better now. It's more difficult than I imagined not getting you every moment I want, but it's getting better."

I cup his cheeks and stare into the endless blue depths of his eyes. He doesn't have to say anything else for me to know that he might've been struggling with the new levels of my relationships I'm exploring with his brothers. And I can't really blame him. I'm not sure how I'd feel if I were in their positions no matter what was agreed upon. Even though this feels incredibly right and normal already, I know it goes against the possessive nature of vampires.

"Everett, next time, will you just talk to me? While this

was...so, so hot, I don't want you to hold your feelings in," I say. "Is this the real reason you blew up at Jameson over the attack?"

He tightens his jaw. "Now *that* I will apologize for."

I slide my fingers over the scruff of his face until I comb my fingers through his hair. "I want you to know that what I have with you means a lot to me, okay? I've never felt like this with anyone. You have no reason to be jealous. And if you do get jealous, let me know. I know a cure for that."

He rests his forehead to mine. "You're not obligated to do anything. This was our agreement. I'm happy to have this with you."

"I'm happy too, and I know I'm not obligated. I want to." I glide my tongue over his bottom lip and pull it into my mouth. "Especially if they turn into moments like this."

"Yeah?"

"You're so incredibly sexy. The way you—" I shiver. "So good."

He kisses my throat. "And you're amazing. I wish I could savor you more, but then it'll give our little secret away."

I grin. "We can't have that now, can we? I mean, those are the rules."

He eases off of me and scoops my ripped thong from the floor. I laugh and bat his arm as he tucks it into his pocket and picks me up to take me to the bathroom to get cleaned up. Everett fixes my messy hair for me, tucking the strands behind my ears.

"You're the best, Lady Tori," a feminine voice says from somewhere in the hallway outside the room.

"You must be quick, Xochitl. The misters might not be with the Royale Coven for much longer. I heard them discuss the new arrival," another woman responds.

"Don't worry. I'm sure he won't take long." Soft laughter sounds through the air. "He was quite ready to go when I had the chance to tease him at dinner. You should have seen the way he looked at me. I will be pregnant in no time, and Fabiola will finally get knocked a notch down."

I groan and look at Everett. "This is a weird-ass household."

"Could be worse."

I backhand his shoulder. "That's what Jameson said."

He chuckles. "We're guys. Do you know how many have to spend their whole lives mastur—"

I press my finger to his mouth to cut him off. "Don't you dare even say it."

"You're right. We don't have to. We'd do it anyway," he says with another laugh.

Groaning, I shake my head. "Okay, enough."

"But it's fun to make you blush."

I stick out my tongue. "I'm sure you can figure out another way. I do not want to think about guys—especially my brothers—jerking off or having sex or passing on the dhampir gene."

"Oh, shit," Everett says, his eyes widening.

I furrow my brows in confusion. "What's wrong?"

"The dhampir gene." He picks me up off my feet before I have a chance to react. "Your brother can pass it on. Here. Now."

"Ugh. We have to stop him."

"I never thought I'd want to cock block anyone besides my brothers."

I can't help but laugh. I know he doesn't intend to be funny, but it helps ease the oncoming anxiety tightening my chest. "He'll survive. Plus, if you knew everything about my family and my past. You'd totally agree that he deserves it."

15

RUDE INTERRUPTION

"OHMYGOD, WE'RE TOO LATE," I whisper into Everett's ear.

I thought I was occasionally loud, but it's nothing compared to the noise coming from behind the closed door where Ms. Stephanie said my brother was staying.

"It might be foreplay," Everett says, meeting my gaze, struggling to keep an even expression.

I bare my bottom teeth in a grimace. I shake Everett's shoulder. "Fuck. This is the worst. You do it. I'm not going in there."

He whips his head back and forth. "The woman might be naked."

"So might my brother," I argue.

"From experience—with you, I might add—it's far better to see your family naked than one of the females of another vampire's staff. Especially if she's under the care of Lady Tori."

I narrow my eyes at him. "So not true. I know you're worried about my jealousy. Not having to see the reason for all those sex noises is worth it to me."

"Think of the woman, Gwen. Would you have wanted some strange vampire guy walking in on us?" He twists his lips, a dash of cockiness in his expression. And damn him for being right.

"You better have something in your medical bag to wash my eyes out with," I mutter.

He chuckles.

"Something stronger for my head."

He nudges me. "Hurry. I hear a headboard banging."

"Shit."

Squeezing my eyes shut, I let Everett thrust open the door to the room. I charge in like a freaking lunatic, but nothing happens. No yells or screams. No outrage. But all the moaning. And Everett was right about the headboard banging. Also, a strange-ass smell engulfs me—like sweat and perfume, musk—and I cover my mouth with my hand. My dumb dhampir senses really go crazy. I knew things smelled differently, but ugh. This isn't the yummy scent of my guys.

"Fuck," I whisper. "Is this what we're like?"

Everett laughs into his hand, keeping out of the way of the open door. "I guess that would depend on who you ask."

Another moan sounds through the air, and begrudgingly, I snap my eyes open.

Big fucking mistake.

The mirrored walls and ceiling of this strange room gives me a complete view of a gorgeous woman with cascading black hair and only wearing stilettos. She nearly bounces as she rocks on my just-as-naked brother, who lies half propped up and tied to the wall, wearing a pink, silky blindfold. I try to avert my gaze and get a side view of the two of them, where I see it's my brother's head hitting the wall while he sucks on the woman's boobs.

"If you're going to be here, you might as well join us," the woman, who I remember hearing being called Xochitl, says. She tips her head back and smiles at me. "There are some toys in the chest over there for you to play along."

"Toys?" my mouth squeaks the word out.

"He shouldn't be the only one to cum now, should he? If you get me off before him, I'll return the favor. Because, as you see, his hands are a little tied."

Fuck. My. Life.

My brother moans again.

"Come on, mi amor. You better hurry," Xochitl says, curling and uncurling her fingers at me.

Fisting my hands, I stride toward her. Her smile widens, and she waves to a giant wooden chest against the wall. Instead of going to it, I stomp my way across the room, dying a little inside with each of my steps. Because fuck. The scent of their sex grows more potent. The noise louder.

Xochitl cups my brother's cheeks and kisses him. "I'm going to turn around and ride you like the wild animal inside you."

"Wait, I'm going to cum." My brother stretches out the word with a moan.

I'm nearly certain my life flashes before my eyes. "Fuck, Everett! Help me."

"Throw a blanket over her," he calls.

Xochitl doesn't have time to react as I grab the end of the blanket strewn across the floor and throw it over her. Everett knocks her off my brother, and she screeches. What happens next is something I could've lived the rest of my life without ever witnessing.

I slap my hands over my eyes and spin around. Xochitl flies at me. Everett scoops me up and out of the way, but she wasn't charging to attack. She dashes toward the bed again and lands back on top of my brother.

Ripping off his blindfold, she squeezes his cheeks in one hand. "Again. You will watch this time."

"Oh, no you fucking don't," I say, holding my hands

over my eyes.

"Gwen? What the—holy shit. Fucking A. Get out of here!" Silas yells.

"Not until she gets off you," I snap.

Everett strolls with me away from them, keeping his eyes trained on me. "The likelihood of fertilization at this point is slim."

"But she's humping the hell out of him again." I don't even have to look. I can hear it.

"A male donor his age has a refractory period that averages about ten to thirty minutes. It could be less," Everett says, using his health keeper voice. "But I highly doubt your brother would be an exception, even if it's been a while since his last ejac—"

"TMI, Everett," I say, covering his mouth.

"I'm sorry. You usually have a lot of questions, and I know how little sexual education is taught to humans." He rubs his lips together. "I can't help myself."

I groan. "Still. We need to do something."

Everett slides his hands to my ass. "We are doing something. We're waiting for my brothers to return. It shouldn't be long now."

"Everett, please."

Heaving a sigh, he murmurs, "Okay, fine. But you need to hold the female back."

"If this is what being part of the team is like, we might need to reconsider a few things," I grumble, fake-glaring at him.

Everett smirks. "I'll make it up to you, but you better make it up to me."

"Deal."

Turning around, Everett darts with vampire speed and grabs Xochitl off my brother. I find myself standing in front of her a second later. I throw my arms around her, restraining her to me. I try my best not to think about what kinds of nastiness might be getting on my clothes and instead focus on keeping her still.

"Please, you have to let me go," she says. "I need this."

I don't think I've ever heard such desperation, not even someone pleading for their life. "But why?"

"It's my turn. If I don't get pregnant in the next month, the girls will change my status. I'll be a staff donor for a year. This is my chance to make something of myself."

I grimace. "You don't want to expand the donor population with him."

"He's in excellent health. Good looking."

A carrier of the dhampir mutation. I don't say the words, but I think them.

While the chances of birthing a female, one who becomes symptomatic, are low, it could still curse another woman like me in the future. Most dhampirs don't even live past infancy due to the nature of their needs. One would have to know such things, and most humans and vampires don't. Like Bronx said, my existence was sort of a story to him. His brothers didn't even have a clue.

"He's a criminal. A Blood Rebel." I hate that I say the words, but Xochitl is this immersed in a vampire household, then she would know such people exist.

"I don't care." Her voice comes out as a whine, grating on my nerves.

A sudden alarm booms through the air, and I release Xochitl to cover my sensitive ears. The blast of sound erupts shadows in my vision. Swinging her arm back, Xochitl elbows me in the stomach. I bow forward with the movement.

Everett releases the most threatening growl I've ever heard from him. Xochitl freezes in place, her human fear instincts kicking in at the threat Everett poses her. He materializes in front of her, flashing his fangs. I can't even react as he leans in and cups her face.

"Never touch my girl again. When you leave and Lady Tori asks about Silas, tell her he tricked you into freeing him. He ran. Now forget we were here and leave."

Everett releases her and rushes to my side. He crouches down and motions for me to climb on his back. Going to the bed, he retrieves my brother, who now lies unconscious. I suppress the mixed emotions rising inside me about Everett's mind manipulation and instead take a few deep breaths against his neck.

The world blurs and a burst of fresh air engulfs us. The sirens wail even louder, and it takes everything in me to hold on. Everett sneaks around the massive structure, keeping close to the walls and running under the trees whenever he can.

We reach a tall concrete wall, and Everett sets my brother on the ground and rips a few bushes of the unkempt foliage on the outskirts of the property to camouflage him with. It helps that the evergreen sheet Everett wrapped Silas in blends in well with the surroundings.

"We will come back for him," he says, flipping me off his back to carry me in his arms.

I twist my lips. "We can't just leave him. I can stay. I'll hide too."

He shakes his head. "Absolutely not."

I open my mouth to argue that if he thinks it's safe enough to leave Silas, then it's safe enough to leave me, especially because I can and will fight. Everett kisses me and takes off, not giving me a chance to make my point.

Bright light cuts across the sprawling lawn. The security detail of the Hunter Coven scours the area—probably for an intruder that they don't realize is us. Everett retraces our steps, choosing to scale up a tree near a balcony. He tosses me over the guardrail and soon follows. Motioning me to the wall, he stands facing me, caging me in with one arm while using the space between us to pull out his com device.

He taps a few buttons. "We're going to be okay. I'm sending Mikkalo the info to all the cameras we passed so he can delete the feeds."

"But someone still saw us. The alarms—"

"Were activated because I freed your brother. While he looked like he enjoyed being tied up by Lady Tori, it was her way of imprisoning him until she could assure he wouldn't run," he says, keeping his voice low.

His com device beeps, and he glances at the screen and releases a breath. "It's all good. I need you to take a few deep breaths."

I inhale and exhale with him until my tight nerves relax. The shock of the night wears off, and we meet each other's gazes. I laugh first and rest my head on his shoulder.

"The things I'm willing to do for you," he murmurs.

I snuggle my face against the softness of his shirt. "Let's try not to do this ever again."

"Hopefully you only mean in regards to the most awkward interruption of my existence," he says. "Because the other stuff...did you know the refractory period with vampires only takes a few minutes. With some, it could be seconds."

I raise my eyebrows, a laugh threatening to bubble from my throat. "Are you the latter?"

He presses me harder into the wall. "Would you like to find out?"

This time I do laugh, and he chuckles, running his cool fingers along my warm cheek. Even getting all technical and in health keeper mode, Everett still manages to be sexy.

"Depends. I'm suddenly feeling more curious. What

else can you teach me?" I lick my lips and smile.

He bends down, getting close to my ear before grazing his lips to it. "Now what's the fun in telling you? I'd rather show you."

"Careful, Everett. If your brothers hear you, they'll know your secret. That behind your kind, easy-going, sweet persona is a panty ripper that I definitely don't mind sneaking around with." I draw my finger along his chest. "And I kind of like that little secret."

"Only kind of?" he murmurs, kissing my throat.

"I'd have to experience it again just to be sure."

He releases a throaty hum that sends a burst of tingles through me as he sneaks his hand down my pants just to feel my warmth. I return the favor and tease him through his clothes. While Mikkalo teased that Jameson would try to always keep me in his room, I'm nearly certain it's going to be Everett. And right now? I totally want to let him.

"Next time don't wear pants," he whispers, his breath sending tingles through me. "I don't care what Bronx says. If it's my time, I want you my way."

Oh, shit. I never thought such words could excite me. I've never been one to let someone tell me what to do, but something in Everett's silver flashing eyes makes me nod my head. I lick my lips and kiss him, moaning softly as he continues to touch me. The sound of a door slamming is the only thing that stops us from proceeding. Everett slips his hand from my pants and sucks his finger into his mouth, closing his eyes for a second.

"I hope you let me taste more of you later," he says, smirking.

I just gape at him, my eyes wide, my face hot as hell.

He takes my hand and pulls me toward the glass doors that lead inside the same guest room Ms. Stephanie brought us to. I hadn't even realized that's where we were. If I ever got separated from my guys, I'd be so screwed. I need to figure out how to pay more attention to my surroundings. It's just hard with someone always holding me close.

Bronx, Mikkalo, and Jameson stand near the door with various expressions on their faces. Amusement on Jameson's, suspicion on Mikkalo's, and fury on Bronx's. I can't stop the memory of our fight earlier from flitting to my mind. It hasn't been more than an hour, but the way he looks at me and Everett, like we have somehow fucked up again, pisses me off.

"Brother, what happened to the plan?" Bronx asks, keeping his voice at a whisper.

Everett remains calm. "There was an incident."

I clear my throat. "Apparently one of the girls wanted to use my brother as a sperm donor, you know, since she isn't a vampire."

Jameson cracks first, his amused expression turning into a full-blown smile. "I thought I smelled sex."

I roll my eyes. "Please don't remind me. I had no idea it had a weird smell."

"I wouldn't call it weird," Jameson says, giving me a once-over. "Not with you."

Bronx swings out and clocks Jameson in the stomach, knocking him back. The surprise punch forces him into the wall where he pushes off and launches at Bronx. The two of them blur in a fight that Everett spins me away from. It takes Mikkalo intervening to get them to pull apart.

I clench my fingers into fists, the fragrant scent of blood wafting toward me. "What the hell is wrong with you, Bronx?" I turn to Jameson. "And you, Jamie. You didn't have to retaliate. You split Bronx's lip."

Bronx touches the blood dripping from his mouth. I stroll toward him, but he disappears into the bathroom and returns with a wad of tissue. The action freezes me in my tracks. I gawk at him while Jameson, Mikkalo, and Everett gape at me. A whirlwind of emotions swirls through me. He's not only on edge about the change in plans, he's also still mad. I don't have to ask him to know. He totally wasted his blood on purpose. I hadn't planned on licking his wound or anything, but the fact that he obviously doesn't want me close to his blood speaks volumes.

And I'm hurt.

The painful ache inside me nearly makes me cry, but I suck it up, cross my arms, and stride past him toward the door. No one moves, the heavy silence of the room weighing all of us down. I'm not sure how to handle this mess, and Bronx and Jameson don't even try. I don't think any of us thought about the possibility of a disagreement or how to handle it. Do I let Bronx and Jameson work it out? Get in the middle? Bronx and I obviously have our own shit to deal with.

"Gwen, where do you think you're going?" Bronx asks.

I swivel and glare at him. "Where do you think?" Turning toward Everett and Mikkalo, I add, "You're going to have to lead the way, Everett. Mikkalo, I want you to carry me."

"What about me, Gigi?" Jameson asks.

Bronx steps in front of the door, blocking my way. "You're staying here. We're all staying here. If we leave, it might cause suspicion."

"Then it causes suspicion. I don't care." I stride toward the balcony. "Whoever catches me, carries me."

Bronx doesn't try to stop me this time, and his brothers don't stay behind. They follow me.

With my heart in my stomach, I jump.

16

THE BARONS

MIKKALO CARRIES ME THROUGH THE dark property, following closely behind Everett. Jameson circles us, keeping a look out as we head toward where we left Silas. Shadows move and dance in my vision, the blurring world around us hard to focus on. I can't tell if it's the wind stinging my eyes or unbidden tears. Either way, I continue to blink and clench my jaw, praying that the knots in my stomach don't get the best of me.

"He's over here," Everett says, speeding ahead to the wild terrain he camouflaged Silas with.

Everett pulls off a few bushes, and I release a relieved breath to see my brother's unconscious form still lying under the green blanket. Standing straight, Everett shifts on his feet to face us. His calm features help ease my building nerves, but even though he smiles, I still feel as if my heart might fall out. Bronx should be here with us. I thought he'd give in and follow, but he didn't.

"Jameson, why don't you hop the wall? I'll throw Silas over to you," Everett says.

Without hesitating, Jameson launches himself at the wall, effortlessly catapulting to the top. He smiles at me and winks, probably sensing the wild emotions hurting me. But no one talks about Bronx. They keep their focus on the task at hand.

Everett looks at us. "Mikkalo, you're in charge of our girl."

Mikkalo nods. "Jameson, catch."

I don't have a chance to brace myself as Mikkalo tosses me into the air. Jameson grabs my hands and swings me up and onto the wall. I wobble on my feet, disoriented by the motion. Mikkalo lands beside me and steadies me with a smile.

"You're getting better at not reacting to sudden relocations," Mikkalo says.

I clutch his shoulder and gasp. "Too fast to...even make...a sound." The words come from my mouth in bursts.

"Get ready for the drop down." Mikkalo hooks his arm around me and jumps from the wall. He lands with ease on his feet, not even jostling me in the process.

We smile at each other, and I hug him close for a second, just feeling the good weight of his arms around me. If a growl didn't sound through the air, I would have kissed him too. Spinning on his feet, Mikkalo unsheathes his dagger and searches the area.

"Someone's here—"

Everett grunts and snarls from the other side of the wall. Without hesitating, Mikkalo throws me back into the air where Jameson catches me. He hands me a dagger while holding onto me, making sure I don't fall.

"Shit, is it the Hunters?" I ask, peering down at Everett blurring in a fight with another vampire.

Mikkalo's booming voice draws my attention behind us, and I tense at the sight of five vampires emerging from the trees. One looks up at me and waves, baring his teeth in a smile that sends dread down my back. Not because of the way he smiles, although creepy, but because I notice a naked dude on his shoulder—and not a stranger. It's Silas.

"Looks like the bastards followed us," Jameson says. "One was hiding under the blanket as a decoy."

"What do we do? We're outnumbered," I say. "That asshole has Silas."

Jameson doesn't get the chance to respond to me. A burly vampire, taller and bulkier than even Bronx, lands on the wall next to us. Jameson jabs his dagger, stabbing the vampire in the stomach, but he barely reacts. And then he shoves Jameson into me.

The wall falls out from under me, and I screech and brace myself to collide into the ground. A familiar vampire catches me and flashes his fangs. It's the same guy that attacked our car the other night.

Jameson rams into the both of us, knocking the guy off his feet. I tumble over the rough terrain, losing my dagger. Somehow, I manage to somersault to my feet to get a better view of the area. Jameson and the guy fight, sending waves of dirt and debris flying through the air. I scour the ground for something to use as a weapon. I spot a pretty hefty tree branch and race toward it.

A black boot steps on my fingers as I try to pick it up. Without thinking, I swing out and punch the asshole right in the dick, sending him to his knees. I lock my fingers around the branch, striking him in the face. He falls on his back, stunned from the action, and I hurtle away from him and toward the towering wall.

"Gwen, don't fight." The other familiar vampire from the other night materializes in front of me. "I don't want to hurt you, but I don't care about your brothers."

I pretend that I'm going to knee him in the balls but instead sucker punch him in the nose. I only get a few feet away. The vampire rams into my back, knocking the wind from me. I never touch the ground. He tosses me on his shoulder and takes off.

Gripping his shirt, I yank it up and scratch my nails into his back. He only grunts and readjusts me, locking my arms underneath me. I attempt to bite him, snapping my teeth at his back, but I just can't get close enough. He zooms me farther and farther away that I can't suppress the fear billowing inside me.

I slacken my body for a minute, pretending to give up. If I relax, he might. I can then catch him off guard.

"Why are you doing this?" I ask, trying to keep my voice even.

"We have a contract. You belong to the Baron Coven."

"I do not."

He hums his disagreement. "You do. And had my obnoxious brother used his head, you could've been properly transitioned into our household. You'd have never been claimed by a coven far less superior or powerful."

Fury ignites inside me, and I buck my body so hard that the guy can't catch me from falling. I spill to the dirt and skid across the overgrown terrain, ripping my clothes and scraping my hands and cheek across the ground.

"Fuck, Gwyneth. You could've been seriously hurt." He bites his arm. "Here, drink my blood."

I flare my nostrils, the strangely familiar scent of his blood wafting over me. "No."

"Come on, you're probably hungry. When was the last time you had blood?"

"It's none of your business."

He smirks. "So recently. Who knew your brother was right about your...willingness to do what it takes to survive."

That fuckhead.

Jerking my leg up, I try to kick him in the junk, but he grabs my foot. A shadow materializes behind him, but he's so focused on me that he doesn't see the figure approach. My heart nearly explodes at the sight of Bronx raising two daggers, preparing to cut the guy's head off.

I brace myself to catch the asshole's head, but my body's reaction gives me away, and the guy turns. He drops low and charges at Bronx, taking a dagger to the back. He doesn't stop, running so fast that Bronx hits his back on the tree.

The guy disappears, choosing not to fight, and Bronx looks ready to chase after him. But he doesn't. He rushes to my side and scoops me off the ground, cradling me in his arms. I don't even care if we had gotten in a fight or if he's pissed at me. He's here and that's all that matters.

"Are you okay?" he asks, his voice gruff, his muscles rippling as he flexes with his movements.

I lick my lips. "I think so."

"Can you walk?"

"Yeah."

A sense of emptiness engulfs me as Bronx sets me on my feet, putting space between us. My heart crashes back to my stomach. I blink a few times, gawking at him. He doesn't look at me, keeping his attention on our surroundings. He leads the way through the trees until I spot our car idling on a smooth road.

"Silas?" I ask, spotting my brother slumped against the door in the backseat. "You got him."

"That was Everett," Bronx says.

With his comment, Everett emerges from the trees with Jameson and Mikkalo. The three of them rush to me and engulf me in the most amazing vampire sandwich. Even though my body screams with the aches from falling, my heart explodes with relief.

"What's their status?" Bronx asks, his deep voice cutting through me again.

"One dead, the rest gone. Think there were seven total," Mikkalo says.

Bronx nods. "We'll look into them when we get home. I now have seen their faces."

"And I have their coven name," I say quietly.

Bronx glances at me. "At least that's something." Motioning to the backseat, he adds. "Everyone in. Gwen, you're going to have to share a seat unless you want your brother in the trunk."

"Okay," I murmur.

"Good. Now, let's get home."

Silas sits on the edge of his bed in a guest room on the second floor. An empty plate rests beside him, and I balance my still full plate on my knees. Bronx, Jameson, and Mikkalo retreated to their rooms the second we returned, and I haven't seen any of them since. They've left me and Everett alone to deal with my brother.

The one thing stopping me from succumbing to the wave of emotions inside me is that I don't want Silas—or Everett for that matter—to see that I'm still upset over the whole ordeal with Bronx. Or that I had expected them to come to us for dinner. But they didn't. And then they missed breakfast too. And dinner again.

I'm nearly certain that Bronx won't come to get me for my time with him, though I'm not sure I even want him too. The awkward as hell, quiet car ride home with him did nothing to help my fragile nerves.

"Gwen, may I talk to you?" Everett taps on the door. He left me to stay in the hallway to give me some time to talk with Silas. I feel bad that he's spent our time together dealing with this, but I'm also so thankful he hasn't complained once.

Silas looks at me. "I'm fine, little sis. I'm not going anywhere."

I swallow and bob my head. "I know this is a lot to take in."

"Yeah, I'm just trying to figure out what's worse—you seeing me jizz all over the place or the fact that you are living with four vampires...by choice."

"Can we never talk about my cock-blocking you again? 'Kay, thanks."

Silas releases a cross between a laugh and a groan and takes the plate that I offer to him. Without the instigation of my other brothers, he seems chill enough. Or maybe he's been through so much that he doesn't have it in him to fight anymore. At least, not against me.

Everett opens the door, hearing my approach, and I join him in the hallway. He combs his fingers through my hair, pushing the strands behind my ears. Leaning in, he brushes his lips to mine like he can't help himself, and I give in to his need and lace my arms around his neck to pull him closer.

"This is going better than I expected," he murmurs against my lips.

I nod. "Silas wasn't as invested in the rebel cause as my other brothers. I think he resented the fact that our dad kept us—or I guess Rochester—kept us away from everything."

"It must've been tough."

I shrug. "I don't even know anymore. I'm still trying to process everything."

"I was hoping that if you'd let me, I could see if your brother would be of any help." He tilts away to check my reaction before I can answer.

"Not if he doesn't want to." I search his blue eyes, trying to figure out his feelings before he says anything to me. He's excellent at hiding his expressions better than any of his brothers.

Everett swings my hand with his. "That works for me. Will you formally introduce me to him? I don't know how much he remembers from the Blood Match Center."

I smile. "I'd like that. My brothers aren't really as crazy as they come off. They got along okay with Laredo..." My words trail off. Of course, I don't know how much of that was real or manipulated into their heads. Or if it matters. I don't want Everett to think about my life with Laredo. I know it bothers him.

"I'll just make sure to keep my hands off you, though the task might kill me in the process." He kisses me again, lifting me up to press my back against the wall.

I rock against him, just to tease the hell out of him. I can't help myself. He thinks he's the one who's addicted, but I'm nearly certain I'm hooked. Even his closeness excites me. Thinking about his passion and desire draws me to him.

"If you don't stop, we're not going to make it." He squeezes my ass, digging his fingers just right into the spot of the bite Mikkalo had left on me. It's already healed but the memory lingers.

And ohmyfuck. It sets me off so much that Everett spins me into another room to muffle the sound of my loud ass moan. Mikkalo wasn't kidding about it being a pleasure bite.

"Shit. I forgot about that. I'm sorry," Everett murmurs, one side of his mouth twitching in what I think is a smile he tries to suppress.

I pant, rubbing my hands over my legs. "It didn't hurt if that's what you're worried about."

He clears his throat and rubs his hand on the back of his neck. "But it's not mine."

"Oh. Is that a big deal? It's barely even a mark now. And even so, it might be Mikkalo's bite, but it's my body."

He chuckles. "It doesn't bother me. I just assumed it might be weird for you."

"It's fine, Everett. Just...be careful. Thinking about you even touching it again turns me on. It's so weird."

Licking his lips, he looks fully prepared to test me. "Serves Mikkalo right for doing that to you not long before my time. Now I get to have all the fun."

I wave my hands at him. "I want to. I mean, I *really* want to. Just imagining what we did earlier...it's taking everything in me not to jump on you." Biting my lip, I smile at the silver flashing in his eyes.

He swallows, his Adam's apple bouncing in his throat. "Come on. We should return to your brother. If we don't go now, I'm not so sure I'll let you."

I open my mouth to tease him, but he tugs me to my feet and kisses me all the way back to my brother's room. I enter in first, turning my gaze to Silas. He stares at his hands in the exact same spot I left him. Something about his sullen expression cuts deeply through me. I don't think I've ever seen him look so hopeless. Empty.

Strolling to the bed, I ease down beside him and drape my arm over his shoulders. He turns to me and returns my hug, squishing the breath out of me. A blip of fear rises inside me, because I know my guys get weird about others touching me, but Everett doesn't react. He doesn't come any closer either, giving the two of us space.

"Silas, I'm sorry I didn't protect you like I should've," I say, patting his leg.

Silas surprises me with a laugh. He pulls back to look into my eyes. Dad used to say Silas had our mom's eyes—golden caramel with speckles of chocolate. I never saw a picture of our mom, but just knowing Silas even has a hint of her makes me feel close with the woman I never knew.

He messes up my hair with his fingers. "Gweny, we were the ones who fucked up. It was our job to protect you not the other way around. I don't care what Grayson or any of the elders say. The fact that you went through all of this for me—" He waves his hand around the room to refer to our situation. "To help us. It means everything. I'm sure it's been difficult. I can't even think about what you've had to do."

"Nothing. I haven't had to do anything I didn't want to. I know that you guys thought the Royale Coven was manipulating me, but they're not. They've been amazing. Better than Laredo ever was. They helped me see the truth."

He frowns. "What do you mean?"

"Silas, we were prisoners. The bunker? Only leaving on

special occasions? Rochester made sure that we were separated from everyone. He used dad. He manipulated him. And now, there are others coming for us. They got Grayson." The words spill from my mouth, and I pout my lip.

Silas stares at me. "I don't understand. Who is Rochester?"

"The monster that killed dad," I say.

"The blood source had a name?"

"Laredo manipulated us to stop us from remembering." Reaching out, I take his hand. "But that's not the only thing. He was Rochester's coven brother and leader. They were the ones responsible for Gwyneth and the Gallagher dhampir gene. I think Rochester loved her or something. I'm not sure. He wanted me to be her."

"But Gweny, how do you know all this?" His brows furrow, his head tilting.

I motion to Everett. "Everett helped me. He was able to break the block on my mind."

Silas regards him suspiciously. "How do you know he didn't manipulate you to believe these things?"

"Because...he would never. He and his brothers give me their blood. None of them would even have a chance to try. You have to trust me. They're different."

Silas doesn't respond but continues to stare at Everett.

I get up and cross the room, taking Everett's hand. "They care about me. Protect me. They're trying their best to reunite us."

Silas flares his nostrils, his brows pinching together. "And what do they get in return? Surely you can't sustain those kinds of dues on your own, Gwen."

I can't blame Silas for thinking that. I'd have thought the same if our positions were reversed.

Everett clears his throat, drawing Silas's attention from me to him. Silas stiffens as Everett approaches, and I squeeze my brother's hand to reassure him that everything is okay. Everett pulls the desk chair to the bed and sits beside me, resting his hand on my knee. I automatically cup my fingers over his cool ones, sharing my warmth.

"I understand that this might be hard for you to believe, but the only thing I have asked of your sister is for some of her time," Everett says, turning his gaze to smile at me. "She's the most interesting human I have ever met."

"And what of her blood?" Silas asks.

"What I choose or don't choose to share with Everett is none of your business. You never involved me in the arrangement you guys had with Laredo. Just know this is far better," I say. "I care for Everett."

My brother groans. "How can you after only a few weeks, Gwen? Help me understand."

I know nothing I say will make this right for him. He doesn't know what it's like to be me. "I don't think you ever can. I'm a dhampir."

"Gwen," Silas hisses.

I hold up my hand to him. "Stop. Everett and his

brothers know about me. They're okay with it."

"They're lying. You're a predator to them." Silas pushes to his feet and links his fingers to the back of his head. "Don't be so naïve, Gwen."

"Maybe you shouldn't be so close-minded. Can't you just trust me? Everett can help you. He can fix whatever Laredo did to you. You'll see more clearly. Maybe then you'll understand." I touch Silas's shoulders. "Please. Trust me. I need you, Silas. So does Grayson. Declan, Porter, Ashton. They're counting on us."

"What about Kyler?" Silas asks.

My heart clenches at the thought. I've suppressed memories of him, of his death, completely. Silas's words rip the lock free, tearing all the heated, awful emotions from me. Shadows crowd my vision, and I turn away to find myself engulfed in Everett's arms. He hugs me close, brushing his lips to my forehead, comforting me the best he can even while Silas's glare burns into the both of us. But I'd never dream of pushing Everett away. I'd never deny him the chance to help me. Not because of Silas.

"Gwen," Silas whispers. "What happened?"

"Kyler made a deal with his Blood Match. He thought he could use the information about my dhampir mutation to free you guys. He traded me for you." My voice sounds so softly I'm not sure my brother can hear me. "It got him killed."

Silas sucks air through his teeth. "No."

"I'm so sorry," I whisper.

"No!"

Silas jerks his hand toward me and locks his fingers to the back of my dress, trying to yank me from Everett. Swinging my arm, I clock my brother upside the head, knocking him hard enough that he trips and falls onto the bed. He yells out, scrambling to find anything he can use as a weapon. Everett intercepts him, dragging him to his feet.

"Gwen! He'll kill me! Do something," Silas says.

I step forward, my knees trembling with every one of my steps. Standing in front of my brother, I cup his cheeks in my hands. "He won't."

"But Kyler."

My heart sinks into my stomach. This is the first time in my life I've ever seen Silas cry. His eyes glass over, and he hangs his head, grief washing over him so intensely that I can feel the weight of it even in my soul.

"It wasn't Everett or his brothers," I whisper. "It was all Laredo's fault. He put us in the position we were in. He tried to steal me away from you. He's the reason Kyler is dead."

Silas sniffles, heaving a breath. "I can't believe it. Laredo was on our side."

"He wasn't. Everett can show you. Will you please just let him? I won't let anything bad happen to you. You have to trust me. Believe me when I say I can take care of you. The Royales assure it." I run my fingers over Silas's scruffy cheeks, begging him with my eyes.

After a long moment, he nods. "Okay, Gweny. For you."

I hug him, sandwiching him into Everett, who remains in complete control. "Thank you, big brother. You'll see."

Everett doesn't waste any time preparing my brother. Not like he had with me. Spinning him around, he locks his gaze to Silas. Silas relaxes, going slack in Everett's hold. The two of them stare at each other, and I lace my fingers around my brother's.

Everett's eyes flash silver as he opens Silas's mind. "Everything you were told to forget will be restored. You will remember what Laredo did. You will know your life as it happened and not as you thought it happened. Remember."

Silas's eyes widen, his slack jaw opening his mouth wider.

He screams.

17

A LITTLE PUNISHMENT

I SNUGGLE MY FACE INTO Everett's chest, just letting him hold me on the recliner. He moved Silas into his room, because he's been out for hours now, and I can't stop glancing at him sleeping motionlessly on the cot a few feet away.

"He's going to be fine, Gwen," Everett says, playing with my hair. "I promise. Why don't you go and get some rest? If I have any problems with Silas, I'll get you."

"Go? Go where?" I press my lips into a line.

"It's already past sunrise and it's your time with Bronx," he murmurs, resting his chin on my shoulder.

"I doubt he wants to see me. He couldn't even look at me." My voice cracks with the words, and I inhale a deep breath. "I think I'll just stay here."

Everett groans. "I might regret this, but you can't stay here. Whatever you're dealing with in regards to Bronx, he's probably dealing with it too. You two have to work it out."

"If he wanted to, he'd have come by," I say.

"You needed space. We agreed we weren't going to overwhelm your brother." Everett tucks my hair behind my ear. "Now give me a kiss and get that cute ass out of here before you test me."

I fake glare at him. "Such a waste of a dress."

He closes his eyes like he regrets ever asking me to wear one. "Next time."

He kisses me tenderly, just enough to show me how much he cares and how much he'll miss me. I squeeze him tightly and let him carry me to set me on my feet by my brother. Leaning over, I press a kiss to Silas's forehead and comb his hair back with my fingers.

"He'll be okay," Everett assures again.

I bob my head. "Call me if you need me."

It takes everything in me to leave Everett and my brother. I glance over my shoulder, catching him smiling at me, and I return the gesture by blowing a kiss. Soft music hums in the hallway, and I peer around, wishing that Everett would at least walk me to Bronx's room because Bronx sure as hell isn't in the mood to pick me up.

As I reach his closed door, I contemplate continuing past to Mikkalo's room, but a quiet moan sounds through Bronx's door, drawing my attention. My stupid feet stop in place and shuffle forward. I don't even have a chance to think about opening Bronx's door before it swings inward under my touch.

His projection screen glows with a movie, and I stand frozen, staring at the couple having sex on screen.

"Mind closing the door, dandelion?" Bronx asks, keeping his voice even.

I turn my attention away from the movie to catch sight of him propped up on his pillows, his raging fucking boner in his hand, jerking off. He doesn't stop or anything as I gawk at him. All he does is raise an eyebrow.

I swallow my nerves and keep my eyes locked on his. "So this is why you didn't pick me up?"

He stops touching himself and grabs a small towel from the nightstand to wipe his hands on. "Actually, yeah. More fun than having you look at me like I'm an asshole. Relieves a helluva lot of stress too. Maybe you should try it."

"You think *I'm* looking at you like you're an asshole?" My voice rises in pitch, the hurt that was clinging to me for the last day now turning into anger. "You're the one looking at me like I'm the fuck up."

"You did fuck up. You put yourself in unnecessary danger. You jeopardized the standing as allies we have with the Hunter Coven," he says, his deep voice digging under my skin. "You made rash decisions with Everett that the five of us should have made together."

"I know," I say, balling my hands into fists. "And I'm sorry."

"You could've been taken from us, Gwen," Bronx continues. "And for what? Your brother? I'm sorry, but no one, and I mean no one, is more important than you are to me. You need to know that. I will do what is necessary to assure nothing happens to our coven. I am our coven leader."

A dozen thoughts whirl through my mind as I replay everything that made me so angry at Bronx—his mind manipulating the Hunter staff member, how he yelled at me for intervening and taking it upon me and Everett to get my brother. How he didn't follow us when we had to get Silas.

"And I'm not," I say, lowering my voice.

"Exactly, despite what you think."

Ouch.

I break eye contact and stride across the room to the leather couch and plop down on it. Everett said that we had to work things out, but right now, I'm not so sure how. Or if we can. I'm like a chaotic mess that just dropped from the sky on Bronx's orderly life. And every time I try to pick my shit up, it just crumbles in my hand and scatters, making it worse.

"Gwen, I'm sorry," Bronx says, swinging his legs off his bed to stroll over to me. "I didn't mean that."

"Yes, you did."

He sits down next to me, and I shift away, and not because his closeness bothers me. I turn because I know if I meet his eyes again, I might fall into his arms and tell him that everything is okay. But it's not.

He sighs and snakes his hands around mine to link our fingers together. "I'm sorry I hurt you, dandelion. I'm not used to this, okay? I was mad that my brothers went against me, but I'm more pissed at myself because I didn't pick you too. I should've been there for you and my brothers."

I swallow my pride and stubbornness to face him. "I'm sorry too. I've always been a bit impulsive, and I might have used my cute little ass to get my way. Your brothers have far less restraint than you do."

He chuckles. "None of us stand a chance against you."

"You can only blame yourselves."

Humming, he slides his hands around my waist and pulls me onto his lap. I smile and press my finger to his mouth, stopping him from trying to kiss me.

"I just want to give you everything you want," Bronx mumbles against my finger.

I drag his lip down with my finger and lean in close but keep an inch of space between our mouths. "I don't know, Bronx. You were dead-set against it earlier," I tease. "I think you deserve a little punishment."

His eyes flash silver, and he tries to kiss me. I pull back and smile, loving how he devours me with his gaze. Sliding off his lap, I saunter toward the bed and pull my dress over my head and toss it at him.

He gets to his feet to follow me, but I wag my finger at him. "Nu-uh. You're going to sit there while I finish this movie in bed. Do you have my thermos? I'd like to have a little drink while I'm at it."

The smoldering stare he gives me heats me up from between my legs and to the rest of me. Things have been so tense that I feel myself about to burst. Something about teasing Bronx, seeing how he lusts for me, sends my whole body tingling, suppressing everything else.

Bronx materializes next to the bed with an empty glass in his hands. He licks his lips and bites his arm, sending a rush of anticipation through me. "I thought Everett would have satiated you before you came. I hope this is okay."

My heartbeat picks up, and I suck my bottom lip between my teeth. "I guess we'll find out."

He stands next to me, his muscular body flexing, his massive erection so close that if I just stretched my arm a little I could graze my fingers along it. I lift my hand and watch Bronx's eyes flicker with silver in anticipation.

I smirk and wave my hand. "Your punishment isn't over quite yet."

He play-growls at me and walks backwards to the couch, never taking his gaze from mine. I slowly bring the glass of his blood to my lips and hum my pleasure, the sweet decadence of his blood exploding across my tongue. Bronx doesn't even blink, his smoldering gaze continuing to burn over me in the best way possible now heightened by the sensation of his blood settling in my stomach.

I lick my lips and set the glass down, leaning my back on the pillows. The side effects of his blood tease me, but it's not enough to send my body flying out of bed at him. It just makes me feel incredibly good and hot.

Bronx inches closer, remaining standing, watching me as I pick up the remote and turn on the movie he was watching. I divide my attention, looking at the TV but really focusing on him. I purposely release a tiny gasp of a moan and shift on the bed, rubbing my legs together.

Bronx intakes a breath as I toss my hair away from my shoulders. Gliding my hands down my clavicle, I run my fingers over the fabric of my bra. I pinch free the front clasp and expose my boobs to him. He takes another step closer, his boner flexing in anticipation.

I hum softly under my breath and graze my fingers over my excited nipples. Trailing my hands lower, I ease them down my stomach and to the hem of my sheer thong. Turning my gaze away from the TV to give Bronx my sole attention, I slip my fingers into my panties and touch myself.

His fangs peek from beneath his lips, and he strokes his hand over his shaft pleasuring himself while I explore my own body. I hold his stare and shimmy out of my panties to give him a better view of me. He strolls closer, and I let him. Climbing into bed, he sits across from me. He leans on one elbow, never taking his gaze away from my body as I try to figure out what I like.

Scooting down a bit, I lie on my back and rest my legs on Bronx's so that I'm sitting between his. I've never masturbated for someone before, and Bronx makes me feel so incredibly hot that I throw my nerves away and relax.

"You're so sexy," Bronx murmurs, squeezing my knee with one hand. "I want so badly to touch you."

I moan just thinking about him doing so. "Not yet."

"This is torture." He scoots his body even closer to mine, grazing the tip of his erection over the smoothness of my thigh as he continues to rub himself over and over again.

"Well, it is your punishment," I tease, peering up at him through my eyelashes.

I continue to draw my finger over myself, shifting and moving my hips under the good pressure I create. Bronx digs his fingers into my leg, his breathing growing heavier by the minute. His touch turns desperate, his hand wandering higher up my body. I let him pull me to him completely until I straddle him, feeling the thumps of his dick as he taps it against my stomach because of our closeness.

"I'm going to cum," he murmurs, squeezing my side with his fingers.

He releases a moan, his face scrunching with his pleasure, and he finishes across my stomach and chest. Bowing into me, he rests his head on my shoulder, his breathing faster than mine, and I cup his chin and guide him up to me for a kiss.

He reacts to my affection with such passion that I find my back hitting the pillow. Grabbing the towel on his nightstand, he quickly cleans me off and kneels in front of me, resting his hands on my knees.

I squirm under the weight of his stare, his still burning desire, and sink deeper into the pillows. Bronx eases onto the bed, his muscular arms flexing with his motion, and he grabs me by the hips and pulls me closer. I moan so embarrassingly loud at the flick of his tongue before he sucks my clit into his mouth.

He holds me still, positioning my legs over his broad shoulders to ease my hips up a bit. The sensation he creates with his tongue leaves me panting and moaning, gripping the blankets. I had no idea how badly I wanted to be close to Bronx or how much I needed and missed him until this moment, our hearts bare for the both of us to see and care for. Pressure builds between my legs, tightening my muscles so much that I curl my toes. I reach down and run my fingers through Bronx's soft hair, my body now so desperate for the release Bronx can bring.

Electricity zings through me, and I throw myself back helplessly into the pillows, my whole body exploding in the best way possible. I moan through my orgasm, clenching my nails into my palms so hard that I break the skin.

Bronx slides his body between my legs to lie on top of me, keeping his weight up with his elbows. His dick presses against my warm skin, fully ready to continue with his hot desire seeming never-ending for me.

"You're bleeding," he murmurs, pulling my hand away from the blanket to see.

"I'm fine. That was intense." I lick my lips and breathe against his neck.

He brings my palm to his mouth and glides his tongue over the drops of blood before kissing my skin. "I want more of you. All of you," he says, swallowing thickly with his words, his anticipation buzzing over me as he waits for my answer.

I rub my lips together and nod my head. "Can't get enough, can you?"

"Never."

Bronx eases upright and positions my feet to his taut chest. I don't know what I was expecting, maybe missionary because it's our first time together, but he looks ready to take me to a state of utter bliss.

"Is this okay?" he asks, spreading his knees a bit so that my ass rests between them.

"I can't be certain yet," I say, smiling.

His eyes flash silver, and he aligns his body with mine, just testing me with his tip, feeling my excitement for him. And the desire darkening his eyes shows me how much he enjoys even teasing me a little. Lacing his fingers around my elbows, he waits for me to do the same.

Starting slow, he enters me with a moan. The sudden pressure of his intimidating girth makes me gasp, and I close my eyes to feel and experience every inch of him. He picks up his motion, swinging into me while using my arms as support. I moan with every deep penetration, my whole body feeling the passion of his desire.

His eyes stay locked on mine, and we watch the pleasure rolling over our features. He glides in and out of me, the constant movement feeling so incredibly amazing that I gasp and moan, digging my nails into his arms, just holding on tight as Bronx enjoys my body as much as I enjoy his.

"You're so stunning, Gwen," Bronx whispers. "Perfect. Beautiful. Everything I ever wanted."

I hum, my voice refusing to spit out coherent words through my ecstasy.

"You mean so much to me. I want you to know that. I never knew I could feel this way or that life could be this way. You've changed me."

Easing my legs open, he sinks between them to close the space. He kisses me passionately, holding one of my legs up to assure I get every ounce of pleasure he has to offer.

"I didn't know I could feel this way either," I whisper. "You're not the only one changed. I just—I care so much for you. The other night killed me, you know. I never want you to feel that way. I never want to feel that way again."

"I'll do better," he says through another kiss.

"I'll try not to be such a pain."

He moans softly, kissing my throat. "Only the good kind, dandelion."

Heat and desire, a pleasure so intense that we both fall quiet to savor it, explodes between us. Bronx takes his time enjoying me, kissing me, exploring my tongue with his, holding my hands to feel even more connected. What started as hot and intense and full of need turns into a moment where I'm certain I can feel his soul. A moment we blend together to be one, experiencing each other on an emotional level I never knew existed. A level I hadn't realized how much I craved.

Bronx whispers my name into my ear, grazing his fangs along my throat and to my shoulder. He nips my skin, and I moan and bend my neck, giving him silent permission to bite me if he wants. He pricks me, the pinch fading the second his tongue glides over my skin and he sucks just for a minute until he thrusts harder into me with his climax.

"I didn't drink too much, but you should bite me in case," he murmurs.

Nerves grip me as I think about what happened the last time I bit him. Bronx must see the hesitation in my eyes because he rolls beside me. Biting his arm, he eases it around me, cuddling me from behind. I suck hard enough to make him moan, feeling his erection harden more between my legs. I hum, astounded that he's ready to go at it again.

"Can you imagine it being like this with us forever?" he whispers. "Is that something you'd want?"

It's then that I realize the heaviness of his words.

What they mean.

I also realize that forever might not be possible. I was bitten by Laredo and never transformed.

But I can't bring myself to say the words. I don't want to ruin this amazing moment. I don't want to see the sadness or worry cross Bronx's handsome face.

So instead, I say, "I don't know if forever is long enough."

18

BROTHERLY DISAPPOINTMENT

"YOU GET ENOUGH TO DRINK?" Bronx asks, standing in front of the bathroom sink while he shaves his face.

I swirl my nearly empty glass of his blood in my hand, watching the ruby liquid coat the sides. "I'm going to wait for the rest of your brothers if that's okay with you."

He turns around, giving me a complete view of his hot, muscular body. "That's probably a good idea. I'm not sure I could resist asking you to bite me."

I can't stop my heart from racing, seeing his boner pointing in my direction. How he still manages to be so horny after the day we had? Fuck, I might never walk normal again.

I didn't realize how achy I was because Bronx had carried me into the shower and then back to the bed where we slept for all of an hour. It wasn't until I tried to get up to get ready for breakfast and to check on Silas did I realize the good consequences of giving in over and over again to our desire.

Stretching my leg up, I watch as foamy bubbles trickle from my toes and back into the citrus fragranced water. "You'll have to come to me. I'm not leaving this amazing bath for at least another thirty minutes."

His eyes flash silver. "Careful, dandelion."

I don't get a chance to respond because Bronx jerks his head toward the bathroom door at the sound of muffled voices. I can't distinguish who they belong to over the soft music playing through the surround sound, but they draw closer.

Snatching a towel from the rack, Bronx wraps it around his waist and strides to the tub. Leaning down, he meets me for a kiss and says, "Stay in here as long as you want. If you need something for your aches, I'll call Everett if you need me to."

I crinkle my nose, most definitely not wanting that. I nip his lip. "I like the reminder."

He releases the sexiest noise from his throat. "I'll be right outside."

Bronx disappears into his bedroom, and I rest my head on the soft bath pillow and close my eyes. But the peace surrounding the bathroom doesn't last long. Something crashes in Bronx's room, and he yells a couple of creative swear words that tense my muscles. A door slams, his angry voice fading. I try to listen to what's going on, but it's nearly impossible unless I get out of the tub.

I use the side of the tub to pull myself up, my knees wobbling like jelly from the crazy-ass stretches of our passion. I make a note not to let so many days pass without some sort of exercise, especially with how creative Bronx is.

Suddenly, the wall of the tub looks a billion times taller than when Bronx set me in. Unlike with Mikkalo's tub, Bronx's doesn't have any steps to get in and out. I suck in a breath and swing my leg up, groaning in the process. The bathroom door swings open, startling me, and I slip and fall back into the tub.

Two hands pull me from the water, and I laugh out in embarrassment as Jameson holds me against him, squishing my wet boobs to his chest.

"Damn, Gigi. I'm totally not sorry for scaring you. This was exactly the welcome I wanted," he says, smiling at me with his fangs.

I pat his damp shirt and shake my head. "You're...something else. What are you even doing here?"

"Bronx said you were planning to stay in the bath for a while longer and asked me to wait for you. I couldn't stand just sitting in the bedroom—which, damn it, Gigi. I can smell your sexiness everywhere, and I'm incredibly jealous." He licks his lips.

"Jamie," I say, twisting my mouth.

He kisses me. "I'm just kidding...mostly. I'm more anxious than anything."

I can't stop the cross between a moan and a groan as my vagina decides to clench and tingle at the thought. I'm both excited and scared by his anticipation, because really, I never thought I'd experience so much pleasure in my life, and I don't know how I'll handle it all.

Raising his eyebrows, he gives me a look that screams he sees my sudden nervousness. Instead of calling me out on it, he adds, "I have the best time planned. I was hoping you'd help me with a new art piece for our room. I can't get it just right without you."

"What is it?" I ask, smiling at him. I want so much to smother him for his consideration and determination to make sure I'm great without me having to tell him. I'm nearly certain he can read me better than even my own family ever could.

"A surprise. But don't worry. It's nothing intense. Relaxing."

I slide my arms around his neck. "That sounds perfect."

"I thought you could also come with me to introduce your brother to the kitchen staff. He's probably not ready just yet, but I think it would be good for him to see the humans here so that he knows we don't have a dungeon of donors on tap or whatever it is you guys used to imagine."

"We didn't imagine it," I say, pursing my lips.

He grimaces, knowing that I speak the truth. I've seen humans in chains with my own eyes, and recently. Corona had others imprisoned near me. "I just want everything to be good for your family."

I hug him. "Me too. I appreciate everything you're doing. I know it isn't exactly ideal or easy. I just hope Everett and I got through the worst of it with Silas."

"Want me to call Everett for an update?" he asks, roaming his hands down my slippery back but never taking them past my waist.

"Silas was still sleeping not that long ago. I'd rather he rest."

He smirks at me. "You're right. Less douchey that way. At least, I know that for me from experience. The two things that leave me in a bad mood are being hungry and tired."

"Yet you pull all-dayers with me," I tease.

He chuckles. "It's worth it."

"He's right about that." Bronx's smooth voice draws my attention from Jameson, and I offer him a smile as his gaze trails over my soapy, wet body like he didn't just see me.

Jameson eases away, and I take a few steps, trying to walk like I didn't discover some never before used muscles.

Bronx closes the space to me and wraps a towel around my shoulders. He scoops me up into his arms and carries me back into the bedroom. I meet Mikkalo's gaze as he sits on the leather couch with his feet propped up on the coffee table.

"Hey, Mikkalo," I say, wiggling my fingers at him. "How was your day?"

"Not as exciting as yours," he says, teasing me.

I wag my finger at him and laugh, letting Bronx carry me into the wardrobe. I hear Jameson join Mikkalo in the sitting area but keep my focus on Bronx. He sets me on the seat and strolls to my drawers to pick out some undergarments for me.

I raise my eyebrows, surprised that he picks out a bra that will actually support my boobs. He's been paying attention to my preferences, and I can't stop myself from smiling.

"Are these okay?" he asks me, holding the bra up to his chest.

I crack up. "Try it on and tell me if it's comfortable."

Bronx laughs and shakes his head. "I don't mind if you decide you'd prefer to go without."

I stick my tongue out at him. "Only if you swear to carry me all day without bouncing me. Promise I won't have to do any running, climb stairs, or get cold."

"Deal."

I laugh and snatch the bra from him to put it on. He kneels on the floor in front of me and slides a pair of cotton boy-shorts styled underwear up my legs. Lifting my hips, I let him pull them up all the way. He eases my legs open and onto his shoulders, bending in close to kiss me between the legs on top of my underwear where I'm most sensitive. He grins at my reaction and works his way up my stomach, follows my cleavage, and meets my lips.

"You make it tempting to turn in the paperwork that announces Zaire's death so that I can forget about the region and spend the rest of time experiencing and savoring every inch of you." He says the words too quietly so that his brothers wouldn't be able to hear him.

Something about his words prods at me, and I guess I must make a face because he tilts his head, searching my eyes. "You don't like the thought of that."

I blink a few times, trying to gather my jumbled mess of emotions suddenly coursing through me.

"I'm moving too fast," he adds, almost like he's warning himself. "I'm sorry, Gwen."

My eyes widen, and I reach out and cup his face. "Oh, no. It's fine."

"I forgot that time feels different for you," he continues.

I kiss him to stop him from rambling. I haven't ever seen him act nervous like this before, and I realize that the step we took in our relationship was a huge one—but especially with him. I know how guarded he keeps himself. How much his life before me revolved around doing everything for Zaire and the region. For power. But now? This decision of being with me—it was for himself.

"I know that. I kind of feel it being around you guys. Things feel almost timeless—like so much yet so little passes," I say, smiling. "And I don't feel as if you're moving too fast. I like that you keep imagining me to be part of your future."

He relaxes and kisses me again. "You sure? The face you gave me...what was it for then? The only times you've looked at me like that was because I fucked up."

"You definitely didn't mess up. I just—is everything going to be okay with your brothers now? I mean, I'm not going to have to remind you that I love giving them my time too?" I bite my lip as I say the words, though they're not exactly what was on my mind. Bronx didn't get all possessive seeing me with Jameson in the bathroom. But it's like my mouth refuses to say what I'm really thinking.

Bronx's forehead wrinkles with his frown. "I know that, Gwen. I'm more okay with it than I thought possible. After today...I have no doubt in my mind about any of this. It amazes me how you make me feel like I'm not only getting a part of you."

"Because you're not. I'm all in with all of you." I link my fingers through his, bringing his hands up to my chest so that he can feel my heartbeat. "It feels so natural. Perfect."

"It does, doesn't it?" he says. "Even when you're being a

pain in my balls."

I laugh and smack his taut shoulder. "Hey now."

Bronx chuckles and pulls away to dress. He picks out some athletic pants and a tank top for me and insists on dressing me. I do the same for him, finally getting my ass together to push through the muscle aches until I barely notice them.

"You guys are seriously doing this?" Jameson asks, waving his finger at the two of us when we step out of the wardrobe.

I tilt my head. "Would you prefer if we stay naked?"

Jameson smirks, cocking an eyebrow.

Holding my hand up, I say, "Never mind. Don't answer that."

Mikkalo howls a laugh and whacks Jameson on the shoulders. "He means the coordinated clothes."

"You jealous?" Bronx asks, sliding his hands around my stomach.

"Nah, I know our girl hates that." Mikkalo grins at me. "I just think you two look so damn adorable together. I might have to go change to join in."

Bronx releases a low growl at his brother's teasing, and I spin around to face him and clutch his face to pull him to me for a kiss.

"Bronx is adorable, isn't he?" I say, talking to Mikkalo while smiling at Bronx. "And sexy. Hot. I mean, these muscles. I can't stop touching him." I stand on my tiptoes and kiss his neck. "Or kissing him."

Jameson heaves a dramatic groan. "Okay, Gigi. We get the point."

"Maybe you'll let me bite you a little?" I continue, grinning at Bronx.

He chuckles and spins me off my feet before plopping with me on the couch between his brothers. I somehow land on my stomach across the three of their laps with my face right on Jameson's bulge. Mikkalo slaps me on the ass in the spot where he had bitten me, and I shoot up in surprise. Even though the bite mark completely healed without even so much as a scar, I still feel a whisper of pleasure from him touching the spot. I flip over and arch my back, covering my eyes with my hands.

"Fuck, she's so fun to tease," Mikkalo says, linking his fingers to the side of my hip.

Bronx slides his arms under my arched back and curls me toward him to snuggle his face into my boobs. Jameson takes advantage and kisses me tenderly. I hum under my breath, his lips so soft and sweet that he has to ease away first because I'm not going to.

"Damn," Mikkalo whispers under his breath.

I sit up and smile, twisting on Bronx's lap, feeling his arousal as I meet Mikkalo for the kiss I know he wants. He kisses me far more passionately than Jameson, tasting my mouth with the caress of his tongue, devouring my affection.

"The only thing that would make the perfect start of my day even better would be if Everett were here too," I say, patting Mikkalo's cheek. I smile at Bronx and Jameson. "I just love this."

A small tap on the door draws my attention. Bronx calls out for Everett to come in. Everett smiles at me, his handsome face lit up. "You wanted me?"

I slide off of Bronx to get to my feet. Everett closes the distance, not letting me take more than a step. I hug him and press my chin to his shoulder, giving him the attention he wants. "Always. How's Silas?" I ask, tipping my head up to meet his blue eyes.

"He's in the shower. Pretty calm, all things considered," Everett says, glancing to his brothers.

It makes me dart my gaze to them. I flick my attention to Bronx. "So what was all the yelling over earlier?" Jameson distracted me so much that I nearly forgot that Bronx left me in the tub.

"Nothing important, dandelion. Brooklyn called with another warning. Apparently the Hunter Coven broke off their alliance with the Anderson Coven because of our arrival last night. Brentwood kept his word on keeping our appearance secret, but Corona suspects something is up. Brooklyn overheard him talking to Francisca. She's supposed to call Everett."

I turn back to Everett. "Want me to punch her heart out?"

I don't know what he was expecting—that maybe I'd be annoyed or jealous considering that he has history with the gorgeous blonde—but it definitely wasn't what I suggested. All four of them break out into laughter that makes this whole situation seem less dire. I know Bronx said it was nothing important, meaning he was taking care of it, but I don't even have to know vampire politics to know that breaking an alliance is some serious shit.

"Tell her yes," Mikkalo says. "I don't think I've ever heard anything so sexy."

I scrunch my nose at him. "I guess I'm going to have to work on that."

Everett groans and hugs me, lifting me off my feet to squeeze the two of us on the couch between Bronx and Jameson. "As much as I want to let you, I don't think that's the best idea."

"That's no fun," Jameson says. "That bitch tried to take my heart."

I pout my lip at him. I can't stand even thinking about that horrible moment and how Jameson was willing to die for me.

Jameson nudges me with his foot. "But luckily, I got you back."

A weird-ass coo noise escapes my lips, and I pull the front of his shirt to get him to kiss me.

Bronx clears his throat. "We will deal with her appropriately when the time comes. I promise you that, brothers.

But for now, I must agree with Everett. Francisca arranged the exchanges for Gwen's brothers. We need her alive to narrow down the placement of Declan, Ashton, and Porter. They've been taken out of our region."

"I promise to get the information, Gwen," Everett says, snuggling his nose to my throat. "It's just taking longer because..."

I peer at him straight on. "Because why?"

"Ev won't bone her like he used to," Jameson says, answering for him.

Everett releases a scary-ass growl at his brother, and I plant my mouth to Everett's to distract him long enough not to start a fight. He sinks into my kiss, tightening his hold on me until I ease away.

I turn to Jameson. "I hope you didn't suggest that he should, Jamie. Because Everett's mine and that would be a pretty shitty thing to even mention."

It's Everett who distracts me this time, gently pinching my chin to get me to shift the weight of my gaze from Jameson and his wide green eyes. "He didn't, Gwen."

"Then why did you get mad?" I ask.

"I don't exactly want you thinking about me with anyone else," he murmurs. "You're our girl and nothing in the past matters to me."

I smile at him. "I agree with that, and I understand you had a life before me—a long one. Plus, I'm not a stranger to the male species. Hello, you did help me cock-block my brother, remember?"

He kisses me again, chuckling against my mouth. "You're so perfect, you know."

"I'm not, but I'll try to be for you—all of you." I stretch my arms out in an attempt to bring the four of them closer to me. "I hope you always know that."

Everett looks at his brothers. "See? Perfect."

Bronx leans in and kisses me next. "You don't have to tell me that."

Thudding footsteps sound from outside Bronx's door, and Everett lifts me to my feet with him. Bronx gets up with us, but he motions to Mikkalo and Jameson to remain on the couch. Because none of their staff members are allowed onto their floor, I already know the footsteps belong to Silas.

"Think he's looking to escape?" Bronx asks Everett.

Everett shakes his head. "He's looking for Gwen. He wouldn't leave her. I saw as much from the glimpse into his head."

Strolling ahead of them, I get my achy legs to stay up with my mind, and Bronx lets me beat him to the door. I swing it open and pop out of the room, startling my brother enough that he swings out at me. Bronx tugs me back by my shirt and into his rock-hard chest. A soft growl escapes his mouth, and I elbow him in his abs, regretting the decision immediately. Because hell. He's an amazing cuddler, and I had no problem falling asleep in his arms, but right now his body feels like a brick wall full of tension.

"Shit, Gwen. You surprised me," Silas says. Luckily, he didn't catch the soft growl directed at him.

I try to pull away from Bronx, but his hand remains locked on my stomach as he goes into protective mode against my brother. Stepping on Bronx's foot, I attempt to snap him out of it without making it obvious to Silas. I'm afraid how he'll react if he finds out that I allowed my guys to claim me. He'd probably lose his shit, and I need him to keep his shit together.

"Sorry, Silas," I say, keeping my voice even. "Everett heard you coming down the hall and thought you might be looking for me."

"Brother, you have to let Gwen go," Everett whispers to Bronx too quietly for Silas to hear, but he smiles at him.

"He might hurt her," Bronx whispers back.

I want to tell Bronx that I'll be fine, but I don't trust my voice to whisper. I might have super hearing, but I really suck at whispering.

Stepping back, I nudge Bronx to move a foot away. I realize that Silas shifts on his feet, probably sensing the weirdness between us.

I clear my throat and smile. "Are you hungry, Silas? Jameson makes the best pancakes. They have syrup."

He tries to look past me but can't see into the room with Bronx's massive form blocking the way. "It's dinner time."

"Not for me," I say, twisting my lips. "I follow a night schedule now."

Silas tightens his jaw and tips his head a bit, motioning to me that he wants to have a word. I glance to Everett and Bronx and say, "Will you give us a moment?"

I think the only reason Bronx relents is because with super hearing and a now quiet, music-less hallway means that nothing Silas says to me will go unheard by any of them. Everett slides his arm over Bronx's back and guides him inside the bedroom and closes the door.

Silas reaches out and takes my hand, pulling me away. A blip of fear ignites inside me at his sudden movements, but he stops about twenty feet away and bows closer to me. He knows about a vampire's super hearing as well, but I don't think he really knows the extent of it.

"Gwen, I know you think you like it here, but we can't stay," he whispers.

Uh-oh.

I'm pretty sure Mikkalo growls this time.

"And where will we go?" I resist Silas tugging me along.

"I don't know. But please, Gwen. You have to listen to me. Something isn't right. I saw the way Everett looked at you and then that other dude. He looks like he'll start a fight, and you don't want to get in the middle of it." Silas yanks my hand harder, forcing me to budge a foot.

I try to pull out of his grip, but damn it, is he strong. Stronger than I remember. "Bronx will never hurt me. Neither will Everett. Nor will Mikkalo and Jameson for that matter."

His face twists in what I can only describe as disgust. "You're kidding me, right?"

I blink. "Why would I lie?"

He bares his bottom teeth, flaring his nostrils. "Shit, no. Which one of them are you fucking, Gwen? I'm not stupid. I know how you used to get with Laredo when consuming his blood. Don't think we didn't know you were sneaking around."

Ice slides down my back, and I don't respond to him.

"Funny how much I remember now," he adds. Linking his fingers around my other wrist, he pulls me closer. "So tell me, which one of those assholes are you fucking? That way the Baron Coven can kill him first."

Four threatening, super scary growls reverberate through the air so deeply that I can feel the vibration of my guys' voices in my bones. Goosebumps prickle over my skin as fear trickles through me. But I'm not scared of them. I'm scared for my brother.

"You're fucking *all* of them? Gwen, are you insane?" Silas digs his nails into my skin and forces me to turn around to look at my guys.

Anger rushes over me, and I jerk my arm back and ram my elbow into Silas's stomach. He heaves a breath and lets me go. I spin and shove him away hard enough that he stumbles and lands on his ass in the middle of the hallway.

A strange expression crosses his face, one I don't recognize, and he pushes back to his feet. "Dad would be so disappointed in you. Do you even realize what we went through for you? Dad died because of you. How could you do this?"

"Shut up," I say.

Silas glowers at me. "Kyler died because of you."

"He didn't."

"Now, if you stay here, Grayson will die because of you."

"I said shut the fuck up!"

Without thinking, I launch at my brother and wrap my hands around his neck.

I squeeze.

19

SURVIVE ON EACH OTHER

TWO HANDS LOCK AROUND MY waist, yanking me off Silas. He yells out and tries to punch Everett, but Everett hoists him against the wall and locks him in his stare. Silas slackens in Everett's arms, and I turn my head to hide my face in Jameson's chest.

"Sleep," Everett commands Silas. A second later, he sets him on the floor and turns to me with a look of worry, knowing how I feel about mind manipulation.

"Take him back to your room," Bronx tells Everett.

Everett disappears without another word.

"Jameson, take Gwen to your room. Make sure she gets something to eat." Bronx closes the space and touches my cheek, getting me to look at him. "Dandelion, something feels off with your brother. I want your permission to open his mind again."

I swallow. "I want to be there."

He shakes his head. "No. Not happening. What he said to you—"

"I don't care," I say. "I want to be there. He's my brother."

Bronx's eyes flash silver as we stare at each other, both of us too stubborn to give in. I know what he's doing. He's trying to protect me from getting my feelings hurt again, but he also doesn't want me to see him manipulate Silas's mind.

"Gwen."

"Bronx." I wiggle in Jameson's arms until he sets me down. "Stop arguing with me. I'm going to be there. What Silas said to me—it only hurt because it's true."

"Fuck that, Gigi. The hell it is," Jameson says. He clenches and relaxes his fingers like he might scoop me up and take me to his room despite what I want.

I place my hands on my hips. "We're wasting time."

Mikkalo steps next to me, closing the circle my guys make around me with their bodies. I fully expect Mikkalo to agree with his brothers. Both Jameson and Bronx stare at him in a silent conversation, trying to have a discussion in front of me without actually saying the words.

"I think we should let Gwen see," Mikkalo says, surprising me. "We're a team, and this involves her."

Everett appears in the hallway. "I'm with Mikkalo."

Bronx groans and shakes his head. "You better not hold this against me, dandelion. Silas is a threat to you."

I blink a few times. "You're giving in?"

His jaw twitches. "Not exactly, and I don't like it, especially after your reaction with the Hunter's staff member."

I grasp his hand. "I might've overreacted then."

He shrugs. "Still. But anyway, Mikkalo is right. We're a team. So majority rules. You can come."

"Majority?"

"Yeah, dandelion. You get a say too."

I can't stop the smile from crossing my face. Throwing my arms around Bronx, I hug him and attack his face with my lips, kissing him a dozen times all over his cheeks and forehead. His arms tighten around my waist, pulling me into his body.

"He's a goner," Jameson says to Mikkalo. "He finally sees why I plan never to deny our girl of what she wants."

I crack up and pull away from Bronx to smack Jameson on the shoulder. "It's not about giving me what I want."

Jameson raises his eyebrows. "But it should be. All the other stuff? You're our girl. It shouldn't be a surprise that you get a say in what we decide."

I smile at him. "Come here. I want my mouth all over

you."

Everett whacks Jameson's back. "Careful, she looks hungry."

I snap my teeth at Everett. "So let's hurry and do this. I plan on devouring all of you. Maybe give you a little taste in return."

Mikkalo grins. "I fucking love our girl."

Warmth washes through me at his words, sending my heart racing. All four of them have admitted to caring for me and loving things about me, but this is the first time I've heard anyone say that they love me. They're right about how meaningless time is with how deeply connected I feel on every level with them.

"How could you not?" Jameson says, smirking at me.

Everett slides his fingers through mine. "It is quite impossible, isn't it?"

Bronx tucks my hair behind my ear and holds my gaze with his dark depths. "You're right about that, brothers."

I don't even know what or if I should say anything, so I just keep smiling and soak in all the attention until Bronx breaks their circle and tugs me along with him. Everett holds my other hand and Jameson and Mikkalo stroll behind us. When we reach Everett's door, I consider asking if we can eat first. My nerves and the crazy emotions my guys summoned from my very soul threaten to consume me in the best way possible. I don't want anything to ruin what suddenly feels like the most perfect moment in my life even if we just stand here, doing nothing.

Bronx squeezes my hand. "I'll be careful, Gwen."

I bob my head. "I know."

"I'm also warning you now. If you show any signs of distress, Jameson will take you out of here. I can't risk you turning...wild on me."

"I got your back, brother," Jameson says. He winks at me. "Her wild-ass will be handled exactly how she likes."

I blush like crazy. "I'll be fine."

Bronx nods and releases my hand. He enters Everett's room first without another word and walks ahead, straightening his broad shoulders like he's steeling himself for what's to come. I realize I mimic him, clenching my jaw so that I can remain expressionless. I wouldn't put it past him to have Jameson take me out of here if I so much as puff my lip. I want to prove to Bronx—and the rest of them for that matter—that I can handle this.

Everett sets Silas on the cot. It's so strange to see him like this especially after he just told me I'm basically the death of my family. I want to be furious with him, but it's hard to have it in me if there is even the slightest chance that something is wrong. He was fine before Everett unlocked his mind, if not just a little freaked out, but something changed.

Jameson guides me to one of the recliners, stopping me from following Bronx. I try not to frown over the fact that I can't sit next to my brother and Bronx. Mikkalo joins us in the other chair and reaches out to hold my hand. Everett glances at me from his spot near Bronx, and I offer him a small smile.

Bronx inhales a deep breath and motions for Everett to prop Silas up and to restrain him. I squirm on Jameson's lap in anticipation, and Jameson grips my thighs, holding me in place.

"It's going to be fine, Gigi," he says, pulling me into him so he can wrap his arms around me completely and snuggle his chin into the crook of my neck.

I don't respond to him, unable to turn my gaze away from Bronx and Everett. They have a silent conversation with each other for a moment, and then Everett gives Silas a firm shake, startling him awake from the mind manipulation. Bronx grabs his face and leans in, intercepting Silas's mind before he has a chance to freak out and react.

"Tell me your name," Bronx says, leaning in. His closeness to Silas stirs anxiety inside me but not for Silas. I'm worried that Silas might somehow snap out of the manipulation to hurt Bronx.

"Silas Gallagher," Silas says, his body slackening so much that he sinks against Everett.

"How old are you?" Bronx asks.

"Twenty-five." Silas's robotic voice stirs something strange inside me.

"What do you know of the Baron Coven?"

My eyes widen at Bronx's question. I hadn't thought

much about Rochester and Laredo's coven since getting Silas.

Silas doesn't respond to Bronx's question.

Bronx leans closer. "Tell me what you know about the Baron Coven."

Silas's eyes water, but he still doesn't respond.

"Why do they want Gwen?"

"She's the first female to be born in our family since the uprising."

"What do they plan to do with her?"

I cringe at the question, afraid of the response.

"Fulfill the contract. She will Blood Vow to their leader to ensure power in the Baron Coven's future. It will free our family from donor life."

"What does any of that even mean?" I ask.

Silas doesn't respond to me because of Bronx's mind manipulation.

"What happens if she doesn't?" Bronx asks instead.

"Our family will owe a blood debt to the coven until the next female is born, and Gwen will die," Silas says. "It is her duty to proceed. She will give the Baron Coven what they want."

"We won't let that happen," Jameson murmurs to me.

"But why a Blood Vow?" Bronx asks.

"Power."

"Explain."

Silas doesn't respond.

Bronx's muscles flex, and he leans in so close that his nose practically touches Silas's. "Explain."

Silas yells out in pain, startling me. Jameson hugs me against him, and it takes everything in me not to lose my shit.

"I can't," Silas says, his voice cracking.

"Explain," Bronx repeats.

Silas yells again.

This time I break free of Jameson's hold, but I don't make it more than a foot.

Bronx breaks his stare on my brother and turns to us. Furrowing his brows, he gives me a once-over as Mikkalo blocks my way. "Get her out of here."

I scowl. "No, I'm fine."

Bronx's eyes flash silver, and he tightens his lips. "I said get her out."

I don't even get the chance to argue before Jameson carries me away. I land on his bed with a thump, the world still spinning. He sits on the edge, keeping a few feet of space between us, probably because I glower.

"Seriously, Jamie?" I ask, still trying to orient myself to the swift relocation.

"Bronx told you that was the deal. You can't be mad at us," he says, keeping his voice even. "I wasn't going to risk having to pull you off my brother. I don't like to do that shit."

I dig my nails into my palms and inhale a few deep

breaths. "Sorry, Jameson."

"You don't need to apologize."

"But I do."

He frowns. "For what?"

"For this."

I launch at him, knocking him off the bed with me. The speed and strength of my sudden movement catches him off guard so that I manage to shove off him and get to my feet. I race toward his bedroom door in an attempt to run back to Bronx's room, but Jameson cuts me off.

"Not cool, Gigi," he says, crossing his arms.

I groan. "What you're doing isn't cool. I need to be with Silas."

"What you need is to calm your ass down. Silas is fine."

I glare. "Bronx was hurting him. He was pushing too hard."

"It's the only way to get the answers we need. Bronx was right about something being wrong. Everett managed to unblock some of his memories, but it looks like the block was stronger than we thought."

I purse my lips. "Or he didn't know the answers."

"Silas would've been quick to say so if that were the case. He was silent, which means that he has the answers and can think them, but someone powerful really did a number to lock them inside him."

"Then maybe they locked them inside me too," I say.

"Well, if Mikkalo and Everett didn't pull them out of

you, then we'll never know," he says. "Bronx won't touch your mind, and he's the only one strong enough to break through something like that."

"Then I'll make him." I swipe my leg and kick Jameson's feet out from under him.

Dodging past him, I make it into the hallway this time before he links his fingers to the back of my tank top and drags me back into the room. I scream out as he tosses me to the bed. Grabbing a pillow, I chuck it at his head, and he ducks and releases a growl at me.

He races to me and tries to grab onto me, but I launch from the bed to evade him. Catching me by the wrist, he pulls me closer. I throw my weight at him, knocking him back. Landing on top of him, I straddle his waist with my thighs and tug his arms over his head to restrain him.

"Stop enjoying this," I say, narrowing my eyes at him, feeling his erection pressing between my legs.

"Then stop looking at me like you're going to ravish the hell out of me."

"You mean ravage," I say, leaning in close.

"I don't care which one." Jameson stretches his head to the side, prodding at my very nature with his attempt to distract me.

And it works.

Bending down, I glide my tongue to his neck, tasting the sweetness of his skin. He moans softly, turning me on, and I can't stop myself from sucking on the sensitive skin of his throat. My fingers tighten around his as I graze my teeth along the collar of his shirt. I roll my body into his, feeling the length of his shaft through his clothes.

"Gwen," he whispers into my ear. "We have to stop."

I shake my head and meet his lips for a kiss. "Just a little bite."

He groans and nods, letting me break from his mouth to trail my lips over his jaw and to his neck. I grind against him, the anticipation burning through the both of us. I hadn't realized how badly my need for Jameson was until he whispers that he's ready into my ear.

"Damn." Mikkalo's voice cuts through the air. "Should we intervene?"

I snap upright and let go of Jameson's hands and throw myself off him. I hadn't realized that the door to his room was wide open. Mikkalo and Bronx stand in the door staring at us, and I cover my hands with my face in embarrassment. What am I even doing?

Jameson chuckles and sits up, rubbing the huge-ass hickey I left on his neck. "That's up to Gwen if she wants you two to join, but I have to warn you, she's pretty dead-set on biting. And dry humping."

My whole face warms with embarrassment. "Jameson."

"None of that. You shouldn't be ashamed of your needs." Jameson laces his fingers around my wrist and pulls my hand from my face. "It's breakfast time anyway. Let us take care of our girl after the bullshit your brother put you through."

I can't stop myself from glancing at Bronx. "Is he okay?"

Bronx presses his lips into a thin line. "Yes, and I can take you to him to see for yourself if you want. I'm sorry for snapping like I did, Gwen. The whole situation has me on edge."

"Did you find something out?" I ask, worry washing over me.

"Why don't we wait for Everett, so we can all talk about this together?" Bronx asks, glancing to Jameson.

Jameson nods and waves the two of them in. "We can feed our girl while we wait. What do you say, Gwen? But you know I don't like putting it in a glass."

Bronx meets my gaze. "Is that okay, Gwen?"

I want to say no and to ask him to take me to Everett's room because the anticipation of what Bronx found out digs deeply into me. But I bob my head instead. I'm not exactly sure if I'm ready to know.

"Yeah, but no glass for you either," I say, giving him a once-over.

Bronx's eyes darken. "Okay."

I turn my gaze to Mikkalo. "Or you."

Mikkalo raises his eyebrows. "Anything for you."

I lick my lips. "You guys sure about this?"

Jameson scoops me off the floor and tosses me onto his bed. "Only if you don't make me sit at the table and feel like a meal."

"You know I'd never consider you food. Only that I can survive on you," I say, biting my lip.

Jameson has always been clear about his feelings of a blood exchange needing to be based on taking care of each other and not just because we're hungry. He won't even give me his blood in a glass unless his brothers insist like with the thermos Bronx likes to keep around.

"I'd kind of like to survive on you too, Gwen." Jameson smirks at me, waiting for my reaction.

"Is that so?" I ask, my body doing all sorts of crazy things considering that Jameson has never bitten me before. "Maybe a little bite when Everett gets here. I want him to join us too."

He blinks. "Really? I was only teasing, Gwen."

"That's too bad." Shit. My. Rebellious. Mouth. What am I getting myself into?

Bronx sits down on the bed next to me and touches my knee. "Don't get too excited, brother. She loves to tease."

Jameson flicks his gaze to Bronx before looking back to me. "Our girl is serious."

Bronx's eyes turn silver, and I brush my hair from my shoulders.

I swallow my nerves and nod. "Extremely serious but a little nervous too."

Mikkalo releases a long breath and sits on the end of the bed. "Why? What are you nervous about?"

I love how he asks me why instead of just telling me that I have nothing to be nervous over. "It's a lot of bites. And...are you sure you guys are really okay with this? You won't get jealous or possessive or anything? Because I can't handle that right now. I just—I want to feel loved by all of you."

Mikkalo grabs me by my ankles and tugs me to him, making me laugh. Leaning over me, he brushes my hair from my face. "You have my word that I'm good. Even if you change your mind or want to stop—whatever. I'm good. You're our girl."

Jameson flops forward to lie on his stomach next to me. "He's right, Gwen. We can take it slow. You can bite us first, and if you only want Bronxy or Mik to give you a love bite and not me, I won't have any hard feelings. I know we haven't gone there yet."

I shift my gaze to Bronx. "Are you sure you can handle it?"

He nods with a smirk. "Are you? You can't devour us all."

"Wanna bet?" I tease.

"Don't take her up on that," Everett says from the doorway. "She's as competitive as you when she wants to be."

Jameson waves Everett in. "You're just in time. Our girl is starved and needs all our cuddles after that shit show this evening. If you are not fully prepared to be cool with some extreme bonding—"

"Then we're going to wait until you are," I say, smiling up at Everett.

"No need to wait," Everett says, shrugging his shirt off to toss it on my head. "I'm good. Let's do this."

I laugh in shock, landing on my back under his weight. Everett kisses me without letting me see him until I gasp. Swiping the shirt off my eyes, I bring it to my nose, inhaling a breath of his incredible scent. He grins at my reaction, knowing full well where my mind wanders as I drink in the curves of his muscles.

"Ev's first," Jameson says, knocking his knuckles into Everett. "He just put our girl into savage mode."

I snap my teeth at Everett. "I won't bite you unless you want it, but I'm pretty set on sucking somewhere that isn't your arm."

Bronx hums under his breath. "You're going to give him the wrong idea, dandelion."

I giggle and squeeze his thigh. "Of course you twist my words."

"Damn," Mikkalo says.

I stick my tongue out at him. "Save that thought for later."

"You know I will," Jameson says, flashing his fangs at me with his excitement.

Ah, hell.

Everett holds his arms out, motioning for me to close

the space to him. I inhale a small breath, rubbing my lips together. I can't believe I'm doing this. Or how much I want to do this. Sitting between Everett's legs, I curl my body around him, letting him pull me so close that I can feel his desire through his pants.

"Show our girl how tough you are," Mikkalo says, playing with my hair.

Bronx and Jameson each touch one of my legs, remaining close. I know the act of a blood exchange like this is rather intimate, letting me drink from them, and the fact that they all surround me instead of looking away touches my heart in a way that I know they love me, even if they admitted it only to each other.

"Don't listen to your brother. You don't have to be tough for me," I whisper into his ear. "I want you to enjoy it."

He hums deep in his throat, shifting under me as I explore his muscles with my fingers before leaning in to kiss his skin. I work my lips over his shoulder and up his neck until I reach his mouth. Everett sucks my bottom lip and nips me so that he gets a tiny taste of my blood.

"Where do you want me to bite you?" I ask, dragging my fingers down the planes of his stomach.

He twines his fingers with mine and guides my hand to stop on his chest above his nipple. "Here." His choice tells me that this isn't about feeding my nature but feeding into my desire. Playing with his.

I push Everett back on the pillow and bend down to kiss him again. I savor the taste of his lips while feeling the pressure of his brothers' hands roaming across my body. Their attention turns me on, and I reach down and stroke Everett's erection through his pants, getting him to moan for me.

"Is this okay?" I ask Everett.

He hums.

Mikkalo draws his hand around my side to touch my breast. "Is this?"

Both Everett and I say yes at the same time, and I smile through another kiss. I work my way down his neck, kneeling between his legs to reach the spot he wants. His boner pulses against my hip, and I stroke him some more.

"Ready?" I ask.

"Yeah."

With his word, I sink my teeth into his chest hard enough to draw blood. He moans and tangles his hands into my hair as I suck his skin, tasting the sweetness of his blood. Bronx, Jameson, and Mikkalo remain quiet but their breathing picks up with their anticipation over hearing Everett's reaction.

I stay with Everett a few minutes longer after I release him, just kissing him softly. Mikkalo kisses my shoulder, drawing my attention to him. I reach out and touch both Jameson and Bronx so they know that I haven't forgotten them. Mikkalo smiles at me, his eyes flashing silver with his desire. I hook my fingers to the hem of his shirt and tug it over his head, taking a moment to appreciate his smooth, muscular body. He kneels with me and combs his fingers through my hair to caress his full lips across my throat.

"Show me where," I say, my voice coming out low and sultry.

He guides my hand along the ridges of his stomach and up the hard planes of his chest. I tease him with my fingers, grazing them along his skin until he stops on his shoulder blade. I lean in and brush my lips to the spot, gliding my tongue back up his neck for another kiss. Mikkalo lifts me up so that I wrap my legs around him, pressing our chests together. He slides his hands to my ass cheeks and squeezes the spot he bit me before.

I moan so loud at the sudden wave of tingles that explodes through me from his touch that I hang onto his neck with one arm to reach between us with my other to slide my fingers into his pants.

Jameson's hands squeeze my hips, and he presses into my back. "You're so beautiful, Gwen. Is this okay?"

I nod my confirmation, bending my head some to feel the softness of his lips on my throat. Bronx kisses me from over Mikkalo's shoulder, and I nip his lip.

"I'm ready, Gwen," Mikkalo murmurs, his breathing hard under the touch of my fingers.

I bite his shoulder, closing my eyes as his blood coats my tongue. Latching on, I mold my lips around my bite and suck hard enough that Mikkalo knocks me onto my back between Jameson's legs.

Jameson smiles down at me from over Mikkalo's shoulder. "Be easy on him, Gigi. He won't tell you to stop."

It probably doesn't help that I'm still rubbing his dick, determined to give him a pleasure bite like the one he gave me. I moan softly, working my hand over him without drinking his blood anymore. I'm only sucking his skin, getting him off, not even caring about what will come next—hopefully him.

"Gwen," Mikkalo says, my name so hot and breathless on his lips.

"One more bite, please," I say, bringing my mouth to his to kiss him.

He nods and moans, trailing his fingers to my breasts. I catch Jameson's gaze above me as he watches my expression. His eyes flash silver as we watch each other.

"Gwen." My name sounds desperate coming from Mikkalo's mouth, his muscles flexing, his body tensing with his oncoming release.

I bite him again on his other shoulder, and he cums on me. He sinks down, resting his head on my shoulder with his panting breath. I kiss the bite mark, making him shudder, and I can't stop the huge-ass grin crossing my face.

"So good," I say, licking my lips.

Mikkalo flips over, pulling me with him. Without commenting, Jameson tugs my shirt over my head and tosses it on the floor. Now that my mind is catching up with my body, I'm so relieved none of them mention the fact that I jerked Mikkalo off in front of them. Jameson meets me for a kiss, and I giggle into his lips.

"Where do you want me to bite you, Jamie?" I ask.

Jameson suddenly stiffens without responding. Instead, he jerks his hands up and covers my ears.

An alarm screams through the air.

20

LIVING DANGEROUSLY

MIKKALO HOPS OFF THE BED and rushes to the wall cabinets behind the table. He grabs a couple of weapons out and tosses a dagger to Bronx. Jameson throws me to Everett, and I don't have a chance to brace myself as he relocates me into the bathroom with him.

The alarm snaps off, leaving my ears ringing. Everett strokes the length of my back, pushing away the trembles coursing through me.

What the actual fuck?

"It's probably nothing," Everett whispers, keeping his

voice low. "The alarms are overly sensitive for a reason. A bird could've hit a window or something on one of the upper floors."

"Really?" I ask.

"Damn it, Brooklyn. I told you not to come. You're putting us all at risk." Bronx's booming voice comes in through the closed bathroom door.

Looks like Everett was wrong. And damn it am I mad at the rude interruption. Everett must sense it, because he plops me on the counter and spreads my legs to stand between them.

"Let me distract you," he whispers, cupping my cheeks.

"*Me?* You're the one risking everything." The sultry voice of Brooklyn rises with the same anger lining Bronx's growls. "And I didn't want to come here, but Corona asked me to. He thinks you are taking too long in giving him the information about the rebel nest. He's starting to think you might be lying and turning other covens against him."

"Tell him to fuck the hell off," Jameson says, his voice low and threatening. For the first time, I think he might sound scarier than Bronx. "We'll get him the shit he wants when we're ready."

"Also tell him we've done everything he wanted, and it's not our fault he can't handle one family of Blood Rebels," Mikkalo adds.

"Gwen," Everett whispers again. He digs his fingers into my hips, putting just enough pressure to pull my attention back to him. "Please, let me kiss you."

I give in to his velvety plea and slide my hands around his neck. His soft lips mold to mine, starting slow and sweet and teasingly as Everett tests to see if I'll offer him more of my affection. I squeeze him between my thighs, wanting nothing more now than to ignore the yelling outside the door. It prods at my fear instincts.

"Do you want me as much as I want you?" Everett murmurs, sliding his hand between my legs to graze his fingers over the fabric of my athletic pants.

"I can't promise to be quiet."

He kisses my throat. "I'd never ask you to. And after seeing you with my brother..." His voice trails off.

I pull back. "What?"

Biting his lip, he grins at me. "It just makes me want a little more."

Something crashes in Jameson's bedroom, not giving me the chance to respond. Bronx and Brooklyn continue to yell. More things crash.

"Just let me talk to her," Brooklyn snaps.

My eyes widen.

Bronx growls. "No."

Now I wish I had been listening.

"Don't be an idiot, brother."

Mikkalo grumbles next. "He's not you're brother, Brooklyn. He hasn't been for decades. Do not try to use your mortal bonds on him."

"You're making a mistake, Mik," Brooklyn says.

"Just get out before I throw you out," Jameson says, his voice more threatening than I've ever heard it.

Brooklyn hisses, sounding scary as all get-out. "If you don't let me talk to her, then this is over. You will no longer get my help, Bronx."

"We don't need her help," Mikkalo says.

Bronx groans. "Brooklyn, sit down. We need to take a vote."

The door to the bathroom swings inward, and Bronx leads Mikkalo and Jameson inside, but keeps the door cracked to keep an eye on Brooklyn. Everett steps away from me so that his brothers can see me fully. I don't get a chance to slide from the counter before Bronx takes Everett's place between my legs.

He leans in to press his lips to my ear. "I'm sorry this was ruined for you."

I rest my hands on his side. "It wasn't. Can we just get rid of her so I can get to devouring you?"

He chuckles, relief relaxing his hard features. "She wants to talk to you."

I crinkle my nose. "What for?"

"I don't want to find out," Mikkalo says.

Everett nods. "Agreed."

Jameson steps closer to me. "I'm too curious. I'd like to know what the hell she wants to tell you."

"I agree with Jameson," Bronx says. "Brooklyn doesn't

go out of her way often. So it's up to you, Gwen."

I flick my eyes to Jameson. "I want to know too."

Mikkalo and Everett both groan.

Raising my palms up to them, I cut off their complaints. "I know you guys are worried, but if she's willing to test you guys, it might be important."

Bronx lets me slide off the counter, but he stays right at my side. Jameson takes the spot at my other side, linking his fingers through mine. Mikkalo leads the way, while Everett walks so close behind that he holds my waist, keeping with my steps.

Brooklyn sits at Jameson's table, her long, tan legs crossed at her knees, showing off her smooth thigh from the slit in her dress. Jewelry sparkles from her ears, neck, wrists, and fingers, catching the light from the ceiling fixtures. She looks even more gorgeous than I remember.

Parting her plum-painted lips, she offers me a cross between a smile and a sneer like she's trying her best to keep her cool even with her nature probably wanting nothing more than to attack, especially with how protective my guys act.

I force myself to smile. "Hello, Brooklyn."

She doesn't greet me right away, just boring her stare into me. She drinks in Bronx, Jameson, Mikkalo, and Everett, studying them with a strange expression on her face.

"What is it you wanted to tell me?" I ask from over Mikkalo's shoulder. "We were in the middle of something, so I don't want to waste any time on small talk."

Her eyes flash silver at me. "Watch how you speak to an Anderson Heir, little dhampir."

Ah, hell.

My guys react, unleashing all the scary growls. I can feel each of their voices vibrating in my bones.

Brooklyn straightens her shoulders, not letting them intimidate her. "I'd like a word with Gwen alone."

"No," Bronx says without thinking.

Mikkalo tenses, still clutching the weapon he took from Jameson's cabinet. He looks seconds away from attacking, and if he does, it might not end well.

So I take a breath and dodge around him before my guys can react. I don't know if they thought I would just stand there and let them negotiate my time for me or what, but I could never truly be alone with Brooklyn. I'm sure they would listen in from a mile away if they had to.

I hold my finger up, stopping them from trying to close around me again. "Just five minutes and across the room. We won't be going anywhere." I direct my words to my guys but look at Brooklyn's pretty brown eyes.

Her features sharpen, her gaze darting from me to my guys. "Fine."

I step closer to her and take a seat at the table, motioning for my guys to step back a few feet. They begrudgingly listen and return to the bed. I wish I didn't watch them, because my heart picks now to ricochet around my chest in anticipation to join them.

"I had assumed you were with Bronx," Brooklyn says, leaning on her elbow.

I don't confirm or deny her words.

"But after my last visit and now seeing this—what you're doing, Gwen. It's wrong," she says.

My mouth drops open. "You think what I'm doing is wrong? Maybe you should take a long, hard look at your own damn coven."

She extends her fangs, and Bronx closes the space and puts his big hands on my shoulders.

"Get out," he says. "You do not get a say or get to have an opinion in the infrastructure of our coven. It's none of your business."

"You're making a mistake, brother," she says. "It'll tear you apart."

No one gets the chance to respond because Brooklyn vanishes, slamming the door behind her. Mikkalo follows her out, probably to make sure she leaves, and Bronx pulls out his com device and taps the screen a few times. Jameson scoops me off the chair and carries me back to the bed, plopping me down.

"Now where were we?" he asks, smiling at me, acting like Brooklyn wasn't even here.

I laugh, my voice breathy with my nerves.

Bronx sits on the edge of the bed and scrubs his face with his hands to rake his fingers through his hair. Everett drapes his arm over his shoulder, and I can't stop the smile from crossing my lips. The small act alone proves that Brooklyn is utterly and completely wrong.

"Brace yourselves. Gwen's gonna tackle you both from behind," Jameson says.

He lifts me up and tosses me, making me screech. Bronx twists and catches me, and I crack up as he lays me on my belly across his lap. Everett squeezes my ass, and I squirm until I flip back over to meet their three gazes.

"She's wrong, you know," I say. "We work perfectly."

"Yeah, we do," Jameson says, hanging his arms over both Bronx and Everett while sticking his head between theirs to peer at me. "I mean, look how happy our girl is."

"You guys make me happy," I say, arching up to kiss Bronx because his lips are the closest. "And hungry."

"Is that so?" Bronx murmurs, curling me up some more.

My boobs push into Jameson's face, and he licks my cleavage. "I think you need to give her what she wants, Bronxy."

Everett presses a kiss to my hip, and I inhale a breath. "He's right."

Mikkalo clicks the door closed, drawing our attention away from each other. "She's gone."

I arch in Bronx's arms, tilting my hips more up to Everett, letting him tug my waistband a little lower. "You have perfect timing."

He smiles at me and bends down, brushing his lips to mine. "Is it our turn?"

I wag my finger at him. "Not quite. Soon." I reach out and touch Jameson's cheek. "You were next."

He snaps his teeth at me. "I'm going to save your bite for later. Let Bronx have his turn."

"Are you sure?" I ask him.

He hums and nods. "I can't wait to get my own fangs on you."

I shiver at the low, sexiness of his voice.

"So tell our girl where you want her mark, brother," Everett says, digging his fingers more into my hip. "Because I'm with Jameson."

Fuck. Me. My body already loves the idea. I should be freaked out at the thought of the four of them biting me, but I'm not. Tingles already course through me in anticipation. Their desire ignites mine further, and I bring my mouth to Bronx's throat and lick from his jaw to his collarbone.

"Not there, dandelion," he murmurs.

I stretch and flick my tongue over his nipple and over the taut planes of his chest.

"Not there either."

Bronx lowers me another few inches, and I continue to lick and kiss and suck my way down his stomach until his prominent erection presses into my side. I lace my fingers around it through his clothes and smirk up at him.

"Damn, Bronxy. Living dangerously," Jameson says.

I raise my eyebrows. "Not there."

Bronx chuckles. "No, but here." He guides my hand to his thigh and pushes my fingers into his leg, just feeling the pressure of my hand. "If that's okay."

My smile widens, and I nod, a bit nervous and excited of getting to bite somewhere completely new to me with him. This is probably what Mikkalo felt when he wanted to bite my ass cheek. It's a little weird but thrilling. Unexpected.

I ease myself off him and Everett and slide between his legs. Bronx's eyes flash silver again, his jaw twitching with a lusty smile. Jameson, Mikkalo, and Everett burn their gazes into me, and I shift on my knees.

"Breathe, guys," I say, a giggle escaping my mouth.

"Don't get carried away, Gigi," Jameson teases. "You look extra bitey."

Blush warms my cheeks, and I tug Bronx's pants down just enough to push up his boxer briefs to kiss his thigh. I lean forward, blocking everyone's view with my hair to slip Bronx's hard-on out of his underwear to suck into my mouth, teasing him a bit. He digs his fingers into my shoulders and releases a moan.

"Damn," Mikkalo whispers more to himself. "I'm risking that spot next time."

I smile to myself and work my way over Bronx's hip and to his thigh. Grazing my teeth over his skin, I nip him, testing him for a reaction. And hell does he give me one, combing his fingers through my hair, his breathing quickening in anticipation. I love how much he wants it.

Lacing my fingers around his boner, I stroke him while I build up his anticipation more with my mouth.

I bite him where he asked, and he releases a cross between a grunt and a moan, pulling at my hair but not to move me away. He wants to look. Four intakes of breath fill the silence as Bronx combs my hair up for all of them to see. I hum and suck, my body burning under their intense gazes.

Tingles blossom through me, and it takes all my willpower to ease my mouth away from the delicious taste of his blood. I carefully fix his clothes and smile at the four of them, loving how none of them can take their eyes off me. I feel so hot and sexy. I can't wait to let them bite me in return.

Bronx holds his arms out to me and helps me to my feet. He encircles my waist and rests his head to my chest, hugging me. "Thank you for trusting us enough to do that."

I lick my lips. "Was it okay?"

"So hot," he murmurs.

"You're really testing our restraint, Gigi," Jameson teases.

"Is that so?"

He plops down next to Mikkalo, and I lie back across their laps, feeling four majorly hard boners poking me, showing me exactly how much they enjoy my attention.

"So much so that I'd bite you at the same time as my brothers if you'd let me." He plays with my blond hair, twisting it in his fingers.

I squirm at the thought.

And inhale a shuddering breath.

"Whoa," Mikkalo breathes. "You like the idea."

"I think we could safely do it," Everett says, lifting up my hips to kiss me just below my navel. "I mean, if you want and everyone agrees."

"Shit," I whisper under my breath.

"I'm good with it," Jameson says.

Bronx licks his lips. "Me too."

Mikkalo bends and kisses my cleavage. "Hell yeah."

They all look at me for my reaction, and I stretch back, arching up. "Be gentle, please."

Jameson caresses my cheek. "Always."

Everett gets to his feet, and Bronx lifts me up to him so that he can move me to the middle of the bed. Jameson props his back on the pillows and pulls me closer. I relax against his chest, feeling the thrums of his heartbeat against my back. He kisses me sweetly, whispering how amazing I am in my ear. How much he wants to take care of me. See me smile.

Bronx and Mikkalo take their places on both sides of Jameson, stretching my arms up. Mikkalo kisses my wrist, just caressing my skin, and Bronx sucks my skin without biting me, leaving a small hickey.

I gasp at Everett choosing a place between my legs.

He touches the waist of my pants, and I ease my hips up until he undresses me, leaving me in my bra and panties. The four of them drink me in, drawing my attention in four different directions but never completely apart.

"I want to make it feel as good as possible," Everett murmurs.

I don't even have to ask him to know what he wants to do. I ease my legs open in silent permission. He smiles up at me, and I shift between Jameson's legs, feeling his boner press into my lower back.

Bronx bends my knee and Mikkalo follows his lead. I feel like I'm going to explode from anticipation.

"You're so perfect, Gwen," Jameson murmurs, sliding his hand into my bra to feel the hardness of my nipple.

I tilt my head so that he can meet me for a kiss that turns into a gasp as Everett shifts my panties without taking them off, bringing his lips between my legs. I moan so fucking loud at the exploding sensations rippling through my body. Bronx and Mikkalo bite each of my arms, but I don't feel the pinch, only the wave of pleasure bursting through me. I press harder into Jameson, already barely able to contain myself.

He kisses my throat, rubbing his fingers over my nipples as he bites my shoulder. I don't know if it's having so much attention on me, experiencing all of their bites, or if Everett is just so good with his mouth, but he takes me over the edge faster than ever, and I arch into Jameson with my orgasm, my toes curling, my skin buzzing. My muscles clench and release, and Everett bites my hip, sliding his finger inside me to feel my body pulsing because of him.

"I swear no one better high five him," I say, catching Everett flick his gaze from me and to his brothers.

Mikkalo chuckles. "That was hot."

"So sexy," Bronx says.

Jameson kisses the spot where he left his bite mark on my shoulder. "Incredible."

Everett slides his tongue over his bottom lip. "Delicious."

I shift and pull him up and between my legs. The four of them hug me, knowing exactly what I want. To be close. To feel their arms around me. To savor their touch and desire. Their need.

None of us hear the door open.

Silas makes it halfway across the room before Mikkalo jumps to his feet. Loud pops echo through the air, startling me. A figure blurs in from the door.

I brace myself for the shit show to come.

A familiar vampire flies at me.

21

MARKED

"GET GWEN OUT OF HERE," Bronx says to Everett.

Everett wraps me in the blanket and cradles me against him, darting in the direction of the table to go around it while Jameson and Bronx head toward the vampire. The guy evades them in an attempt to cut Everett off.

"Gwen! Gwen! Help me!" Silas yells, drawing my attention to him. Mikkalo slams my brother's back into the wall, shattering one of Jameson's framed drawings.

"Mik, back up Everett," Bronx commands.

Mikkalo drops Silas and zooms toward us as Jameson

blurs and tackles the intruder. More gunshots ring through the air. Silas shoots Jameson in the back, giving the vampire the chance to catapult to his feet.

He rushes to where Mikkalo left Silas and picks him up. "Gwen, come to me, or I'll kill him right now."

Silas flares his nostrils. "You fucker. We had a deal, Thaxton."

"The deal was only complete if you held them off. And you misinformed me. You said she was only with one. They have all marked her."

Silas pulls his shit together and searches the room, settling his gaze on me. "Gwen, how could you?"

I turn my head away. I can't even look at him.

"Please, little sis. You said you'd protect me. Thaxton isn't lying. He'll kill me."

Bronx materializes at my side. "Gwen, let us handle it."

I tighten my jaw and turn my gaze back to the vampire, Thaxton, and my brother. Thaxton holds a dagger to Silas's throat. Silas's watery eyes plead with me to give in. To help him. To keep my promise to protect him.

My lips tremble as I force the words free. "I asked you to trust me, Silas."

"It's them I don't trust!" he shouts. "They're going to leave us all to die. You just watch."

Hugging Everett tighter, I hide my face in his shoulder. "Go ahead, Bronx. Take care of them. Silas made his decision, and I will not be punished for his mistakes."

Silas yells and Thaxton roars. Everett spins me away, pressing his hand to my ear to muffle the sound. Silence falls over the room, sinking deep inside me. A part of me dies a little as I face the truth of my life. My family will be forever broken and in shambles. Everything I thought I knew about loyalty and unconditional love is a total crock.

Everett shifts on his feet, and I brace myself to see Silas's bloodied body on the floor, but the room is empty. My guys aren't here either.

"Come on. Let me get you cleaned up," Everett says, carrying me into the bathroom.

"Where did they go?" I ask, my voice low.

"My brothers will take care of Thaxton. They will bring Silas back." Everett drops the blanket and kicks his pants off, never setting me down. He carefully undresses me and strolls us into Jameson's shower, filling it with steam. I just hug him, wrapping my legs around him, resting my cheek to the bite mark I left on his chest.

"Oh." It's all I can say.

He adjusts me in his arms and peers at me. "How did you know Thaxton was bluffing about killing your brother?"

I press my lips together to stop them from trembling. "I didn't." And I feel like shit for it. But I'd rather feel like shit than risk a lifetime away from the life I just created with my guys.

Everett's brows pinch together, his blue eyes searching

my face for a moment before something shifts in his gaze. Leaning in, he kisses me so passionately, sliding his hands down my slippery back to pull me in as close as possible. I release a breathless laugh, gasping in the warm steam.

"I thought I was only falling in love with you, but I realize I'm already madly in love with you. I can't spend another second without telling you. I love you, Gwen." His eyes capture mine, his words sinking deep in my bones. "Thank you for choosing a life with us."

I don't know how to respond or if there are any words I could say that would resonate as deeply with him as his words do with me, so I kiss him instead. I kiss him with as much love as he poured onto me, letting him devour my affection.

My back hits the wall, and I gasp into his mouth. I reach my hand between us and align his body to mine, feeling the pressure he builds with his weight. He enters me, squeezing my ass to hold me in place as he thrusts hard and deep and desperately, never breaking his lips from mine.

I hold on tight, scratching my nails into his back, the feeling of his body so intense that I can't control the scream of pleasure that rips from my mouth. Everett pushes away all of my bad feelings and replaces them with everything I feel like I need to survive, his love for me a sweet whisper into my ear over and over again until I bend my neck and let him bite me again.

I never wanted to fill his needs so badly in every way I

know how. Something about tonight, about the bonding time we spent together, about the new level of intimacy we reached brings out a rush of adrenaline and an indescribable feeling that takes me to a cliff I'd gladly dive over knowing Everett would never let me crash and break into the ground.

Our moans come in short, loud bursts, our hearts and bodies in perfect rhythm. The incredible sensations warm my skin, filling me up in such a way I want to drown myself in everything that Everett is. Everything he does to me.

He finishes with a moan, leaving my body buzzing like crazy. I pant against his damp shoulder and let him hold me and stroke his hand up and down the length of my back, making the world seem so right.

"I want it to be like this forever," he whispers, kissing my throat again. "You're my forever." He leans away and searches my eyes.

I blink a few times, suppressing the emotions threatening to spill from me. I open and close my mouth, but the words stay locked in my throat.

Everett frowns. "Is that not something you want?"

My heart clenches, and I shake my head, strands of my wet hair clinging to my cheeks. "Everett, I don't think forever is possible for me."

Silver flashes in his eyes. "Why do you think that?"

"I couldn't transition."

Moving to the inlaid bench, he sits and slides me off his lap but keeps my legs over his. A dozen thoughts cloud his eyes as he thinks about my words.

"Why would a coven fight so fiercely to possess you and bestow you with a Blood Vow if you couldn't?" He asks the question more to himself.

I don't know what a Blood Vow is, but I can think of a few reasons, and I say as much. "Because they want to cage me. Drain me over and over again because I heal quickly? Power? I don't know. There are so many reasons. Corona had similar ones."

He slumps and hugs me. "Maybe. I don't know. But I'm going to find out."

"I'll do whatever I can to help you...because, I want forever with you too."

He links our fingers together. "You do?"

I nod. "Yeah. I want it more than I realized."

Pulling me closer, he kisses me again. "You make me the happiest man."

I grin. "I think I can make you happier."

"Not possible."

Meeting his blue eyes, I touch his cheek. "I think it is. You know why?"

He smirks at me, waiting for me to continue.

"Because I'm falling in love with you too."

By the time everyone returns, Everett and I are dressed and sitting at Jameson's table. We watched the guys pop up on every security feed on Everett's tablet as well as tracked a few of the mysterious security details that monitor the property. At one point, Everett had to close the feed, trying to stop me from seeing Mikkalo lay it on someone, probably because Thaxton should've never made it inside.

No one says anything as they slide into the chairs around me. I try not to pounce on them for information and take a bite of the yogurt and fruit Everett pulled out of a refrigerator hidden inside Jameson's wall cabinet.

"We need to reassess security," Bronx says, leaning his elbows on the table. "The fucker slipped past all but one of the cameras."

Mikkalo scrubs his face, looking like he wants to beat himself up. "We either have a traitor among our staff or the Baron Coven has been here many times before Gwen moved in. Thaxton must've been watching and waiting for a while. He took advantage of Brooklyn's arrival. It's how he slipped past us."

I drop my spoon, and it clanks in my bowl. "Shit." Just the thought that he managed to get in leaves me on edge. "What if another one of his coven brothers is still here? They're never alone."

Mikkalo tightens his mouth. "He was this time."

"How do you know? What if one of them is hiding in one of your rooms? They could attack us in our sleep."

Slumping forward, Mikkalo thunks his head on the table and takes a breath. A moment later, he disappears without a word.

I stare in surprise at his empty seat.

Bronx and Everett both disappear next, leaving me in confusion alone with Jameson. He changes seats to take the spot Everett sat, and then he pulls me to him so that I sit on his lap. Grabbing my spoon, he feeds me a few more bites of yogurt in silence like he needs time to get his thoughts together.

Jameson brushes the hair from my shoulder where he had bitten me and kisses the spot. His lips tickle, but my skin feels like normal because of the numbing cream Everett applied to all of the bites just in case since it was the first time I've ever had so many.

A loud-ass growl sounds from the hallway, and I stiffen in Jameson's arms. He relocates me to the bathroom and stands in front of the door protectively but doesn't take his eyes off his room.

Another guttural rumble cuts through the air, and I can't stop hugging Jameson from behind to peer over his shoulder. The noise doesn't come from any of my guys, but it sounds just as threatening. My fear instincts ignite inside me, sending goosebumps over my skin.

Jameson growls deep in his throat, the sensation vibrating against my chest. "You were right, Gigi. Someone else got in."

I inhale a sharp breath.

I don't get the chance to say anything as Everett appears in the doorway, his eyes flashing crazy silver, and what light I had elicited inside him from our moment of lovemaking has now vanished into shadows that leave me on edge.

"Bronx found someone in his room," Everett says, keeping his voice even. He doesn't look at me as he says the words but keeps his gaze trained on Jameson.

I clench Jameson's shoulders. "Ah, hell."

"Bronx wants you both to join us in Mikkalo's room for the interrogation. The guy hasn't said a word, but Gwen's appearance might strike a nerve." Everett finally meets my gaze.

"Fuck no. I don't want our girl anywhere near this douchebag," Jameson says, lacing his fingers through mine like I'm the only thing that'll stop him from exploding.

Everett remains expressionless. "It's an order."

"An order?"

I squeeze Jameson's hand, stopping him from lashing out at Everett, knowing that he's just the messenger. Tugging Jameson closer, I slide my arms around him and bury my face in his chest, just breathing in the sultry scent of his skin. He relaxes after a moment and rests his chin to my shoulder, soaking in the calmness I try to project to him.

"This dude's going to regret ever coming here," I say, tilting my head up to meet his green eyes.

"Damn straight," Jameson mutters.

He takes another breath and straightens his shoulders,

silently guiding me across the room where Everett awaits. Everett slides his fingers through my free hand and offers me a cute smirk, probably loving how I intervened as my way of protecting him from Jameson's anger that's mostly directed at the world but Everett just happens to be here to face it.

"I don't want you within ten feet of this douche," Jameson says, speaking up in the hallway.

I frown. "How am I supposed to punch his heart out then?"

Jameson fake-glares at me. "Not happening. We're taking care of him."

"We'll see," I say, smirking at him.

He play-growls and smacks me on the ass, moving from next to me to slide his arms around my shoulders protectively while Everett shifts to the front of our little line. I hesitate at the open door leading into Mikkalo's room, suddenly feeling more scared than I have in a while. And I hate how even the mere presence of this Baron brother sets me off before I lay my eyes on him.

"We got you, Gigi," Jameson whispers, feeling my body tense against his. "Don't let him see that he can get under your skin."

He's right about that. If the dude even suspects he can get to me by using my human rationale against me, he will try.

Straightening my shoulders, I summon my nerve,

channeling my deep-seated nature as a predator. I tighten my fingers on Everett's hand, trying to borrow a bit of his strength to get me to keep my shit together. I'm not some weak, scared donor. I'm a fierce, sometimes wild, dhampir with a whole lot of muscular goodness to back me up if I need it.

A strange noise hums through the air, drawing my attention away from my thoughts and to the handsome creep with a weird-ass collar on his neck now chained to Mikkalo's wall. I knew Mikkalo had a lot of weapons, but I had no idea he could actually imprison someone in his bedroom.

I try to remain expressionless, but I dart my gaze to Mikkalo in silent question. He responds by twisting his lips to the side while making a face that reads he'll talk to me about it later.

"My Gwyneth." The claim snaps my gaze from Mikkalo and to the creep.

I stiffen. "You did not just fucking try to claim me."

No one has time to react as I dash forward, fueled by my annoyance and anger. Mikkalo could intercept me, but he doesn't. He grabs the guy by the shoulders and restrains his arms. I knee the douchebag in the balls, making him holler. If he thinks that hurt, he has no idea what's to come.

Bronx hooks his arm around my waist and hoists me back before I can show the guy. "You can have your fun in a couple of minutes, dandelion. We need him to be able to talk."

I thrash once on purpose in an attempt to threaten the guy again. Bronx spins me around and holds me to him by my ass, his eyes lighting silver. His chest presses into mine, his body practically puffing with pride. A smile twitches on his lips, but he keeps his jaw clenched as not to react though I can totally feel that I turned him the hell on.

"I need you to use that cute ass of yours against him," he murmurs.

I suck in my bottom lip between my teeth and nod, kissing him softly on the lips. He sets me down and spins me back toward the guy, now staring at me like seeing me in Bronx's arms causes him physical pain.

I saunter to Mikkalo and take his hand, pulling him in close to kiss him next. "Thanks for letting me do that."

He hugs me. "Anything for you."

The creep full-on roars, thrashing against his restraints and snapping his teeth at Mikkalo. My affection to Mikkalo set him off, turning his eyes a crazy flashing silver. He looks like he'd try to tear Mikkalo apart if he managed to get free.

"Don't touch her!" the guy yells. "She doesn't belong to you."

Pulling away from Mikkalo, I strut closer to the guy. Bronx intercepts Jameson, stopping him from trying to get in front of me. Everett hovers nearby, ready to rush me, and Mikkalo grips the chain attached to the collar on the guy's neck.

I clear my throat, meeting the creep's dark eyes.

They're devoid of flecks of color I catch in both Bronx and Mikkalo's, his pupils barely noticeable even in the overhead lighting. I search his face, taking in his features, trying to figure out if I've ever met this vampire before. But I don't think I have. He might've been there when the Baron Coven tried to attack us when we went to get Silas, but I can't be sure. I didn't get a good look at any of them.

The vampire freezes under my closeness, his eyes trying to lock onto mine, but I don't let him. "You don't belong to them, Gwyneth." His soft voice prods at my mind, and I tense as not to react.

I lick my lips, drawing his attention to my mouth. I can feel the burning intensity of my guys remaining statue-still and silent around me, but I decide against looking at them. I don't want to risk setting him off when Bronx wants me to try to get answers. If only I knew the questions to ask.

"Then who do you think I belong to?" I capture his stare, proving that I'm not afraid of him despite looking into a vampire's eyes being the most dangerous thing a human can do.

"Me."

"You? I don't even know you." Like, seriously? Who does this douche think he is?

"Laredo had no right to keep you away," he continues, tilting his head slightly. "He was not next in line. Look what he did to you. Nearly wasting such a beautiful gift intended to..." His eyes flicker silver. He lets his voice trail off and licks his lips. "Let me take you home. I know you have it in you to free me. To get rid of those who don't understand you like I do."

It takes everything in me not to knee him in his junk again. "I don't know," I say. "I don't even know your name."

"Galveston." He stretches his neck, trying to close some of the distance. Clenching his jaw, he releases a strange noise from his throat.

And then I see it.

Blood trickles from the collar, setting off my senses. I flare my nostrils and can't stop myself from watching as a drop streams down his throat to disappear into his shirt. Noticing my reaction, he leans forward again, causing more of his blood to spill.

"You like that, don't you?" he murmurs.

I don't respond.

He flashes his fangs. "Do you want to taste?"

"Gwen."

Bronx doesn't get a chance to say more as my rebellious feet take me forward. Galveston snaps the restraints on his arms far too quickly for anyone to reach me. He yanks me into him, chomping down so hard on my shoulder that a scream rips from me. Tears blur my eyes as a burning sensation explodes over my skin, edging my vision in shadows. All four of my guys yell and roar and growl, and Mikkalo jerks Galveston away.

Except it doesn't work. His fangs pierce deep in my bone, longer than any fangs I've ever seen on a vampire. Even when his body falls away from me, his head remains attached. I scream and punch him in the nose, knocking his severed head to the floor.

Bronx catches me in his arms, pulling me against him.

Everett says my name.

Pain radiates too intensely through me that all I do is blink.

The last thing I see is Mikkalo and Jameson tear the rest of Galveston apart.

22

UNTAMED

"HURRY, LITTLE DHAMPIR. I NEED you to hide and remain as silent as possible." Laredo pushes me toward a large chest positioned at the end of his bed. "No one can know you're here."

I climb inside the chest and curl my knees to my stomach, lying on my side.

Laredo holds his index finger to his lips, reminding me to be quiet. A knock on the door draws his gaze from mine, and he shuts the lid, leaving me in darkness.

"Laredo, something has happened," a deep, smoky

voice says, muffling to me. "The Gallaghers are gone. The dhampir killed Rochester."

"Why?" Laredo asks, his smooth voice stifling the nerves threatening to leave me quaking.

Rochester was the only vampire I knew before Grayson showed up a few days ago with Laredo in tow. It took me over a day to even look at him, but when I finally did, I could tell by the look in his eyes that he was nothing like my previous blood source.

"I can only assume it had to do with Jerry's final donation and the revelation of a contract none of us agreed upon. He lied to us. Rochester never intended to propose. The contract Thaxton drew up remains unsigned," the other vampire says.

"I see," Laredo says, not reacting. He knows all of this already and insisted we leave everything as it was in the bunker. "What a shame dear brother wouldn't listen to me about Rochester."

"Thaxton thought Rochester was trying to grow a relationship with her," the other guy snaps. "Maybe the new contract was to help. You know how Jerry was. He couldn't see her as we do."

"Or she wasn't interested, which seems to be quite obvious now."

"That doesn't matter."

"How can you expect such an exquisite being to accept such a life Rochester had planned without her consent? I bet *he even called her Gwyneth. No woman wants to be held in comparison to another. He didn't handle the situation with care."*

"You say that like you could've done better," the guy says.

Laredo hums. "I know I could've, Galveston. And I can't wait to prove it."

A growl sounds through the air, setting off my fear instincts. "You're last in line, little brother. I'll have her vow before you."

"She'll rip you apart. She'll kill all of you."

The slamming of a door startles me, and light erupts in my vision as Laredo opens the chest. I peek up at him, his words swirling through my mind.

"My apologies, Gwen. I didn't intend for you to hear that." Laredo offers me his hand and helps me to my feet.

I glare at him. "You should've told me that you were part of Rochester's coven."

"Your brother would've never accepted my proposal if he had known."

"Your proposal?"

He shrugs. "Nothing to worry about." Holding out his hand, he waits for me to take it. "Now, come along. We must hurry. We have to get as far away as possible unless you want to seal your fate as one of my other brothers' intended. They would never treat you as I do. They want nothing more than to control you."

I frown.

He hooks his arm around me and lifts me to my feet. "Dreadful, I know. That's why we must show them that you can never be tamed."

Warm liquid coats my tongue, drawing me from the dark recesses of my mind. My body reacts to the taste of Jameson's blood, and I grip his arm, pulling it close enough that I can latch my mouth around the puncture wounds.

"That's it, Gigi. Drink what you need. That asshole bit you with venom," he murmurs, trailing his hand across my stomach.

I moan under my breath, my body tingling like crazy, reacting to his words. His voice sounds so sexy in my ear that it awakens my lust before my mind can fully orient itself to what the hell is going on.

I flutter my eyes open and peer around the dark car. Confusion washes over me, and I manage to pull my mouth from Jameson. He snuggles his face near mine, his soft breath blowing strands of my hair away from my cheek.

"Where are we going?" I finally manage to spit out, unable to focus on anything clearly. It's like my mind clings to the memory I had of Laredo and Galveston, refusing to let me process much else. Jameson does nothing to help either. Because I'm still so hungry. Starved, really. I want nothing more than to—

"Here, Gwen. Drink some more," Mikkalo says from next to me.

My gaze darts to his bleeding arm, and I wiggle on Jameson's lap so much that he releases me. I scoot from his lap and on the spot between the two of them. Mikkalo's delectable blood tantalizes my senses, and I end up on his lap with my back to his chest. It's me who restrains him, clasping his arm in both my hands. I draw my tongue over the pooling blood and hum, the fire burning through me dwindling the more I drink.

"I'm so sorry I failed you, Gwen," he whispers into my ear. "That bastard should've never gotten his hands on you. I underestimated his strength."

"We all did," Bronx says, his husky voice grabbing at my attention until our gazes meet in the rearview mirror.

A gentle hand touches my knee. "As soon as you're done, I'm going to switch places with Mikkalo and examine you. Your subconscious wouldn't let any of us get close to the bite he gave you."

I frown.

Everett holds up his blue and black hand.

"Oh, shit." I drop Mikkalo's arm to scoot forward for a better look.

"Yeah, apparently you're tough even in your sleep," Bronx says. "You broke three of his fingers."

"Fuck," I breathe.

"And one of mine," Jameson says, showing me his

bruised index finger.

"You bit the crap out of Bronx," Mikkalo adds, leaning forward to smack his brother on the shoulder.

It must be bad because Bronx tenses.

"Only Mikkalo came out unscathed," Jameson says, bumping his knee to mine.

I blow out a ragged breath. "What the fuck?" I intend to say the words only to myself, but I can't control the pitch of my voice.

Mikkalo chuckles. "You came close."

"I don't remember any of this," I say, trying not to freak the fuck out. How on earth did I manage to cause so much damage in my state of unconsciousness? What if I had hurt them worse? The thought alone sends a chill through me, and I cover my face with my hands.

Mikkalo rubs his hand in circles on my back. "Hey, none of that."

"I could've killed you without even realizing it," I murmur.

Jameson squeezes my knee. "Highly doubt it. You were just a little wild. Nothing we can't handle. I'm pretty sure Bronxy enjoyed every second of your teeth sinking into him."

Bronx shifts in the seat to look at me. "He's right about that."

I blush crazy hard, their reactions toward my savagery helping extinguish the fear and guilt tightening my chest. I don't know if they're being calm for my sake, but it helps.

"Apparently vampire venom heightened your dhampir mutation," Everett says.

I scrunch my nose. "That's why it hurts so badly?"

He nods. "We thought you were in a state of transition."

"But you wouldn't drink the human blood," Jameson says. "Spit it right in Bronx's face."

"Which is how I got bit."

I close my eyes, trying to remember what the hell happened after I blacked out, but nothing comes forward in my mind. Sinking back in the seat, I turn my gaze to my hands. Jameson and Mikkalo crowd me in the best way possible, just giving me the comfort I so desperately need.

"Gwen," Everett says softly. "May I examine the bite now?"

I turn my gaze up to his and consider telling him no, but he looks like he might just die if I deny him the chance to make sure I'm okay. Bobbing my head, I give in and slide forward instead of making him and Mikkalo switch seats. He helps me into the front, and Bronx pulls my legs onto his lap so that Everett can get a better look.

"Make it quick, Ev," Mikkalo says from the backseat. "I got something on one of the feeds."

I frown and look at him. "Is that what we're doing in the car? We're tracking someone? Did you find another one of my brothers?"

Bronx taps a few buttons on the navigation screen, turning on the autopilot. He swivels in his seat to face me. "Not exactly."

Everett shifts my hair off my shoulder, ripping my attention away from Bronx. I snatch his hand and stop him from tugging my strap down to get a better look. A small growl sounds through the car, and Mikkalo bursts into laughter in the backseat.

I realize the noise comes from me.

Covering my mouth with my hand, I meet Everett's amused expression. He motions for me to pull my own damn strap down, which I can't blame him for. I'm fucking out of control. He wasn't joking about the venom enhancing my instincts. I'm pretty sure I'm even stronger now.

Bronx squeezes my knee. "Anyway," he continues, pretending like I didn't almost snap at his brother. "I discovered that Lady Tori had put a tracker on Silas. Brentwood called not long ago, because a few of his staff members went missing."

I raise my eyebrows. "Ah, hell. There are tons of guys out there. Why are they trying to get my brother?"

"Who knows, really," Everett says, answering for Bronx. "Could be something in the mutation since he's a carrier. Could be alluring to females like you're alluring to us."

I groan, trying not to think about the fact that he might be right. My brothers never had a problem finding women to sleep with according to them. I never met them personally.

"Maybe that's why there are seven of you," Jameson says. "I mean, I'm not going to lie. I can't stop thinking of sleeping with you. You're lucky we can't procreate. Pulling out isn't that effective and—"

I shift and scowl at him. I don't want to think about any of this. "Seriously? You are not imagining the possibility of impregnating me."

Jameson leans closer and smirks. "I like kids."

Mikkalo punches him. "Knock it off, Jameson. You're freaking her out."

I meet Jameson's gaze, keeping my face expressionless to his comment. "I'm not freaked out. I just don't want to talk about how he thinks the world wants to bone my family because of something in our genes."

Bronx laughs and covers his mouth with his hand. Jameson doesn't even try to suppress how funny he thinks it is. Mikkalo shakes his head, rolling his eyes.

Everett pulls my shirt back up, drawing my attention from all the amusement. Jameson's words were enough to distract me from the exam, but now I have all sorts of crazy thoughts spinning through my mind.

"It would kind of make sense," Everett says, speaking up. "At least for humans. Dhampirs are a threat to vampires, a natural predator, yet they don't cause any harm to humans. It's not like vampires will purposely try to create someone who can destroy them."

"I think it's both. I've never been so attracted to someone or as horny for someone as I am with Gwen in all of my existence." Jameson leans forward and kisses my cheek from over the seat. "You can't tell me you don't feel it."

Everett clicks a button on the seat, sending it shooting back at Jameson, squishing him. "Of course I feel it. But if I have to explain why to you, we would have a lot of other things we might need to worry about."

I laugh this time, making Jameson play-growl at me. "Don't worry, Jamie. The feeling is mutual." I wink at him. "And while I don't have experience with kids, I think I'd like the idea of having them if it were possible with you. One day. When everyone isn't trying to cage me."

The others look at us, various expressions crossing their faces. I wonder if I took my teasing too far.

"We can continue to test out the possibility until then." Jameson purrs, the noise sending tingles between my legs. "So come back here. Don't let my brothers ruin our fantasy for the future."

"I kind of like the idea, too," Everett says. "And since Gwen's sitting with me..."

I wag my finger at him. "Not in the car."

Jameson chuckles. "Don't worry, Ev. You can seduce our girl on your night."

"He can try," I tease, joking with Everett, because now I'm pretty certain his brothers assume we haven't slept together despite the amazing oral he performed on me.

Everett slides his hand between my legs, squeezing my thigh. "Mmmhmm."

I squirm. "Behave." My words come out soft enough for only him to hear.

"You should've worn a dress."

I release a breath.

"Damn, what did you say to her, Ev?" Jameson asks from the back.

Shifting, I shake my head at him. "Nu-uh. No asking."

"She's right. We're coming up to our destination anyway," Mikkalo says, tapping away on his com device. "Pull over up there, Bronx. Where the orange trees are."

"Whoa," I murmur, drawing my attention away from Jameson to peer at the outside surroundings. "Are you sure this is where Silas is?" A small blip of fear trickles through me. I should've been paying more attention.

Mikkalo nods. "Unless they surgically removed the tracker. Apparently Lady Tori wasn't chancing him taking it off."

"Shit," I breathe, swiveling to look out the window more. I almost don't believe it. Why would the Baron Coven bring my brother here?

"What is it, Gwen," Bronx asks, touching my knee, pulling me from my thoughts.

Swallowing, I meet his dark gaze. "I know this place."

He frowns. "You've been to the Baron Coven's estate

before?"

I nod. "Yeah, but I don' think this is it."

"What do you mean?" Bronx puts the car in park and shuts off the engine.

Jameson and Mikkalo lean forward in their seats, and Everett snuggles close to me. They give me their undivided attention as I piece together a memory from a couple of years ago—one before Dad died.

"This is rebel land," I say, waving to the orange grove. "There is a community here that's been a haven since the uprising."

The car shakes, and a cloud of dirt rains around us outside the car. A strange rumble muffles through the windows, and the car quakes again. Bronx's eyes widen, and Everett twists me in his arms, handing me to Mikkalo. Silence falls between us as my guys listen and stare at our surroundings.

The windshield shatters.

Mikkalo swears and thrusts his door open. He yanks me with him and into the trees. Gunshots pop through the air, startling me. I try to peer around from Mikkalo's arms, but he runs too fast, blurring the world.

"What's going on?" I ask, clinging onto Mikkalo as tightly as I can so that he can keep his arms free. Everything happens so fast. My brain can't catch up.

"We're under attack," he says, flashing his fangs with his heavy breathing. Another explosion booms through the air, the weapons used far more powerful than the guns rebels usually favor, but this is their land. They'd do anything to protect it. They probably saw us coming.

"The rebels won't follow us. They're just trying to protect their home," I say.

Mikkalo spins, and I screech. A figure blurs through the trees. Bronx materializes in front of us, holding a dagger in his hand. He and Mikkalo share a look with each other, but neither says anything to me.

Jameson whistles, waving his arms. "Everett's down. Quick."

My heart pounds in my chest, the edges of my vision shadowing. Mikkalo tosses me to Jameson, and I cover my mouth with my hand, spotting Everett on the ground, his throat spilling his blood all over the place. That wound doesn't look like one from a rebel. They could never get close enough to do that much damage.

"Oh, God. Put me down," I say to Jameson. "He needs my help."

Jameson doesn't argue and sets me on my feet, but he stays close to me. Mikkalo puts pressure on Everett's neck to staunch the bleeding the best he can. The more he bleeds, the weaker he'll be and the longer it'll take for him to heal.

"Easy, Everett," Mikkalo says, pinning his brother in place. "Our girl's got you."

I kneel on the ground and lean in. "Be gentle."

My arm barely touches Everett's lips when a loud boom rings through the air.

"Brothers, cover me. We have to move him," Bronx says.

Bronx hoists me and Everett into his arms like we weigh nothing, and I have to awkwardly arch my back as I lie on Everett while Bronx cradles him. Everett sucks on my arm, holding my stare with his silver flashing eyes. I try my best not to panic at the dread washing through me.

"We need shelter," Bronx says. "Anything."

"Keep heading south in the grove. We'll reach the community in a few miles," I whisper.

"If we do, we'll lead them right to the rebels," Bronx says.

"Lead who?"

"The Anderson Coven."

23

WAR

"I FOUND AN ABANDONED GAS guzzler," Jameson says, materializing next to us. "It should do."

The world blurs as Bronx follows Jameson through the trees until we reach a small open space with a dirt road. A black van hides under a bunch of tree branches, probably waiting for a rebel to return for it. Jameson pries the locked door open, revealing an empty cargo space.

"I want you to stay here with Gwen and Everett," Bronx says. "Make sure Gwen gets more of your blood. Everett drank a lot from her."

Jameson nods and climbs into the van, holding his arms out. He helps me in first before taking Everett, who I nestle between my legs to let him rest his back to my chest. He clutches my hand so tightly that my fingers lose their feeling, but I don't even consider trying to pull away. Seeing him on the ground like that—it got to me. I'm terrified even to let Bronx venture out again.

"Where are you going?" I ask Bronx before he disappears. "Where's Mikkalo?"

"We're going to scout the area. See what we're dealing with. Corona must've been informed about the tracker on your brother and thought he'd lead him to you," he whispers. "He could've bought access to the feeds from a traitor to the Hunter Coven."

My lip trembles. "Fuck."

"Take a breath, dandelion," he murmurs, kissing me. "Don't devour Jameson while I'm gone."

I clutch his face to stop him from leaving. "Be safe."

He nods once and slides the door closed, vanishing into the night. Jameson crawls behind me, sandwiching me to Everett. His arm snakes around my neck with an offer of blood, and I automatically latch on and suck, listening to his even breathing pick up.

"Would it be inappropriate to suggest you let me distract you?" Jameson whispers, keeping his voice at a pitch only I can hear.

"Totally inappropriate," I murmur, hugging Everett's

chest. "I'm not getting caught butt-ass naked by our ene-mies."

"Another reason for you to wear dresses." Everett's voice comes in a breathless whisper.

Jameson chuckles.

I graze my teeth to Jameson's arm. "You guys. Stop. Someone will hear us."

"We'll be fine." Jameson sneaks a kiss to my throat. "Knowing my brothers, we're probably the bait anyway."

I stiffen. "Seriously?"

Everett sits up and twists to look at me. Color returns to his face, and the nasty wound on his neck coagulates as he heals. He squeezes my hand, forcing a smile in an attempt to calm me down.

Someone slams their hands on the window, cracking the old glass under the pressure. Jameson covers my mouth to muffle any sounds threatening to come out. I glare at the unfamiliar jerk flashing his fangs at me.

"Stay calm," Everett whispers, shifting to glance at Jameson.

Jameson releases a low growl. "Bronx or Mikkalo will take care of him."

"I hope you're right." I can't stop my voice from sounding out. "I did not agree to this bait bullshit or being separated."

Hugging me closer, Jameson kisses my neck a few more times, ignoring the vampire smashing through the glass.

"Don't be mad, please. Bronx knows what he's doing."

I hiss at the guy, flipping him off. "Of course I'm mad. I wasn't prepared for this shit."

The vampire shoves his arm through the glass, and Everett tugs a dagger from beneath his jacket and slashes it at the guy. The vampire pulls back before Everett severs his arm and snarls. A gunshot pops through the air, and Jameson jerks me to the floor. He rolls on top of me, squishing me with his weight to shield my body the best he can. The ringing in my ears spins my head. It takes me a second to realize that a bullet hole fissures the window opposite to where the vampire stood.

"Shhh, Gwen," Jameson whispers. "I got you."

My heart thuds against my ribs. Jameson's weight smothers the trembles threatening my body. Fear prickles over my neck, growing more intense by the second. I hate this. I hate waiting to see what happens. Not fighting back.

"Everett, get Gwen to the back. Bronx's taking too long. Something's wrong," Jameson says, shifting off me only enough that he can help me roll over to Everett. The gunfire stopped, but it could mean a lot of things, not that we're safe.

Everett tightens his jaw, pulling me with him. His eyes flash crazy silver. His nostrils flare at my closeness, and without having to ask, I know he still needs more blood, but he won't ask. He won't risk leaving me vulnerable.

My heart races the longer the silence drags on. I can't

shake the feeling of impending doom. Jameson is right. Something is completely and utterly wrong. But I don't think it has to do with Bronx. My human instincts go off like crazy in warning.

"Guys, we can't stay here," I whisper.

Jameson and Everett look at me, studying my face.

Jameson cocks his eyebrow, drawing his gaze toward the broken window. He growls, the noise low but intense, vibrating through me even though he hunches down a foot away. Everett sets a cold, heavy blade in my hand, and I curl my fingers around it.

"Go out the front. We'll leave out the back," Everett says.

Jameson nods. "Don't stop for anything. I'll be right behind you."

Everett and Jameson bump knuckles, and Jameson squeezes my hand. He abandons the van first, and I catch sight of a figure blurring at vampire speed to crash into him. Everett covers my mouth and drags me toward the back, forcing the hatch open with his shoulder.

Cool air engulfs us, and I wrap my legs and arms around him, holding on as tightly as I can. We don't make it far before a strange vampire speeds in our direction. I tense, and Everett pushes to move faster, but he's not fast enough.

The vampire flies past us to cut Everett off, and Everett spins, slashing his dagger out. The vampire catches his arm and drags him forward. I brace myself to collide into the guy, possibly get bitten, but Everett manages to spin and ram into him backwards. The vampire extends his fangs longer than normal, and bites Everett in the shoulder, making him grunt.

A guttural noise escapes my lips, and I jam my own dagger into the asshole's eye, making him screech so loud that my ears ring. The vampire stumbles away and disappears into the trees. Everett doesn't stop to chase him. Instead, he sprints forward in the opposite direction and keeps going.

Screams sound through the air the deeper Everett takes me into the orchards. Not just men yell. Women. Children. All of them human. Vampires don't scream in terror. They scream in rage and in pain.

"Everett, head toward the community," I say, my stomach twisting and turning.

"We can't. It's not safe." He doesn't slow down to even consider my command.

"They'll be slaughtered." I pinch his shoulders, trying to push myself upright, but he clutches me tightly against him.

He glowers but not at me. "They put a death sentence on your head."

"I know," I say, burying my face into the crook of his neck. "But this wasn't how we were going to handle it." We might've planned on giving Corona information about the

Blood Rebels, but it wasn't about this community. It was one filled with soldiers, fighters for the elders, and not people like this who risk the wild to survive in a world outside of vampire law.

"If we go, we risk someone recognizing you. We'll have no choice but to go to war. Everything in our region will fall apart. We could lose it altogether."

Everett's words battle against my humanity. Against my need to prove to the Blood Rebels that I'm not against them despite choosing this life. Despite loving vampires. But because of the love that grows stronger each day, my humanity fades more and more.

A soft whistle sounds through the air, and Everett relaxes a bit. Mikkalo materializes in front of me and greets me with a soft kiss to slow my out-of-control heart. Twisting, Everett hands me to Mikkalo, who squishes me into his rock-hard body like he just needs to feel my closeness to know that I'm okay.

"Everett, are you good to fight?" Mikkalo asks, slowing down until we take cover on the side of a rundown shack that looks as if even the lightest gust of wind could knock it over. Knowing Blood Rebels, it's probably been here since before The Divide, maybe even the uprising.

Everett risks leaning on the side of the shed, catching his breath. "I'm weak. Not exactly in the best shape."

Mikkalo sets me on my feet but doesn't take his hand off me, just scouring my body to make sure I'm uninjured.

Everett combs his hand through his messy blond hair and peers around, never taking his gaze away from our surroundings.

"Okay, then you'll back Jameson up." Mikkalo turns to me. "You're going to back me up. Think you can handle it?"

I blink a few times. "You want me to fight?"

"No, but someone's gotta rescue Bronx's dumb ass." Mikkalo jerks his neck, cracking it with the motion.

My eyes bulge, fear rushing over me. "What happened?"

"Nothing serious. The rebels got him. They're far more strategic than we realized." He remains expressionless. "They have some serious weaponry too. Enough that the Anderson Coven is regrouping. They think you're hiding in the main structure."

"Where's Jameson?" Everett asks.

"Here." Jameson throws his arms around me, kissing me on the lips.

"And the Anderson Coven?" Mikkalo asks.

"Surrounding the place." Jameson pulls out his com device, displaying a sloppy hand-drawn map of the area. "There are two here. One here. And five coming up on the far side." Jameson draws lopsided circles onto the screen.

Mikkalo studies it for a minute. "There are rebels guarding here and here." He swipes two Xs on the screen. "If we come up here, we'll avoid the Anderson Coven and might miss some of the guards. It's the straightest shot. But we'll have to move fast. The second Corona realizes we're here, he'll change his focus."

"What about the asshole who attacked us?" I ask.

"Dead," Mikkalo and Jameson say in unison.

I puff out a breath. "What about my brother and the Baron Coven? I don't understand why they're here."

The three of them look at each other. "We don't have the answer to that. We haven't seen any other vampire outside of the Anderson Coven."

I frown. "What if—"

"Our priority is getting Bronx so he doesn't have to kill a bunch of people and then get you out of here," Mikkalo says. "Everything else? We can't risk it. There are too many unknown factors."

I consider opening my mouth to argue, but he's right. "Okay, but if we see my brother—"

"We'll get him," Jameson says.

I crinkle my nose, torn between wanting my brother safe and also wanting to kick him in the dick for being such a fucking ass. It's tempting to give him back to the Hunters. Maybe sterilize him first. Damn, I can't believe I even think those words, but he really hurt me. Whatever relationship we had has been trashed. And for what? It's almost painful even to want to go through this over and over again with my other brothers. I'm not sure my heart can handle it. It makes me miss my dad more than ever. He'd clobber them upside the head for even thinking something bad about me.

Mikkalo squats in front of me. "I want you on my back. Everett and Jameson will be behind us."

I climb up and squeeze his waist with my thighs, wishing with everything in me that Bronx would show up and tell us that he handled everything and we could go home. But no such luck. Mikkalo breaks out into a speed run, and I keep my face tucked between his shoulder blades to help with the whipping wind. My hair blows all over the place in a tangled mess, and I try to think about what a pain it'll be to brush later instead of the whispering of voices growing louder as we draw near.

"Jameson, you and I will disarm them. Everett put them to sleep," Mikkalo says. "Gwen, I'm going to need you to distract."

"You're going to get our girl hurt," Everett snaps, his eyes flashing silver.

Mikkalo slows down and comes to a stop to face his brother. "Our girl is a badass, and she's the least likely they'll attack."

I hop off his back and stroll to Everett. "He's right. Maybe we can use them to our advantage. They could lead me to Bronx."

All three of them fall silent as they stare at each other in contemplation. If I know Blood Rebels like I think I do, they'll want to protect me...unless they know who I am. But this isn't a community with elders or soldiers, and it's one

I've been to before. If I can get in, I might be able to find Bronx and lead the guys to him. They'll keep a vampire alive as long as they don't show signs of aggression. It's probably something Bronx knew. Rebels like to keep blood sources around for a reason.

"If they even try to touch you, I will murder them," Jameson says, unleashing a growl unlike anything I've ever heard from him.

"Jamie."

He shakes his head. "No. This isn't something you can persuade me out of. So don't even try using that sexy pout of yours to get your way." His narrowed eyes prove how serious he is, and for the first time in a while, I might be a teensy bit scared.

I remain expressionless. "Okay."

"Okay?" His eyebrow peaks on his forehead in surprise.

"I want Bronx back, and I don't want to get hurt, so yeah." But I also know that he might not actually go through with it. I mean, as long as I prove that I can handle myself. Jameson hasn't done much training with me, so he doesn't know my skillsets like Mikkalo and Bronx.

Wrapping me in a hug, he lifts me off my feet and kisses me. "I swear you better take care of yourself. If I have to save your ass, I'm going to spank the hell out of it later."

"You're full of shit," I say, smiling.

He groans. "Fine, but don't think I won't kiss the hell out of it."

I blush crazy hard, my face burning. "This is not the time to put that kind of stuff in my head."

He sets me down and spins me around, leaning into my back to whisper in my ear. "Just something to look forward to."

I shiver under Jameson's breath and quickly hug and kiss Everett next. Mikkalo takes my hand and leads me forward until the voices whisper loud enough that I know I'll stroll right in the middle of the Blood Rebels post.

Mikkalo bends down to my ear. "Be safe."

I comb my hair off my shoulder. "I need you to bite me."

He blinks in surprise. "What?"

"Trust me. Just be gentle."

I lick my lips and tighten my fingers around his, feeling the softness of his breath against my skin. The click of his fangs extending sends a good shiver over me, and I brace my free hand on his shoulder.

Mikkalo bites me and sucks on my neck for just a few seconds. I sink into him and moan under the sensation that already has me reaching for his pants like a damn sex fiend. He doesn't help any, reaching down to grab my butt.

"Who's there?" a masculine voice calls.

Mikkalo mumbles for me to be safe and pulls away to disappear behind a nearby tree. I touch my bleeding neck, savoring the tingling sensation blossoming across my chest. I release a weird-ass cross between a moan and a whimper at his sudden absence. Footsteps thud in my direction, the noise drawing whoever is nearby closer.

I drop to my knees and hunch forward, making myself appear smaller, less threatening.

"Hey, Leo. Over here. Quick." The thudding footsteps pick up pace, and I force another whimper from my mouth. "It's another female. She's been bitten."

"Watch it, Dirk. It could be a trap. Blood suckers don't just leave, especially if they catch a woman."

I grimace at his words and pull out the dagger Mikkalo gave me. Luckily, it's covered in vampire blood. "Stay back," I say, whining a little. "I'll stab you like I did the other asshole."

The men stop in their tracks. "It's okay, sweetheart. We're not damn blood suckers. Where did you come from anyway?"

A dozen thoughts swirl through my mind as I think of a response.

"You come with the humans looking for Silas?" the man asks.

I blink a few times and nod. "Where are my sisters? We got separated."

The older of the two guys steps forward and holds out his hand to me. Jameson's words flash through my mind, and I shake my head and push to my feet on my own. The guy drops his arms at his sides and peers around behind me like he expects a vampire to come flying out from hiding.

He's lucky I didn't risk allowing him to help me up. Jameson's clinging onto the edge of control that I don't know if I trust that he won't react.

"What's your name, sweetheart?" the man asks.

"Gigi," I say, speaking the first name that pops into my head.

He reaches into his pocket and pulls out a dirty rag and waves it to me. "I'm Leo. This is Dirk. We have somewhere safe you can stay the rest of the night."

I take the gross rag from him and cringe as I press it to my neck. Mikkalo growls too lowly for anyone to hear, and I try not to glance in the direction he left in. I bet it drives him crazy that I comply and cover the bite. He probably won't mention it, but I know how possessive my guys get, and they're only good with each other.

The two men motion for me to stroll between them. They stand on guard, weapons drawn, peering through the dark orchard. I notice they keep to a particular path that sometimes forces the three of us to merge into a single-file line.

A strange noise sounds through the air, causing the rebels to stop.

"Gwen, run!" Mikkalo shouts, his voice yelling through the air.

The ground quakes, exploding somewhere nearby. Dirt and debris rain down on top of us, and Dirk pushes me forward.

Leo releases a loud whistle through the air, a call of sorts to whoever stands guard nearby. Fear courses through me, and I pick up pace. Running as fast as I can, I push past the two men. A figure materializes in front of me, and I skid, trying to slow down. I eat shit on the rough terrain and scrape my hands across the ground. Leo and Dirk fire their weapons, the loud pops leaving me seemingly deaf with only ringing in my ears.

I don't get up, bowing my head, trying to pull my shit together.

"Oh, little dolly." A feminine voice trickles to me through the cacophonous noises echoing through the air. "I'm so happy to have found you." Francisca materializes next to me, paying no attention to the guys shooting at another vampire.

I push up, scrambling to my feet. I search the ground for my discarded weapon, catching sight of it only a few feet away. I don't respond to Francisca and lunge at the dagger, landing on top of it so that it takes more effort for her to disarm me.

She hums under her breath and nudges me over with her stiletto. "Come along, dolly. Corona said whoever found you will get ten minutes to play. I don't want to waste any time."

I swing my arm out and jam the dagger into her leg. She screeches and kicks me so hard that I roll a few feet. Pain explodes through me as she steps on my chest, digging the sharp heel of her glittering shoe into my sternum. All it would take is a bit more pressure and she'd impale me.

I scream, locking my fingers to her ankle. "Stop!"

She ignores me, smiling as she continues to force her heel down.

I thrash, unable to stop my mouth from screaming my lungs off. The pain is far more excruciating than anything I've ever felt. What's worse is that I'm certain she'll kill me at any second, and my guys haven't even shown themselves.

Something cracks inside me, and I beg my body to black out as warmth trickles between my breasts. My ear-piercing shouts ring through the air. I'm sure every vampire within the vicinity can hear my screams of agony.

Francisca hisses, stepping off of my chest to peer around the dark orchard. The guys that were helping me lie motionless on the ground, and I heave a breath, trying to get my body to curl in on itself.

"The dhampir is mine," a deep, guttural voice says, the words nearly incoherent through the growls escaping another guy's throat.

Francisca and the male vampire square off, strategizing their next moves. Neither pays attention to me, and I take advantage of the situation. Kicking my leg out, I clock Francisca hard enough to throw her off balance. She roars, reaching for me at the same time the guy flies at her.

I jerk my hand up as the man shoves her down, and blood cascades over me. Francisca screams and thrashes, and the man smiles at me from over her shoulder, readying his blade to sink it into her back.

He doesn't get a chance.

Francisca drops her weight on top of me as I rip out her heart.

24

DUTY AS A DHAMPIR

THE VAMPIRE STANDS OVER ME, tilting his head to the side. Something comes over me, and I bring Francisca's heart to my mouth and lick it. I know it's gross. My mind screams at my body to knock it the hell off. But damn it, she tastes good enough. Not mouthwatering, but acceptable, and my body craves the reprieve consuming extra blood does for my injuries.

And this bitch.

I shove her off me, my strength throwing her at least ten feet away and farther than I should be capable of doing.

The dude just gapes at me, darting his gaze from Francisca's dead body and back to me. Something strange darkens his steel-blue eyes, and he clenches his fingers into his palms.

Holy shit. I know that look. I've given that look. He's scared of me.

"You have five seconds to get your douche ass out of here before I take your heart next," I say, wiping my hand on my pants.

All the guy does is take a few steps back, keeping his intense gaze locked on me as I push up to my feet. My legs tremble like crazy, and I bow forward for a couple of seconds to try to get my nerves to settle. The fact that he hasn't tried to attack or kidnap me leaves me on edge. His familiarity digs into me, but I can't tell if I've seen him at Corona's house or somewhere else.

"You have a remarkable similarity to Gwyneth," he murmurs, daring to inch closer.

Just the mention of Gwyneth erupts fear in my heart. Spinning on my feet, I try to dash away, but the vampire materializes in front of me. He stops me in my tracks and leans in, brushing loose strands of my hair from my face.

"So perfect. Strong," he murmurs. "You'll create such marvelous power for our future."

I slam my palms to his bone-hard chest, but he doesn't budge. "Back the hell up."

He doesn't. "Please, Gwen. I've waited so long for my chance to meet you. Do not deny me the opportunity to introduce myself."

I glare into his eyes, trying to pull a memory that refuses to break free from my mind.

"I'm Freeport, first in line of the Baron Coven, and your future mate," he says, stroking his fingers across my cheek. "I look forward to the chance to get to know you on every level you need."

Future mate? Is this guy for real?

Anger rushes through me. The asshole has the nerve to lean in for an uninvited kiss. I snap my teeth on his tongue, ripping out a cross between a groan and a growl. He pulls back, unfazed by my attempt to bite his tongue off and only smiles.

"I suppose I should've given a taste to you first," he murmurs, sinking his teeth into his arm. "I'm sure you'll be very pleased with what I have to offer."

I gawk at his bleeding arm and dart my eyes back to his. His grin softens his hard features to where I might call him handsome if he didn't sound like such a creep. "Okay, asshole. There is no way my mouth is going anywhere near your blood. Now back the hell up."

His eyes flash silver, and he jerks away like I slapped him. "My dhampir, you must be so confused. What did my brother do to you to make you this way?"

"Laredo?" I ask. "Or Rochester? Maybe Galveston? Thaxton? All of them were douches."

"I cannot speak for Rochester or Laredo, but Galveston

and Thaxton were only trying to help me bring you home where you belong," he responds, tightening his jaw.

I scrunch my features, trying my best not to lose control. "Where I belong? Are you kidding me?"

"You have a duty as the heir of Gwyneth Gallagher to fulfill your place at my side. She did not lose her life for you to throw the gift she passed down to you away. We cannot afford to wait more decades for another descendant with the dhampir mutation. We must act now." Freeport closes the space to me again, but this time he keeps his hands to himself.

"What the hell are you talking about?" I ask, wishing with everything in me that my guys are nearby. Where the hell are they anyway?

"If you're looking for the blasphemous Royales, they will not be coming for you." He flicks his gaze past me to search the dark orchard. "The war they started with the Anderson Coven put your very existence in jeopardy. They must be taken care of appropriately before word travels. For your sake. If anyone found out about you—"

"They'll kill me? Cage me for the rest of my life?" I place my hands on my hips. I know I shouldn't let him continue on. I know I should run and fight for my life. To search for my guys. But he seems to know more about me than I know about myself, and my dumb curiosity gets the best of me.

"For the rest of eternity," he says, keeping his voice low.

"You cannot die naturally."

I blink, a wave of emotions washing through me. "What?"

He rubs his lips together. "You didn't know."

I don't answer him.

"There is so much for you to learn," he says, extending his hand out to me. "Let me take you home. You'll be exceptionally happy. I vow that. I know I'll do right by you and help you successfully fulfill your duty as a dhampir."

He keeps saying that: My duty.

"I will not be feeding you or whatever it is you think is supposed to be my duty."

His lips quirk into a smile. "Oh, but it's so much more. You'll bear the power I have to offer. A new life will be born."

I blink a few times, unsure what to think about his words. What the hell does that even mean? Bear power? A new life will be born? Is that what a Blood Vow is? He thinks I can transform into a vampire?

A strange noise hums through the air, drawing his attention away from me. I don't get a chance to react as his hands encircle my waist and hoist me onto his shoulder. The world blurs for a few seconds, and I orient myself, fear colliding over me, stealing my breath away. My instincts take over, and I pound my fist so hard into Freeport's back that I throw him off balance.

He drops me, the both of us tumbling across the hard

dirt. My body kicks into action, and I catapult to my feet, darting away faster than I have ever moved in my life. It's like my dhampir mutation suppresses my humanity, leaving me in a strengthened state. Freeport yells my name, begging me to stop.

I don't. I can't. I run, breathing hard, my whole body aching. My eyes water in the wind, blurring my vision. I focus too hard on the world around me that I don't see the dark shape of a headless body lying in the dirt until it's too late.

I trip over the hulking form and land on my stomach, my eyes widening as the back of a severed head appears in my vision. The familiar, tightly cropped hair and smooth dark skin on a thick neck steals the warmth from me.

Scrambling away, I crab walk back to the body. The guy is dressed in all black, his shirt pulled up slightly to reveal a couple bluish-black lines tattooed on his back. Lines I recognize.

"Mikkalo!" I scream, my heart exploding, the realization sinking in. "Mikkalo!"

Something hits me in the back of the head, sending me sprawling across the ground. I land with my cheek in the dirt, facing the open empty eyes of an unfamiliar vampire. My heart skips a beat, my wild emotions paralyzing me.

I start bawling my eyes out, relief rushing through me. It's not Mikkalo. I don't know who it is, but it doesn't matter. As long as it's not Mikkalo, I know he's out here somewhere, strategizing how to get to me.

"*This* is what Corona broke an alliance for?" a masculine voice asks, spilling dread through me. "I'm underwhelmed. She looks nothing like a predator to escalate our power."

"Agree. If anything, she'll cause us to lose it."

I stiffen at the familiar female voice.

Tipping my head up, I look at Brooklyn and another vampire standing several feet away from me. Brooklyn remains expressionless, cold even, as she stares at me with eyes I shouldn't find relief seeing considering she's nothing like Bronx.

"What do you say we just give her final donation and claim it was an outcast? Perhaps we can still salvage a relationship with the Royales and Hunters. I'm sure you'd appreciate not being at war with your brother." The guy strides forward and glares down at me.

A guttural noise draws their attention from me and to the trees where I catch sight of Freeport as he rushes to close the distance. Blood drips down his face, his nose crooked, broken from some sort of fight that left blood spatter speckling his shirt. Panic ignites through me, my instincts going wild. I can't tell if it's because the guy looks ready to kill everyone in the universe to get his hands on me or if it's because I'm right in the middle of an impending battle. Either way, fuck this shit.

Pushing to my feet, I scramble past Brooklyn and her

companion and race in the opposite direction of Freeport. I don't make it far. The guy with Brooklyn materializes in front of me, and I crash into his chest. He thrusts me back, and I slide across the dirt.

Freeport roars, snarling and snapping his teeth. The douche vampire returns his threat by pulling a dagger from his jacket. He kicks me out of the way and blurs in a fight against Freeport. Two cool hands grip my waist, hoisting me up.

Brooklyn stifles my yell with her hand. "Be quiet if you want us to get out of here alive," she whispers. "You have a price on your head that's tough for even me to refuse."

I frown, flaring my nostrils as I try to gasp in a breath.

She eases her hand away. "Now tell me. Where is my brother?"

"I don't know," I whisper, trying to control the pitch of my voice. "Something went wrong. The rebels got him."

She flashes her fangs. "You're lying. He'd never get bested by a bunch of donors."

"I'm not. He doesn't want to hurt anyone. I was on my way to get him when I was attacked. Mikkalo, Jameson, and Everett were all with me, but I don't know what happened." The words tumble from my mouth, and I try not to freak out. The dead body I thought was Mikkalo flashes through my mind again, twisting my stomach.

Brooklyn drops me as I heave, my stomach wanting nothing more than to expel its contents. Turning onto my side, I breathe deeply through my nose and watch Brooklyn abandon me to disappear into the trees. Freeport squats down beside me and pats my back.

"Don't touch me," I snap, swatting his hand away.

"You're hurt. Let me help you up. We need to go. My brothers are waiting for the exchange," he says, ignoring my demands.

Swinging my arm out, I punch him right between the legs hard enough to send him sprawling back. I push through the pain and knots rippling through me and bolt away. I brace myself to get ripped off my feet at any second, but he doesn't chase me. Silence falls through the orchard, the growls of vampires fading. Soft light sparkles through the trees, and I head in the direction of the community.

I slow down and duck behind a tree to search the outskirts the best I can. A few bodies lie in piles on the ground, but they're vampires and not humans. I don't understand. Rebels aren't that great at fighting vampires. Not this many. One or two, maybe. But the three bodies I see turn out to be only the first pile. There are three more piles further down.

I cover my mouth with my hand and inch forward, unable to resist searching the piles. I heave a few bodies away from their place, terrified of spotting one of my guys. I don't recognize anyone. An eerie sensation crawls up my back, and I spin around, expecting to see Freeport. But he's not there.

"Gwen."

I startle at the sound of a familiar voice, and swivel on my feet. Grayson stands with his arms crossed a few dozen feet away. He clenches a bloody silver stake in one hand, ready to fight. His right eye sports a purpling bruise, and blood stains the collar of his plain white T-shirt, dripping from a bite on his neck. I spot another bite on his arm, but it looks older. Maybe a couple of days.

I hesitate, trailing my gaze to the rest of him. Rubbing my palms over my eyes, I wait a second to see if he's only part of my imagination. But he steps closer, giving me the same intense once-over I give him.

"Grayson? I don't understand." My voice cracks with the words. "What are you doing here?"

He strides to me, opening his arms. A frown deepens his face when I'm not quick to react. I step out of his reach and peer around the area. I thought I'd be happy to see Grayson. I thought I'd be relieved. But all I feel is all sorts of wrong.

"What are you doing here, Grayson?" I repeat, straightening my back.

"I live here," he finally says, attempting to coax me to him again by wiggling his fingers. "And I should be asking you the same thing. You were supposed to be gone. Did Freeport not find you?"

My muscles tense at the asshole from the grove's name. "He did..."

He groans, rubbing his hand through his hair. "Please don't tell me you killed him. He was only trying to protect you. It seems Silas brought a war to our door...no thanks to you."

I slap Grayson across the face, unable to control my reaction. "You asshole!"

Anger bursts through me, and I contemplate running back into the grove. But I have no idea what's going on or where to go. All I want is to find Bronx. I know he's gotta be around here somewhere, and most likely in one of the underground cages where a community like this would keep a blood source.

Grayson surprises me by swinging out and punching me in the face. Pain explodes in my cheek, shock and hurt sending me reeling along with the force. I nearly eat shit but manage to catch myself. Charging forward, I plow into my brother and knock him off his feet. Fury shadows the edges of my vision, and I attack him right back, clocking him in the nose so hard that he yells. Blood floods from his nostrils, and it sets me off even more. I'm so pissed that I can't see straight.

"Gwen! Gwen, stop it! You're going to kill him." Silas's voice rings through the air, and I jerk my attention in his direction. I catch sight of Thaxton looming behind him, his tall, sinewy form extinguishing my fury, cooling it into panic. Searching the ground, I find Grayson's silver stake a few feet away. I scramble off him and dive for it. A muscular arm encircles my waist, hoisting me up to dangle me like a doll.

I attempt to stake Thaxton in the groin, but he jerks his body back, and I narrowly miss him. Spinning me around, he disorients me, sending my stomach rolling. I have no choice but to stop fighting. The world shifts and moves around me, dizziness leaving me weak.

"Is she always this feisty?" Thaxton asks my brothers, smiling down at me.

I glower, digging my fingers into the ground to scoop up dirt. I throw it at him, but he darts to my other side. The cloud of dirt dissipates before I realize he moved.

"No," Grayson responds. "Something's different. I hardly recognize her. My sister would never attack me."

"It was the Royales. They got to her," Silas says. "You should've seen it, Grayson. They were all feeding on her."

Warmth blossoms in my cheeks. "Shut the hell up. They were not."

Thaxton tightens his jaw. "It was far worse. Nearly broke my heart. I assumed Laredo had taught you better than to fall into bed with those beneath you."

Is this guy for real?

I clench my fists, my body preparing to attack again, but Thaxton lands on top of me. He pins me down, freaking me the hell out with how he yanks my hands over my head. A smile splits his lips, turning into a leer the longer he studies me, familiarizing himself with my features.

"It's one thing to screw a human—"

Breaking free of his hold, I shove him hard enough to send him flying off me. I somersault backwards to my feet and dash away. Fear bats at my chest. I feel as if I'm trapped in some twisted game of predator and prey, but my body refuses to accept that I'm the bigger threat. All it wants to do is run.

"Gwen," Thaxton calls. "You're going the wrong way. If you're looking for the Royale Coven, you won't find them in the grove."

I freeze at his words.

"Unless you would prefer to chance it with one of the Andersons, though, it's only the few too coward to try to free their leader. We have him too." Thaxton releases a laugh. "Such a fool to think he could ever contain you. That he was worthy of even gracing the same room as the one we'll assure bears the greatest power of the future. Only a Baron can provide the Blood Vow necessary."

How do I even respond to this bullshit? I knew that Blood Rebels always referred to me as a gift to humanity, but what the hell does this guy mean about me bearing great power? And again with the Blood Vow.

"I don't know what the hell you're talking about, but no fucking thanks," I say.

"If you do not agree, we will take the region by force. You will not give us a choice. Word cannot get out about your precious gift. Everything counts on it, little dhampir."

Thaxton closes the space and cups my cheeks in his hands. "You will leave us no choice but to end the Royale Coven, and seeing as their loyalty grows for you, we thought they would serve our cause well as long as they know their place."

I think of a dozen ways to take the asshole down, but if I do, then what? He could be lying about having my guys, and Corona for that matter, but I can't be so sure. I have no other explanation as to why no one has shown up for me.

"What will it be?" Thaxton asks, rubbing his thumbs over my cheeks. "Perhaps if you see them, your decision will become clearer."

The world blurs, and I land on my ass in the middle of a sprawling lawn outside of a towering brick, wood, and stone mansion. Light shines through the tinted glass windows and ivy vines climb all the way to the roof. I don't take in the enormity of it for long because a dozen figures sit on the wide steps, bound and peering in my direction.

I fly to my feet, only making it half of the distance to Bronx, Everett, Jameson, and Mikkalo. Freeport appears in front of me, blocking my view. I try to back up, but I hit Thaxton's chest. Six more vampires materialize out of seemingly thin air, closing the space around me. They each take turns drinking me in, making me squirm on my feet.

"She's so perfect," one of the unfamiliar guys whispers. He tilts his head, sending chestnut brown hair across his forehead.

I realize they don't know that I now have super hearing.

"Right, Wesson? I can't get over how much she looks like Gwyneth," another guy says, his blue eyes burning the side of my face with their intensity.

A bearded guy with dark hair and eyes risks touching my shoulder. "Or that she's finally here."

Thaxton raises his arms. "Careful, brothers. She's agitated. It seems she's bonded with the Royale Coven."

"So soon?" The vampire, Wesson, inches closer to me, his eyes flashing silver.

The guy with a beard tenses. "Which one? I want his head."

"Easy now, Cortland," Thaxton says. "That's unnecessary."

"The hell it is," Blue Eyes says, his voice sending a shudder down my spine. He disappears from the group and stands in front of my guys. None of them look at him, all training their eyes on me.

Thaxton cuts him off. "Duncan, I said it was unnecessary."

"But if she—" Duncan takes a deep breath. "They could destroy everything we've worked for. Any impurities could ruin things."

"What the fuck?" I ask, unable to control my rebellious mouth.

The Baron brothers ignore me, keeping their attention on each other.

"He's right. I'm not willing to risk it." Freeport touches my cheek and disappears to stand behind my guys.

Thaxton tries to intercept him, but one of the other brothers—a guy with auburn hair—tackles him. Wesson snatches my hand, stopping me from running forward. Freeport pulls a blade from his jacket and grabs Bronx by his dark hair.

"I'm going to assume it was you, Mr. Royale," Freeport says, stretching Bronx's neck.

I release a small cry, drawing Freeport's attention to me. He flashes his fangs like I just confirmed his thought.

"Close your eyes, dandelion," Bronx says, meeting my gaze.

I shake my head, refusing to look away from the sparkling blade in Freeport's hand. Flashing his fangs, he smiles at me. I've never seen someone look so happy to cause me pain before.

"Would you like to taste him one last time, Gwen?" Freeport asks, scratching the blade across Bronx's throat hard enough to make him bleed.

I bob my head, my mind whirling.

Freeport's smile widens. "Wesson, bring her here."

Wesson growls. "No. If she wants a taste, just give me his head."

25

BRAVE

"NO!" I DRAG WESSON FORWARD with me, surprising him with my strength.

He pulls back to stop me, and I swing my arm, punching it hard into his chest. Bones crush under the force, and warmth blossoms around my wrist as his blood pours from the hole I create. Wesson's eyes widen, his gaze flicking down to my arm impaling him. It shocks everyone so much that no one reacts right away.

Two hands lock onto my shoulders, and another one grabs my wrist, keeping me in place. Thaxton digs his nails into the skin of my wrist, releasing a scary-ass growl that causes me to squeeze Wesson's heart harder in my hand.

"Don't let her pull," Wesson yells, snapping his teeth at me.

A roar sounds out from where my guys are, and I turn my gaze in their direction, catching sight of Bronx throwing his body back into Freeport's gut. Bronx jerks his restraints into the dagger Freeport grips in his hand, sending the blade clattering across the concrete.

"Fuck. Cortland, help him," Thaxton says. "Kill them."

I scream out, squishing Wesson's heart harder, feeling his insides slide through my fingers as I pulverize the one thing that keeps that asshole alive.

Wesson jerks, his body giving out on him.

"Keep her with him, Morgan," Thaxton says to the guy standing behind me. "We've already lost Galveston. We're not losing Wesson too."

I land on top of Wesson, thrashing to pull my arm free. His brothers have a death grip on me, stopping me from jerking my hand away. And then Thaxton unsheathes a blade. Fear pours through me as he aims it at my arm.

"Gwen, ease your fingers off his heart now. If you don't, I won't hesitate to sever your arm. You don't need it to be an intended." Thaxton aligns the knife with my arm.

"Are you fucking kidding me?" I screech, my breath coming out in pants.

"Five seconds," Thaxton says.

My body wants to test his resolve and to discover whether or not he's bluffing. I want more than anything to jerk my arm back and remove this douche's heart, but just the idea of the agony Thaxton is willing to inflict on me leaves my blood running cold. My mind whirling. But, still my hand won't release.

"Four." Thaxton taps the sharp blade on my skin hard enough to make me wince.

"I'm going to kill you next," I say, grinding my teeth together.

"Three."

Ah, hell.

Fuck.

"Two."

I squeeze my eyes shut.

"One."

I brace for unbearable pain in silence, refusing to give in to my fear or my body's sudden need to start sobbing.

"Last chance, Gwen," Thaxton says, drawing my attention to him. "I mean it."

Thaxton and Morgan are so focused on me that neither of them sees the hulking form of Bronx materialize behind them. Bronx's sudden presence gives me the burst of bravery I need, and I glower and try to jerk my arm free of Wesson's chest.

Thaxton raises his arm, his fangs extending, readying to send enough force down to cut my arm free. He wasn't bullshitting me after all. This guy is a lunatic.

Bronx blocks Thaxton's blow with a bloody dagger, swinging it up and toward Thaxton's neck. Morgan releases me to attack Bronx to stop him from beheading Thaxton. I automatically pull my arm free of Wesson's chest cavity still squeezing the warm, bloody organ. Thaxton roars, fighting Bronx harder. He manages to knock Bronx into the side of the house. Too many figures blur around in a fight, and I scramble to search for a weapon on Wesson's dead body. I tug a knife free, and concentrate on who I could possibly fight in this mess.

"Damn it, Gwen," Grayson says, reaching down to grab me.

I swipe the blade at him, stopping him in his tracks. "Stay away from me."

"You're going to get killed out here," he snaps, trying to close the space again.

His distraction works, because Silas hooks his arms around me from behind, pinning me against him. Grayson disarms me and grabs my chin to hold my head in place. He glares into my eyes, his brows furrowed, an almost feral look in his eyes capturing me. I don't know who the hell this guy is, but he's not Grayson. Grayson would've never set me up like this.

"Stop fighting us, Gwen," Grayson says. "You need to get your shit together and listen. We're not the enemies. We're your family. The Barons are your family."

I suck my bottom lip between my teeth to stop it from quivering. My voice remains locked in my throat. I don't know what I could say to him to get him to realize that he sounds utterly crazy.

"Gwen!" a familiar voice calls from behind us.

I twist in Silas's arms, trying to break free at the sound of Mikkalo's voice. "Help me!" I scream.

Mikkalo yells, and something crashes. I can't see anything from my spot in Silas's arms. Grayson pulls out a gun and fires it, and I startle with each pop. My ears ring, quieting the noise until all I can hear is the sound of my beating heart.

It's like the world slows. My vision blurs with tears, betrayal running so deeply through me that it feels as if Grayson takes a dagger to my stomach and rips it up through my heart and neck and to my mind, destroying everything. I had no idea I was capable of hating my brother, but it's more than that. I don't only hate him, I despise him.

A whistle sounds through the air, cutting apart the silence muffling the world around me. Thaxton, Freeport, and Morgan appear beside us a dozen feet away. Everett, Bronx, and Jameson materialize on the other side with me and my brothers in the middle. I've never seen so many vampires hurt, the fragrance of their blood wafting through the air, blending into a perfume that stabs at the wild, savage predator inside me.

"You will never overpower us, Royales," Thaxton says.

"Not without your brother."

"Zaire was not what brought us power and strength," Bronx says, tightening his hand on a dagger. Blood splashes across his shirt, but I can't tell if it belongs to him. His split lip looks like it heals already, and apart from a small cut on his throat, most of his injuries consist of bruises.

Everett and Jameson look far worse. Jameson's eye is so swollen that it remains closed. I'm nearly certain that Everett's arm might be broken by the way he holds it close to his body, his handsome features seemingly permanently pinched in an expression that mirrors my own despair.

"Is she worth it?" Freeport asks. "You have no idea what you're getting into. You will never maintain the life you have as long as you possess her. She will die due to your inability to not only protect her but handle everything that comes along with her."

Jameson growls and flies forward, not giving a damn that Grayson fires his gun at him. The Barons fly toward us in a race of who can get to me first. I swallow my fear instincts and ram my head back into Silas's nose. He swears, unable to hold me any longer. Instead of running away like my body wants, I scramble to run toward my guys.

A figure blurs between us, and I scream out at the sight of Corona flashing his fangs. He shocks the hell out of me by locking his hands around my waist only to throw me into the air like the little doll Francisca claimed me to be.

"I got ya, Gwen," Mikkalo says from somewhere under

me.

His muscular arms envelop me, cradling me against him. He darts away and into the orchard. Setting me on my feet, he searches over me, making sure I'm okay. I throw my arms around him and hug him. I don't give him a choice but to pick me up again. He keeps his eyes open, paying attention to our surrounding as I kiss him.

"I was so scared," I whisper into the crook of his neck.

He hugs me tighter. "I'm sorry, Gwen. We underestimated the power of the Baron Coven. We haven't heard of them because they're unregistered. Half of them are from before the uprising. It takes all four of us to overpower one of those assholes."

I shudder a breath, groaning. I had no idea. Laredo was the youngest and created after The Divide. But if some of his brothers are older than the uprising? Shit. They're probably responsible for it. I always thought it was Donor Life Corp, but it seems that everything I thought I knew has been muddled by a lifetime of my mind being manipulated.

"We have to help them," I say to Mikkalo.

He shakes his head. "No. Bronx will kick my ass."

"If they're as powerful as you say they are, then if we don't, he won't get the chance to be pissed off at you. Come on, Mikkalo. We're a team. I can handle myself. You know that." I cup his cheeks in my hands, feeling his stubble under my fingers. I beg him with my eyes.

He tightens his jaw. "I'm not letting go of you, Gwen.

You want to fight? We fight together."

I nod and kiss him, tasting the sweet tang of dried blood on his healing split lip. Mikkalo carries me to the edge of the grove surrounding the vast property. It's so strange seeing the mansion in a place I know Blood Rebels reside, the community around here somewhere.

The fight between my guys and the Barons continues at full force. I'm nearly certain it won't end until everyone on one side is dead. Without hesitating, Mikkalo sets me on my feet, clutching my hand. I'm of better use on my legs than in his arms. This isn't my first fight after all, just my first against a whole bunch of incredibly powerful vampires.

"Thaxton, there she is," Freeport calls, pointing in our direction.

"Damn it, Mikkalo," Bronx shouts. "Get her out of here."

Everyone's attention falls on me, and I grip Mikkalo's hand tighter, bracing myself for the fight now flying at us inhumanly fast. Thaxton closes the distance first, risking trying to snatch me away. Mikkalo swings me off my feet and spins me a full circle so fast that I don't realize it until my body collides into Thaxton's back, and he stumbles off his feet.

Thaxton lands in the dirt and rolls over to catapult up, but Mikkalo's quick to kick him down. He jabs his dagger into his shoulder blade so hard that it stabs all the way through him, imbedding in the compacted dirt.

It's enough to slow Thaxton down so that he can't get to his feet. Mikkalo goes in for the kill blow, swinging his arm to add enough force, but Freeport knocks Mikkalo off balance, sending him crashing into me. I hit the dirt with a thud, the breath escaping my lungs. Mikkalo rolls on top of me, acting like a shield as the two vampires close the distance, preparing to retaliate with what I can only assume to be a fatal attack.

Something inside me snaps, and I thrust against Mikkalo so hard that I throw him off to switch places. A knife jabs into my back, and I scream out in pain, my eyes blurring with shadows.

"Gwen!" Everett yells.

My surprise move freezes the Baron brothers, my loud voice enough to distract everyone from the fight. Growls reverberate through the air, and Bronx, Jameson, and Everett take advantage of their hesitation. They rush toward us so fast that Thaxton shoves Freeport and the two of them disappear. So do the other brothers. I don't think anyone was prepared for the fact that I chose Mikkalo, Bronx, Jameson, and Everett. I didn't just choose to be with them. I chose to be part of their team, to fight with them, to die for them if it came down to it.

A massive explosion shakes the world around us, and Everett scoops me into his arms. Bronx helps Mikkalo to his feet, and Jameson leads the way away from a billowing cloud of smoke wafting into the glittering night sky.

I squint through my blurring vision at the orange and yellow flames eating away at the mansion. I don't know exactly how it happened or who started it, but I do know that the place belonged to the Baron brothers, and I can't help wondering if it was their doing.

"Everett...my brothers?" The question comes out softly, just a breath on my lips.

He adjusts me in his arms, careful to keep pressure on the wound on my back while hugging me against him. "They took them."

I rest my cheek on his shoulder. "I don't understand any of this. What happened?"

"We were all set up. Both our coven and the Anderson Coven," Bronx says, answering my question.

I rest my face on Everett's shoulder, my mind whirling but my body wanting nothing more than to give into the sudden exhaustion consuming me.

Everett strokes the small of my back, the sensation feeling so incredible. "She needs blood, but I don't think she's strong enough to bite me."

"Mind if I help? I know it's awkward as fuck—"

"Anything for our girl, Bronx," Everett says.

I expect Bronx to shove his arm between my mouth and Everett's shoulder, but instead, he leans over and sinks his teeth into Everett's other shoulder. Everett shifts me again, filling my senses with everything he is. Blood coats my lips, and I find the strength to latch onto him. His blood tingles down my throat and sends a burst of energy through me. I suck harder, digging my fingers into his shoulder, making him moan softly.

"Stay close," Bronx says. "No one let our girl out of arm's reach. We're meeting with the remaining Anderson Coven members outside the rebel nest."

I blink a few times, trying to wrap my mind around his words. "Wh-what?"

Jameson pops in my view. "Don't worry, Gigi. Common enemies sometimes salvage alliances. At least temporarily. Don't look at or say anything to anyone, okay?"

It's not like I'd want to. I wish we weren't meeting them at all.

Everett kisses my temple. "I know it's not ideal, but no one will dare mess with the strong, fierce, dhampir who can rip a heart out."

"And eat it," Mikkalo says, forcing his mouth to smile.

I release a sigh and nuzzle my face into the crook of Everett's neck. The four of them slow at the soft murmur of voices. My chest clenches, hearing the husky voice of Corona. And then I hear the soft cries of people.

I tense, my stomach flip-flopping, threatening to expel Everett's blood. It didn't even dawn on me that there would be captives. It claws at me worse than I expected, especially because these people somehow found themselves in the Baron brothers' clutches.

"The rebels will not be hurt, Gwen. I promise." It's like

Bronx reads my mind, or maybe he hears my suddenly furiously beating heart. "I didn't risk our safety for them to end up dead."

"What will happen? Will you take them to Crimson Vista? Add them to the donor pool?" Because if that's the case, they're dead. No Blood Rebel would ever submit to such a life. They think death would serve a greater purpose, reminding humanity what things have come to.

"Ms. Gallagher, is that what you want for the people who deemed you a traitor to her own kind?" Corona's voice stabs into me.

If Everett didn't squeeze me tighter, I would snap at Corona. I'd thrust myself away and take his heart, crushing it like he did to mine when he murdered Kyler. When he separated my brothers. When he blackmailed my guys.

"It's Ms. Royale, and do not speak to her," Bronx says, his voice deepening with threat. "Do not look at her."

"Do not even fucking breathe near her," Jameson adds.

Bronx holds his arm up, stopping Jameson in his tracks. The command doesn't stop Mikkalo. He strides closer and swings, punching Corona in the face. The vampire flies off his feet and hits the dirt with a snarl. But he doesn't get up or try to fight back. He doesn't even meet my gaze as I pull away from Everett to peer behind me.

"Mr. Royale," a sultry, feminine voice says. Brooklyn saunters from her spot near the side of a small house. "Is that really necessary? You have already shown my father his place. He will not test your power again."

Father? What the hell?

"He's not actually her father," Everett whispers. I realize I might have murmured my confusion out loud. "Every coven has a different infrastructure. Some leaders choose to treat their members as their children, funneling power to only them instead of spreading it evenly."

"That's so weird," I say.

Everett chuckles. "It works for some. Not for others."

"...no idea. Be grateful that he's still breathing." Mikkalo returns to our side, and I reach out and touch him. I missed half of what he said, but from the silence filling the air, it was enough to shut Brooklyn up.

Bronx closes the distance to Brooklyn and whispers something too lowly for me to hear into her ear. She nods and returns to her spot without as much as another look. Mikkalo and Jameson close in tighter around me, their muscular bodies shielding me from anymore looks. Stepping away, Bronx assesses the situation, strolling to the captive humans.

"The Hunters' humans will be returned to Brentwood immediately after we wipe their memories of tonight. They will have only found an abandoned community."

Bronx squats down and extends his arm to the familiar, beautiful woman who was determined to bone a baby out of my brother. Xochitl's bottom lip trembles, and she opens her palm to take what Bronx offers. I inhale a sharp breath at what looks like a chunk of flesh. Xochitl whimpers and closes her hand without dropping it.

"She will return Mr. Gallagher's tracking device."

I groan, drawing Bronx's attention to me.

"The Barons removed it," he says to me, remaining expressionless.

Bronx continues to instruct the surrounding vampires with orders. Something about his authority leaves me gaping at him, entranced almost. I've seen him act as a leader for his brothers, but seeing him control the Anderson Coven too kind of turns me on. He looks sexy as hell with his straightened shoulders, rippling muscles, and dark eyes that turn to me every few seconds like he has to assure I'm okay at this short distance away.

"What will happen to us?" a human man asks, daring to speak.

Bronx rubs his lips together, looking at me once again. "You will continue living as you are."

Corona raises his brows. "Mr. Royale—"

"Do not question my decision. You and your coven may leave. Check in once the humans are returned to the Hunters. If Brentwood has the need to retaliate for your fuck-ups, you will accept it without complaint. You will also give me the locations of the remaining Gallaghers. If I retrieve them all unharmed, I will consider allowing you to maintain power. But betray me again and you'll see what I'm truly capable of. Understand?"

Corona nods. "Yes, Mr. Royale."

Bronx flashes his fangs. "And speak of the Barons to no one. The offense will be punished by death."

The vampires scatter, taking the three women from the Hunters with them. Everett finally sets me on my feet, but Jameson quickly scoops me up to nuzzle his nose to mine before he kisses me softly. I sink into him, devouring his affection like it's the one thing that can ease the ache inside me, filling the cracks and holes the shit show of tonight left behind.

"Brothers, take care with their manipulations. We cannot afford any fuck ups. All of them must believe that they saw Gwen die tonight. We have enough to worry about without having Blood Rebels continuing to threaten Gwen. Until we know what the Barons' next move is, we must take every precaution we can. Also, do whatever you can to gather as much information short of causing permanent damage." Bronx pats Everett and Mikkalo on the back, sending them toward the people.

Jameson squeezes me to him like he's never going to let me go, and Bronx doesn't ask him to either. Instead, he stands behind his brother and touches my cheek, kissing me on the lips. I stretch my arms out and half hug him from Jameson's arms, just breathing in his scent, filling my lungs with the calm and safeness his presence exudes.

"You okay, dandelion?" he asks softly, searching my eyes.

I shrug. "I don't know. I'm so confused. Mikkalo said these guys were more powerful than you." I crinkle my nose at the thought.

He tightens his jaw. "Only together. But don't worry. We're going to tear them apart one by one. You're our girl, and I'm not letting anyone think otherwise."

My lips pull into a smile. "As your girl, I demand you guys take me home."

He chuckles. "Yeah?"

I tighten my lips. "I want a hot bath, a massage, something hot to eat, including the lot of you, and snuggles."

Jameson purrs in my ear. "You heard our girl, Bronxy. Get to it so we can get the hell out of here."

I wave my hand. "He's right. I'm going to devour him otherwise."

Jameson tilts his head, exposing his neck. "You better be true to your word."

"Always." I graze my teeth along his throat until I reach the spot I know he likes. I bite down, and he releases the sexiest noise, holding me close.

"Damn," Mikkalo whispers. "Me next."

I laugh, licking the blood from my lips. "I have the perfect spot in mind."

Everett chuckles and whacks him on the back. "All right. I'm after."

Bronx shakes his head. "Careful, Gwen. They're all going to want to return the favor."

I toss my hair over my shoulder. "If you can finish in five minutes, I might even let you on the way home."

Mikkalo materializes in front of me and kisses me. "Best plan ever."

I can't help but agree.

26

SURPRISE

WARM WATER STREAMS DOWN MY chest as Mikkalo rinses the shampoo from my hair. I lean back into him, enjoying the slippery feeling of his body against mine in the bubble bath he drew the second Everett, Bronx, and Jameson retreated to their rooms after dinner. I could tell they wanted to stay longer, but I knew I'd probably never sleep then. It'll be hard enough trying to with Mikkalo as he slides his fingers over my nipples, gently pinching them while kissing my throat.

I hum under my breath, tilting my head back to feel

the cool air sending goosebumps across my skin. "That feels so good."

He brushes his lips on my shoulder, tracing his fingers to my stomach. "What about this?"

I inhale a breath as his hand slips lower, and he rubs between my legs. I moan my response, shifting in the water under the pressure he creates that sends my whole body buzzing. The stiffness of his arousal glides against my lower back, and I run my fingers up and down his legs, unable to sit still a moment longer.

"Mikkalo," I say, his name moaning from my mouth. "Let's get out. I can't stand going another moment without showing you how much you mean to me."

He lifts me from the bath, grabbing a towel from a hook. "I know how much I mean to you," he says, adjusting me in his arms. "You saved my life. I've never been so scared of anything until I thought someone would take you from us. So let me show you exactly how much you mean to me, Gwen. I love you. I love you more than my own existence."

I grin at his words, kissing him again. "So you're kind of mad that I did what I did?" I tease.

His eyes flash silver. "Furious. But damn was it hot. I've never been protected like that."

"I hope you know I'll always protect you. I love you too, Mikkalo. More than my own life."

My back hits the soft bed, and Mikkalo sinks against me, kissing me with so much passion that I can feel the heat of his love deep in my soul, burning away the cold pieces of fear and dread arisen from the Baron Coven.

His mouth breaks from mine, and he explores my neck with his lips and tongue, sucking and licking his way down to my breasts. He slips his finger between my legs, teasing me enough to make me arch my back from the pleasure he sends spiraling through me. Everything about this moment with Mikkalo is so utterly perfect. The heat of my skin warming him. The softness of his mouth trailing over my stomach as he memorizes every inch of me with his lips. How our hearts beat in sync almost as if we're a soul split in two finally coming together as we belong.

Mikkalo shifts his body between my legs and hooks his fingers to my hips. He rolls me on top of him so that I'm straddling his broad chest, my knees resting on both sides of his neck. I release a breath, anticipation making my body tremble. Mikkalo retracts his fangs and smiles at me, easing me closer to his head so that I now straddle his face.

A loud-ass moan escapes my lips, and I bend forward, pressing my palms to the wall to keep myself from smothering him. He digs his fingers into my ass cheeks, gently guiding my hips back and forth as he kisses and sucks and licks my clit in a way that makes me pant. He closes his eyes like he enjoys every bit of me, and I savor the explosion of pleasure rushing through me.

Mikkalo continues to explore my body with his mouth, lifting me up a bit to reach the spot where he had given me a pleasure bite. My body tenses in anticipation, and he releases a deep, throaty cross between a moan and a growl at my reaction. The buzzing sensation sends my body over the edge, and he digs his fingers right into the spot still tingling with the memory. I jerk forward with one of the most intense orgasms of my life, my thighs clenching Mikkalo's head as good spasms rush through me, curling my toes. He slows down and licks his lips, his desire prominent as he slides me lower.

He sits up, resting his back on the headboard, aligning my body with his. I shudder and moan, feeling the pressure of his thick girth tease me, testing me, just slowly enjoying me like he wants us to savor every moment of our first time together.

"You're so sexy," Mikkalo says, the click of his fangs sounding in my ear. "So delectable. I love everything about you."

I moan, bowing my head to his shoulder to kiss his now heated skin. Grazing my teeth along his tight muscles, I nip him just hard enough to make him release what sounds like a deep purr from his throat. "I've been thinking about this moment with you. Everything is better than I imagined."

He nudges my chin so that he can meet my eyes. "Let me watch. I want to see you enjoy me."

I breathe through my parted lips, anticipation growing with the pressure of his erection sliding into me. I dig my nails into his shoulders, releasing a breathless moan at how deep he sinks into me. He closes his eyes, tightening his fingers to my hips, rocking me a few times until I take over, gasping every time my thighs meet his hips.

He kisses me softly, stealing the moans from my mouth, running his fingers from my hips and up and down the length of my back. His fingers twist in my hair as he holds me close, taking over when my legs turn to jelly. He eases me onto my back, never separating from me, positioning my legs onto one of his shoulders. He picks up his speed, thrusting into me, his moans matching mine. He links his fingers of one hand with mine while holding my legs with his other, keeping his eyes on mine as I arch my back and enjoy every minute of pleasure.

Mikkalo's eyes flash silver, and he sucks in his full bottom lip between his teeth, biting it with his orgasm. He opens my legs to rest on me, kissing and teasing me with a few drops of his blood coating his lip just for me. I moan and kiss him deeper, my heart and body so content that all I want to do is lie here and listen to Mikkalo's breathing and his rapid heart beating, thumping against mine.

We savor the silence, the closeness of our entangled bodies long after we finish, just enjoying the comfort and happiness we bring to each other.

"I want this forever, you know," Mikkalo says, watching me stroll from the bathroom in only one of his T-shirts. "I never want to experience another day without you."

I smile and kiss him, sliding back into bed. "I'd love that."

Mikkalo drapes his arm over my shoulders and pulls me into his body so that no space dares remain between us. "We'll make it happen."

I puff a breath of air through my lips. "You talked to Everett." Except now I worry that my forever will end by the hands of the Barons despite what Freeport told me about my supposed immortality, which I'm not even so sure I believe.

Mikkalo kisses my temple. "I did. And I thought you should hear it again from me, Gwen." Shifting, he smiles at me. "We will get forever together."

I bob my head. "I believe you."

He smiles. "Good. It's my vow to you."

Turning my head, I peer at him. "A Blood Vow?"

His smile widens at my reaction. "You're dying to know what that is, aren't you?"

"Well, yeah. The Barons—" I stop talking at the frown crossing his face. "Never mind. I don't want to give them even another second of my thoughts. You're all I want to think about."

"We'll talk about Blood Vows later, my vow is more...a Gwen Vow. And you're all I want to think about. All I want to taste. To hear. To feel." He hooks his arm around my side and pulls me close so that I can lie on top of him. I cage his head between my elbows and give him the affection he craves, kissing him with the same fervent passion emanating from his every touch and kiss and gasp of breath. Mikkalo consumes my senses, fogging the world around us so it's just me and him together.

But the sound of heavy footsteps breaks the wall of love we surround ourselves in.

He sits up with me, keeping his hands on my lower back, and we both hold our breaths to listen to the clomping of definite human feet. No vampire would ever be that loud. I expect the shock alarms to go off at any second and even cover my ears in anticipation, but Mikkalo pulls my hands from my head.

"The alarms only go off with intruders," he says, reaching over to swipe his com device from the nightstand. "That's one of the staff members."

I slide onto the bed next to him to glance at his com device as he brings up the security feeds of the property. We're greeted with a bunch of blank screens. Half the feeds aren't showing. Mikkalo stiffens and abandons me on the bed, rushing to his office. I scoot to the end of the bed and dangle my legs off, watching him lean on his desk and peer at the dozen screens on the wall.

He rubs his chin, his muscles bulging and flexing with his movements. "What the hell," he mutters to himself without looking at me.

A soft tap on the door draws my attention away from him. "Mr. Royale? I need to speak to you." A masculine voice sounds through the door, setting off my fear instincts like crazy.

Mikkalo ignores the guy at the bedroom door, even when he tries to turn the knob. Mikkalo continues to study his security screens, not paying attention to the guy turning desperate with his knocking.

"Mr. Royale!" the guy yells.

Fear trickles over me, and I hop out of bed and pad across the room to join Mikkalo. He hooks one arm around me, pulling me close without a word. I try to see what he's looking at, but there's a lot of jumbled words and images that I can't decipher.

The guy bangs and kicks on the door, and I squeeze Mikkalo tighter.

"What's going on?" I finally ask, sensing that Mikkalo might not offer me the information otherwise. He's currently consumed with his monitors. "Are we under attack? Is that why the feeds are down?"

He breaks his gaze on the feeds to look at me. "No one triggered the perimeter barriers, and the security cameras are all coming back." He taps the screen to get me to look. "And I can't see anything wrong. Can you?"

I blink a few times, surprised that he asks me. I bend forward, resting my palm on the desk, and search each feed one by one for something out of the ordinary. The only thing I notice is a strange man in the hallway outside our door. His twisted features display panic across his face, and he even jumps up and down, now waving at the camera.

"Am I imagining this dude?" I ask, tapping my finger to the screen.

Mikkalo tightens his jaw. "No."

"So...are you not going to answer the door?" I find it weird that we just remain here.

He nods. "Not with you here. I'm waiting for my brothers. They're almost done with the sweep."

He points at one of the feeds, and I spot the three of them standing together just outside the door that leads to the path to the gym building. They hide in full sun protective gear under a pop-up awning that shelters them from the bright sunlight pouring through the property.

Just the sight of them outside makes me nervous as hell. "Hurry up, guys," I whisper, more to myself.

Bronx shifts and looks at the camera. "We're fine, dandelion. Nice and toasty if anything."

Jameson chuckles from beside him. "Hot as fuck."

"But safe," Everett says.

Mikkalo hugs me tighter, sensing my nerves. "Just hurry up. Our girl is stressing out. We have a visitor at the door."

The three of them disappear from sight, and I release a breath at their appearance outside our door. The guy doesn't even look at them, continuing to bang on the door, calling for Mikkalo. Bronx waves his hand, motioning for Mikkalo to answer the door. Jameson stands tense behind the guy, looking ready to tackle him. Everett waits off to the side, just studying the guy, remaining expressionless.

"Stay here," Mikkalo tells me, pointing at the rolling chair.

I plop down on it and nod. "Got it."

As much as my curiosity nags at me to follow him, my good senses scream that I better keep my ass planted on this chair and watch from the safety of the feed. I can't see Mikkalo, since there isn't a security camera in the room, so I continue to stare at Bronx, Jameson, and Everett.

"Mr. Royale, I need to speak with you." The guy's voice booms through the room. "Where is Ms. Gallagher?"

I shiver at the sound of my human-given name, despite knowing that the staff wouldn't usually call me that. I became a Royale the second I arrived here, even before I fell for my guys and let them claim me.

"That is none of your business, Mr. Geoff. Do not forget your place in our household." Mikkalo's deep voice reverberates through me as he uses the tone I've only heard him use to intimidate others.

I can't stop myself from frowning at his referral to the guy, Mr. Geoff's, place either.

Bronx materializes in the doorway and strides to my side, not giving me a chance to get to my feet before I find myself in his arms and sitting on his lap as he steals the chair from me. He swivels and looks at the feeds without a sound, hugging his arms around me.

"I'm sorry, Mr. Royale. Please forgive me. It's just important that I speak with Ms. Gallagher," Mr. Geoff says.

"What is this regarding?" Everett asks, keeping his voice even compared to the soft warning growls erupting from Mikkalo.

"Where is Ms. Gallagher?" Mr. Geoff repeats, ignoring Everett. "I need to speak to Ms. Gallagher."

The desperation in the guy's voice makes me push against Bronx, but he holds me in place on his lap. I twist and frown at him, and he tightens his jaw and matches my glare. Bronx has the nerve to lean in and kiss me, even with my annoyance from him pinning me. And damn my body. I totally devour his lips, tasting the sweetness of his kiss. He smiles the cockiest smile in all of existence like he just knew a kiss would work to keep me from trying to bolt out there. So I wiggle my ass on his lap, shifting and moving and rubbing against him until I feel the bulge of his boner.

"Careful, dandelion," he murmurs into my ear. "I take your teasing seriously."

Fuck. Me. I don't even know why I try to play games with him. It always seems to backfire. "I bet you do."

He hums, tightening his fingers to my legs. "I don't know if I can wait another two nights to be with you."

"Ms. Gallagher!" Mr. Geoff's voice echoes through the air, pulling our attention away from each other.

Jameson materializes in the doorway, resting his arms on the frame. "He's not going to stop. He's been manipulated."

Bronx releases a growl in my ear. "I don't want him near our girl."

"Then what do you want us to do? If we try to break it, it could cause brain damage," Everett says from behind Jameson. "Geoff is our best staff member. He has family. I'm not willing to risk it."

I swivel and touch Bronx's cheek. "What he said."

Bronx narrows his eyes at me. "No."

"No?" I repeat.

Jameson groans. "Now you've done it, Bronxy."

I glare at him next. "Jamie."

Jameson sticks his tongue out at me. "We don't want you to speak with Geoff because if he's had his mind manipulated, he could have been commanded to do something insane like attack you. Then we'd definitely kill him. Like Everett said, we don't want to risk jeopardizing him."

I sigh and scrub my face with my hands. "Then what do we do?"

"Maybe through the com line would suffice. Most vampires don't think the specifics like that through. He might've been commanded to do something upon sight of our girl," Mikkalo says from his spot near the door. I can't see him, but I can still see Mr. Geoff pacing the hallway because Mikkalo blocks him from getting in.

Bronx heaves a sigh and taps the screen a few times. Mikkalo's face appears on the screen in front of us, his eyes flashing silver in agitation. I can't blame him. I'm annoyed as hell too by the interruption of our most perfect day together.

"Gwen, you don't have to say anything. Just listen to what he has to say," Mikkalo says.

I bite my lip between my teeth and nod.

Tapping the screen, he disappears and Mr. Geoff comes into view. Mr. Geoff freezes in place, finally calming down. Mikkalo's idea worked.

"Ms. Gallagher, thank you for seeing me," Mr. Geoff says almost as if I'm standing right in front of him. "There is a package waiting for you in the entryway. It must be opened at once."

My heart falls into my stomach at his words. All I can think is that our home is about to explode at any second. Bronx must think so too, because he flips me onto his shoulder and the five of us abandon Mikkalo's room.

Standing outside in the shade, I squint in the bright sunlight. It's been a while since I've been outside during the day. A part of me thought I'd miss seeing and feeling the sun, but I don't. All I can think about is how vulnerable my guys are and how it's up to me to protect them if shit is about to go down.

"I don't want to split up," Bronx says, adjusting to cradle me in his arms. "If this is a setup, they'll expect that."

Mikkalo moves his weight from foot to foot. "I agree."

Jameson growls and punches the wall. "We can't just

stand around here. If someone's watching, they can't think they can intimidate us."

"We don't even know what the package is," Everett says.

"Not it," Jameson, Bronx, and Mikkalo say in unison.

I frown. "Not it for what?"

Everett shakes his head. "Looks like I'm going to be investigating your gift."

My mouth forms an O, and I look at each of them. They can't be serious. Everett could get hurt or worse. "Nu-uh. I don't think so. Can't you call Corona or something to do it?"

Mikkalo tips his head back and laughs. "I love our girl."

Bronx clears his throat. "No. I'll do it. It must be taken care of now."

"No, I'll do it, Bronxy. Our region needs you more than me. Gwen needs Mikkalo and Everett more too." Jameson pushes his fingers through his hair and doesn't meet my gaze.

I wiggle in Bronx's arms until he sets me down. "Oh, shut up, Jamie. I'd starve without you. Who will make me that delicious pasta I love?"

A smile lights his face. "You know how to cook."

"But doesn't mean I need you any less." Swallowing my nerves, I decide to do the stupidest thing in existence. I know it's stupid. My head screams to stay in place and let my guys handle it. But the package is technically for me.

Darting my eyes to the two feet of shade before the direct sunlight, I count silently to five while my guys look at each other. I squeeze my eyes shut and rush away from them, heading to the path that will lead me to the front of the mansion.

No one yells at me or calls my name. They don't even follow. I run past a guy on a lawnmower and slow down at the lush garden blooming with colorful flowers. I've never seen so much color together in my life.

I shake my head and focus on the path before me, winding along the gorgeous property until I see the arched, covered drive with the outdoor chandelier. The ground sparkles with minerals, and I can't help but appreciate how grand everything is. And now I'm worried I'm going to lose it all.

A small package sits on the ground in the entryway just outside the open door to the foyer. Bronx, Jameson, Everett, and Mikkalo stand in the doorway, and we stare at each other from the twenty feet of space between us.

"Gigi, stay back," Jameson says.

I place my hands on my hips. "No. We're in this together."

Everett abandons his brothers and blocks my view. "For one, you're not as resilient as us. And two, it's not an explosive like we expected."

Standing on my tiptoes, I peek over his shoulder to study the small, weird shaped package. It's then that I notice the blood staining the tiles under it. "What the hell?"

"Let Mikkalo take you back inside. We can handle this," Everett says.

I purse my lips. "I'm not afraid. I've seen a lot of nasty shit over the years. You don't have to protect me."

Mikkalo materializes in front of me next. He reaches out and brushes the backs of his fingers to my cheek. "We know that, ball kicker," he says, teasing me. "But we want to anyway. It's from the Barons."

I suck in a sharp breath, my mind reeling with all sorts of panic. "Ah, hell."

I shove past Mikkalo and Everett and close the distance. Bronx snatches the package off the ground, and my eyes flick to the bloody note beneath it. I hunch down and read the perfectly scripted line over and over again.

"Your brother for ours," I say out loud, my voice quivering.

"Shit," Jameson growls.

Jerking out my hand, I grab the bloody package from Bronx. He lets me take it, knowing full well that I might attack him for it. I carefully rip the paper free and stare at the heart in my hand. I scream out in anger and chuck it away. It splatters against the window and leaves behind a streak of blood.

"Those bastards!" I yell, spinning to cover my face with my hands. "I'm going to kill them all. I'm going to rip their hearts out and make them eat them for doing this to us."

My guys surround me, sandwiching me in a hug that keeps me together as I try not to fall apart. Fury floods over me like a tidal wave of molten lava. I've never felt such hatred in my life. What did I do to deserve this?

"Damn-fucking-straight you are," Jameson says, petting my long hair. "And we're going to help you."

I bob my head and stretch to kiss him. "You better."

Mikkalo presses his face to my shoulder. "Hell yeah."

"You're our girl. Ours." Bronx flashes his fangs, peering at the world around us.

"You hear that!" I yell, projecting my voice. "I'm theirs! And they're mine!"

Everett releases a soft hum. "That's never going to get old."

I kiss him. "Hope not, because I plan on saying it forever."

"Yeah?" they all ask me in unison, various expressions crossing their handsome faces.

I nod. "Maybe even longer than that."

Epilogue

NO LONGER SAFE

JAMESON SITS AT A SMALL table, sketching away on a thick piece of paper. I stare at him without moving, my naked breasts rising and falling with every breath. He drops his pencil and strolls to me, grazing his finger across my clavicle to push my hair over my shoulder.

"We'll take a break in a couple of minutes," he murmurs, drawing his finger between my cleavage and down the plane of my stomach. He stops short of my lacy panties and traces his finger along the band.

I smile at him and spread my legs an inch. "I'm not

sure I can wait. When you asked me for help, I thought it would be less torturous than this."

He slides his hand into my panties and feels exactly what he does to me with his finger. "Mmm. The wait will be worth it."

He returns to his table and sits down. I'm nearly certain he intended the words for himself because his eyes flash silver, and his heart picks up speed. He licks his lips, turning his gaze back to me, and I swivel my body on the lounge chair in his studio and sit up.

"Gigi," he murmurs, dropping his pencil. "What are you doing?"

Lifting my hips, I grin as I shimmy my panties down. "I can't wait any longer."

His mouth parts open with a breath of desire, but he doesn't rush to me. He swallows, tightens his jaw, and picks his pencil back up. "I'm going to have to start over now."

I giggle and reposition my body to how I was posed. "Not like that, you aren't. Is this how I was?"

He presses his lips together, hiding his smile. "Your hair needs to move."

I slowly comb it off my shoulder again. "Like this?"

"Perfect." He hums deep in his throat, and I totally take advantage of his intense gaze, drawing my own hand over my breasts and down my stomach. I peek over at him, catching him drinking me in, his pencil just hovering in his hand, his drawing forgotten. I lean back on the lounge chair, closing my eyes, and touch myself, moaning in exaggeration just to get a reaction out of him. His silhouette blocks the overhead light, and I can't stop the smile from crossing my face as he sits down and covers my hand with his, just feeling and watching as I explore myself.

"If you're trying to seduce me, it's working," he says, gliding his fingers away from mine to slip one inside me. "Even your fake moans are sexy as hell."

"It's not fake," I say, moaning again with the pressure he creates.

"Wanna bet?"

Oh, boy.

I don't even get a chance to say anything as Jameson twists his wrist and wiggles his finger inside me, touching me in a way that sends a burst of tingles through my body as he adds to the pleasure I elicit myself. I moan so loud that he chuckles and leans in, kissing the noise from my mouth.

"See," he says, grinning against my lips.

I link my fingers to the hem of his shirt and tug it up until he bends closer for me to pull it off. "Do it again," I say, sucking his bottom lip into my mouth.

He chuckles and brushes his lips to mine, sliding his tongue into my mouth to deepen our kiss. His hands trail lower, and he explores my body, touching me in different ways to see what I like the most. I squirm and shift, so turned on that I can't take another second of his teasing. I unbutton his pants and pull out his erection, lacing my fingers around it to rub up the stiff length of his shaft.

He moans, quickly losing his pants to get between my legs. Lifting me up by the ass, he positions me on a pillow to sit up higher so that he can kneel in front of me, easing my legs open wide enough to meet his hips completely to my thighs.

I gasp as he rocks into me, holding onto the back of the chair to assure I get to experience every inch of him. Grabbing his tight ass, I cling onto him with every deep thrust that leaves my whole body buzzing with pleasure. He draws one of his hands between us and rubs my clit, creating a crazy amount of good pressure paired with the bursts of sensations with his thrusts that I know I'm going to orgasm.

Jameson moans my name into my hair, whispering how good I feel. How much he enjoys every second of our time together and how lucky he feels that I'm with him. I bask in the sexiness of his voice, how amazing his touch is, how perfect our bodies feel as one. I tense and arch forward with my orgasm, sinking my teeth into his shoulder in the process just how he likes.

Thrusting into me a few times, he cums with a low moan, pinching my hips as he slows. He lets me drink from the bite I left on him, breathing heavily while grazing his lips over my neck. I ease away when I can't suck anymore and meet his startling green gaze. He looks so hot with his messy hair and pouty bottom lip, puffing with each of his breaths. Being with Jameson helps me forget the world outside of his arms.

"Gwen, I—"

The door of his art studio swings open, and Everett rushes in, covering his eyes with his hand. He kicks the door closed, and Jameson doesn't rush to move. He scoops a blanket from the back of the chair and drapes it around the two of us.

"Get dressed. Now," Everett says without looking at us.

"What the hell is going on?" I can't stop my voice from rising.

Everett winces. "Gwen, I'm sorry I interrupted."

Jameson lets me go as I pull away from him and get to my feet. I swipe my underwear from the floor and put it on. Padding across the room, I grab my shirt from the back of Jameson's chair and slip it over my head.

I close the space to Everett and touch his shoulder. "It's okay, but you didn't answer my question."

Jameson strolls up behind me butt-ass naked and wraps his arms around my shoulders. "This better be good, brother. We were in the middle of...some art." He smirks at me and motions toward the table where I glimpse the half-finished photo-realistic sketch of the upper-half of my body. And whoa. Seeing what I look like through Jameson's eyes has me all sorts of crazy about him.

"Jamie," I murmur.

He covers my eyes with his hand. "No looking yet."

I reach down and grab his cock, getting him to let go

but only to lift me onto his shoulder, hanging me upside down. I pinch his ass, making him jump and set me back down.

The door to the art studio swings open again, and Bronx hovers, silhouetted in the shadows. "What's taking so long?"

Everett snaps his gaze, still lingering on Jameson's sketch, appreciating it like it's the most amazing piece of art he's ever seen, toward Bronx.

Mikkalo shows up behind Bronx. "Don't get too mad, brother. Gwen makes it easy to get distracted, especially wearing that." He drinks me in from my bare legs up to my lacy panties and short shirt exposing a few inches of my stomach.

Bronx groans. "We have to go. Come on. It's not safe here."

Jameson releases a growl, throwing on his clothes. He tosses me my pants from the floor, and I shimmy them on, using Bronx's hulking arm to brace against. I stand up on my tiptoes and kiss him when I'm dressed, and Jameson picks me back up.

"What are we facing?" Jameson asks, tugging a weapon from one of his cabinets. He hands it to me to hold. "The bastards back?"

No one responds to him right away.

I swallow my nerves. "Did we get another package?"

The lack of response speaks volumes, and I rest my

head on Jameson's shoulder and take a deep breath.

"It wasn't one of your brothers," Bronx says lowly.

Everett reaches out and touches my cheek. "Neither was the heart. It was human, but the tests didn't match what we have in the system. It was a warning."

My eyes widen. "What? Are you sure?"

Nodding, Everett offers me a half smile. "I'm positive."

"But that doesn't mean much," Mikkalo says. He straightens his shoulders. "Now, come on. We have to go."

The world blurs around me, and I land in the backseat of the car idling on the narrow road that leads back to the mansion. Jameson helps buckle me in and squeezes my hand, seeing the dozens of thoughts swirling through my mind.

Bronx hits the throttle, sending the car barreling forward at a speed that makes me a bit nervous. I clutch onto Mikkalo's leg and grip Jameson's hand so tightly that he keeps wiggling his fingers.

"We're going to head into Crimson Vista for the next few days," Bronx says, glancing at me in the rearview mirror. "There's been another security breach, and the only way to take care of it is to relocate all of the staff and bring in new people. The Barons were...thorough."

I scrunch my nose. "What the hell is that supposed to mean?"

Bronx slams the brakes without responding. The tires screech as we skid to a halt a couple hundred feet from the wrought iron gate that leads off the property. Jameson's too slow to cover my eyes, and I catch sight of a group of people strolling at a human's pace in our direction.

"Fuck, you've gotta be kidding me," Mikkalo says, his words coming out with a growl. "That's everyone left."

I dig my fingers into Jameson's wrist until he drops his hand. Leaning forward against my restraints, I search over the group of humans illuminated in the car's headlights. I gasp and cover my mouth with my hand. A few of the people carry severed heads in their hands—not humans, but vampires. Some I think might have been part of Mikkalo's security team.

"Gwen." My name trickles through the air, the eerie sound of the crowd's voices in unison twisting my insides. "It's time to come home. You have five seconds to leave the Royales. If you do not, more will die."

The people drop the vampire heads and tug daggers from their jackets. Bronx, Mikkalo, and Everett abandon the car, and Jameson unbuckles me and pulls me to him.

"Five," the crowd says. "Four."

Bronx disarms the first guy on the right while Mikkalo and Everett take two others.

"Three." There are too many. They count too fast. "Two."

Bronx raises his hands up, waving at us.

"One."

Jameson twists me in his arms to block my view, but it

doesn't help. We're surrounded. From the back window, I catch sight of more people behind the car. They hold blades to their throats, trapped in powerful mind manipulation.

Shoving from Jameson, I jump out of the car and raise my hands. "Wait!"

But I'm too late.

I drop to my knees, hanging my head.

A dozen thuds of bodies hitting the dirt soon follow, and there's nothing any of us can do.

To be continued...

Thank you so much for reading *Rebel Dhampir* and hope you love the series so far! Don't forget to check out *Rebel Match*, the third book in *The Royale Vampire Heirs* series.

Want more of the *Vampire Heirs World* and haven't read *The Divine Vampire Heirs* or *Academy of Vampire Heirs?* Check out *Blood Match* and *Dhampirs 101*.

To stay up-to-day on new and future releases, follow Ginna on Amazon or Bookbub. By signing up for Ginna Moran's newsletter at www.ginnamoran.com or joining her Facebook Group PARANORMAL CENTER FOR MATCHES AND MATES, you will also gain exclusive access to special content on her website.

OTHER REVERSE HAREM NOVELS BY GINNA MORAN

THE VAMPIRE HEIRS WORLD

La Vega Vampire Showstoppers:
Vampire Nights
Bloody Nights

The Divine Vampire Heirs
Blood Match
Blood Rebel
Blood Debt
Blood Feud
Blood Loss
Blood Vows

The Royale Vampire Heirs Series:
Rebel Vampires
Rebel Dhampir
Rebel Match
Rebel Heir
Rebel Fight

Academy of Vampire Heirs Series:
Dhampirs 101
Blood Sources 102
Coven Bonds 103
Personal Donors 104
Blood Wars 105

THE MATES OF MAGAELORUM WORLD

The Pack Mates of Lunar Crest:
The She-Wolf Games
The Wolf-Mate Trials
The Omega Hunt
The Witch Chase

Fated Mates of the Dragon Clans:
Caged by Her Dragons
Freed by Her Dragons
Saved by Her Dragons

SEVEN SINNERS WORLD

Her Personal Demons
Her Deadly Angels
Her Darkest Devils
Her Sinful Saints
Her Twisted Sinners

About Ginna Moran

GINNA MORAN IS the author of over fifty novels, including the popular The Pack Mates of Lunar Crest, The Divine Vampire Heirs, and The Royale Vampire Heirs Why Choose novels.

She always carried a fascination for all things paranormal and wrote her first unpublished manuscript at age eighteen. Her love of the supernatural grew stronger through her adult life, and she now spends her days with different creatures of the night. Whether it's vampires, werewolves, dragons, fae, angels, demons, or mermaids, Ginna loves creating and living in worlds from her dreams.

Aside from Ginna's professional life, she enjoys binge watching TV, crafting and design, playing pretend with her daughter, and cuddling with her dogs. Some of her favorite things include chocolate, mermaids, anything that glitters, learning new things, cheesy jokes, and organizing her bookshelf.

Ginna is currently hard at work on her next novel and the one after, and the one after that.